P9-AOX-514

"Rich characterization, passion and romantic adventure . . . Chapman is unmatched and unforgettable."

—*Romantic Times*

PRAISE FOR NEW YORK TIMES BESTSELLING AUTHOR JANET CHAPMAN

. . . and her captivating contemporary romances

THE MAN MUST MARRY

"Offbeat and charming. . . . Chapman's gift for creating characters you love spending time with is on full display."

—*Romantic Times*

"Ninety-percent laughter, ten-percent tears, and one-hundred-percent romance. Nobody writes a luscious romantic comedy like Janet Chapman. . . . Superb."

—ReadertoReader.com

"Chapman excels at creating a melodious story of one heroine meant for only one hero."

—Compuserve Books

THE STRANGER IN HER BED

"A thoroughly enjoyable tale of a modern-day knight and his feisty ladylove set in the rugged mountains of Maine."

—*Booklist*

"More hot passion and danger in the wilds of Maine. . . . When you crack open a Chapman book, you are guaranteed pure reading pleasure."

—*Romantic Times*

THE SEDUCTION OF HIS WIFE

"A charming story of love, growth and trust."

—*Romantic Times*

"Chapman presents a cast of rugged characters in rural Maine who enact a surprisingly tender romance."

—*Booklist*

THE DANGEROUS PROTECTOR

"One thing that Chapman does so deftly is meld great characterization, sparkling humor and spicy adventure into a perfect blend."

—*Romantic Times*

THE SEDUCTIVE IMPOSTOR

"Chapman's skills as a storyteller just keep getting better. Utilizing warmth and humor, she makes this thrilling romantic tale both funny and scary. Great reading."

—*Romantic Times*

"One of the best books I've read in a long time. . . . A fun, sexy read!"

—*Old Book Barn Gazette*

"Engaging romantic suspense . . . surprising twists . . . Janet Chapman seduces her audience."

—The Best Reviews

Don't miss her thrilling new paranormal romance series . . .

MOONLIGHT WARRIOR

"Plenty of good humor . . . lovable characters, [and] a sweet romance."

—*Publishers Weekly*

"A warmhearted tale of love and magic. . . . Full of warmth, danger and romantic passion."

—*Romantic Times*

"Will knock your socks off. . . . A must read. . . . I couldn't put it down."

—*Winter Haven News Chief*

"A magically believable story brimming with imaginative scenarios and unforgettable characters."

—SingleTitles.com

"A charming tale with sympathetic and quirky characters. . . . Great fun."

—A Romance Review

"Chapman's romantic fantasy is a sweet and silly mythical mélange with a dark magic center. . . . Brimming with interesting, well-crafted characters."

—ReaderToReader.com

. . . or her charming Highlanders series

SECRETS OF THE HIGHLANDER

"Liberally spiced with mystery, this story has warmth and genuine love that make it the perfect antidote for stress."

—*Romantic Times*

ONLY WITH A HIGHLANDER

"A mystical, magical book if there ever was one. . . . A perfect 10!"

—Romance Reviews Today

These titles are also available as eBooks

ALSO BY JANET CHAPMAN

A Highlander Christmas
Moonlight Warrior
The Man Must Marry
Secrets of the Highlander
The Stranger in Her Bed
The Seduction of His Wife
Only with a Highlander
The Dangerous Protector
Tempting the Highlander
The Seductive Impostor
Charming the Highlander
Loving the Highlander
Wedding the Highlander

Available from Pocket Books

And look for Janet Chapman's
next contemporary romance

TEMPT ME IF YOU CAN

Coming soon from Pocket Star Books

WEDDING
THE
HIGHLANDER

JANET
CHAPMAN

POCKET BOOKS
New York London Toronto Sydney

Pocket Books
A Division of Simon & Schuster, Inc.
1230 Avenue of the Americas
New York, NY 10020

This book is a work of fiction. Names, characters, places, and incidents either are products of the author's imagination or are used fictitiously. Any resemblance to actual events or locales or persons, living or dead, is entirely coincidental.

Copyright © 2003 by Janet Chapman

All rights reserved, including the right to reproduce this book or portions thereof in any form whatsoever. For information address Pocket Books Subsidiary Rights Department,
1230 Avenue of the Americas, New York, NY 10020

This Pocket Books trade paperback edition January 2010

POCKET and colophon are registered trademarks of Simon & Schuster, Inc.

For information about special discounts for bulk purchases, please contact Simon & Schuster Special Sales at 1-866-506-1949 or business@simonandschuster.com.

The Simon & Schuster Speakers Bureau can bring authors to your live event. For more information or to book an event contact the Simon & Schuster Speakers Bureau at 1-866-248-3049 or visit our website at www.simonspeakers.com.

Manufactured in the United States of America

10 9 8 7 6 5 4 3 2 1

ISBN 978-1-4391-8715-9
ISBN 978-0-7434-8010-9 (ebook)

To Delbert Byram,
for a lifetime of unbelievable patience and gentle
devotion, and for always being a safe place to land.
I love you, Daddy.

And in memory of Ella Byram,
for her empowering guidance and love, her unique
and always curious outlook on life, and for being
the foundation I stand on today.
I love you, Mom. And I miss you greatly.

Acknowledgments

I wish to thank Sihaya Hopkins for showing me the painstaking skill involved in working with glass. My visit to your Glass Blossom Studio in Harborside, Maine, was fascinating, and the generous gift of your time is greatly appreciated. Your jewelry is simply beautiful, and I cherish the glass Snowy Owl you made for me that day.

I also wish to acknowledge the Christmas Tree growers here in Maine, most especially FinestKind Tree Farm in Dover-Foxcroft, and Piper Mountain Christmas Trees in Dixmont. I don't know how you do it, but no matter which tree gets chosen, the magic of the season always comes with it. Thank you for opening up your farms each year, and for helping create memories that bind generations together in a warmth of tradition.

And thank you, Esther and Chick, for your love, your beautiful photos that make my webpage come alive, and for your overwhelming support. Robbie and I are truly blessed by your friendship.

WEDDING
THE
HIGHLANDER

Chapter One

Pine Creek, Maine, October 22

A shout woke him as he spiraled through the horrific void, twisting and clawing to find something of substance to hold on to. But there was only blinding white light and the terror of knowing his fate was beyond his control.

Michael MacBain opened his eyes, held himself perfectly still, and listened to the silence broken only by his own labored breathing. He slowly sat up and scrubbed the sweat from his face, then untangled his legs from the sheet, threw back the cover, and stood. He walked to the window, lowered the top sash, and took slow, metered breaths of the crisp October air, letting it wash over his quivering muscles.

A full two minutes passed before his heart finally calmed and his head cleared. Michael sighed into the night. All was right with the world; he decided as he stared into the darkness; the moon-washed mountains still cast their shadow over his farm, the stars still shone from the heavens, his house stood peaceful. And his son, Robbie, was safe in his bed, and John was sleeping downstairs.

Michael scrubbed his face again with tired impatience. The dreams were becoming more detailed. And far more frequent.

They started with Maura—with her funeral. In the dream, Michael would see himself crouched on the hillside, hidden from the MacKeages, watching them bury his woman outside the fence that separated the sinners from the decent.

Ian MacKeage was placing his daughter in unhallowed ground. And as they covered Maura with unholy dirt and the dream progressed, Michael would relive the anger and utter impotency he had felt that day.

She hadn't killed herself—she'd wandered onto the rotten ice of the *loc* by mistake because of the snowstorm. She'd been coming to him, running away from her clan to get married, so their child would be born with the blessing of the church.

And from there, the dream would change to his confrontation with Ian MacKeage that fateful day eight hundred years ago. Michael's feelings of heartbreak had been compounded by Ian's harsh reprisals. Michael had walked away, unable to reason with Maura's father.

Aye, it was then he had decided to go to war.

The dream would shift rapidly, this time to a *gleann* not far from the MacKeage keep. Greylen, Ian, Morgan, and Callum MacKeage were on their way home from talks with the MacDonalds, looking smug in their success at gaining the other clan's aid against the MacBains.

And so Michael and his five warriors had attacked— and his dream turned into a nightmare hellish enough to curdle a warrior's blood.

The storm descended upon them without warning. The sounds of battle turned into a frenzy of shouting men, screaming horses, and deafening thunder. A godless wind came first, roaring down from the heavens, uprooting trees, and churning up dust that clogged their throats. Lightning sizzled through the air, and the rain started, ruthlessly pounding against them. And the last thing Michael remembered seeing was a small, aged man standing on the bluff above them, watching in horror.

Sometimes—if he were lucky—he'd wake up then. His own scream of terror was enough to jolt him from the nightmare, and he'd find himself in his bed, in the twenty-first century, safe but no closer to understanding how ten men and their warhorses could be hurtled forward eight hundred years through time.

Nor, even after living in this modern world for twelve years now, was he any closer to understanding why.

But sometimes he didn't wake up, and the nightmare continued, settling back into a less violent but just as disturbing dream, with him standing on the summit of TarStone Mountain, at sunrise on Summer Solstice eight years ago.

In the dream, Michael was casting the ashes of Mary Sutter, Robbie's mother, onto the gentle breeze, watching it carry her away. He was holding their infant son in his arms, surrounded by the MacKeage warriors who shared his fate, Mary's sister, Grace, and Mary's six half brothers. The priest, Daar, was there as well—the same man he had seen on the bluff in the storm eight hundred years ago.

Michael rubbed his now dry chest and looked toward TarStone Mountain. Daar was actually a *drùidh* named Pendaär. He lived halfway up TarStone now, hiding behind his priest's robes and neighborly smile.

The four MacKeage warriors were also his neighbors, their ancient war superseded by their need to survive in this modern time. The blood tie of the eight-year-old boy sleeping down the hall now bound them together.

Greylen's wife, Grace Sutter MacKeage, was Robbie's aunt. And to the man, the old *drùidh* included, Robbie's happiness came first.

Michael continued staring out the window, but his focus suddenly shifted to the soft footsteps coming into his room, and he waited until Robbie was about to pounce before he spoke.

"Ya best be heavily armed, son," he said softly, still not turning around. "And prepared for the consequences."

The footsteps stopped.

Michael looked over his shoulder and smiled at the boy standing three paces away, his hands on his naked hips and a scowl on his young face.

"A noble warrior does not use a weapon on an unarmed man," Robbie countered, obviously insulted. His scowl suddenly changed to a diabolical smile as he raised his hands and wiggled his fingers. "It was a tickle attack I was planning."

Michael closed the window, picked up his pants, and put them on. He faced his son as he slipped into his shirt. "How about you get dressed instead," he suggested, "and we head for the summit now?"

"Now?" Robbie echoed, lowering his hands back to his hips and looking at the clock by Michael's bed. "But it's only two in the morning."

Michael reached into the top drawer of his bureau for socks. "We might make it by sunrise," he offered.

Never one to need an excuse for an adventure, Robbie clapped his hands. "Can we bring the swords?" he asked.

"Aye," Michael agreed as he sat on the bed to put on his socks. "Dress warm, and bring our packs when you come downstairs. I'll put together some food to take with us and leave John a note."

Robbie was out the door and running down the hall before Michael could finish giving his orders. Michael stood up and tossed the sheet back over the mattress, which was still damp with his sweat.

His shout must have awakened Robbie. And being far too astute for his age, the boy had known his father was dreaming again and had tried to distract him with a tickle attack.

Michael stared at the rumpled bed. This was the third time he'd had the dream in the last six weeks. Before that, he'd relived the horror only occasionally.

It wasn't the dream itself that disturbed him but more its escalating frequency. Michael walked back to the window, rested his arms on the top sash, and stared at TarStone. Were the dreams a precursor to something?

The nightmare retold his past, not his future.

Was another vision about to be added to the sequence?

More importantly, did he hold the power to control the outcome this time? He'd made a new life for himself here and now had a son to guide into manhood. Nothing must come between him and Robbie, not an aging wizard and most especially not the magic.

"Come on, Papa. I'm dressed, and you haven't even packed anything yet," Robbie said from the doorway. "I want to be on the summit by sunrise."

Michael gathered up his sweater from the back of a chair and walked into the hall, gently prodding his son ahead of him. "Do we ride or walk?" he asked.

"Walk," Robbie quickly answered, skipping down the stairs, the empty packs slapping against the banister. "Stomper is too old to wake up this early, and Feather's too lazy." Robbie stopped at the bottom, looked up at Michael, and said in a lowered voice so he wouldn't wake up John,

"I'm not up to fighting that stubborn pony this morning. Besides, he doesn't like my sword. I think it pokes him when I'm riding."

"How about the four-wheeler?" Michael asked, his voice also hushed.

Robbie shook his head. "Too noisy. We won't see any of the night animals."

Michael gave his son a nudge toward the kitchen. "You write the note for John and fill our packs. I'll get our swords."

"Can I use Robert's sword?" Robbie asked.

Michael lifted a brow. "You're too tired to fight with Feather but willing to hike to the summit of TarStone carrying Robert's sword?"

The boy thought hard on that prospect, then slowly shook his head. "Nope. It's too heavy." He suddenly brightened. "You could carry both."

After another nudge to get him moving toward the kitchen, Michael turned and headed to the library. "Nay, son. A warrior carries his own weapon," he said over his shoulder.

Michael continued into the library, came to a stop in front of the hearth, and studied the three swords hanging over the mantel. Two of them were as long as the hearth was wide and flanked a smaller sword designed for a much younger hand. He reached up and took down Robbie's weapon, feeling the balance as he ran one finger along the smooth length of the blade.

He'd had it made especially for Robbie and had given it to the boy on his fourth birthday. Robbie's aunt Grace had been appalled. The MacKeage men had been impressed. Well, except for Greylen. Laird MacKeage had taken on a yearning, almost pained expression as he'd held the small weapon and looked at his three young daughters.

Robbie had immediately named his sword *Thunderer,* which was a loose translation of what Michael called his own sword, and had rushed outside to battle the bushes. Since then, with both amazement and a great deal of pride, Michael had been teaching Robbie the skills of a warrior.

Learning to wield a sword was only a small part of his lessons, but it was the most enjoyable part for Robbie. The boy was unbelievably capable, in charge not only of his young mind but of his quickly growing muscles as well. With the confidence of youth backed by an unusually keen intelligence, Robbie was fast on his way to becoming a remarkable adult.

Still, Michael was not willing to relax when it came to his son. Nor did he trust this new life and new land, even after twelve years, for he knew from experience how quickly it could change. And that was why, as he guided his son into manhood, Michael also kept a tight rein on himself.

He minded his own business, ran his Christmas tree farm with a strong and careful hand, and stayed friendly but guarded from the community of Pine Creek. He took care of John Bigelow, the original owner of the farm, and tried to soothe the old man's pain at losing his wife of fifty-seven years.

They all missed Ellen, especially Robbie. She'd been a surrogate grandmother to the boy, and the three of them were finding it difficult to cope with their bachelor lives since Ellen had died two months ago. He was going to have to give in, he supposed, and hire a housekeeper before they got stomach rot from all the burnt food they'd been eating.

Michael reached for *Tàirneanaiche,* wrapped his fist around the hilt of the sword, and took it off the wall. He closed his eyes and sighed at the familiar weight of the weapon that had been an extension of his right arm for the greater part of his life. For the last twelve years, he'd felt naked without it strapped to his back, and now he spent his time cleaning the dust off *Tàirneanaiche* instead of his enemy's blood.

He looked up at the mantel again, at Robert MacBain's sword. The old warrior had not been able to adjust to the twenty-first century and had chased thunderstorms in the hopes of returning home.

Michael's grip tightened on *Tàirneanaiche* at the memory of his old friend's death ten years ago, on the highlands of northern Nova Scotia; desolate and desperate, only the two of them remained of the original six-man war party. Robert had died instantly from the bolt of lightning that had traveled down his sword and into his body. He hadn't made it home, and Michael could only hope the old warrior had finally found peace.

"You're in an odd mood this morning, Papa," Robbie said from the doorway. "Aunt Grace says if something is bothering me, I should talk about it. That talking will make it better." He moved into the library, his now full pack slung over his shoulders, and stared up at Michael with concerned, deep gray eyes. "You could tell me about your dream, and that might help."

Michael set *Tàirneanaiche* on the overstuffed chair and settled Robbie's sword into the sheath sewn into his pack, making sure the hilt didn't impair his movement. He smoothed down Robbie's hair, lifted the boy's face to his, and smiled.

"I dreamed that I was standing on TarStone, holding you, as we said good-bye to your mother eight years ago," he told him, deciding a half-truth was better than an outright lie. "It must be this hike we had planned that made me dream of Mary."

Robbie wrapped his young arms around Michael's waist and hugged him tightly. "We don't have to go, Papa."

"Aye, we do," Michael said softly, hugging him back. "We're both needing to visit Mary's favorite place."

"No, Papa," Robbie said, pulling back to look up at Michael. "Mama's favorite place was in your arms."

Feeling like a sledgehammer had just hit his chest, Michael hugged Robbie against him so the boy wouldn't see how hard his words had landed.

"Can you keep a secret, Papa?" Robbie said into his shirt.

"I can."

"I have a new pet."

"What sort of pet?"

"A snowy owl."

Michael looked down at his son and raised an eyebrow. "And just how long have you had this dangerous pet?"

"She came to me on my birthday, last January."

"She?"

Robbie nodded, completely unaware of Michael's concern. "I call her Mary," he whispered.

The sledgehammer struck again, this time almost doubling him over. "Mary? You named your pet after your mother?"

"Aye," Robbie said, nodding. "I was wishing real hard for my mama on my birthday, but I got an owl instead. So I named her Mary."

Michael stepped away and picked up his sword. He slowly digested the news, thinking about an eight-year-old's imagination and an owl's propensity to be drawn to the child. "Why haven't I seen this owl?" he asked, looking back at Robbie. "Where do you meet with your pet?"

Robbie pointed out the east window of the library. "There. On TarStone. When I ride my pony, Mary likes to follow me." And now that his secret was out, Robbie rushed to tell his tale. "She glides through the forest like the wind, Papa, on silent wings. And she's a good hunter. She catches rabbits and shares them with me." Robbie scrunched up his face. "Mary won't eat the rabbit, though, when I burn it."

Michael took a step back, more awed than concerned. Since Grace had placed his son in his arms eight and a half years ago, he and Robbie had walked these woods, camped, fished, hunted, and cooked their dinners over an open fire. He had not been aware, however, that his son was in the habit of cooking his own dinners.

Or that he'd made a pet of a snowy owl.

Michael turned Robbie and urged him toward the kitchen. "Do you have your knife?" he asked, deciding to wait until they were hiking up TarStone to explore the subject of Robbie's pet more closely.

His son reached into his pocket and pulled out a folded jackknife, holding it up for Michael to see. "When can I have a big one like yours?" he asked.

"When I decide you should."

"I could have a straight blade and keep it in my boot like you do."

"No, you can't. A folding knife is safest," Michael instructed, reaching into his pocket and pulling out his own knife. "The one in my boot is a weapon, Robbie. The knives we carry in our pockets are tools."

"And a warrior doesn't even need a knife to survive in the wilderness," Robbie quoted by rote, tucking his knife back into his pocket as they headed through the kitchen and out onto the porch. "Papa, are you going to die?"

Michael softly closed the door behind them with a slightly shaking hand, careful not to show how much Robbie's innocent question unnerved him. He slipped his

own pack onto his back, adjusted Tàirneanaiche so that
the hilt sat just behind his left shoulder, and walked down
the steps. He was not surprised by the question. Since
Ellen's passing, the boy had been full of questions about
death, and Michael had found himself at a loss for answers
more often than not.

"I am going to die," he finally said, keeping his tone
even. "But not today. Nor tomorrow. I'm a warrior, Robbie.
And it's my duty to live long enough to guide you into
manhood."

"And will I be a warrior when I grow up?"

Michael headed toward the upper field, setting a brisk
pace. "Yes and no," he answered honestly. "You will have
a warrior's knowledge and skill and the heart of a
Highlander, but you will live here and help me run our
Christmas tree farm when I grow too old to do it myself."

"Grampy's sons didn't stay and help him," Robbie countered, falling into step beside him. "But I won't leave you,"
he promised, taking Michael's hand as he looked up with
sincere gray eyes. "And I won't die before you do."

Michael nodded. "Aye. You'll not die first," he thickly
agreed.

"Maybe . . . maybe you should get yourself some more
sons," Robbie whispered, letting go of Michael's hand so he
could adjust the straps on his pack. He looked up. "Just in
case I do die."

"That will not happen," Michael growled, stopping and
turning Robbie to face him. "And babes are not pulled
from thin air. I would need a wife in order to get these
sons."

"You got me without a wife."

Michael frowned. How had this conversation turned
from death to sex? "I was trying to marry your mother," he
explained. "And if Mary had lived, we probably would

have had more bairns. But things don't always work out the way we would like, Robbie. Sometimes life interferes with our plans."

"Then why don't you just find another woman to marry?"

Michael started walking again, weaving his way through the rows of Christmas trees until they came to the woods. "A man doesn't decide he wants to get married and then simply pick the first available female. A man and a woman need to love each other first."

"Like Aunt Grace and Uncle Grey."

"Aye," Michael said softly. "Like Grace and Grey. And Callum and Charlotte, and Morgan and Sadie. A bond must be formed first, and love must grow from there."

"But you can't form a bond with a woman, Papa, if you don't never try." Robbie looked up, his eyes shining in the moonlight with the mischief of a boy on a mission. "And because Gram Ellen is gone, it's my duty to speak for her. And she says you need to go on dates."

"And my answer to you is the same as it's been to Ellen for eight years. I don't want a wife."

"Because your heart is broken, Papa. But Gram Ellen always said the right woman could mend it." Robbie stepped over a log in the path, then turned and walked backward as he continued. "And I can help."

"How?" Michael asked with wearing patience, moving past his son to take the lead. It appeared this recurring discussion had not ended with Ellen Bigelow's death. Apparently, his son was taking up her cause.

Along with Grace MacKeage. What was it with women that they couldn't stand to see a man remain single?

"I've already started, Papa."

"How?" Michael repeated, his patience turning to wariness. "Has it something to do with all the time you've been spending at Gu Bràth with Grace this last month?"

"Aye," Robbie said. "Aunt Grace helped me place an ad on the Internet."

Michael stopped walking. "What sort of ad?" he asked, staring at the moonlit forest in front of them, wondering if his son and Grace had advertised on one of those sites for lonely singles.

"An ad for a tenant," Robbie clarified. "I'm going to rent my house."

Michael didn't know whether to laugh with relief or shout with surprise. "You're wanting to rent your mother's home?" he asked softly, turning to face his son. "Why?"

"Because it shouldn't sit empty. A home needs to be lived in. It needs to be alive."

Michael actually could hear Grace's words coming from Robbie's mouth. "It will be lived in," he snapped. "When you grow up and get married."

"But that's too far away. The house needs to be alive now. When I go there, it's terribly quiet, Papa. And lonely. It needs to be needed."

Michael turned and started walking again, taking long strides that made Robbie have to jog to keep up. "It's a house, son, made of wood and glass and stone. It doesn't have feelings."

Robbie tugged on Michael's pack to get him to slow down. "It does too, Papa. I can feel the loneliness when I visit."

Michael narrowed his eyes on the path ahead. "Explain to me how renting your mother's home has anything to do with finding me a wife."

"Because I'm going to rent it to a special woman. And she'll fix your broken heart, you'll get married, and I'll get a new mama and some baby brothers."

Michael stopped walking again. He took the boy by the shoulders and hunkered down until they were face to face.

"You do not shop for a wife on the Internet," he said softly. "Nor for a mother. When we get back tonight, you and I are going to see Grace and have her remove the ad. You do not want strangers living in your mother's home."

"No, Papa! It's too late. I already have it narrowed down to three women."

Michael didn't shout, he roared. He straightened and turned and started walking back home. Goddammit. Aunt or not, Grace MacKeage had overstepped her boundaries—again.

Robbie ran to catch up but bumped into his father's back when Michael suddenly ducked to avoid being hit by a white blur of feathers. The owl's silent approach changed to an angry whistle as it lifted one wing and turned toward them again.

Michael grabbed Robbie and threw them both to the ground as he rolled to tuck his son beneath him. The owl landed on a fallen log just three feet away, and Michael found himself staring into the yellow-gold eyes of a predator.

A fist punched him in the ribs as his son squirmed to get free. "Mary!" Robbie shouted, scrambling to his knees. He knelt between the owl and Michael. "Don't be afraid, Papa. Mary won't hurt us."

Michael had lost the woman of his heart almost nine years ago, and hearing her name still tightened his chest. He sat up and pulled Robbie onto his lap, away from the bird, and stared at the snowy.

The owl stared back, its huge eyes unblinking in the moonlight, its beak slightly open as it chattered in a high-pitched rattle. Talons, more than an inch long, clung to the moss-covered log. The bird stood nearly two feet tall, and, as if it wanted Michael to complete his inspection, it stepped to the side and opened its wings to an impressive span of nearly five feet.

A very lethal, very efficient predator.

His son's pet.

Which Robbie had named for his mother.

"Mary, you stop that," Robbie scolded. "This is my papa."

The snowy owl folded its wings, ducked its head, and changed its rattle to a gentle chatter.

"Isn't she the prettiest thing you've ever seen, Papa?"

"Aye," Michael quietly agreed. And she was. The owl's sleek white feathers ended in solid black tips that appeared like lace over the snowy's entire body. Her face was a heart-shaped disk of solid white, with large, crisp yellow eyes encircled by thick black lines that might have been drawn by a heavy pencil. Strong legs ran into broad toes, completely covered with white down that ended where the powerful, sharp talons began.

A magnificently packaged predator.

"It's okay, Papa. Mary just heard your roar and thought I was in danger. See, she's calm now," Robbie said, holding his hand toward the bird.

Michael grabbed Robbie's outstretched hand and held it safely against the boy's belly. "Have ya touched her, Robbie? When you visit each other, do you get close to . . . to Mary?"

"Aye, Papa. She likes to sit on my shoulder when I ride my pony. I can whistle, and she'll come to me."

"And she's never clawed you?"

"Nay. She's very careful." Robbie stood up, found his pack, and settled it back over his shoulders. "Come on,

Papa. Mary wants to join us on our hike to the summit. She can help us decide."

"Decide what?"

"Which woman I'll rent the house to."

Michael rubbed his hands over his face. They were back to finding him a wife. Clearly a product of the mother he'd never known, Robbie could give stubborn lessons to a mule. The boy would be relentless now that he had decided on a course of action.

Michael stood up and once more headed toward the summit of TarStone Mountain. "Then we'll continue our trip," he agreed. "And spend the day discussing your need to rent your house to a stranger."

The snowy took flight and silently glided through the forest ahead of them, as if knowing their destination. Michael inhaled the smell of the night woods as the fallen leaves crunched beneath their feet. It was nearing the end of October, and the land was preparing itself for another winter—just as he must do soon. Ellen Bigelow's death, coming suddenly but peacefully in the night while she slept, would make their upcoming Christmas season all that more difficult.

Ellen had been the driving force of the Christmas tree farm. Even last year, at the age of eighty-three, the woman often had shamed the men with her energy. Ellen had been able to put unbelievable meals on the table three times a day, make wreaths, hand out saws so the customers could cut their own trees, sell decorations, dispense cider and doughnuts she made every morning, and still have time to keep up with the town gossip.

Michael had spent the last ten years, since coming to Pine Creek and buying the Bigelow farm, in awe of the woman.

"Papa, are you upset that I named my pet Mary?"

"Nay, son. Mary's a good name for such a fine pet."

"But you are upset that I want to rent my house."

"It's not so much your wish to see the house lived in," Michael clarified. "It's the fact that you've set your hopes on finding this special woman to rent it to. What happens if she turns out to be a disappointment?"

"She won't," Robbie said with all the confidence of an eight-year-old. "I'll be real careful when I choose. Aunt Grace is helping me write e-mail letters to them."

Michael snorted, letting his son know what he thought of Grace's contribution to his insane plan. "And just who is going to be the landlord to your tenant?" he asked. "When the water heater breaks or the furnace quits, are *you* going to make the repairs?"

"Nay, Papa. You are."

"I see. I would bet that was your aunt's idea as well."

"Nay, it was mine."

"Well, if I get called to the house at two in the morning, know that I intend to wake you up and take ya with me. If you're wanting to be a landlord, young man, you're going to have to carry the responsibility."

"Does that mean I can rent Mama's house, then?"

"Wouldn't ya rather find a family to live there? And get yourself a new playmate out of this endeavor?"

"I don't need a playmate nearly as much as you need a wife, Papa." Robbie stopped and looked up into Michael's eyes again. "She's going to make you smile."

Michael messed his son's hair and then pushed him forward along the trail. "Tell me about the three women you've found."

"Not until later, during breakfast. But I will give you a hint about one of them. Carla is a widow with three children." Robbie turned and wiggled his eyebrows. "She must be nice, if some man loved her enough to marry her. And with Carla, we would both get something. You'll get a wife, and I'll get new playmates."

"And where is this Carla from?"

"Florida."

Michael snorted again. "Are ya not worried she won't like our winters?"

"I do have that worry, Papa." Robbie was quiet for several minutes as he strode ahead. "Maybe I should cross Carla off the list," he said without turning around.

"So that leaves only two. What of them?"

"But there might be more," Robbie countered. "I haven't been able to check my e-mail for two days."

E-mail. Internet ads. Choosing a tenant before meeting her. What a different world his son was growing up in, compared with Michael's own childhood eight hundred years ago.

"Do you want to go to Gu Bràth with me tomorrow and check my e-mail?" Robbie asked as he ducked under a bent maple sapling.

"Nay, Robbie. I will leave that craziness up to you and Grace. I need to start preparing for the Christmas season and for the snow that'll be coming soon. And I'll have to keep John busy as well, keep his mind off his loss."

"Grampy won't go to Hawaii and live with his son, will he?" Robbie asked.

Michael was about to respond, but his chest suddenly tightened again. A prickle of cold ran up his spine and raised the hairs on the back of his neck.

Robbie's pet—the owl his son called Mary—had just glided past them again through the forest. The snowy landed on a branch in front of them, and damn if the air around the bird did not glow with the warmth of a gentle blue light.

The same blue light Michael sometimes saw in Robbie's

room when he checked on his son before going to bed himself.

The same blue light he had seen on West Shoulder Ridge eight years ago when the *drùidh's* magic had saved Grace MacKeage.

The exact same blue of Mary Sutter's beautiful eyes.

Chapter Two

Los Angeles, California, October 22

Elizabeth Hart stepped through the door of her town house and let her briefcase slip from her hand without regard for its contents. She used her hip to close the door, kicked off her shoes, and abandoned her raincoat to the floor as she headed down the hall to the kitchen.

Where had she put that bottle of Scotch?

Elizabeth searched through several cupboards and finally found the unopened bottle tucked in the back of the pantry. She grabbed a tumbler from the sink, opened the freezer, and filled the glass with ice. With an unsteady hand, Elizabeth poured the tawny liquor nearly up to the rim. She took a sip, coughed to catch her breath, then carried her drink as well as the bottle into the living room.

Guided only by the glow of the streetlights streaming through the windows, Elizabeth made her way to the couch and sat down. She set the bottle of Scotch on the coffee table and picked up the remote.

Leaning back, she took another sip of her drink, clicked the remote, and watched flames appear between the perfectly arranged ceramic logs. Fake embers started to glow at the base of the logs, and Elizabeth strained to hear . . . nothing.

Other than a slight whoosh on ignition, the fire was silent.

And odorless.

And very, very clean.

She had bought the town house five years ago, choosing it not for its proximity to work or its architecture or even its exclusive neighborhood. She had bought it because it had a fireplace.

Only at the time, the hearth had been built to burn wood.

They'd all ganged up on her, though—her mother, her father, and the guy she'd been dating. For the life of her, she couldn't remember if it had been Paul or Greg. Wood fires were dirty, labor-intensive, and smelly, they'd told her. Natural gas would fit her lifestyle so much better.

Grammy Bea had been her only ally against them. But living an hour's drive away in the mountains was not nearly enough to help counter the pressure presented by the united front of her parents and her boyfriend. The gas logs had been installed before Elizabeth had moved in.

There was something intrinsically primal in tending a wood fire. On her winter breaks through college and med school, Elizabeth had spent weeks holed up in the mountains with Grammy Bea. Setting kindling to paper, hearing the crackle of burning wood, and cleaning out ashes were daily rituals Elizabeth had cherished. A wood fire meant warmth, both physically and emotionally, and required patience to build and nurturing to sustain, creating a humanizing rhythm for the day.

Elizabeth clicked the remote, and the flame in her hearth disappeared. She clicked it again, and it whooshed back to life.

She took another, longer drink of the Scotch, relishing the burn on the back of her throat. Her stomach warmed. Her muscles prickled with the release of tension.

The train derailment had occurred just ten miles north of the city. Forty-three passengers had been injured, six of them critically.

Elizabeth had dealt with three of the most badly injured passengers.

Two of them had been almost routine, if such a thing could be said of trauma cases, and Elizabeth had worked with her usual efficient skill. The young man with the ruptured spleen and another man with broken ribs and a punctured lung would live, and heal, and go back to their lives which had been interrupted so rudely by fate.

The Scotch was because of patient number three.

Elizabeth would remember Esther Brown and her husband, Caleb, for as long as she lived. The elderly couple had been traveling to Seattle to visit their daughter and grandchildren.

Caleb had been lucky, coming away from the train wreck with only cuts, several bruised ribs, and a swollen knee. Esther had sustained injuries that were life-threatening to a seventy-eight-year-old woman: a shattered leg, a broken wrist, and internal bleeding.

But before Elizabeth could take Esther to surgery, Caleb had insisted on praying with his wife.

And he had insisted that Elizabeth pray with them.

Prayer was not foreign to Elizabeth, having grown up in the shadow of Grammy Bea. She was well aware of its power, and praying with Esther and Caleb did not mean she was getting emotionally involved. It only meant that she was a surgeon willing to use whatever means possible to help her patient deal with the trauma of surgery.

And so Elizabeth had stood beside Caleb, placed her

hand on Esther's arm, and added her own will that the woman would live.

But something had happened then.

Something unexplainable.

Elizabeth's body had started to warm. Her skin had tightened. Her heartbeat had slowed, and the trauma room had faded from her sight until only light had remained.

An array of colors in their purest form had surrounded her. A rainbow had swirled through her head in a brilliant display of laser-sharp beams. And Esther Brown had been there with her.

Only Elizabeth hadn't seen Esther, she had *become* her. She had felt the blood rushing through Esther's veins and the beat of Esther's heart, and she had taken each breath with the woman. And she had felt Esther's determination to live.

Elizabeth lifted her trembling hand, examining its silhouette in the light of the hearth. It still tingled with lingering warmth.

Elizabeth knew Grammy Bea was up in heaven, laughing her head off.

Elizabeth had not only loved Grammy Bea, she had adored her. While her parents had been off vacationing someplace or attending never-ending conferences, Elizabeth had been quite content to bask in her grandmother's attention.

The only time Bea had agreed with Elizabeth's parents was when Katherine and Barnaby Hart had announced that their daughter would grow up to be a doctor. That prophecy had come at Elizabeth's birth, and everyone, including Bea—and later including Elizabeth herself—had worked for thirty-one years to see that it happened.

The only discord was when her dad had announced that Elizabeth would train as a surgeon. Bea had spoken up then, rather forcefully, claiming that, yes, her granddaughter was destined to be a healer, but she should study for general practice instead.

Surgery was too constrained, Bea had argued. Too focused on body parts and not the whole patient. Bea claimed Elizabeth had been born with the gift of healing, carried down through her family's maternal line, and being in general practice was her destiny.

A healer? As in the mumbo-jumbo of magic?

Bea had insisted the solid white streak in Elizabeth's hair was a sign of her gift, but Elizabeth thought it was nothing more than a genetic anomaly. It wasn't even all that uncommon.

She was not a healer. Such a thing was not possible.

Or so Elizabeth had thought before today.

By the time they'd gotten Esther Brown into the operating room and Elizabeth had gotten herself prepped for surgery, the change had occurred.

At first, Elizabeth had been too focused on the procedure she was set to perform to pay much attention to the whispers. The surgery team usually whispered as patients were going under, and Elizabeth had learned to block out the unimportant chatter.

It wasn't until her scalpel was poised over Esther Brown that one of the nurses stopped her. Elizabeth had looked up to find a sea of panic-widened eyes staring at her over their masks.

And then everybody started talking at once. The patient's vitals were normal. There was no sign of a shattered leg or a broken wrist, and her once distended stomach was flat.

Elizabeth had grabbed the chart away from one wild-eyed attendant, cursing the entire trauma team for anesthetizing the wrong patient.

Dammit. She'd nearly cut into a perfectly healthy woman.

For more than half an hour, they checked every monitor and took several more X rays. Admissions was called, and Esther's wristband was read and reread and electronically scanned several times. Elizabeth had finally pulled off Esther's surgery cap and oxygen mask and studied the woman's face.

It was her. Her hair was a bit whiter, and her features were no longer drawn in pain, but the woman on her operating table was the same woman she had prayed over less than an hour ago.

Elizabeth could only stare at her silent team then. Something had gone terribly, terribly wrong.

Or wonderfully right for Esther Brown.

Oh, yes. Grammy Bea was surely laughing her head off, telling everyone in Heaven about the miracle. And, like a house of cards facing a gale, Elizabeth saw her career as a surgeon being scattered to the wind.

She had walked away from the operating room without saying a word to anyone. She had started to leave the hospital, but something had compelled her to push the up button in the elevator instead of the one that would take her down to the lobby. The elevator door had opened on the children's ward, and Elizabeth had found herself walking to young Jamie Garcia's room.

That morning, Jamie had arrived with a head injury he'd sustained when his bicycle had rolled into the path of a car. He was in a coma, and the prognosis was bad.

Elizabeth had sat beside Jamie, taken his young hand in hers, and quietly willed him to wake up. And again her body had warmed, her skin tightened, and her pulse slowed. The rainbow of brilliant colors had returned.

And Jamie Garcia had opened his eyes and smiled at her.

Elizabeth hadn't walked away that time. She had run.

She refilled her tumbler with Scotch and took the drink with her as she paced to the window. She stared out at the skyline, at Cedars-Sinai Medical Center. She could just make out the surgery unit, where she had always felt so comfortable, vital, and in charge—of herself and of any situation she faced.

Until today.

In one blinding moment, as she'd stood facing her trauma team over the anesthetized body of Esther Brown, Elizabeth had realized that she wasn't in charge at all.

In her flight from Jamie's room, and for the entire ride down to the lobby, she had fought the urge to run through the hospital and pray over patients. The need to heal had been so overwhelming that Elizabeth had felt as if she might explode. The only world she had known for thirty-one years was unraveling around her in a maelstrom of swirling colors, tugging at her until she felt herself being consumed by the chaos.

Yes, she had been completely out of control.

She needed to figure out what was happening. All of her life, Grammy Bea had told Elizabeth about the women in her family who supposedly had this gift. The last one had been her great-aunt Sylvia, who had died almost twenty years ago. All the women with this gift had had some sort of oddity or physical anomaly. Elizabeth's great-great-grandmother, she'd been told, had two different colored eyes. Great-aunt Sylvia had been born with hair down to her waist, and throughout her life, it had continued to grow at an amazing rate. Elizabeth remembered being taken to Sylvia's funeral when she was only eleven or twelve and seeing her great-aunt's braided hair all but filling the casket.

Elizabeth tugged on her own white lock of hair, pulling it forward and lifting her gaze, then blowing it back into place with a sigh. She'd laughed at Grammy Bea's stories as a child, dismissing them as tales designed to add excitement to a lonely girl's life.

Well, she wasn't laughing anymore.

She couldn't go back to the hospital. Not with all of those sick and injured people tugging at her. Not if she wished to keep her sanity.

The phone rang, blaring into the silence of the town house. Elizabeth turned with a start, sloshing her drink onto her hand, and stared at the phone on the table by the couch.

She didn't want to talk to anyone.

It rang five agonizing times before the answering machine finally picked up. Elizabeth listened to her own voice tell the caller to leave a message and then caught her breath when James Kessler's voice suddenly filled her living room.

"Elizabeth. Are you there? Pick up the phone, Elizabeth, I want to talk to you."

There was ten seconds of silence.

"Elizabeth! Pick up the phone, and tell me what happened to Jamie Garcia. I know you were in his room this afternoon. His monitors went off, and when Sally Pritchard ran to check on him, she saw you leaving."

Another ten seconds of silence, and then, "Elizabeth, pick up the phone!"

She took a step forward but stopped. James Kessler was a neurologist and family friend, and Jamie Garcia was his patient. He wanted an explanation from her, but what could she tell him? That she'd laid her hands on the boy and magically healed him?

"Dammit, Elizabeth. You call me the minute you get home."

The answering machine beeped, and the red message

light started flashing the moment James broke the connection. Elizabeth took another sip of her Scotch.

She had to get out of there. Hell, she had to get out of California. There was no way she could face James or her colleagues or even Esther Brown. How could she explain to any of them what she couldn't explain to herself?

She needed time to think—and some distance wouldn't hurt, either. Until she could come up with an explanation that wouldn't get her committed to a sanitarium, she had to avoid everyone.

But did that include her mother? Katherine knew their family history, and, like Elizabeth, she preferred to believe their female ancestors had been eccentric rather than gifted. Having hair that grew excessively, two different-colored eyes, or a white forelock was not damning, it was—well, it was the stuff of family legends.

Of course, Elizabeth had talked to her mother on more than one occasion during her childhood about Grammy Bea's tales. Katherine had been quick to dismiss them as wishful thinking, saying Bea had always been jealous of Aunt Sylvia's claim that she had been the one blessed with the gift. Bea thought of herself as an Earth Mother and had grown and gathered and processed herbs that she sold on her small farm up in the mountains. And since Bea had only one daughter, and since Katherine didn't have any "sign" of being special, Bea was simply projecting the gift onto her granddaughter.

Made sense to Elizabeth.

Or it did at the time.

But it certainly didn't explain what had happened today. Even now, her body still quivered with a strange energy. Her head felt as if it was stuffed with cotton. Her living room, cast in shadows, seemed to pulse gently with an unnatural light that was more in her mind's eye than visual.

Elizabeth sat back down on the couch and stared at the fire. All these years, Grammy Bea had been trying so hard to give her a glimpse of something beyond surgery. Up until Bea's death just two months ago, she had committed herself to grounding Elizabeth in the natural—or, rather, the unnatural—world.

And that had driven Barnaby Hart crazy until the day he himself had died four years ago. Her father used to complain that it took him two weeks to straighten Elizabeth out when she returned from a visit to her grandmother's farm. She usually came home with a suitcase full of medicinal herbs, tinctures, and balms and would have to hide them before her dad could throw them away.

She would place them in with her mother's toiletries, having figured out early that hiding something in plain sight was best. Besides, Katherine knew the value of herbs, being Bea's daughter, and used them whenever she felt a cold coming on or a wrinkle dared to show itself on her beautiful face.

The phone rang again, startling Elizabeth a second time. She held her breath for all five rings, listened to her voice tell the caller to leave a message, and then heard only silence.

"Elizabeth," her mother finally said. "Please, if you're home, pick up. James just called looking for you. He, ah, he said something strange was going on at the hospital. Something about people being—being mysteriously healed. Pick up, Elizabeth," Katherine said, her voice rising in demand.

Elizabeth quietly picked up the phone and set it to her ear. "I must be crazy, Mom, because it's true. I healed two people just by touching them."

There was a good thirty seconds of silence.

"Mom?"

"Did anyone see you do it?" Katherine asked softly.

Elizabeth set her drink down on the table and gripped the phone with both hands. "I don't think so," she whispered. "My surgery team was prepping when I prayed with the lady. Her—her husband was there, but nothing outwardly happened. The chaos was all in my head. I just left the room after and went to scrub up for surgery. Mom, I didn't even know what had happened until the lady was in the OR. Everyone just thinks there was a mix-up, because so many patients were coming in from the train wreck."

Another few seconds of silence, and then, "What about James?" Katherine asked. "He said you were in his patient's room and that the boy suddenly woke up from a coma. And that he shouldn't have. That he was about to be declared brain-dead."

Which was why James was trying to reach her. They'd always known each other, since their fathers ran a medical practice together. And having grown up on Grammy Bea's stories with Elizabeth, James was now suspicious about her.

"I—I healed him, Mom," Elizabeth whispered, closing her eyes against the sting of tears, as the impact of saying it out loud echoed through the silent living room.

"You didn't, Elizabeth. You couldn't."

"I felt it, Mom. I felt them—Esther Brown and Jamie Garcia. I went right inside them and—and healed them."

There was absolute silence on the other end of the phone.

"What do I do?" Elizabeth whispered, swiping at a tear running down her cheek. "What happens now?"

"You lie," Katherine said succinctly. "You can't have this get out, Elizabeth. Your life will be ruined, your career will be over, and the media will turn it into a circus."

"I have to leave," Elizabeth added. "I can't stay here.

I—" She took a shuddering breath. "I can't go back to the hospital, Mom. I thought I was going crazy. I could feel people tugging at me, begging to be healed."

"Oh, baby." Katherine cried softly. "I'm so sorry. You're right, you have to leave—but just for a little while, until this whole thing dies down. With nothing concrete to go on, James will have to let it go."

Elizabeth gripped the phone tighter. "No, he won't. Not as long as we're both up for that grant. He'll use this against me." Elizabeth sighed into the phone. "It doesn't really matter now, Mom. I have to pull myself off the grant. Even if we can keep this a secret, I can't work in a hospital anymore."

There was a gasp on the other end of the phone. "You're a surgeon, Elizabeth Hart," her mother said evenly. "You can't just walk away."

"But I can't go back. Don't you understand, Mom? It was overwhelming."

"I realize that, dear. I mean, I don't understand any of this, but I imagine it must be difficult. But Elizabeth, you're not thinking straight right now. You can't know that your career is over. Take some time. You're right, you probably should leave, but don't do anything you might regret."

"Why did this happen, Mom? Why now, without any warning?"

"I don't know, sweetie. I'm as shaken as you are."

"How is it possible?"

"It's not," Katherine firmly assured her. "You can't heal a person by will alone, no matter what Bea wanted you to believe. Don't let her stories affect you this way, Elizabeth. There has to be an explanation for what happened. And I'm sure once you put some distance between yourself and the hospital, you'll be able to reason it out."

"Where should I go?"

There was a hesitation on the other end of the phone, a deep sigh, and then Katherine finally said, "You can't go to the farm. James knows about it, and that will be the first place he'll look for you."

"I'll write a letter to the chief of surgery tonight and have it delivered tomorrow," Elizabeth said, deciding she'd figure out her destination later. "I'm going to tell him I have a family emergency and need a leave of absence. I'll imply that it's on Dad's side of the family, so it won't look strange that you're still here."

"I could come with you."

Elizabeth hesitated. "No, Mom," she said gently. "I need to get away by myself and think this out. I'll call you as soon as I find a place to stay."

"Elizabeth? Are you going to be okay?" Katherine asked softly. "I'm worried about you just heading off all alone, without a plan of some sort or even a destination."

"I'm a big girl, Mom," Elizabeth said brightly, trying to sound more confident than she felt. "I promise, I'll call you as soon as I find a place to stay."

"I don't like it," Katherine said with a sigh. "But I think it's best, considering your alternatives. You simply can't stay here right now. Not until this dies down and you've come up with a reasonable explanation."

Whatever that was, Elizabeth thought.

"I've got to go now, Mom. I want to pack and get out of here before James decides to come looking for me. There's too much money and prestige at stake for him to let this go."

"I love you, Elizabeth."

"I know, Mom. I love you, too. Please don't worry about me. I'm very good at taking care of myself."

"Still, you call me the minute you're settled. And meanwhile, I'll take care of James on this end. I still have a few strings to pull at the hospital."

Elizabeth smiled into the phone. "Then pull them, Mom. I gotta go now. I'll keep in touch, and you can let me know what's happening here."

"I—I love you," Katherine repeated.

"I love you, too. 'Bye."

Elizabeth gently set the phone back in its cradle and stared into the fire. She had to find someplace to go, and she had to go now. She stood up, a sudden sense of urgency pushing her into the bedroom.

She dug in the back of her closet, pulled out her suitcase, opened it, and threw it on the bed. On one of her trips from her bureau to the suitcase, her arms laden with clothes, Elizabeth stopped as she passed her computer and turned it on. She continued to pack while it booted up but suddenly had a thought, tossed her underwear into the suitcase, and all but ran to the kitchen.

She walked to the intercom and pushed the lobby button.

"Dr. Hart?" came Stanley's voice over the speaker. "What can I do for you?"

"Stanley, if anyone comes here asking for me, could you please tell them I'm not home? I don't wish to be disturbed for the rest of the night."

"Not a problem, Dr. Hart," Stanley cheerfully promised. "That's why they pay me the big bucks, to make sure no one's disturbed if they don't want to be."

"Thanks, Stan. Oh, and I'm going out of town for a while. Mom will be coming in to water my plants and stuff. Take good care of her for me, would you?"

"You got it, Dr. H. Have a good trip."

"I intend to, Stan. Thanks."

Elizabeth pushed herself away from the intercom and headed back to the bedroom. She stopped at her computer and logged onto the Internet. While the modem dialed up, she went to her closet and stared at her clothes.

What should she take? Damn, she needed a destination. She'd bought herself a bit of time with Stanley if James decided to come looking for her. The National Guard couldn't get past her doorman now that he knew she didn't want to be disturbed.

Elizabeth went back to her computer and surfed the Internet for real estate ads for houses to rent, suddenly deciding the opposite coast just might be far enough away.

New England sounded good, quaint and unhurried and very, very real. A place in the mountains where she could feel the earth wrapping securely around her.

As her search engine complied listings in Maine, New Hampshire, and Vermont, Elizabeth headed back to the closet and pulled out warm clothes. She returned to the computer and found 846 listings of houses for rent.

She narrowed it down by population, requesting a small town, which brought the total to 320. She trimmed the list further by limiting the search to rentals with wood-burning fireplaces.

Elizabeth sat down at her desk with a tired sigh. She'd have to read 106 ads. She was creating a new life here, and she intended to do it right.

One hour later, Elizabeth straightened in her chair and blinked through blurry eyes at the listing in Pine Creek, Maine. It was a hundred-year-old farmhouse set on sixty-four acres, with a fireplace, a farm kitchen, and a two-bay garage. It had outbuildings for animals and a view of Pine Lake from the porch, all backed up against TarStone Mountain. Rent was four hundred dollars a month plus utilities.

But it was the pictures, not the outrageously low rent, that caught Elizabeth's attention. There were four digital photos with the ad, and Elizabeth immediately fell in love with the house, Pine Creek, and the boy who sat proudly on a pony in front of a field of Christmas trees.

The first photo was of the house, a stately, two-story, white clapboard New England farmhouse with a slate roof, two chimneys, and a porch that wrapped around it on three sides. The second photo was taken from a distance and nicely showed off the setting. The house sat away from the road and was nestled against brightly colored maple trees contrasted by dark evergreens rising steeply up the side of TarStone Mountain.

Elizabeth assumed the third photo was taken from the porch of the house. It showed an unbelievable autumn vista of more mountains surrounding a very large body of water that must be Pine Lake.

But it was the fourth photo that tugged at her heart. A child eleven or maybe twelve years old sat on his pony and grinned at the camera. His chest was puffed out, his deep auburn hair was blowing in his eyes, and he had a lopsided smile on his face that was more arrogant than sweet.

Proud. Handsome. And apparently wanting to rent his mother's house, according to the write-up, which stated that the house had sat empty for almost eight years now.

She could give the old house its life back. Heck, she even had a way to make a living in Pine Creek.

Since the age of twelve, Elizabeth and Grammy Bea had kept their hobby a secret, simply because jewelry making would not be a noble pursuit in her father's eyes. And if he had known and had somehow approved, well, her dad would have nagged Elizabeth to know why she wasn't using gold or silver if she wanted to play at being a craftsman. No, Barnaby Hart would not have understood that creating jewelry out of glass was just as inspiring, and just as rewarding, as using more expensive material.

Elizabeth decided she could open a studio and sell her creations from her own little shop. Pine Creek was in the mountains, and Maine was known for its great skiing.

Surely there was a resort town within a reasonable commute where she could set up a shop.

Her equipment was at Bea's home in the mountains, so she'd have to drive up there tonight, pack it up, and ship it to Pine Creek. She figured she had two, maybe three days before James grew impatient enough to make the drive up there to find her.

And so Elizabeth clicked the response button at the bottom of Robbie MacBain's ad and typed:

Dear Mr. MacBain,

I was very taken with your ad to rent out your home and would like for you to consider renting it to me. Right now I live in California, but I wish to move to New England. There is no snow where I live, but I have spent a lot of time up in the mountains, and I love snow.

I also love your home. It is my hope to move to Pine Creek and get a few cats and some chickens. I also like your pony, and I think I might like to have my own horse to ride in your beautiful woods.

I enjoy growing things and would love to plant an herb garden next spring. But mostly I think you should know that it's the house itself that draws me to Pine Creek. It's a beautiful home your mama lived in, Robbie. It looks to be well built and very cozy. I especially love the fact that it has a fireplace.

And I think you're right, a house is only a home when it's lived in. I'm glad you wish to rent it, and I'm hoping you'll rent it to me.

I am a jewelry maker and would like to set up a studio in town or in a town close by. I make glass jewelry inspired by nature—birds, flowers, acorns, leaves, and animals.

I'm sorry that I can't send you my phone number so that

we can talk in person, but I'm going to my grandmother's home before traveling to Maine—and to Pine Creek, I hope, if you'll have me.

I will still be able to check my e-mail on a regular basis and am looking forward to hearing from you.

Sincerely,
Elizabeth Hart

Elizabeth reread her letter. She thought for a minute, clicked on her name at the end, and quickly changed "Elizabeth" to "Libby." Grammy Bea had always called her Libby, and if she was creating a new life for herself, a new name was a great way to start. And so Elizabeth—no, Libby—set the mouse pointer on the respond button, took a deep breath, and sent her letter spiraling through cyberspace toward young Robbie MacBain.

There. It was done.

Chapter Three

Pine Creek, Maine, October 28

*D*riving *definitely would have been easier* if Libby could have kept her eyes on the road. And the trip wouldn't have taken nearly as long if she hadn't had to stop every half hour to get out and stare at the landscape.

But the country was beautiful. Rugged. Overwhelming.

The trees went on forever; fluorescent red and yellow and orange blanketed the mountains, broken only by the deep green of pine and spruce and hemlock. Cliffs of solid granite pushed up through the vivid colors, hinting at the massive foundation that lay beneath the forest.

Since renting the small compact car at the airport in Bangor and heading northwest on Route 15, Libby had felt herself climbing, rising into the mountains until they wrapped completely around her. The tension of the last week slowly seeped from her body, and *home* became a whispered mantra that repeated itself with every beat of her heart.

After taking nearly three hours to travel the eighty miles from Bangor, Libby crested yet another hill and just barely

caught herself before slamming on the brakes. The sight of
Pine Lake, with its vast waters contained only by the sheer
strength of the mountains, stole her breath. Libby guided
her car to the shoulder of the two-lane road, shut off the
engine, and stared through the windshield.

Islands, some the size of houses and some several acres
in size, dotted the large cove that fingered in from the lake
toward the small town nestled on the shore. Mountains
rose from the water's edge like watchful guardians, several
of their peaks shrouded by low clouds as they marched
into the distance.

Her life up until this moment seemed no more than a
dream as she stared at the great reality in front of her.
Miracles lived here. This was a realm of possibilities, whispering the promise of sanctuary to her fragmented soul.

Her flight from California had ended. She'd been
driven—or pulled—to this magical place by a guiding
presence that needed no reason other than rightness. How
and why and what would happen next did not matter.
Libby simply knew this was where she belonged.

She had never given much thought to mystical powers—
not until a week ago, when she'd found herself holding
that very power in her hands. She was a surgeon who
could suddenly heal people without a scalpel.

Libby finally tore her gaze away from the lake and
picked up her collection of printouts from Robbie
MacBain. She shuffled the papers until she found the digital photos that had accompanied Robbie's Internet ad. She
stared at the young boy sitting on his pony in front of a
field of Christmas trees and tried to decide what it was
about him that had made her choose to come here.

His mother's home was certainly enticing enough. And
the mountains held their own allure, if only for their illusion of security.

But Robbie MacBain had been the final deciding factor. There was something about him, something almost other-worldly. He was a child with the eyes of an ancient soul. There was a presence about him, as he sat so proudly on his pony and looked directly at the camera with a subtle, I-know-a-secret smile lifting his lips and the promise of magic shining in his young, pewter-gray eyes.

Libby shuffled the papers again and found Robbie's last e-mail to her. "Head northeast out of Pine Creek," he'd written, "and drive until you see a large field of Christmas trees on your right. I think it's about five miles from town. I know it's not a very long ride on the schoolbus, so it shouldn't take you too long to find my home."

Libby adjusted the rearview mirror so she could see herself, brushed a stray curl from her face, and gave a quick fluff to her short, wavy hair. She blinked her huge brown eyes as she examined her reflection, hoping that her light touch of makeup wasn't too much, and smiled to make sure a stray piece of lettuce from the sandwich she'd gotten in Bangor wasn't stuck in her teeth. She wanted to look at least presentable when she met her new young landlord, so he wouldn't realize that he'd rented his mother's home to a desperate woman with secrets of her own.

Satisfied that she looked like a sane, sensible, thirty-one-year-old jewelry maker, Libby started the car, waited for a pickup truck to drive past, and pulled back onto the road. She drove slowly through the tiny town of Pine Creek, noticing with interest the few stores and three dozen or so people going about their business. She also noticed that her little car was dwarfed by the many pick-ups and huge logging trucks. She saw only one other car, squeezed between dust-covered pickups in front of Dolan's Outfitter Store.

She stopped at the intersection in the center of town

and tried to decide which way to turn. She didn't have a compass, but there were only three ways out of Pine Creek, and Libby picked the graveled but obviously much-used road that put the sun to her left, figuring it pointed her northeast.

She traveled for six miles and still didn't see a Christmas tree. Libby picked up the *Maine Atlas and Gazetteer* she'd bought at the airport in Bangor, but her attention was quickly drawn back to the road when a streak of white swooped past the nose of her car. She slammed on the brakes and jerked the steering wheel to the left to avoid hitting the large bird.

She was traveling too fast, and her car skidded toward the ditch. Libby jerked the wheel back to the right, and again she slid on the frozen gravel, fishtailing into the sharp curve that suddenly loomed before her.

She might have been able to maintain control if that damn suicidal bird had not flown past her windshield again. She cut the wheel to the right this time, only to skid on a puddle of ice at the edge of the road. Her car hit the ditch, shot up the embankment, and suddenly became airborne.

Libby shielded her face with her arms as she plowed through a stand of evergreens, her scream of surprise cut short when the small car slammed into the frozen farm pond on the other side of the trees. Both airbags exploded, punching Libby in the chest and face with the force of a cannonball.

She slapped the slowly deflating airbag away, coughing on the packing powder that had shot through the interior of the car when the airbags deployed. Water and ice cascaded over the hood, seeping into the cracks in the windshield, and the sound of the hissing engine and gushing water turned Libby's shock to terror.

The car settled deeper into the pond.

Libby grappled with the buckle on her seat belt as freezing water rushed over the floorboards. She finally got free but couldn't open the door. It was locked, and she couldn't find the release button on the new-model rental. She tried rolling down the windows, but they were electric and wouldn't work, either. So she pulled her wet feet up onto the seat and started kicking at the driver's side window. After several forceful kicks, she realized there was a man wading through the water toward her. His steely glare followed the path her car had taken, and then his piercing gun-metal eyes came to rest on her.

The car settled deeper into the pond.

The idiot. Why wasn't he rushing to help her get out before she drowned? Libby kicked the window harder and yelled at the man to do something.

But he only continued to glare.

Until finally, and ever so slowly, he tried to open the door, only to find it was locked. He pointed at the gearshift and motioned for her to put the car in park.

Sitting upright, Libby pushed on the gearshift until it was in the park position. She heard the distinct sound of all four locks clicking open. She immediately lifted the door handle and tried to open the door, but it still wouldn't budge.

And the car continued to settle deeper into the pond.

Libby started beating on the window again.

The man broke more of the ice around where he stood, braced one booted foot to the right of the car door, and took hold of the handle. With a powerful tug, he pulled open the door, and gallons of water rushed into the car, sweeping Libby into the passenger seat. She banged her head on the opposite window and cursed.

But she quickly shut up when her ungracious and still

glaring rescuer ducked into the car. The guy was huge, the most ferocious-looking man she'd ever laid eyes on.

And he was cursing back at her.

Something about murdering his prize Christmas trees.

Or was he wanting to murder her?

"You little fool," he growled as he reached toward her. "You won't drown because the pond is not deep."

More shaken by his attitude than his size, and deciding she wanted to escape him as well as the sinking car, Libby drew up her knees, planted her feet on his chest, and shoved.

Her action was so unexpected, the giant reared up, bumped his head on the roof, and went sprawling backward into the pond with another colorful curse of his own. Libby scrambled over the seat and out the door before he could recover, only to find that her legs refused to hold her up.

She fell on top of the giant.

Powerful arms wrapped around her. They both sank under the surface this time, and Libby swallowed half the pond as she struggled to get free. His strength mocked her efforts. And with one of his viselike arms wrapped around her waist and his other hand cupping her bottom, he simply stood up.

Libby instantly stilled when she found herself looking into deep gray eyes that were no longer glaring.

They were laughing.

And the giant's hand on her bottom felt more like a caress than an attempt to secure her.

So much for first impressions. She was a soaking wet, shivering mess who couldn't even keep her car on the road, and he was a knock-down-gorgeous mountain of man who couldn't even control his hormones long enough to fish her out of a pond without copping a feel. But before she could tell him what she thought of his anything but heroic rescue, the chaos of the crash finally caught up with her, and Libby slumped forward and very quietly—and most unwisely—fainted.

The whispering woke her.

And the throbbing in her temple caused her to moan.

The whispers immediately ceased, and Libby opened her eyes, only to let out a scream of surprise that made her sit up and grab her head. Two strong hands reached out and took hold of her shoulders, keeping Libby from toppling over. Her head swam, making her dizzy, and she grasped the arms holding her steady, only to find herself looking into the deepest, darkest pewter-gray eyes she'd ever seen.

Eyes that were dancing with amusement.

"I fainted," she said lamely.

"Aye."

Libby blinked. *Aye?* "Aye?" she repeated aloud.

The giant nodded.

Libby felt the heat of her blush travel up her neck to her cheeks. She also felt a flutter in the pit of her stomach.

"Papa, can't you see how huge her eyes are? You're scaring Libby."

Libby turned to the child who had spoken. The boy was sitting beside his father on the coffee table in front of the couch, grinning at her. She immediately recognized him from the picture in the ad on the Internet.

He patted her knee. "It's okay, Libby," he said. "My papa's just afraid you'll faint again."

His papa was most likely getting ready to cop another feel, Libby thought. She looked back at Robbie MacBain's father and gave him a good glare to let him know what she thought of his chivalry. She quickly decided she'd rather deal with the younger MacBain when Robbie's papa simply smiled back.

"You know who I am?" she asked Robbie.

The boy nodded but lowered his eyes. "I knew you were Libby Hart the moment I saw you, but Papa looked in your purse just to make sure."

Libby shot the man another glare. He finally let go of her shoulders and leaned away, crossing his arms over his chest, his deep gray eyes still dancing with lazy humor.

The word *giant* came to mind, but somehow even that label seemed inadequate. *Goliath* might fit better. Libby imagined Goliath had looked just as intimidating.

This giant was wearing a flannel shirt that clung to an impressively broad chest and strongly muscled arms. There was a towel draped around his neck, which obviously had been run over his still damp hair to dry up the pond water. The shadow of an emerging beard covered his angular jaw, and his high cheekbones were tinged red as his body worked to replace the heat he'd lost to the pond.

Libby couldn't decide if he was ruggedly handsome or simply imposing in a very male way. He did make her pulse race, but then, that just might be her body trying to warm itself up.

Libby decided to give her attention to Robbie.

But Robbie was looking at his father. "See, Papa. She's already making you smile. And you laughed at the pond."

Libby looked back at the giant, who had lifted one brow at his son. "Aye. She did make me laugh," he agreed. He shot Libby a grin. "She's the smallest fish we've pulled from that pond all year."

Libby snapped her gaze down to her lap, brushing her wet clothes as she felt heat climb back to her face. Oh, he was a nasty man, making fun of her size.

"Do ya think we should throw her back and let her grow

a bit more?" the older MacBain continued, humor lacing every word.

"No, Papa. I want to keep her."

Libby reached up to push one of her short, damp curls behind her ear.

"Well, Papa? Can I keep her?" Robbie asked.

"You're a jewelry maker?" the older MacBain asked.

Libby dismissed his question with an absent nod and directed her own question at Robbie. "Does your papa have a name?"

Robbie grinned at her. "Aye. It's Michael."

Libby snapped her gaze to Michael MacBain. Surely this man had nothing in common with that great angel. But then again, maybe *Michael* did fit. The archangel he was named for must be large and powerful and ferocious-looking if he was capable of defending Heaven.

Michael MacBain looked capable enough.

"What happened to your hair?" Robbie asked. "Did you have a terrible fright when you were young that turned some of it white?"

Libby reached up to touch the white streak of hair over her forehead and smiled. "No, I didn't have a fright. I was born with it that way."

Libby noticed that Robbie leaned forward in interest and that Michael MacBain leaned back in . . . well, in suspicion. She considered both of their reactions rude but refrained from saying so.

Libby let her hand trail down from her hair to rest on a bump on the left side of her forehead. It felt as large as a goose egg and made her head throb when she touched it.

"Can you tell me if ya're hurt anywhere else?" Michael asked with a grin that made him look more devilish than angelic. "I noticed your knee appears to be swollen," he said, looking down at her wet trousers clinging to an obviously swollen knee.

Her knee did feel swollen and hurt when she tried to bend it. She must have hit it on the dash when her car slammed into the water. Her left shoulder and chest felt bruised—from the seat belt, most likely. But other than a few bumps and a pounding headache, she felt relatively intact.

"How long was I out?" she asked, wondering about a concussion.

"Maybe ten minutes," Michael said.

Libby forced herself to look at her rescuer. "Thank you for pulling me out of the pond," she ungraciously muttered, remembering how he had taken his damned time to do it. She gave him a less than warm smile. "I'm glad you finally realized that I wouldn't grow any bigger and decided to fish me out."

Michael stood up. "And now I must go fish out your car," he said, giving her an equally ungracious smile. "And see what are left of my Christmas trees."

He leaned over, placed one hand on the back of the couch, and set his face uncomfortably close. "Your little accident has cost me first place at the state fair next year, lady," he whispered. "And I intend to see that I'm compensated."

With that warning—or maybe it was a threat—Michael MacBain straightened and walked out of the room. Robbie immediately scooted along the coffee table until he was sitting beside her and patted her arm.

"Don't let him bother you, Libby. Papa likes to growl a lot, but he don't mean anything by it." He suddenly grinned and held out his hand. "Hi. I'm Robbie MacBain."

Libby took the young man's offering. "It's nice to meet you finally, Robbie MacBain," she said, shaking his hand, trying not to notice that it was nearly as large as hers. Or that she probably outweighed the boy by only twenty pounds.

She couldn't decide how old he was. He spoke and acted much younger than he looked, and there was an aura of eager innocence about him. Did eleven- or twelve-year-old boys still call their fathers Papa?

"How old are you, Robbie?"

The boy puffed up his chest. "Eight," he told her. "But I'll be nine in January."

Libby didn't believe him. He was nearly as tall as she was. And his eyes, for all the innocence she saw in them, also hinted at a wisdom usually found in adults.

"Eight?" she repeated. "You're sure?"

He frowned at her. "Of course I'm sure," he said, as if she were simple-minded. "I was born the year of the ice storm."

Libby hadn't heard about any ice storm, but she nodded agreement. It was possible the boy was just large for his age, especially considering the size of his father. Michael MacBain must be nearly six and a half feet tall.

Libby stood five-foot-three in heels.

She still couldn't believe she'd actually attacked the man in the pond. It must have been temporary insanity induced by her fear of drowning. Or maybe the cold water had momentarily frozen her brain.

"Ah, Robbie? Do you think you can find me something dry to wear?"

He thought about that and said, "Gram Ellen's clothes are still here, but I don't think you should use them. It might upset Grampy if he sees you in them."

"Grampy?"

Robbie nodded. "Grampy John. He's not really my grampy, but he likes that I call him that. He's not here right now, but he lives with Papa and me 'cause he used to own this farm. But he sold it to Papa before I was born."

"And your Gram Ellen? Where is she?"

"Dead," he said, lowering his eyes. "Papa and Paul buried her in the cemetery up back two months ago."

"Oh, I'm sorry, Robbie," Libby said sincerely. "Who's Paul?"

"Grampy's son. But he's gone back to Hawaii now."

"I see. Then maybe you're right, I shouldn't borrow your Gram Ellen's clothes. How about something of yours?"

He stood up. "I'll go get you one of my shirts." He looked up and down the length of her lying on the couch. "I got some jogging pants that will fit you," he added. He headed for the door. "I'll bring you some socks, too."

As soon as he disappeared up the stairs, Libby sat up and swung her feet over the edge of the couch, pulled up her pants leg, and looked at her knee. It was indeed swollen and red. She flexed the knee several times, stood up, and put some weight on it.

It hurt but still worked well enough. Libby straightened and put one hand to the small of her back, leaning backward to flex her muscles. She ached all over but suspected it was nothing compared with what she would feel tomorrow.

She was lucky. Her injuries could have been much worse, considering that she probably had totaled the car.

Libby looked around the huge living room and soon realized that this was an all-bachelor household now, since Gram Ellen had died two months ago. There was so much dust covering the furniture that Robbie and Michael's handprints were clearly visible on the coffee table.

Robbie had mentioned in one of his e-mails that his mother had died when he was a child. And apparently there was no new Mrs. Michael MacBain in residence. Or, if there was, she wasn't much of a housekeeper.

Libby limped over to one of the windows to look out, only to gasp in surprise.

She was standing smack in the middle of Christmas.

The snow that had threatened all day during her drive here had finally arrived. Huge, fat, cotton-ball flakes floated down over the landscape, sticking to everything they touched. Rows upon rows of Christmas trees covered the field for as far as she could see.

She had traveled to Wonderland.

Movement caught her attention, and Libby watched as Michael MacBain drove his tractor up to the edge of the car-eating pond. He climbed down and waded into the water until it reached his chest.

The man didn't so much as flinch, much less hesitate to enter the freezing pond. How could he do that? Libby shuddered in her own wet clothes at just the thought of how cold he must be. Heck, she knew from personal experience.

She watched, intrigued and maybe in awe, as Michael pulled a cable from the front of his tractor and dove under the back bumper of the car to attach it. Libby held her breath and didn't release it until he resurfaced.

The man was amazing. Or suicidal. Was he even aware that he could get hypothermia and not even know it until it was too late?

And why was he doing this dangerous and unpleasant chore for her, anyway? Especially considering how mad he was at her.

She had mowed down some of the prize Christmas trees he'd been growing for a state competition. Anyone in his situation would have simply handed her the phone and told her to call a wrecker. But Michael was working in freezing water to clean up the mess she'd made.

And for that, Libby felt guilty.

She was deeply indebted to Michael MacBain.

And that worried her. She wasn't used to owing people. Especially tall, ruggedly handsome men who could turn her insides into warm liquid mush with just a look. Libby hugged herself, remembering the feel of Michael's hands on her shoulders. Truth told, she'd been downright flustered in a very feminine way. Dammit. She was going to have to watch herself if she wanted to make a go of it here. She couldn't get starry-eyed over the first good-looking mountain man she met.

Nor could she let herself get too attached to his son.

She'd come here to build a new life for herself, and she couldn't risk getting involved with her landlords because, above all else, she had to protect her terrible secret.

Michael surfaced from the pond and tossed his head back to clear the water from his face. He waded to the driver's side of the car and pushed on the door until it clicked shut, then looked in the backseat of the nearly submerged compact and shook his head. All of Libby Hart's belongings were soaked, including what looked like a computer floating around in a black briefcase.

The woman was damned lucky to be alive. If he and Robbie hadn't been home or had been up back in the twelve-acre field, she could have frozen to death before she escaped.

Michael snorted. Woman? he thought with another shake of his head. Libby Hart looked more like a boy than a woman, with her short curly hair, tiny body, and childlike large brown eyes. The only thing big about Libby was her temper.

Michael caught himself smiling again. The woman had been so flaming mad at him that she'd come out of the car cursing at him. Which meant her courage was bigger than she was, for her to go up against a man twice her size.

Which also told him that Libby Hart was reckless.

What had his son gotten them into? For the last four days, Robbie had been so excited about Libby's arrival, it had been all Michael could do to keep the boy from bouncing off the walls.

So he'd put his son to work getting Mary's house ready for its new tenant. And he'd shamed Grace MacKeage into supervising Robbie, since she had played such a large role in this unsubtle conspiracy to find him a wife.

Well, hell. Somebody should have asked for a picture of Libby Hart. The woman barely came up to Michael's chest.

But Michael had to admit that she was all woman. He remembered the feel of her nice little behind as he'd lifted her out of the pond. He'd also noticed her flawless skin and long, elegant neck peeking out of her half-buttoned blouse when he'd carried her into the house. He'd had to button that blouse back up after sending Robbie to get a towel, when he would have preferred to strip it off her instead.

Michael felt his blood beginning to stir, only to realize that he'd gone numb from the waist down. He waded back out of the freezing water, climbed onto the tractor, and put it in gear. He slowly released the clutch to coax the car gently out of the pond, but his memory of Libby's body proved a distraction. He popped the clutch, and the tractor lurched back, jerking the car with it until Michael and the two vehicles rolled out onto the road.

And still the image of Libby persisted.

Dammit. He had no use for small, reckless women.

Aye, Libby Hart was going to be trouble.

Chapter Four

Robbie sat in Libby's newly rented house, his elbows on the kitchen table and his chin resting in his palms as he supervised her unpacking. He examined every item as it came out of her soggy suitcase and guilelessly announced whether he thought it was ruined or not.

The ruined pile was growing quite large.

Libby gave up trying to save her belongings and stuffed a lot of things back into the suitcase. She carried it over to the kitchen door and dropped it onto the floor.

"What day does the trash get picked up?" she asked her helper as she set her computer case on the table.

"Picked up?" Robbie echoed, giving her a quizzical look.

"The trash truck. What day of the week does it come around?"

"We don't have a truck that picks up our trash. You gotta take it to the dump."

Libby blinked at her landlord. "I have to take it myself?"

Robbie nodded. "Yup. The dump is open every Saturday."

"I don't suppose that your taking my trash to the dump is included in the rent?"

As Robbie thought about that, his eyebrows lowered in a deep frown. Libby laughed and waved her hand at the air. "Never mind. You come with me next Saturday and show me where the dump is. If I'm going to live here, I might as well get used to the way things are."

Libby opened her computer case but had to step back when a gallon of water spilled out, covering the table and running onto the floor. Robbie scrambled away from the mess and whistled.

"I don't think your computer survived, Libby. Aunt Grace says never get electronics wet."

"Aunt Grace?"

Robbie walked back to the table and looked at the soggy computer. "She's my mama's sister," he told her, finally looking at Libby. "They grew up together in this house."

Libby stilled in the act of reaching for her computer. "And how does your aunt feel about my living in her family's home?"

Robbie gave her a huge grin. "It was her idea. That I rent it," he clarified. "It was my idea that I rent it to you."

"And I thank you for that," Libby said with a grin of her own. She looked around the huge old kitchen. "I've already fallen in love with this place. It feels . . ." She looked back at Robbie. "It feels homey. I'm going to enjoy living here. And thank you for having the firewood stacked in the garage. I can't wait to use that beautiful hearth."

Robbie suddenly turned serious. "I found ya some kittens, but Uncle Ian said they won't be ready to leave their mama for a few more days yet. I can bring them here after school one day next week, if that's okay with you."

"Oh, that will be wonderful. Is Uncle Ian your mama's brother?"

"No. He's not really my uncle, he just likes that I call him that. He's really Uncle Grey's cousin."

"Uncle Grey?"

"Aunt Grace's husband," Robbie said with an exasperated sigh. "There are four MacKeage men. Grey, Ian, Callum, and Morgan. They own TarStone Mountain Resort, on the other side of that ridge over there," he explained, pointing at the kitchen window.

"Grey is married to Aunt Grace, Morgan is married to Sadie, and Callum is married to Charlotte," he continued, apparently feeling the need to list his extended family. "Ian's not married to no one, 'cause he says he's too cantankerous to be married to a woman," he finished.

Since Robbie was being so informative, Libby decided to pry a bit more. She wanted to know about her new neighbors.

"Does your father have any brothers or sisters?"

"Nope. It's just him and me. And John. But I already told you about Grampy."

"And do you have any cousins on the MacKeage side?"

Robbie grinned again, then suddenly scrunched up his face. "Aunt Grace got all girls. Six. And she's pregnant again and says this one's going to be a girl, too." He brightened back up. "Aunt Sadie and Uncle Morgan got three boys and a girl, but they need to grow up some more before I can really play with them. And they don't trust me alone with Jennifer anymore. Not after I nearly killed her. But Aunt Charlotte and Uncle Callum's got a boy, and I play with him a lot."

Libby looked up in surprise. "You nearly killed a girl?"

Robbie nodded, then quickly shook his head in denial. "Naw. Papa told me they just said that 'cause they were scared. They didn't understand that I was holding on real tight to Jennifer. She wouldn't have fallen."

"Fallen from where?" Libby asked softly.

"Off my pony. Jennifer wanted a ride for her birthday."

"And how old is Jennifer?"

"Two. Or she was. She's two and a half now."

Being very careful not to let her horror show on her face, Libby sat down, only to wince when she sat in a puddle of water.

"Oh, about your wanting to have a horse," Robbie said, completely unaware of her distress.

"What about a horse?" Libby asked, shaking away the picture of Robbie riding his pony with a child on his lap.

"I've been thinking that you don't gotta buy your own horse, Libby. I was planning for you to ride Papa's. But he told me that after seeing you, you better ride my pony and for me to ride Stomper."

Determined to ignore Michael's insult to her size again, Libby asked, "And just how big is Stomper that your papa thinks you would be better off riding him?"

"Oh, Stomper's a warhorse. But he's used to me and behaves most of the time. It's only when Papa rides him that he gets a little wild."

"A warhorse?" Libby whispered. She didn't know what breed a warhorse was, but it sounded large. And mean.

"Stomper's really old." He tried to console Libby, patting her knee. "And he's not a warhorse anymore. But Papa won't let him pull the Christmas sled, 'cause he says it's beneath Stomper's dignity."

The boy was a fountain of information—some of which sent shivers down Libby's spine.

There was a knock on the porch door, and Libby stood up, but she stopped to pull her wet pants away from her bum, which is why Robbie beat her to the door.

A beautiful and very pregnant woman walked in carrying a sack of groceries. "There's more in the truck, Robbie," she said, setting the bag down on the counter. She turned and held out her hand. "Hi. I'm Grace MacKeage, Robbie's aunt."

Libby took the offered hand and shook it. "It's good to meet you, Grace. I'm Libby, and I've been hearing all about you from Robbie."

Grace snorted. "I just bet you have." The fortyish woman put her hands on her back to support her swollen stomach as she looked around the kitchen. "So. What do you think of the old homestead? Meet your standards?"

Libby nodded and rushed to pull out a chair from the table. She checked to make sure it was dry, then waved her new neighbor over. "It's beautiful. Please, sit down. I don't have any tea to offer you yet, but we can at least visit."

With a nod of thanks, Grace waddled over to the chair and sat down with a sigh of relief. "Thanks," she said, patting her belly with both hands. "I swear she's playing soccer in there."

Libby nodded at Grace's stomach. "Your seventh, Robbie said?"

"Yup. Another healthy and happy girl, having a grand old time at my expense."

"When are you due?"

Grace cocked her head to the side and grinned at Libby. "December twentieth, this year."

"This year?"

Grace held up four fingers. "Four pregnancies, not counting this one, and six daughters. All born either on December twentieth or twenty-first, depending on when Winter Solstice was that year." She waved at the air. "I don't keep track of the date, just the day."

"All your daughters were born on Winter Solstice?" Libby asked. She pointed at Grace's belly. "And you're expecting this one the same day?"

Grace gave a small laugh. "Why not? It's convenient, having all the birthday parties at once."

"But you can't expect all your children to be born on the same day," Libby impolitely repeated. "It's improbable."

"Said the doctor to the mathematician," Grace quietly agreed with a slow nod, leveling her gaze at Libby.

Libby gasped. She felt the bottom drop out of her new life. "But . . . how . . . how did you know?"

"That you're Elizabeth Hart, renowned trauma surgeon from Cedars-Sinai?" Grace asked, lifting one brow. "Did you expect me to let my nephew rent his house to a complete stranger off the Internet?"

Libby returned her visitor's level stare. "Who else knows besides you? Michael? Robbie?"

Grace shook her head. "No. Just my husband." She shot Libby a conspirator's smile. "Since you didn't mention that fact in your e-mails, I assumed you didn't want it advertised." She shrugged. "I don't know why you've come here, but I don't really care, Libby. As long as you continue to be the level-headed, intelligent woman my sources say you are, I don't have a problem with your wanting to hide here. Pine Creek is a haven to more than one lost soul."

"I'm not hiding," Libby softly defended. "Except maybe from myself," she admitted. She smiled at her new friend, immediately deciding she could trust Grace. "I thought I might be one of those lost souls you mentioned, but if I had doubts about what I'm doing, I don't anymore. The closer I got to Pine Creek today, the louder the voice in my head told me I was finally where I belonged."

Grace set one hand on her knee and the other on the back of the chair and awkwardly pushed herself to her feet. She walked over to Libby and engulfed her in a warm, sisterly hug. "That's good," she whispered. " 'Cause this town can use a woman of your talent."

Libby leaned back. "I . . . I'm through with doctoring."

Grace gave Libby a wink as she pulled away. "I wasn't talking about your talent with a scalpel," she said softly.

Robbie came through the door with his arms loaded with paper sacks. Libby rushed to help the boy, wondering what her new friend meant by her comment,

"You shouldn't have done this for me, Grace," Libby scolded. "It's a tiring chore for someone in your condition."

Grace snorted. "It's less tiring than keeping six girls entertained. I'll have to go rescue my husband from them soon, but I have time for tea," she said, reaching into one of the sacks and pulling out a box of tea.

"Did you buy any water?" Libby asked, looking through the other bags.

Grace laughed. Robbie gave Libby a quizzical look. "You don't buy water at the store," he told her. "You turn on the faucet."

"It's well water," Grace clarified. "And the sweetest in the country."

Libby felt a blush creep into her cheeks. "I'm not such a city girl that I'm unredeemable," she said lamely. "I just had a momentary brain cramp."

Grace patted Libby's arm as she walked past her with the teakettle. "It took me months to reacclimate," Grace assured her. She put the kettle on the range to boil and then walked over to the table and picked up Libby's soggy computer. "This doesn't look good." She turned to Libby. "What happened?"

"She decided to give her car a bath in our pond," Robbie answered before she could, laughing at his own joke. "Remember? I told you Papa had to fish her out." He shot a devilish look at Libby. "We thought about throwing her back, though, so she could grow some more."

Grace messed the boy's hair. "Your father's sense of

humor is not something to emulate, Robbie," she chided. "Go look it up in the dictionary in the living room," she added at his questioning frown.

Grace turned her attention to Libby's own questioning look the moment Robbie ran into the living room. "When he's not acting like the eight-year-old he really is, he can be quite brilliant. And often quite scary."

"He must be in, what, second grade?" Libby asked.

Grace nodded. "He reads at an eighth-grade level, thanks to Michael. And his grasp of mathematics is well beyond that, compliments of his Sutter genes," Grace said with a proud smile.

"He looks much older than eight," Libby said, still skeptical.

"That's thanks to Michael, too. But then, you've met his father," Grace added, a twinkle brightening her eyes. "I heard you were about to take a swing at him."

"I only managed to make him laugh."

Grace patted Libby's arm and then opened a cupboard and took down two mugs. "And that, Libby Hart, is a miracle," she said. She nodded her smile of approval. "I've probably seen Michael laugh only twice since I've known him. And both times were at another person's expense. Once at my own."

"The man sounds wonderful," Libby said.

Grace MacKeage suddenly turned serious. "He is wonderful," she declared with all the loyalty of a sister-in-law. "They don't make men like Michael MacBain anymore."

"You mean big and ferocious-looking?" Libby asked, deciding to lighten the mood.

But Grace nodded agreement. "Yes, Michael can be intimidating, if you let him." She looked up and down Libby's small body, and Grace's smile suddenly returned.

"You might have to stand on a chair, but I think you can give back just as good as you get."

Libby didn't disagree. She did decide that she was supposed to be the hostess here, even though it was Grace's family home. She took over the chore of making the tea and waved Grace back to her seat.

"But I'm supposed to emulate my papa," Robbie said as he walked back into the kitchen. "It means to try to be equal to, if not better than, a person. I want to be just like Papa."

Libby carried the mugs of tea to the table and sat down, amused by her new landlord.

"You can grow big like your papa," Grace agreed, pulling Robbie up against her belly to hug him. "And you can even emulate Michael's manly swagger." She took hold of his chin and forced him to look at her. "But you will be more civilized, Robert MacBain, when it comes to women."

"Papa can be civilized," he countered, grinning up at his aunt. "He buttoned Libby's shirt up so I wouldn't see her breasts. That was civilized, don't you think?"

Libby had just taken a sip of her tea, but instead of swallowing, she spit it all over the table. She slapped her hands to her flaming cheeks and stared in horror at Grace.

Grace lifted a brow and smiled at Libby, then looked back at Robbie and nodded. "That was a very civilized thing for Michael to do," she agreed. She set the boy away and gave him a pat on his backside. "Why don't you go arrange some paper and kindling in the hearth? I'm sure Libby would like to light a fire this evening to stare at while she contemplates just what she's gotten herself into here."

Robbie ran back into the living room, eager to do his important chore, and Grace turned laughing eyes on Libby.

Libby continued to stare in horrified silence.

"I'm scared to death to tell you how similar our arrivals to Pine Creek are," Grace said, shaking her head. "For fear you'll turn around and run back to California."

That cryptic remark brought Libby out of her stupor. "How similar?" she asked, blinking at Grace's very pregnant belly, wondering just how similar their lives would continue to be.

Grace nodded toward the kitchen door at Libby's ruined suitcase. "I also had an accident arriving here, and everything I brought with me was ruined."

She smiled as she said this, and Libby became intrigued. "What sort of accident?"

"My plane crashed," Grace said, waving it away as if it were unimportant. She nodded at Libby's computer. "Even my laptop was ruined, like yours. But that's not the point of this story. I was also unconscious in the arms of a very large, very intimidating man." She patted her belly. "That was eight years and almost seven babies ago."

Libby was back to being horrified.

Grace laughed and awkwardly stood up. "You've come to a good place, Elizabeth Hart. This house will keep you warm and cozy, the land will recharge your batteries, and the people will welcome you." She walked to the living room door to watch Robbie lay up the fire, then turned to Libby again, an impish smile lighting her eyes. "And Michael MacBain is going to drive you crazy, but that won't stop you from falling in love with him anyway."

Chapter Five

*L*ibby *spent the first night in her new home* tossing and twisting in her bed as unsettling dreams ran through her mind. In her mind's eye, she could see a huge white bird fluttering against the ceiling over her head, its beating wings charging the air with a pulsing blue light; a large, snorting, out-of-control horse galloping through the woods with her clinging to its back, screaming in terror for someone to help her; and a giant, with hands like forged steel and eyes as deep and dark as the granite of the mountains, shouting over the howl of the wind.

Libby opened her eyes and screamed at the top of her lungs.

A large hand covered her mouth. "My God, woman, but you do love to holler," Michael MacBain whispered, his face mere inches from hers.

The heat of his hand, the feel of his warm breath brushing her cheeks, and the weight of his large, very male body pushing against her sent prickles of awareness through every nerve in Libby's body. The howl of the wind from her dream continued, the rain driving against the bedroom windows only adding to the chaos of her reeling emotions.

"I'm going to remove my hand," Michael said, his eyes reflecting off what appeared to be the beam of a flashlight lying on the bed beside them. "And if you scream again," he continued softly, "I just might shut you up with a kiss this time. Do you understand, Libby?"

Libby frantically nodded.

What in hell was he doing there in the middle of the night?

But, more important, why wasn't she afraid?

She should be scared to death, waking up to find a man she'd only met yesterday in her bedroom. But truth be told, Libby was more afraid of herself at the moment. It had been a long time since she'd felt the kind of energy that sparked between them.

And it was then that Libby realized why he was there.

Michael MacBain felt the energy, too, and it scared him just as much as it scared her. He was in her bedroom in the dead of night, hoping to unnerve her enough that she'd run back to California before that energy created a very big problem for both of them.

Oh, she was sorely tempted to call his bluff.

As if he could read her thoughts, he suddenly stood up.

Libby sat up in bed, hugging the blankets to her chest.

Michael took a step back and ran his hand through his hair. "Dammit, woman. Why in hell aren't you slapping my face?"

Libby couldn't help but smile as she ran her own shaking hand through her hair. "I can be contrary that way," she told him. "When I think a person has an ulterior motive, I have this need to call his bluff more often than not."

"My God," he breathed. "You're reckless."

"I'm not afraid of you, Michael."

"You should be," he growled, taking a step toward the bed. "Do you not realize what could have just happened between us?"

"Nothing would have happened, Michael, so stop posturing. You didn't really come here to mess up my sheets."

He gaped at her, clearly at a loss for words, then scrubbed his face with his hands. He gave a growl from deep in his chest, and suddenly he was on top of her again—only this time, he wasn't sitting, he was lying beside her, trapping her under the blankets.

One of his hands wrapped around her shoulders, and the other hand caught her hip as he pulled her tightly against him. Libby found herself nose to nose with the giant, staring into his turbulent gray eyes.

It was probably time to panic. Michael MacBain was obviously not used to having his bluff called. And truth told, Libby was not used to being manhandled by large, angry men.

Yes, she should have been scared. And she would have been, but for the simple, telling act of Michael carefully moving away from her swollen knee, using his leg to trap her thigh instead.

"Don't mistake me for one of your civilized California men," he said softly, contradicting his action. "It's not only distance you've traveled to get here, Libby Hart. Men in these mountains have a tendency to finish what we start, and we don't allow anyone, especially a tiny thing like you, to call our bluff."

"What's your point, Michael?"

"Dammit, Libby. Do you even realize why you were lured here?"

She shouldn't smile. But Libby simply couldn't help herself. "Your son is looking for a new mama," she told him. "And he seems to think I might be a good candidate."

He reared back to glare at her. "So you admit you're hunting for a husband?"

Her smile turned into a laugh. "I am not."

It was obvious he didn't believe her when his hand tightened on her backside. Libby quit smiling.

"So you admit you came here tonight to scare me away?" she asked, turning his question back on him.

"I came because I was worried about you in this storm."

"What storm?"

He let out a sigh strong enough to move her hair. "The snow has turned to a driving rain," he explained with growing impatience. "The electricity's gone out."

"You came all the way over here, broke into my house, and woke me up to tell me the power's out? How very sweet of you."

He leaned more of his weight on her. "Are you always this reckless when you have a two-hundred-pound man pushing you into the mattress, lady, or do you merely have a death wish?"

"I haven't been on a mattress with a two-hundred-pound man in a very long time," she told him, wiggling a bit so she could breathe more easily. "Are you going to get up?"

"I haven't decided," he snapped, moving back against her. He brushed a curl from her face but stopped and fingered what Libby knew was her white lock of hair. He studied it and then studied her face.

"Why have you come here?"

Libby guessed Michael had decided not to get up but to talk instead. And she didn't know if she should be relieved or alarmed.

"I'm starting a new life."

"What was wrong with your old life?"

"It didn't fit anymore. I suddenly found myself unable to breathe. Like now."

He lifted his weight, but only slightly, as he continued to study her. And Libby's relief slowly turned to alarm. She was beginning to get hot under the covers, and it wasn't from too many blankets.

Michael MacBain had the most beautiful eyes Libby had ever seen. And that little flutter in the pit of her stomach was becoming an internal storm that mocked the one raging outside.

"Are you going to tell me what you did in your former life?"

"No."

"But you are saying that you're not here to find yourself a husband and a ready-made family."

"That's the story I'm sticking to."

"I won't allow you to break my son's heart, Libby."

"I won't, Michael."

He was silent for a bit, his finger again toying with her hair. One corner of his mouth turned up. "Then that leaves us two choices. I can show you how to run the generator, or we can—how did you so nicely put it?—mess up your sheets."

Oh, she was tempted. Making love to Michael MacBain would most likely be the experience of a lifetime.

"I've always wanted to run a generator," she said.

Libby would give him credit, he didn't appear disappointed. His smile was a little crooked, but her answer seemed to please him. Or was that relief she saw relaxing the harsh planes of his face?

She took her first full breath since waking, when Michael finally lifted himself away and stood up. He picked up the flashlight and shined it at her, keeping the beam out of her eyes.

"Dress warm," he told her. "The power's been out for several hours, and the house has grown cold." He tossed the flashlight onto the bed and walked away but stopped at the door and turned back to her.

"And Libby?"

"Yes, Michael?"

"Contrary to what my son is hoping for, I have no intention of ever marrying. But you should know that I do intend to have you. And for that reason alone, you should fear me, lass. Be wise, Libby, and be afraid."

Chapter Six

It was noon, and Libby was sitting in her new living room, watching the wonderfully smelly and messy wood fire crackling in her new hearth. She rearranged the towel of ice more comfortably over her knee and sighed in contentment.

The storm had blown itself out, and the power had come back on not twenty minutes after Michael had left without showing her the generator. He'd warned her of his intentions and then simply walked out.

Yeah. The sky had cleared, but it appeared the electrical storm between them had only just begun.

Libby wasn't sure how she felt about that. She'd been honest when she told Michael she hadn't come here looking for a husband or a ready-made family. She was trying to build a new life for herself. Well, she'd certainly started it off with a bang. She'd not only crashed into a farm pond, she'd crashed into the arms of a very sexy, very large mountain of testosterone.

A mountain who intended to have her.

Libby couldn't remember the last time a man had said he wanted her. And never had it been put to her quite so bluntly—or so honestly.

And that was why she wasn't afraid of Michael MacBain. Truly honest men, even those who thought of themselves as uncivilized, need not be feared. They were throwbacks to a nobler time—becoming quite rare in this day but definitely interesting to deal with.

And she could deal with Michael, if that's what the man wanted. Heck, she'd be crazy not to take him up on his offer. And how dangerous could it be to mess up the sheets with him? She was made of stern stuff. Her heart could handle a flaming affair as long as she knew from the beginning that it wouldn't lead to anything permanent.

Libby opened the towel on her knee and pulled out a half-melted ice cube. She popped it into her mouth and crunched it between her teeth, wondering if the wood fire was getting out of control or if just the thought of getting naked with Michael MacBain was making her hot.

A knock sounded on her kitchen door, and Libby stilled in the act of popping another ice cube into her mouth. Oh, Lord, it had better not be him, she thought. She wasn't ready to face Michael so soon. Not when her thoughts of having an affair with the man were probably written all over her face.

"Hello, the house!" came a booming shout, accompanied by another, more violent knock.

"I'm coming," Libby hollered back, getting up from the chair and limping into the kitchen. She tossed her towel of ice into the sink as she walked by but stopped to peek through the sheer curtain before opening the door.

There was a very large man standing on her porch, with wild, graying auburn hair and a beard that looked bushy enough for birds to nest in. He was glaring at the window as he knocked again, rattling the entire door on its hinges.

Libby pulled the curtain aside and smiled back. "Can I help you?" she asked.

The man's glare disappeared along with his eyebrows into his hairline, when he realized that he had to look down to see her.

"My name's Ian MacKeage, Miss Hart," he said in a gruff and barely understandable Scottish accent as he attempted to soften the harsh planes of his face with a smile. "I've brung ya the hens young Robbie asked for."

Libby immediately recognized the name and opened the door.

"What hens?" she asked, stepping onto the porch when he stepped back.

The man's chin dropped to his chest, his eyebrows rose out of sight again, and he just stood there and stared at her.

"Where's the rest of ya?" he asked, only to snap his mouth shut and duck his suddenly red face. "I . . . I'm being sorry for saying so, lass, but you're a might tiny thing, and I . . . I . . . ." He snapped his mouth shut again and rubbed his beefy hand over his face, as if he could scrub away his words.

Libby was beginning to wonder if she had moved to the land of giants. Ian MacKeage, for all his advancing years, was a brute. He stood a good foot taller than she did, but most of his size was made up of broad shoulders, massive arms, and an impressively large barrel chest.

"I'm sorry," he said again. "It's just that I was expecting someone a bit, well . . ." He smiled and shook his head. "Has Michael seen ya yet?"

Libby wasn't above a good joke, even when she was the brunt of it. "He wanted to throw me back into his pond so

I could grow bigger," she told Ian, enjoying his shocked expression.

"Michael would never do nothing like that, Miss Hart," he quickly defended. "The boy's got more manners than that."

Boy? Ian considered Michael a boy?

"What hens are you talking about?" she asked.

It took him a moment to realize she'd changed the subject. "Oh, the hens Robbie wanted for ya," he said, waving toward his pickup truck. "He insisted on pullets, but I only had eight, so I threw in a few old ones to make up the dozen."

"And a pullet is?" Libby prodded.

"A young hen. They were hatched this spring and have already started laying."

"A dozen?" Libby repeated softly, only now realizing the implication of owning that many hens. "What am I going to do with a dozen eggs every day?"

Ian gave her an odd look. "Ya bake with them, woman. Ya make cookies and cakes and stuff." His eyebrows lifted again when she didn't readily nod agreement. "Ya mean ya don't bake? Does young Robbie know this?"

Libby was also beginning to wonder if she'd come here to start her new life or been lured to be surrogate mother to Robbie and sexual entertainment for Michael MacBain. Was everyone in Pine Creek in on this little conspiracy?

Hell. Even Grace had alluded to it yesterday.

"I . . . I can bake," Libby said, wondering why she was admitting such a thing. "I just can't see using a dozen eggs every day. Who's going to eat that amount of food?" she asked, already knowing what Ian was going to say and not wanting to hear it.

"Michael and Robbie," he said anyway. "And John. They got no one to bake for them now." He shook his head.

"MacBain can't cook worth a damn, and that's a fact. The boy might do okay over an open fire, but a stove defeats him. Young Robbie's been eating at Gu Bràth a lot lately."

"Gu Bràth?"

"That's our home," Ian said, pointing toward the same ridge Robbie had indicated yesterday. "Me and Grace and Grey and the hellions live there."

"The hellions?"

Ian grinned. "Grace's bairns. The lasses," he explained at her quizzical look. "Heather's almost eight, and Sarah and Camry are almost six, Chelsea and Megan will be four, and Elizabeth will be three this December."

He leaned closer and whispered his next words. "But don't call them hellions in front of Grace," he confided with a conspirator's wink. "Although I've heard her call them that a few times herself." He straightened back up and puffed out his already impressive chest. "They're good bairns for girls, though they can talk a man's ear off if he ain't learned to hide quick enough."

"I met Grace yesterday," Libby told him, nodding.

"She said she was over," Ian said. "But it seems she forgot to mention that a good wind would blow ya away."

Libby was getting sorely tired of her size being such a big issue. She puffed up her own—unimpressive—chest and glared at Ian MacKeage. "Don't let the package fool you," she told him. "I'm much tougher than I look."

He raised both hands in supplication, his grin wide enough to show through his beard. "Now, lass, I'm not wanting to hurt your feelings. I'm only teasing you a wee bit. Come on," he said, turning toward his truck. "We'll see how tough ya are when it comes to dealing with a dozen flapping hens."

Half an hour later, Libby felt confident she had passed Ian's test. All twelve hens were now eating their heads off in her coop, and she had only eight or ten peck marks to show for her efforts.

"Do you know where I can buy a truck around here?" she asked. "Something like yours," she said. "Only not quite so big," she added as she struggled to close the tailgate without looking as if she was about to collapse under its weight.

Ian must have realized she was in danger of being flattened, and he flipped the tailgate up with a flick of his wrist.

"I believe Callum's got a truck he's wanting to sell. But it's not a pickup like mine. It's a Suburban."

"Oh, that would be even better. I can haul my product to craft shows without worrying about getting anything wet. How do I get in contact with Callum?"

"I'll have him drop by with the truck tonight," Ian told her. He cocked his head and gave her a curious look. "It's not that old a truck, lass. It might cost a bit more than you were planning on spending."

"I think I can scrape the money together," she told him.

"Grace said you make jewelry?"

"I work with glass," Libby confirmed, nodding. "And I hope to find a shop in town to rent so I can set up a studio. Do you know of anyplace that might be available?"

"There's a couple of empty storefronts that might work. Check with the Dolan brothers. They bought Hellman's Outfitter Store, but it's called Dolan's Outfitter Store now, and I think they own the whole building. There's an empty space at one end of it," he finished, walking around the truck and opening the door.

Libby waited until he climbed in. "Thank you, Ian, for the information and for bringing me the hens. What do I owe you for them?"

"Already been paid for," he said with a wink. "Robbie

hatched them and told me last week they were part of the rent."

He shut the door, started the truck, and rolled down the window. "Stay outta the wind, lass, so we don't have to chase ya clear into the next county," he got off as a parting shot as he drove away, his laughter trailing in the dust of his wheels.

Libby waited until she was sure he was out of sight, then shot Ian MacKeage a very unladylike gesture.

"And I thought I was uncivilized," a deep, laughing voice said from behind her.

Libby whirled in surprise, then gasped and took several steps back the moment she realized exactly what a warhorse was. It was a long-necked, hairy-tailed elephant minus the trunk.

And Michael MacBain was sitting on top of the monster.

He held out his hand.

Libby took another step back.

Michael's smile widened. "Come on, Libby," he beckoned. "Take a ride with me while I go check on an old man who lives on the mountain."

Libby rubbed her hen-pecked palms on her thighs and stared at Michael's outstretched hand. Damn him. He couldn't say what he had said this morning and then come riding in here and expect her just to jump up and go with him.

"I . . . I don't have a riding helmet," she whispered, knowing he heard her. "And nobody should ride without one," she added.

He said nothing to that but merely continued to hold out his hand.

"I have a hundred million things to do."

He still had nothing to say.

"You . . . you don't even have a saddle on that monster."

Again, he said nothing, his hand as patiently steady as his penetrating gray gaze.

"Dammit, Michael, I can't go with you yet. I mean now. I can't go with you right now."

With no signal from its rider that she could detect, the elephant walked forward and stopped beside her. Libby refused to lose any more ground and suddenly found Michael's outstretched hand mere inches away.

"Come with me," he whispered, the deep timbre of his voice raising the fine hairs on her neck. "You've nothing to fear from me, Libby. Not today."

Of its own volition, her left hand rose up and set itself in his. Michael repositioned her grip, firmly grasping her around the arm just above her elbow, and swung her onto the horse behind him so swiftly and smoothly Libby barely had time to squeak.

She closed her eyes the moment the monstrous beast started to move. Michael dug her nails out of his stomach and repositioned her hands around his waist.

Libby discovered that hugging him was like hugging a large tree. The man was definitely just as solid, only much warmer than a tree. He smelled nicer, too.

And so, with her eyes closed, her body crushed into Michael as if her life depended on it, and TarStone Mountain looming ahead, Libby prayed that she had just consigned her soul to an archangel—and not to the devil himself.

Chapter Seven

God save him from reckless women.

Michael couldn't believe Libby had come with him. It was possible she hadn't understood him this morning, but he didn't think so. Which meant that either she was considering his offer, or the woman should be locked up for her own safety.

"So this is Stomper," she said, removing one of her death-gripping hands from his waist and patting the horse's side.

Stomper thought a fly was on him and gave a violent swish of his tail as he kicked up a hind leg to swat it. Libby gasped and dug her nails into Michael's stomach again.

"Wh-who lives on the mountain?" she asked.

Michael heard the worry in her voice but didn't know if it was the horse making Libby nervous or if she had finally realized the dangerous position she'd put herself in, now that they were quickly leaving civilization behind.

"He's a priest who goes by the name of Daar," he told her, prying her nails out of his belly again and patting her hands flat. "He has a cabin partway up TarStone."

"He lives by himself? I thought priests lived in rectories or something."

"He's an old priest and has no church," Michael explained, trying to ignore his passenger's soft breasts pressing into his back. The woman was clinging to him so tightly it felt as if she were trying to melt into his skin.

Now, there was a maddening thought.

Dammit. What had Robbie gotten him into? Or, rather, what had he gotten himself into by agreeing to allow his son to rent Mary's home?

He didn't want to be attracted to Libby. She was too small. Too outspoken. Too . . . dammit, she was too reckless.

Michael had known she would be trouble the moment she'd set her feet on his chest and pushed him into his pond.

And if that hadn't been warning enough, she had threatened to call his bluff this morning when he'd gone to her house with every intention of scaring her off.

So what was he doing bringing her with him this afternoon?

Aw, hell. He had his own reckless streak, which was proving to be just as dangerous as Libby's. Either that, or he had been too long without a woman.

Most likely, it was a combination of both.

But mostly, Michael had invited her along because he knew that sooner rather than later, the old priest would wander down off the mountain and into Libby's yard. Daar was curious about Robbie's new tenant and could be downright meddlesome at times, sticking his nose into places where it didn't belong.

That was why Michael wanted to be there for their first meeting, so that he could control the conversation. He needed to make sure Libby understood that Daar was a bit

touched in the head and that she shouldn't believe anything he said.

"You all have Scottish accents," the cause of his restless
night's sleep said into his back. "I could barely understand
a word Ian was saying. Even Robbie has a slight accent.
Have you all lived here very long?"

"I've lived here ten years," he told her. "Ian and the
other MacKeages have been here almost twelve years."

"What happened to Robbie's mother?"

"She had an automobile accident when she was eight
months pregnant. My son was surgically taken from Mary,
and she died the next day."

"I'm sorry," Libby said softly against his back. "So
Robbie never knew his mother."

"He knows her. Everyone's seen to that."

Michael faced forward again and decided it was time to
redirect this inquisition. "So, what made you move from
California to Maine?"

There was a moment's hesitation before she spoke. "I
was afraid of earthquakes," she muttered into his back.

Michael turned his head, only to find her tiny little chin
lifted in defiance, just daring him to comment.

Which, of course, he couldn't help but do. "So ya're pre-
ferring blizzards instead? No, I'm thinking it's a man you're
running from."

"I am not," she said, shoving at him to turn him around.

She nearly pushed herself off his horse instead. Libby let
out a yelp and kicked her legs to catch her balance, and
Stomper protested by bolting out from under both of them.

Michael had to choose between regaining control of his
still powerful old warhorse or joining Libby for her journey to the ground. He twisted and wrapped his arms
around the flailing, screaming woman and made sure that
when they landed, Libby was on top.

The fact that he was laughing the whole way down was probably what enraged her the most. Michael captured her hands when she tried to shove away from him. And before her flailing knees unmanned him, he rolled them over and placed her safely beneath him.

"You idiot," she hissed, squirming to get free. "That's why you wear a helmet."

"You don't appear to have any broken bones," he observed, pinning her shoving hands over her head.

"I'm walking back."

"Aye," he agreed, nodding. "We both are, by the looks of the ass end of my horse."

"You are not letting your son ride that monster," she told him. "And he should wear a helmet when he rides his pony."

Michael quickly sobered. "I can take care of my son, woman. I don't need you to tell me what's best for him."

"Robbie could fall and be killed," she continued as if he hadn't spoken. "Or end up in a wheelchair the rest of his life."

Michael leaned his face close to hers and said softly, "When I'm needing a lecture on being a parent, I'll go see Grace."

And still she didn't back down. "You're endangering him."

"I'm raising him to be a man. Robbie will not grow up to be one of your weak moderns who's more afraid of dying than living."

She snapped her mouth shut and glared at him. Michael rolled off her and watched Libby scramble to her feet. He didn't know whether to be insulted or amused when she had the nerve to point her finger at him and continue her lecture.

"Robbie won't ever be a man if he's killed in a stupid,

preventable accident." She took a threatening step toward him. "Don't you dare grin at me, Michael," she shouted loudly enough for every bird in the forest to hear. "I can't believe you can be so callous about your son's safety."

Michael hooked his toe behind her leg and brought Libby sprawling forward on top of him. He rolled again, pinning her back beneath him. "And I can't believe you're so callous about your own safety. Libby," he growled when she tried to protest, "you're in the middle of nowhere with a complete stranger. One who is twice your size and who has already warned you of his intentions."

He set his hand over her mouth when she tried to speak. "And this discussion is over. You have worse things to worry about than my son's well-being."

"What things?" she mumbled under his hand.

"Me," he whispered, replacing his fingers with his mouth.

He was not breaking his promise that she was safe from him today; he only wanted to shut her up.

But Libby broke it for him when she kissed him back. She matched his passion with a heat of her own that was so intense Michael began to worry that if anyone should be scared, it was him.

Libby broke the kiss and stared up at him with huge, hesitant eyes. "I . . . I have a confession to make," she said softly. "I really am afraid of you."

"I know, lass," he agreed, gently brushing a leaf from her hair. "But you have no intention of letting that stop you. Am I right?"

Her eyes grew larger and darker, and she slowly nodded.

"Why?" he couldn't help asking. "If your instinct is saying no, why are you ignoring it?"

Libby studied him as she weighed her answer. She took

a deep, shuddering breath. "I-I don't know," she finally said. "What draws a moth to a flame? There's just . . . there's something about you, Michael MacBain, that makes me want to close my eyes and jump in with both feet."

He leaned back. "You don't even know me."

"I know enough." She touched his cheek. "I'm not looking for much. Just a simple affair. No demands. No expectations. No strings."

"Just two people messing up the sheets?" he asked.

She nodded. "Discreetly, for Robbie's sake."

Well, dammit. It appeared his lust had been turned against him. He was damned if he did and crazy if he didn't.

"I know you feel it, too, Michael. That's why you came to my house this morning. You felt it, didn't like it, and thought you could scare me off so you wouldn't have to deal with it."

"Deal with what, woman?" he snapped, feeling defensive that she had seen through him so easily.

Or was it that she felt what he did?

"The energy." She blew out an impatient breath. "Call it chemistry, then. Whatever. Just don't you dare deny it, Michael MacBain." She suddenly tried to push him away. "Never mind," she muttered. "This is a big mistake."

Michael wasn't quite ready to let her up. He pinned her hands with only one of his and used his other hand on her chin to keep her facing him.

"Mistake or not, that doesn't change my wanting you."

"Well, now, isn't this a fine day for a nap in the woods," came a familiar and unwelcome voice from above them.

Libby stiffened.

Michael closed his eyes. "Dammit, old man. You take your life in your hands sneaking up on me," he said, looking up and glaring at Daar.

Daar grinned back, not the least bit worried about his life. "It's a sad day, MacBain, when a crippled old man can surprise a warrior in the prime of his life. Who's your friend?"

Michael looked down at Libby, who was trying to wiggle deeper under him to hide. "Her?" he asked the priest, nodding at the once again still woman beneath him. "This is Libby Hart, your new neighbor. We were just heading up to your cabin so she could meet you."

"Aye, ya looked like ya was heading somewhere," Daar agreed.

A sharp finger poked him in the ribs, rather violently, and Michael rose to his feet, exposing his embarrassed friend.

With her face so red it must hurt, Libby sat up, quickly looked down to make sure all her buttons were buttoned, then took her time brushing the leaves off herself.

Michael watched in silence while she worked up the nerve to look at Daar. But once she did, it took her less than a second to scramble to her feet and start talking.

"We had an accident, Father," she rushed to explain. "We fell off Michael's horse."

Daar nodded. "I seen Stomper. He passed me hell-bent for home a good twenty minutes ago." He pointed his cane at Libby. "You the woman our Robbie brought to live in Mary's house?"

Not caring to see the old *drùidh* pointing his staff at Libby, Michael stepped between them. "She's living in Mary's house," he confirmed for the priest. "And if you're hoping for baked goods from her, you should know that she can't cook."

There was a small gasp from behind him, but Michael ignored Libby and continued to give the priest his attention. "She might supply you with eggs, though, if ya start acting civilized."

Daar moved to the side so that he could see Libby better, then suddenly stepped back and raised his staff again, this time threateningly, his eyes wide with shock.

"Your hair!" he shouted. "Ya carry the mark!"

Libby gasped, and Michael decided he'd had enough. He spun around, took her by the shoulders, and pointed her down the mountain. "Walk," he told her. "I'll catch up with you in a minute."

He was truly surprised when she obeyed him and greatly relieved when she finally walked out of sight. Michael strode up the knoll and stopped only when his chest came into contact with Daar's staff.

"You will leave her alone, old man," he warned.

The priest moved his gaze from where Libby had disappeared and stared at Michael. "Did ya not see the mark, MacBain? She possesses the power."

"What sort of power?" Michael asked. "Are ya saying Libby's a witch?"

Daar frantically shook his head. "Nay, not a witch. I did not feel anything like that."

"Then what?" Michael asked with waning patience. "If she's not a witch, why are ya so rattled?"

Daar scratched his beard with the end of his cane and stared again at the path Libby had taken. "I don't know, exactly," he said, looking back at Michael. "She surprised me, is all. Maybe . . . maybe ya shouldn't be associating with her until I can learn what she's about. Nor should Robbie be spending any time with her."

"No," Michael countered. "It's you who will stay away from her. Libby's not a threat to us. Maybe to you," he speculated, looking the *drùidh* in the eye. "Ya did enough interfering in my life twelve years ago. You'll stay out of it now."

"That was a mistake, MacBain. I apologized for that."

"And you're mistaken now. It's a lock of white hair. Nothing more."

"It's a sign. And I felt her energy."

"And was the energy good or evil?"

"Not evil," Daar said, shaking his head.

Michael took a step closer to the man responsible for bringing him eight hundred years forward in time. "Then see that you tread carefully, *drùidh*. She's under my protection."

Daar squinted up at him. "So the wind blows that way, does it?"

"It does not. But my son brought her here, and that makes her my responsibility. You'll treat her kindly and apologize for scaring her today. And you'll damn well keep your magic to yourself around her."

The old priest didn't care to be lectured, if the glare he gave Michael was any indication. "Exactly when did you stop being afraid of me?" he asked.

Michael couldn't stifle a smile. "When I realized you don't even have the power to cure your own aches and pains. You wouldn't be walking like an old woman if you could do something about it."

"I can still turn a man into a dung beetle."

Michael's smile broadened. "Not if that man has a nobler calling. And having a bairn under the age of fourteen counts."

"I suppose ya read that in one of them blasphemous books ya got in that cluttered room you call a library."

Michael nodded. "It's amazing what eight hundred years' worth of books can teach a person. I have an entire shelf on wizardry."

"And what do your books say about a woman with a white lock of hair, MacBain?"

"That she's strong and brave and reckless and has the

power to turn powerless *drùidhs* into dung beetles," Michael told him as he turned and walked away. "So be nice to her, old man, or learn to sleep with your eyes open."

"Dammit, MacBain. I'll get all my powers back one of these days, and then we'll see how cocky you're feeling."

Michael waved his good-bye without looking back and started jogging in the direction Libby had taken. He wanted to catch up with her before she reached her house and Robbie showed up there from school.

They had to finish their discussion, and Michael decided he wasn't letting it go until it was finished in his favor.

Libby spent the first ten minutes of her walk down the mountain feeling sorry for ever coming up here in the first place. She had made a complete fool of herself. She'd gotten mad at Michael, yelled at him, and kissed him.

And she just might have made love to him right there on the ground if that damn crazy priest hadn't arrived and embarrassed the hell out of her.

She wasn't baking Daar anything, and she wasn't giving him eggs. And she wasn't having an affair with Michael MacBain, and she wasn't letting Robbie worm his way into her heart.

And she was never getting on a horse again.

If she ever caught Robbie riding his pony without a helmet, well, she didn't care what Michael thought, she was pulling the boy off and shooing his pony away.

It seemed the damn critters knew their way home.

Which was why she had to walk down the blasted mountain with a sore knee. It probably would be blown up like a balloon by tomorrow morning.

Had she left her brain back in California?

What had made her think she could just run away, start life all over again, and, just like that, gain back the control she had lost in her operating room?

Libby suddenly stopped walking, held her breath, and stood perfectly still. The hair on the back of her neck rose, and goose bumps broke out all over her body at the realization that she was being watched.

She slowly turned her head and looked behind her to see if Michael was there. He wasn't. She then scanned the forest around her and still saw nothing, until she looked up.

Huge, unblinking yellow eyes stared at her from a tree limb over her head not fifty paces away. Libby would have felt blessed to see such a wondrous bird if it hadn't been for the disturbing dream she'd had last night.

She was looking at the same white owl that had been in her bedroom in her nightmare. She'd been terrified then, and she was terrified now.

The owl ducked its head and opened its wings in a display of silent strength. Libby took a quick and cautious step back, holding her breath.

"Stand still," came Michael's voice from right behind her.

Libby's knees went weak, and she started breathing again the moment his hands wrapped securely over her shoulders.

"Look her in the eye, lass," he said softly. "She's wanting to take your measure."

"H-her?"

"Aye. She's a female snowy, come from far away to visit with us for a while. Look up, and let her see your eyes. Don't be afraid, Libby. Mary will not harm you."

Libby didn't stop breathing, her heart stopped beating instead. "M-mary? You're calling the bird Mary?"

"Aye. She's Robbie's pet, come to him on his birthday last January."

"He named her Mary?" Libby repeated, not able to get past that point.

She was standing in the middle of the woods, being held up by a man introducing her to a bird named after his dead lover, and he expected her to look that bird in the eye? After just rolling around in the forest with him and trying to start an affair?

No. She didn't think so.

His hands on her shoulders tightened. "She'll not hurt you, Libby. Look up."

"She tried to kill me last night," Libby hissed in response.

"What?"

"She was in my room. Or I think she was. I might have dreamed it, but I've seen this bird before. She doesn't like me, Michael. She's . . . she's jealous or something."

Michael slowly turned her around to face him. Libby finally did look up—into turbulent gray eyes.

"Tell me," he said. "What did you see? What was Mary doing?" he asked, looking at the owl and then back at her.

"She was just hovering over my bed, flapping her wings against the ceiling."

"What else? Was there light?"

"Yes. Blue light. The entire room pulsed with blue light."

He thought about that, his attention back on the bird. Finally, he looked down at her.

"Libby, are you telling me you're afraid of this owl because you think it might be Robbie's mother?"

"Yes. No. I . . . I don't know, Michael. A week ago, I would have laughed in your face. But now . . ." Libby dropped her gaze to his chest. "I don't know what's real anymore."

He lifted her chin with his finger. "What happened a week ago?"

"Something I can't explain. Something I'm not ready to talk about."

"Then we won't," he whispered, smiling warmly at her. "But we will settle your worry with this snowy right now. If we don't, she's going to keep haunting your dreams, Libby, until she's satisfied."

"Satisfied how? That I've been scared away?"

He nodded. "Aye. Or deemed worthy of staying and being Robbie's friend. It seems she's a protective owl."

"And possessive?"

"Nay. Her heart beats only for Robbie now, lass."

He moved his finger from her chin to cover her lips when she tried to speak again. Then he turned her around, and slowly, so very slowly, Libby looked up.

The snowy's wings were tucked back against its sides as it stood tall and alert, its eyes direct and penetrating—and searching for Libby's soul.

The owl suddenly let out a short, clear, single-pitch whistle that made Libby flinch and Michael's hands tighten on her shoulders. It opened its wings and stepped sideways on the branch, ducking its head in a circular motion of curious regard.

Libby tried to take a step back, but Michael held her in place. "If she takes flight, stand your ground," he whispered, his breath washing softly over the top of her head. "Show her you have the courage to be Robbie's friend."

"But I don't, Michael."

"Ya do," he softly contradicted, squeezing her shoulders.

Michael's hands suddenly fell away from her shoulders, and he took a step back, leaving Libby to hold herself up.

"Raise your arm, lass. Give a sharp whistle like she just did, and see if she'll come to ya."

The man was certifiably crazy.

Or she was. Dammit. It was a bird, not a demon, not a nightmare, not even Robbie's dead mother. It was an owl. A beautiful, majestic snowy owl. Libby raised her arm, put her fourth and first fingers to her lips, and whistled.

The owl blinked, spread its wings, and dropped from its perch. The snowy silently glided through the clearing and landed on Libby's sleeve-covered arm.

It was surprisingly light for its size. And amazingly gentle, considering it had talons more than an inch long. The snowy clung without drawing blood and opened its beak to let out a series of gently rattling chatters.

"She'll fold her wings if ya quit your trembling," Michael said from a good twenty paces away. "She's trying to balance."

Yeah. Well. She was trying to get used to the idea that she had a lethal bird on her arm. One whose eyes were now dead-level with hers.

"Reach up and stroke her chest," Michael instructed. "Talk to her, Libby."

Libby raised her left hand and slowly, very carefully, petted the bird's chest.

Mary—if Libby could just get used to that name— settled down and folded her wings. Her chatter stopped, and her eyes appeared to soften. They stared at each other for several seconds, and Libby relaxed.

"I will do no harm to your son," she whispered softly enough so Michael couldn't hear. "And I really can bake cookies and cakes."

Mary blinked and gave a gentle, low-timbre rattle.

"I'll buy him a helmet to wear when he rides his pony," she continued, bolstered by the bird's response. "And I'll go to his Christmas play at school if he has one. Let me be his friend, Mary, and I promise not to break his heart."

The snowy went silent and turned just its head to look at Michael. It stared at him for several seconds and then turned back to Libby.

Libby smiled in understanding. "I won't break Michael's heart, either," she whispered. "I promise."

The snowy studied her for several more seconds, then suddenly opened her wings, pushed off, and gently lifted into flight. Mary disappeared through the forest on down-silenced wings, leaving behind only the echo of her single-pitch call and the aura of fading blue light.

Libby's knees buckled, and Michael swept her up in his arms before she slumped to the ground. He lifted her high against his chest and spun them both in a circle, his laughter shaking her like an earthquake.

"Don't ever again say you're afraid, Libby," he said, spinning around and around until she was dizzy. "You're a brave woman, lass. Braver than most men I know."

Libby gripped his shoulders for balance and marveled at this new picture of Michael. He was being playful.

Or was he just relieved that she hadn't been torn to shreds?

"Put me down. I'm going to be sick," Libby pleaded, trying to make her head stop spinning.

He stopped, and slowly slid her down his body until her face was level with his, leaving her feet to dangle a good foot off the ground. "I'm sorry," he said, his shining gray eyes not the least bit contrite. "But I'm just so surprised that you did it."

"Surprised? Surprised," she repeated a bit louder. She swatted his shoulder. "You told me to do it."

He nodded, his eyes crinkling at their corners. "Aye. I've been noticing how well you do what you're told." He turned serious. "Thank you for walking away from Daar without making a scene."

"He's a crazy old man."

"Aye. But he's basically harmless."

"Are you going to put me down anytime soon?"

"I haven't decided. Are we going to finish our discussion?"

"We did."

"No," he countered, slowly shaking his head. "I believe I had just said that I want you."

"I want you, too, Michael. But I'm . . . I'm afraid."

"So you're saying your answer is no?"

Oh, how like a man to see things only in black or white. "I'm saying—I'm—oh, dammit. No, Michael, I'm saying yes."

Chapter Eight

For a man who should be feeling quite pleased with himself, Michael was unusually silent as they continued their walk down the mountain. But then, Libby didn't have much to say herself.

Something was bothering her. Two things, really, that had nothing to do with the fact that she had just committed to having an affair. No, she was curious about something Michael had said to her earlier and something the priest had said when he'd first found them together.

"Michael, what did you mean when you told me you won't let Robbie grow up to be—how did you put it—'one of your weak moderns'? What did you mean by a modern?"

He shot her a look from the corner of his eye, then turned his attention back to the path in front of them.

"Michael?"

"Have ya ever noticed, Libby, how soft the men of modern society have become? How wars are fought but not really won? And how people have abdicated their right to protect themselves to a system that usually doesn't arrive until it's too late?"

"So you're a philosopher?" she asked, grabbing his arm to stop him, so he would look at her. "You're living in these mountains, watching the world from a distance, and passing judgment on society."

"Nay, woman. I judge no one but myself and my son. Robbie will grow up to be strong and capable and will live by the laws of nature and not the rules of man."

"He's still a member of society, no matter where he lives. And those rules are the foundation of our civilization. Without them, there would be chaos."

"There are a hell of a lot more rules now than there were eight hundred years ago."

"Because there are a lot more people," Libby countered, fascinated by this side of Michael.

Fascinated but not surprised.

Wasn't this exactly what had drawn her to him in the first place? Hadn't she sensed this quiet strength?

"Aye. There's a lot more people," he agreed. "Which is why I live here." He raised an eyebrow at her. "Which is also why you came here."

Well, she couldn't argue with that. "Father Daar called you a warrior. Were you a soldier?"

"Aye. I was until twelve years ago."

"What branch of the military?"

"The fighting branch." He gave her a crooked smile. "Where are these questions leading, Libby?"

She shrugged and started walking again. "Nowhere. I just wondered. So, you're saying Robbie shouldn't wear a helmet when he rides his pony because that will make him weak?"

It was Michael who stopped them this time. "He's been astride a horse since birth, Libby. My son knows how to ride, how to fall, and how not to get hurt."

"I know how to drive a car, and I had an accident."

He brushed a curl off her cheek and tucked it behind her ear. "Knowing how to do something and knowing how to do it well are two different things, lass. You're a poor driver."

"I am not." Libby remembered her accident and suddenly stiffened. "It was Mary. I mean, that bird. That bird flew in front of my car and made me crash."

Michael's face lit with a smile. "She must have known where ya was headed and wasn't sure she wanted you to arrive. Now tell me, is your knee paining ya much? I can carry you."

Libby snorted and started walking again.

But this time, Robbie caught up with her first.

The eight-year-old was driving a four-wheeled ATV.

And he wasn't wearing a helmet.

Michael had a lot of nerve calling her reckless.

"Hi, Libby," Robbie said, stopping the ATV beside her. He looked from her to his dad and beamed like a cat who'd just spotted a full bowl of cream. "What are you guys doing up here?"

"Nearly getting ourselves killed," Libby snapped. "Where's your helmet?"

"Enough," Michael growled, lifting her up and setting her on the ATV behind Robbie. He took hold of her chin and made her look directly into his glare. "Let it go, Libby," he whispered. "We will not sit on the porch and watch life go by without participating."

Libby glared back at him and tried to pull her chin free. But apparently, he wasn't done talking.

"Concede this round, woman. Any consequence is mine to live with."

That was the trouble with philosophers; they spent too much time thinking and not enough time seeing the results of an often foolish world.

"Then don't you dare come to me when something happens. I'm not patching your consequences back together."

He let go of her chin, straightened, and gave her a strange look. "Why would I think to come to you?" he asked. "If something happens, I'll go to a doctor."

Realizing her mistake, Libby shrugged and turned and hugged Robbie around the waist. "I'm just giving you a warning of my own. Of course, you'll go to a doctor if something happens. Come on, Robbie. I need to put some ice on my knee."

"Go on, son," Michael said, waving Robbie forward while he continued to keep his thoughtful gaze on Libby. "Go slow. It's likely her first time on a four-wheeler."

But Libby soon decided she didn't want it to be her last. The smart little machine gave a surprisingly smooth ride. The engine puttered along quietly, and Robbie seemed to control it with ease.

Libby decided she was starting a list of all the things she had to do, had to buy, and had to accomplish to start her new life the moment she got home. And the first thing on the list was going to be an ATV.

The second thing would be a helmet.

No, two helmets. She would concede nothing to Michael. Not when it was this important. She was buying Robbie a helmet, and she would bribe him to wear it if she had to, because she had made a promise to a snowy owl that she intended to keep.

That night, Michael sat in his favorite chair in the one room in the house where he spent most of his time. He had a book on his lap but hadn't been able to concentrate on what he'd been trying to read for the last hour.

A brown-eyed, opinionated, and passionate faerie kept interfering with his concentration. Remembering the feel of Libby beneath him kept stirring his blood. Her taste, her smell, her courage and fear; she swam through his senses, creating an urgency of need.

And that was exactly why he was sitting there instead of where he would rather be. There was no place for need in their bargain. No place for it in his own life. It was okay for him to want a woman, but he could never allow himself to need just one in particular.

Not after loving two others and losing them both.

"Papa, can you take this box over to Libby tomorrow?" Robbie asked, walking into the library with a small wooden box in his arms.

"What is it?" Michael asked.

"It's a secret," Robbie explained, setting the box on the stool beside Michael's feet. "And I want your promise not to look in it. I just need you to take this to Libby so she can do me a favor."

Michael lifted an inquiring brow. "And she's volunteered to do this favor?"

"Nay, Papa," Robbie admitted. "But I'll write her a note and ask. It isn't a big favor, just something I need help with." He gave Michael a speculating smile. "Libby must be good with her hands if she makes jewelry."

Michael closed his eyes on the thought of Libby being good with her hands.

"Please, Papa? Can't you take it to her?"

"Why can't you?"

"I've got play practice after school tomorrow. I won't be home till supper." He suddenly brightened with a new thought. "Maybe we should invite Libby over for supper. That would be a neighborly thing to do."

Michael laughed out loud. "Do ya want to befriend the woman or kill her?" he asked. "Or did ya like what we ate tonight?"

Robbie involuntarily shuddered, and Michael nearly did the same. Burnt chicken had a lingering taste and, sadly, one he was getting used to.

Robbie walked to the large desk near the far wall. "I'll write Libby a note, and I think I'll offer to pay her. That way, she won't feel I'm taking advantage, and she can earn money while she starts her new studio."

It was a good plan, from an eight-year-old's perspective, and Michael didn't have the heart to tell the boy that Libby was not lacking for money.

Michael had had a talk with Grace when he'd learned a new tenant had been found for Mary's home. But Grace had been tight-lipped over what she had discovered about Libby Hart. All she had told Michael was not to worry about Libby's finances. The woman was not there to find herself a rich husband.

No. She'd come to plague him instead, to stir his blood, and to awaken feelings better left dead.

"Spell *compensate* for me, Papa," Robbie demanded, looking up from the computer screen.

"You'll write your note long-hand," Michael said. "You don't ask a favor by e-mail."

"I'm not. I'm going to write it on the computer but print it out so you can take it with you."

"Nay. You'll ask in your own hand, Robbie, or you'll not ask at all. When you have a request, you do it personally. And a computer is not personal."

Robbie rolled his eyes but shut off the screen and picked up a pencil. He was quiet for several minutes, concentrating on forming letters that came so much easier on the keyboard.

Robbie might read at a much higher level, but he didn't much care for writing. Michael knew Robbie was big for his age; he'd been to school often enough and seen his son's classmates. Aye, the boy was strong, intelligent, capable, and far too astute for one so young.

Most of the time. But every now and then—more often lately—Robbie would do something to remind Michael that he was still only a bairn. A bad dream, an insecurity, self-doubt over a decision, when he would need the comfort of a good cuddle, a hug, or sometimes only a wink of understanding.

"I'm back to *compensate,* Papa."

"C-O-M-P-E-N-S-A-T-E."

Robbie went back to work, the only sound in the room that of his impatient sighs and the scratch of the pencil.

Michael studied the box at his feet. He could take it over to Libby tonight, after Robbie was safely tucked into bed. John was there to watch over things.

No. He'd better not. She may have said yes this afternoon, but her answer had been filled with doubt. Libby probably didn't even realize it, but Michael knew she wasn't ready.

She would be, though. He would see to it.

"I'm done," Robbie said, coming around the desk as he folded his note. He set it on the box and looked up at Michael and grinned. "I have your word ya won't peek?"

"Aye."

"Then I'm going to bed now," he said, yawning and stretching his arms to get the kinks out of his growing muscles. "I want to get up early and work on the rest of my surprise before school." He gave Michael a stern look. "You haven't been in Grampy's workshop, have you?"

"I've not," Michael assured him. "I'm letting the suspense drive me nuts."

Robbie pushed the book off Michael's lap and scrambled up to replace it. He turned and snuggled against Michael's chest and pulled his father's arms around him.

"Tell me what ya think of her, Papa," he demanded.

Michael gave Robbie a bear hug. "I think we're going to have to mount a flag on the woman, so we can find her in the snow this winter."

"Aunt Grace says good things come in small packages."

"Aye. And some packages are smaller than others. What do you think of her?" Michael asked, turning Robbie's question back on him.

Robbie tilted his head to smile at his father. "I think you think she's pretty."

"I don't know," Michael murmured, looking up at the ceiling while he tried to decide. "She's got short hair. I don't particularly care for short hair on a woman."

"Hair can grow."

"And she's not very curvy," Michael continued, still looking up. "In fact, I'm not sure she has any curves at all."

"She's got perky breasts."

Michael snapped his head down. "Excuse me?"

"Aren't Libby's breasts perky?"

Michael squeezed his son a little harder this time. "Where have you heard that term?"

"At school. Frankie Boggs says men like perky breasts."

"Gentlemen do not discuss women's anatomy."

"I'm going to be a warrior, not a gentleman."

"You can be both."

"Are you a gentleman?"

"Nay. Aye." Michael rubbed a hand over his face. "I try, Robbie. And I don't discuss women's anatomy with other men."

"You only discuss it with women?"

Michael let out a sigh that moved Robbie's hair. "Son, a woman's body should not be discussed. Ever."

"Can it be looked at?"

Michael tore his gaze away and looked at the hearth. It was getting damned hot in there.

He looked back at Robbie. "It can be appreciated," he carefully said, realizing he'd started this discussion by listing Libby's lack of curves. "Men can't help but look. Even gentlemen," he quickly added before Robbie could speak. "But they keep their thoughts to themselves."

"Do ya think Libby can cook?"

Michael breathed a sigh of relief finally to be on safer ground. "If she can boil water, she's doing better than we are."

"Do . . . do ya think she'll stay, Papa?"

Michael stood up, set his son on his feet, and headed them both to the hall and up the stairs. "She might," he told him truthfully. "But ya shouldn't expect it. Things change in people's lives, Robbie. And if Libby must leave, then accept her decision and be glad she came into your life, even for a little while."

"You want her to stay, don't ya?"

Michael stood Robbie in front of the bathroom sink and handed him his toothbrush. "Aye. I won't mind if Libby decides to stay."

Robbie grinned up at him. "That's good, then," he said, nodding. " 'Cause she's going to."

"And why are you so sure?"

"Mary told me."

Michael stilled in the act of squeezing the toothpaste onto Robbie's toothbrush. "When?"

"This afternoon, when I got home from school. Mary was waiting when I got off the bus. She also told me where to find you and Libby and that I should probably go fetch you."

Michael sat down at the edge of the tub. "Explain how your pet told you such a thing. The owl can't talk, son."

Robbie shrugged. "She just told me. She was looking at me, and suddenly I just knew." His uncertain young eyes blinked up at Michael. "I . . . we talk all the time," he confessed.

Michael placed the tube of toothpaste on the counter, then rubbed his hands over his tired face in an attempt to clear the fog from his brain.

He was going up the mountain again tomorrow and having a talk with the *drùidh*. Daar had hinted more than once over the last eight years that Robbie was special. The old priest had not been specific, although Michael had heard him mutter the word *guardian* once or twice. But when pressed, Daar had refused to elaborate. He'd only said that time would tell.

Well, it was time.

"Are ya mad 'cause I talk to Mary?" Robbie asked, looking at Michael with the fragile eyes of a boy mightily in need of his mother.

"Nay," Michael assured him. "I'm glad you have a good friendship with Mary. And now Libby does as well. Mary landed on her arm today."

Robbie gasped. "She did? Truly?" he asked in surprise. "Mary won't even come to you." He suddenly shot Michael a smug grin. "That must mean she likes Libby."

"And that she doesn't like me?"

"Nay, Papa," Robbie said, smacking him in the shoulder with his toothbrush. "Mary's afraid to get close to you because you might try to keep her forever."

Well, hell. From the mouth of a babe. For more than a week, Michael had been bothered that the snowy would not come to him. That the pet his son called Mary virtually ignored him.

And now he realized why.

She was forcing Michael to let go. She was keeping her

distance in order to free him. And today, on TarStone, she had accepted Libby Hart into her son's life.

But had she accepted Libby into his?

Mary had appeared on purpose, most likely because Michael had been with Libby. She had wanted him to witness their interaction and to know that the woman renting her family home had her approval.

He understood this, because in the twelve years since being hurtled through time, Michael had made it his business to understand all sides—visible and invisible—of the world around him. He had learned to open his mind, as well as his heart, to the existence of magic.

Which is why nothing surprised him anymore.

Not even a son who said he talked to an owl.

Michael gave Robbie a fierce hug. "Brush your teeth and go to bed, young man. I'm waking you at five to go work on your surprise. And Grampy John still will likely be in the shed before you are."

"He cut his thumb yesterday," Robbie confessed, as if it were somehow his fault. "I bandaged it for him," he added in his defense.

Michael pushed the toothbrush toward Robbie's mouth. "It's probably time for John to have his glasses strengthened. And it's good you were there to bandage him up."

Satisfied that what he'd hoped to accomplish tonight had been taken care of—persuading Michael to take his box over to Libby and getting the fact that he talked to an owl off his young chest—Robbie was more than ready for bed. He brushed his teeth, stripped himself naked as he ran into his room, and climbed under the covers.

"Aunt Grace bought me another pair of pajamas," the boy said, distaste dripping off the last word. "She's bound I'm going to be civilized, Papa. Can ya make her stop?"

Michael leaned over and kissed him good night. "It would take an act of God to make her stop."

"Then that's what I'm praying for tonight. That Aunt Grace stops buying me pajamas."

Michael walked to the door and turned out the bedroom light but stopped in the hall and nodded. "Aye. Include me, then. I have six pairs in my closet."

Michael left the hall light on, went back down the stairs, and returned to the library. He didn't sit in his chair but stood in the center of the room and stared at the box with the note lying on top.

He walked over and picked up the envelope, only to realize it had been sealed. Not wishing to spoil Robbie's surprise, and hoping that Libby would feel the same way, Michael picked up the box, held it, and stood there and stared.

He threw the box and the letter back onto the stool and sat down in the chair. He found his book, opened it to the bookmark, and took two minutes to realize the damned thing was upside down. He tossed the book onto the floor and stared at the box.

"Aw, hell," Michael growled to the empty room. He swept up the box and the letter and strode to the kitchen.

"I'm going out for a while," he told John, who was poking his head into the fridge, most likely hoping something edible had appeared there magically since supper. "Robbie's in bed."

John straightened, looked at Michael's face and then at the box in his hand, and smiled. "Take your time," he said. "I'll sleep with my door open, in case Robbie needs me."

Michael nodded but didn't move.

John went back to exploring the contents of the fridge. "It's a good night for a walk," he said into the empty cavern. "Maybe Robbie's new tenant would like to join you and have a look at our stars." He lifted his head above the fridge door and shot Michael another grin. "And don't feel you have to hurry back here. I got things under control."

Michael fought for some control of his own but lost the battle. He grabbed his jacket and headed outside, then stood on the porch and took several gulps of crisp night air. He finally shrugged into his coat and set out on the same path he'd taken during last night's storm.

Only this time, his reason for traveling it had changed.

Chapter Nine

Libby repositioned the bag of ice on her knee, then shuffled through the papers on her lap until she came to the page of things she had to buy. She crossed the truck off the list and shuffled again until she found the page of things she had to do. She made a note to register her new truck, then went back to her list of things to buy. She studied it, thought about it, and crossed off the computer.

She needed to prioritize, and a computer wasn't important right now. An ATV was. Two helmets were. Clothes—warm winter clothes. And birth control.

Libby tapped her pencil against her lips and stared into the fire, wondering if there was a doctor in Pine Creek. She hadn't been on the pill since med school. And she had to find something soon, if she had read that look in Michael's eyes correctly this afternoon when she agreed to have an affair with him.

Libby frowned. She couldn't picture Michael using a condom. Not because he was callous or unconcerned, but maybe condoms didn't fit with his concept of living according to the laws of nature. And he'd had a son without having a wedding first, so Libby decided she would be responsible for their birth control.

She looked back at her list of things to do. First thing tomorrow, she had to go to the post office and pick up the jewelry-making equipment she'd mailed to herself, now that she had a truck to load it in. And while she was in town, she'd take Ian's advice and check with the Dolans about renting their storefront.

Libby smiled to herself, thinking how lucky she was to have a ski resort right next-door. Her studio should do okay there, since she imagined beautiful Pine Lake attracted as many tourists in the summer as TarStone Mountain did in the winter.

Maybe she would take up skiing. She was definitely going to try snowmobiling. She'd seen several sporting goods stores on her drive up from Bangor and couldn't wait to try one of the colorful, sleek, powerful-looking machines.

Part of her new life plan was to live a bit more recklessly. Not stupidly, though. She'd wear a helmet and get the proper instructions, and she would ride safely and stay on the marked trails. But it was time to expand her world to include some of the more exciting things in life.

Like having an affair with a sexy mountain man? Heck, Libby couldn't think of anything more exciting than messing up her sheets with Michael MacBain.

She leaned her head back on the couch and closed her eyes on a sigh. She had done a good job of keeping herself occupied these last few days—of keeping her mind off her problem.

Or, to give credit where it was due, Michael MacBain had done a good job of keeping away the memory of what had taken place in her operating room an entire lifetime ago.

She had gotten her mother to check discreetly on her patients before she left California. Esther Brown and Jamie Garcia had walked out of the hospital that day, neither of them the worse for the wear of their ordeal.

No, she was the one who had come away wounded.

Not mortally but definitely shell-shocked.

Libby lifted her head and looked down at the towel of ice on her knee. If it was true—if she really could heal people by will alone—could she heal herself?

And if she could, should she? Wasn't that . . . unethical or something? Was there an unwritten code for people like her that said they couldn't practice on themselves?

"Physician, heal thyself," Libby quoted aloud, waving her hand over her knee like a magic wand.

"So I should call you Dr. Hart, it seems."

Libby bolted off the couch, her surprise erupting in a scream as she spun toward her intruder.

Michael winced but didn't move.

"Goddammit, Michael!" she shouted, throwing her towel of ice at him. He ducked to the side, and the towel hit the wall behind him, ice cubes scattering around the room like shattering glass.

Michael straightened, his expression resigned.

"I'm changing the locks on the door."

"That won't stop me."

"You scared the hell out of me, Michael."

"I thought screaming might be like the hiccups. That a good fright might cure ya." His features suddenly hardened. "But it seems you were trying to cure yourself, Dr. Libby Hart."

Libby snapped her gaze to the third button on Michael's shirt and rubbed her hands on her thighs in an attempt to calm her racing heart. Finally, and with a shuddering breath, she made her decision and raised her eyes to his.

"Actually, it's Dr. Elizabeth Hart."

His stance didn't change. His eyes did—they darkened and narrowed and cut into her like the razor edge of a scalpel.

"What kind of doctor?"

"A trauma surgeon."

"That explains a lot."

"It doesn't explain a damn thing."

"It explains everything," he countered, still not moving, still piercing her with steel-dark eyes. "Like why you feel so strongly about helmets. And," he continued more forcefully when she tried to speak, "why you act decisively and from your gut. A trauma surgeon would be used to making quick and instinctive decisions. Tell me if I'm wrong, Elizabeth, in thinking that you insist on being in control of whatever situation you find yourself in."

"Of course I do. That's what a surgeon does."

"Aye. I understand now, this authority you carry around you like a protective shield, which you've created to keep yourself insulated from your patients—a shield that also keeps you safe from the rest of the world."

"I'm not an ice queen."

"Nay," he softly agreed. "You are pure fire, Elizabeth. And that scares the hell out of you, because something happened in California a week ago that shattered your control."

"I'm not a doctor anymore. And I'm Libby now, not Elizabeth."

Michael finally moved. He walked around the couch and stood in front of her, and Libby craned her neck, refusing to break eye contact with him.

Michael reached out and picked her up before she

could react. He stood her on the hearth so she was at eye level with him, then stepped away and clasped his hands behind his back.

"You don't spend your entire life training to be a surgeon and then simply turn your back and walk away. What happened a week ago, Libby?"

"Some-something I can't explain."

"Try," he gently entreated.

"I can't," she whispered. "I . . . I can't say it out loud, Michael."

He unclasped his hands and cupped the sides of her face, using his thumbs to brush away tears Libby hadn't even realized were running down her cheeks. "It's okay, lass. Your fear will find its own voice when you're ready," he softly assured her, bringing his mouth close to hers.

Libby eagerly met his kiss, wrapped her arms around his shoulders, and clung to him with the desperation of a leaf facing a storm. She opened her mouth and tasted him, felt his vitality, and was consumed by the strength of his response.

He smelled of wood smoke, of mountain air and the crisp autumn night he'd walked through to get there. The man was solid granite under the flannel of his shirt, and Libby dug her fingers into his shoulders as she canted her head to deepen their kiss. He completely engulfed her, both physically and emotionally, and Libby's desperation slowly and quietly turned to passion.

His tongue explored her mouth while his hands sought out the curve of her backside, sending shivers of delight along the path of his touch. Libby pressed her body closer, whimpered when he lifted her against him, and trailed her lips over his chin and down to the base of his throat, glorying in the heat and smell and taste of his skin.

She felt as if she was floating, and it took Libby a

minute to realize that Michael had sat down on the couch. She found herself straddling his lap and couldn't stop herself from moving against him. Heat shot through her at the intimate contact and settled deep in the pit of her stomach. She trembled with urgency as she unbuttoned his shirt.

Michael stopped her by placing his hands over hers.

Libby looked up into storm-gray eyes that shone with the fire of pure male lust. But it was lust held in control by pure male determination. She clasped Michael's face between her hands and kissed him soundly on the mouth, then pulled back just enough for him to see her smile.

"Don't you dare get noble on me, Michael. This is something we both want."

He gathered her hands back and trapped them against his chest. "I was just wondering who's supposed to be in charge," he drawled, his eyes gleaming with humor.

Libby blinked. "We can work as a team."

He lifted one brow in contradiction. "Really? I don't feel like part of a team. In fact, I don't even feel like I need to participate, only just show up."

Libby leaned back. "Are you one of those Neanderthal guys who's got to be in charge in order to perform?"

Michael lifted his hips against her. "I don't think performance is the problem, lass," he said. "And I'm a bit more evolved than a caveman."

"Then what's the problem?"

He cupped her face in his hands, his expression serious. "I didn't come here tonight to make love to you, Libby."

Her cheeks burned, and she tried to climb off his lap.

Michael held her in place. "This is not a rejection, woman. It's a call to our senses. It's too soon for you. And for me."

"Then why did you come here?"

The corner of his mouth lifted in a self-abasing grin. "I intended only to make out with you a bit. To get myself hot and bothered and very frustrated."

"But why?"

He cocked his head at her, his eyes lit with amusement. "I believe it's called foreplay."

Libby smacked him on the shoulder, pulling free and climbing off him, not the least bit contrite when Michael grunted in surprise and had to protect himself from being unmanned by her knee.

She marched to the hearth, got down on her knees, and made herself busy putting logs on the fire while she fought to bring her temper under control.

No, not her temper—her raging hormones.

Damn him. The man was an idiot. She had all but offered herself up on a silver platter, and he had bluntly said no, although he had tried to soften his rejection by claiming it was for her own good.

Well, dammit, she was getting sorely tired of his nobility.

"You're going to start a chimney fire if you put any more wood on," he nobly informed her.

"It's my body, isn't it?" she accused, still poking at the logs, deciding it was the fire heating her face, not shame.

"Excuse me?"

"I look like a twelve-year-old boy."

He said nothing to that. Libby poked the logs more violently. Since the age of seventeen, when she had finally realized she wasn't going to grow another inch and would never have womanly curves, Libby had decided sex was probably overrated, anyway.

Yeah. Well. She wanted those curves now. And six inches added to her height while she was at it. Dammit, he had to stand her on the hearth just to see her face.

Libby jumped when Michael wrapped his arms around her, taking the poker away with one large hand and pulling her back against his chest with the other.

"You don't feel like a twelve-year-old boy," he whispered in her ear, sending prickles of awareness shooting through her. "Ya feel like fire in my hands, lass, when I touch you."

And he did touch her then, lifting his hand to cover her breasts, pulling her more tightly against him, more intimately into the spread of his kneeling thighs. And the evidence of what he thought of her body scorched her back.

Libby took a shuddering breath, which firmed her breast into his palm when he squeezed her gently and brushed his thumb over her nipple. He splayed his other hand across her stomach, his fingers sliding lower to gently touch her woman's place.

Libby's response was immediate. Heat pulsed through her. Moisture gathered. And the nipple he was stroking poked through her bra and shirt, searching for more of his touch.

She tried to turn to face him, to wrap her arms around his neck and stifle her moan in his shoulder, but he held her still and continued to stroke her, sending her into a storm of raging desire.

His hand on her breast moved to the buttons on her shirt, and, with painstaking slowness, he worked them open one at a time. Libby gripped the edge of the hearth and closed her eyes as heat built inside her and moisture continued to gather against his hand between her thighs.

Her blouse finally unbuttoned, he slipped it down her arms, and his lips found the base of her throat.

Libby moaned, threw back her head, and whispered a curse.

Michael chuckled, the sound deep and warm, as he

pulled down the straps of her bra and continued to make love to her neck with his mouth.

He brought both hands up to her now naked breasts, covering them, kneading them, completely inflaming her.

And then he moved to the snap of her pants.

It was all Libby could do to hold on to her sanity. His mouth was driving her into a frenzy, trailing over every inch of exposed skin. He opened her jeans and then slid his fingers inside her panties and caressed her intimately.

Libby cried out and twisted, trying to face him, but he still refused to let her move. He just kept working his magic with his hand, building her desire with his fingers, making her yearn for more.

"Let go, lass," he whispered into her hair. "Burst into beautiful flame."

She didn't want to, didn't know how.

She was scared. Confused. Unsure.

"I'm right here to catch you, Libby," he thickly continued, his lips brushing her ear, his breath caressing her senses, his hands working their magic. "I won't let you fly away, lass. Let go," he tenderly urged, pushing one finger deeply inside her.

And Libby obeyed in a mindless storm that started deep inside her and spiraled outward and upward and escaped from her throat in a cry of pure pleasure. She convulsed around him, and Michael leaned over her, pulled her mouth to his, and captured her scream.

It lasted forever, this wondrous thing, and Libby clung desperately to his hand as pulse after sensuous pulse of pleasure ran through her trembling body.

"Sometimes a woman's scream is like music," he whispered, kissing her, gentling her with tender caresses, slowly bringing her back to reality.

Libby melted against him with a shuddering sigh, willing

her pounding heart to slow down. She finally opened her eyes, blinked at the fire, and blushed all the way to her socks.

Michael laughed, lifting her with him as he stood. Before she could catch her breath, he swept her into his arms and set them down on the couch, cradling her on his lap in a tender cuddle. Libby attempted to pull her blouse closed, but he stilled her action, instead using his broad, warm palm and strong, masculine fingers to cover her breasts.

Libby's blush intensified.

His smile turned smug. "That was your first time," he said with undisguised male satisfaction.

Not quite sure how to respond to that statement and still trying to gather her wits back, Libby remained mute.

He absently caressed the side of her breast. "And that, lass, answers some of my questions but creates a few more."

Libby still couldn't find her voice. It might be because her heart was still racing a mile a minute or because she was sprawled across Michael like a shameless hussy. Or maybe she was afraid that if she opened her mouth she would scream again—and it wouldn't sound like music this time.

"How is it that a woman your age hasn't ever experienced an orgasm?"

Libby flinched at his blunt question and finally found her voice. "I guess the foreplay is over."

He nodded. And smiled crookedly. "It is for now," he drawled. "The moment I realized you were a virgin, I completely disgraced myself like a boy of ten."

"I am not a virgin, Michael. I've had plenty of boyfriends."

His nod was slower this time. "But you are, lass. Or were," he corrected. "Maybe not technically," he quickly added. "But emotionally. It isn't really sex unless both people involved are completely satisfied."

"Then what is it? Really?"

He shrugged. "Use," he clarified. "Or abuse, more likely, when one party is slaked and the other is left . . . hanging."

Michael the philosopher was back.

Libby decided she preferred the sex god.

She tried to pull her blouse closed again, and this time Michael helped her by pulling it over her shoulders. Libby rose to her feet, buttoned herself up, and fastened her pants.

Then she just stood there, staring at the fire.

What was she supposed to do now? What did a woman say to a man who had just given her the experience of true passion for the first time in her life?

Thank you? I hope we can do this again soon?

Like maybe right now? Only this time, could we both please get naked and actually . . . do it?

Libby turned at the sound of papers being shuffled and found Michael reading her lists. Heat climbed into her face when she realized exactly which page he had stopped at.

His gaze went to the side table, and he picked up her pencil and started writing. She leaned over to see, but he quickly shuffled the pages and started writing again.

Libby spun on her socked heel and walked to the kitchen on rubbery legs. She went to the fridge and took out the bottle of wine Grace MacKeage had thoughtfully included with the groceries, then started rummaging through the drawers for a corkscrew. She found one, but the damned thing refused to work properly. So she rummaged through the drawers again, looking for something either to pry the cork out of the bottle or to drive it down inside.

The wine bottle was suddenly lifted out of her hand and

replaced by her pages of lists. Michael leaned against the counter, crossed his feet at his ankles, and slowly turned the suddenly obedient corkscrew into the bottle.

He stopped to use one finger to tap the top page in her hand, then went back to work on the wine. "When ya go shopping for new clothes, buy a blaze orange jacket," he said. "And spend the extra money for Gore-Tex boots. Nothing freezes a person quicker than wet feet."

Libby stared at her list and saw that *birth control* had been crossed out and that *blaze orange jacket* and *waterproof boots* had been added in neat, dark letters. *ATV* also had been crossed out, and the word *snowmobile* was written beside it.

"Rifle season begins tomorrow," Michael said. He turned and opened a cupboard as he spoke. "So don't step outside this house without wearing orange." He took down two tumblers, set them on the counter, and filled them with wine. "Not even to go to your mailbox. Blaze orange is necessary from the first part of November to mid-December."

Libby looked down at her list again, but her chin was lifted by Michael's finger to gain back her attention. "And if I ever catch you outside without wearing orange, lass, I will personally make you sorry you ever left California," he said very softly, his eyes far more threatening than his words.

Libby was more curious than intimidated. "What do you mean by rifle season?"

"Deer hunting."

"Oh." She was buying a lot of orange clothes, then, even orange socks. "Why did you cross *birth control* off my list? Are you trying to get Robbie a brother or sister?" she asked, deciding it was time to rattle his calm. The man was acting as if what had just happened in the living room were an everyday occurrence.

Good God. She'd just had her first orgasm.

But Michael didn't appear rattled by her question, only amused. "I'll take care of the birth control," he told her.

Libby shook her head. "Since this is a consequence I would have to live with, I'll take care of it."

He looked as if he would argue, but instead he handed her one of the tumblers of wine. He clinked their glasses together and nodded. "Then we'll consider the affair begun," he said, his eyes shining with what Libby could only describe as possession.

And that alarmed her, almost as much as his ability to make her body react in ways she hadn't thought possible. She was thirty-one years old, and she felt sixteen, like a reckless, infatuated, trembling teenager experiencing her first case of lust. Libby took a large gulp of her wine, coughed for a good minute, and looked down at her list through blurry eyes.

"Why . . ." She coughed again and started over. "Why did you cross out *ATV* and write in *snowmobile?*" she asked, deciding to move onto safer ground. "I want an ATV."

He shook his head. "You'd only have another week to use it, at best. ATVs are no good in the snow, and they're not allowed on the groomed snowmobile trails."

"Do you have a snowmobile?"

"Aye. And so does Robbie."

Libby wanted to ask if the boy wore a helmet when he rode his snowmobile.

"And we both wear helmets," he told her before she could work up the nerve, his mouth lifting in a knowing grin. "Only suicidal fools ride without them. And they keep us warm."

Libby took another drink of her wine, slower this time.

"I see you bought Callum's truck," he said, nodding

toward the attached garage. "You'll be glad for the four-wheel drive this winter. And for its size. This is the main road leading out of the deep woods, and Monday through Friday you'll meet loaded logging trucks. So stay alert, and don't ever swerve again for an animal. Your life is more precious than theirs."

"Is it because I'm nearly the size of your son that you feel this need to lecture me as if I were a child?" she asked, tossing her lists on the counter and downing the rest of her wine.

Michael moved so quickly Libby barely had time to finish swallowing before she was picked up, spun around, and set on the counter. He took the tumbler out of her hand and put it in the sink, then stood between her thighs, pulling her firmly against him.

"No," he said with maddening calm. "It's because I want you to live long enough for us to mess up your sheets."

She couldn't argue with that. Libby framed both her hands over his face and stared into his gleaming eyes. "I don't suppose you have some birth control in your pocket?" she asked.

"Nay, lass," he said, shaking his head within her hands. "And I doubt what I have at home is any good. It's at least a couple of years old."

Her surprise must have shown on her face, because her hands moved with his grin. He pulled her hips more firmly against him and leaned forward to kiss her gaping mouth.

"Are ya thinking I'm in the habit of having affairs?" he asked just inches from her lips.

"I . . . I thought . . . I don't know what I thought."

"Then think on this, lass. I've loved two women, and they both died, each taking a good part of me with her. All

I have left is just enough for my son. Look only for passion from me, Libby, because that's all I can give you."

"It's enough, Michael," she whispered, pulling his face close so she could kiss him.

He met her mouth with plenty of the passion he'd promised, and Libby thought her hormones were going to erupt into another riot. But he suddenly stopped and stepped back.

He grabbed his jacket off one of the kitchen chairs, gave her one last heated look, and left as quietly as he had arrived.

Libby stared at the curtain settling back into place against the closing door. She covered her racing heart with one hand and reached for the wine bottle with the other. After a long, healthy swig straight from the bottle, Libby let her gaze travel around the kitchen.

It seemed larger now that Michael had left.

It was definitely more peaceful. The man didn't have to say a word, make a sound, or even move for her to feel as if she were standing in the middle of a brewing storm.

Libby took another swig of wine and continued to look around the silent kitchen, her gaze finally landing on a small box sitting on the table.

It hadn't been there an hour ago.

She jumped down from the counter, walked to the table, and picked up the envelope lying on top of the box. She unsealed it, took out the paper, and read the note written in not-so-neat letters painstakingly formed by a young hand.

Dear Libby,

I was thinking you might like to do this small job for me, since you're an artist and are good with your hands. I'm working on a special Christmas gift for my father, but this part of it is too hard for me to do. Could you please paint the word Tàirneanaiche *on the small wooden board? I put some gold paint in the box, too. Don't worry, I'm not asking you for a favor, just giving you a job so you can earn money until your studio is open. I will have Papa compensate you, but don't tell him what it's for, just how much you're charging.*

Thank you,
Robbie MacBain

Libby read the note twice, then broke the piece of tape on the box and opened it. Sure enough, there was a small wooden board inside, about six inches long. Libby picked it up and looked at the note again. *Tàirneanaiche?* What kind of word was that?

She looked back at the wood. It appeared to be a plaque of some sort, its corners scrolled inward and a beveled line running along all four edges. The plaque was made from a soft wood, like pine or hemlock, and had been carefully sanded.

What was *Tàirneanaiche?*

Libby reread the note, looking for a clue to what the word meant or what the plaque was for. But Robbie was being secretive about his father's Christmas gift.

And then she came to the part where he promised his father would compensate her, and Libby laughed out loud.

Hadn't Michael just paid her in full?

She stuck the note inside the box and carried it into her bedroom. She set it on the dresser, thinking about Robbie and Michael's relationship. The boy obviously trusted his father to bring the box to her without peeking inside. And she decided she wanted Robbie's trust, too, and would do his little job and keep his secret. All she'd ask for in compensation was the meaning of *Tàirneanaiche*.

Libby undressed and slipped into the heavy flannel gown she'd grabbed from her grandmother Bea's farm when she had gone to pack up her equipment. She crawled under the bedcovers, tucked her arms under her head, and fell asleep with the smile of a woman who had finally lost her virginity.

Chapter Ten

Libby opened the door, stepped onto the porch, and stared at the wonderland surrounding her. Frost had settled on everything overnight and gleamed in the bright morning sunlight like polished diamonds. One of the hens was out, pecking at the ground beside the coop, puffed up like a strutting turkey in defense of the cold.

Libby was just stepping off the porch to give chase to the escaped bird when she heard the gunshot. She quickly stepped back and looked toward TarStone Mountain as the shot echoed down the mountainside like a crack of thunder.

Rifle season.

Which meant that some poor deer was up there right now, running for its life.

Libby also ran, worried for her own life, back into the house. She went to the bathroom and pulled a bright yellow towel off the rack. It wasn't blaze orange, but she couldn't think of any animal that had curb-yellow fur. She wrapped the towel around her shoulders like a shawl and stepped back onto the porch. Ducking her head like a soldier being shot at, she ran across the yard and bolted into the chicken coop for safety.

Startled by her sudden arrival, the hens went nuts, flapping down from their roosts in a cacophony of frantic squawks and flying sawdust. Waving away the choking dust, Libby opened the bag of feed Ian had provided and filled the pan on the floor. She checked the water dispenser next and poked the skin of ice off the top. Two birds immediately started drinking.

Libby turned to the nesting boxes and peeked inside the three empty ones. She found only one broken egg and lifted it out along with some of the straw. She set the mess in an empty bucket by her feet and then turned her attention to the hen sitting in the fourth nesting box.

The hen stared back, unblinking, and lashed out when Libby reached under her to feel for an egg.

"Ouch, you ungrateful biddy," Libby hissed, rubbing her hand on her thigh. "I'm going to let the hunters use you for target practice if you don't quit pecking me," she said, glaring at all the hens, including them in her threat. "You girls give me eggs, and I feed you. That's how it works around here."

They weren't listening. Half of them were eating, and the others were drinking. There was a faint sound at the coop door, and Libby walked over and opened it. The escaped hen came running inside and joined her coop mates at the feed pan.

Deciding she wasn't going to find her breakfast in there that morning, Libby stepped outside, made sure the door was securely closed, and pulled her bright yellow towel over her head. She ran back to the house and onto the porch, breathing a sigh of relief when she didn't hear any more gunshots.

Talk about strange, having to worry about going outside her own home. She had never considered hunting season in her decision to move to New England.

She wasn't a vegetarian. She liked meat. But she wasn't sure she could eat a cute little deer. She could eat one or two of her chickens, though, if they kept pecking her.

Libby hung her towel on the peg beside the door and went to the bathroom to wash her hands while she thought about the busy day ahead. She had a million things to do, and her checkbook was going to take another big hit.

She considered adding a new bed to her list. She wasn't keen on messing up Mary's sheets with Mary's former lover in Mary's old bed. It was bad enough she was living in Mary's house.

Libby quickly brushed her teeth and fluffed her hair. She gathered up her purse and lists and headed into the garage. She was going straight to the Dolans' store and buying waterproof boots, thick gloves to protect her hands from pecking chickens, and a blaze orange jacket and hat.

She opened the garage door, walked to her new truck and opened its door, and then tried to remember how she had climbed into the damn thing the night before for her test drive.

Oh, yeah. Callum had kindly lifted her in. Then he had kindly suggested she have running boards installed. And he had not-so-kindly laughed the whole time.

Libby had met his wife, Charlotte, and their handsome son, Duncan.

It took her several tries to get into the truck before Libby finally conceded defeat. She looked around the garage and found a wooden crate, then stood it on end to use as a step. Once inside the truck, she reached down and picked up the crate, setting it on the floor on the passenger side. She'd need it again if she wanted to drive the truck home.

Libby spent the next three minutes adjusting the seat, thankful that it was electric and moved up as well as forward. Still, Callum also had suggested—kindly—that she tape a block of wood to the gas pedal so she could reach it.

She fastened her seat belt and started the truck, smiling at the sound of the powerful engine as she looked around the interior. The Suburban was large enough to hold a dance in. Libby shook her head and laughed at herself. Who would have thought, just a month ago, that she would be living in Maine, in the mountains, driving a truck almost as large as her town house?

But Libby quickly sobered. She was guilty of cowardice, of turning her back on her work. But mostly, she was guilty of not wanting a gift that could help people.

But couldn't that gift become her Midas touch? Was she supposed to heal everyone she came into contact with? Where would it end? When she became a one-woman freak show, with hordes of people seeking her out, hounding her, petitioning, begging?

Libby tried to reason with her unsettling thoughts. As long as she kept her gift a secret, she was safe. All anyone in Pine Creek needed to know was that she was a jewelry maker from California. Michael and Grace would keep her secret, she was sure. Neither one of them seemed overly bothered by her unwillingness to confide in them about her past.

And the fact that she trusted them amazed Libby.

She had learned, as early as med school, to be careful around the people she worked with. Oh, most in medicine were dedicated, but no matter how sincere their intentions, workplace politics were always a factor.

Like her competition with James Kessler over the grant

they both wanted. Money and prestige always complicated things.

Their fathers had been colleagues and good friends, and Libby and James had grown up knowing each other. Though James had been two years ahead of Libby, they'd gone to medical school together and had both found positions at Cedar-Sinai.

And they were both after the same grant to develop a new method of minimally invasive microsurgery.

Or they were, up until last week, when the bottom had dropped out of Libby's world. Now she just wanted . . . hell, she didn't know what she wanted. Peace? Understanding?

Her life back?

Or did she want a new life here?

If she wanted an answer to that question, it was time she started exploring the possibility. And she would begin with Dolan's Outfitter Store and go from there.

Libby put the truck in reverse and backed up. She turned in the yard and started toward the road but slammed on her brakes when a large tractor-trailer rig, loaded to the sky with logs, came racing past the end of her driveway. The driver, apparently not the least bit worried about sharing the road with anyone, was looking at her, smiling and waving. He raised one arm and pulled on the air horn, giving Libby a friendly, deafening honk that trailed after him in a cloud of dust long after he'd vanished.

Just as soon as she saw Michael again, she was going to stand on a chair and apologize to the man. He hadn't been kidding when he warned her about the dangers of her new home.

Maybe she should bake him something. A cake or a batch of cookies. Or dinner. She could cook a nice dinner and invite Michael and Robbie and John Bigelow over tomorrow.

Libby reached into her purse and found her list of things to buy. She added a large roasting hen and smiled in satisfaction. She'd show the packaged bird to her girls in the coop before she cooked it and warn them that if they didn't quit pecking her, they'd be joining it in the oven.

With her plans firmly made, Libby checked for traffic up and down the road and finally headed into town.

"You gotta be looking in the kids' section, missy," Harry Dolan repeated for the third time, trying to lead her toward the back wall of the store. "Ain't nothin' gonna fit you over here."

Libby refused to budge. She was too busy rolling up the sleeves on the blaze orange sweatshirt she was wearing. But the price tag, as big as a book and probably costing more than the garment it was advertising, kept getting in the way.

Harry's wife, Irisa, was trying to help. Libby could only make out every other word the woman said, and those were so heavily accented that she couldn't decide if Irisa were trying to help or trying to get her to take the sweatshirt off.

Dammit, she was not shopping in the kids' section. She was old enough to have children who should be shopping there.

"This should fit," Dwayne Dolan said, walking up from the back wall with a sweatshirt in his hand. "And it's got a hood just like that one."

"I don't want a sweatshirt that fits," Libby stubbornly explained. "I want to layer it over a sweater."

Dwayne stopped in front of her and held the sweatshirt against her shoulders, completely ignoring her protest. His unwavering smile was crooked behind a week's growth of whiskers, and he smelled funny. Like pickles or something.

"You can still layer this one, Miss Hart," he said, tossing the sweatshirt over his shoulder and reaching for the zipper on the one she was wearing.

Libby stepped back, and Irisa came to her rescue, shooing the two men away, pulling the smaller sweatshirt off Dwayne's shoulder as he left.

"I think I know," Irisa said in broken English, nodding sympathetically. "Not girl. Woman."

Libby conceded to Irisa's smile. She pushed up the sleeves on the sweatshirt she was wearing to find her hands and unzipped it and took it off. The damn thing came down to her knees, and she knew she looked ridiculous. So she slipped into the smaller one that Irisa was holding out for her, zipped it up, and wiggled her arms to make sure it was roomy enough.

She was looking at herself in the mirror when Irisa plopped a blaze orange hat onto her head. Libby's humor quickly returned, and she laughed out loud.

Now she really looked ridiculous.

As if she should buy a gun and go shoot something.

The hat was made of felt and had a brim all the way around it, with a matching orange ribbon that added a bit of style. Libby tugged on the front, giving the hat a rakish tilt.

It was pulled from her head and replaced by another, this one a northwoods version of a baseball cap. It was orange and black checkered, with ear flaps and a strap that fastened under her chin. The entire cap was lined with sheepskin and felt as warm as toast.

It made her look like Elmer Fudd.

Irisa plopped another hat onto Libby's head, this one knit. It was also blaze orange and had a small pom-pom on top. But it was pulled from her head just as Libby was trying to adjust it and replaced by the felt hat.

Libby looked up into the mirror and saw a red wool jacket standing behind her, covering a broad chest. She recognized the jacket. And the chest.

Libby whirled and came nose to button with Michael. She looked up, having to push her hat back in order to smile at him.

He smiled back. "Now ya look like a Mainer," he told her, tapping the end of her nose. "All you're lacking is a gun."

"I heard a shot this morning, up on TarStone."

"Aye. That was me, lass."

Libby stepped back in surprise. "You were shooting at a deer? But why?"

His smile disappeared. "So we can eat this winter."

"And did you . . . was your hunt successful?"

His eyes softened at her obvious distress. "Aye. But you needn't worry, Libby. It was a clean kill. The buck was dead before he even hit the ground."

It took all of her willpower not to flinch. And a good deal of effort to smile.

Michael reached up and gently brushed her cheek with his knuckles. "It's a natural act, lass," he said softly. "Man is a hunter, and deer are prey. And that's a fact society will never change, no matter how civilized we think we've become."

"I know. And I eat meat like most people. It's just that hunting is so . . . it's so direct."

"Given a choice, would you rather be a steer in a stock-yard or a deer running wild and free?" he asked. "If you're going to end up on someone's table anyway, which life would you choose?"

"The deer."

"Aye. So would I. And so would the buck I killed this morning, Libby. Please try to remember that when you bite

into one of his steaks this winter. Have ya ever had veni-
son?"

"No. Will you give me a steak?"

"Aye. And a roast or two, if ya want."

"Oh," Libby said, suddenly remembering her earlier
decision. "I'm cooking a chicken for supper tomorrow and
thought you and Robbie and John would like to come over
and share it with me."

For the life of her, Libby could not read the expression
that suddenly came into Michael's eyes. "Are ya stuffing the
chicken?" he asked thickly, stepping closer. "And making
gravy and mashed potatoes?"

Libby stepped closer herself, nodding. "I was also thinking of baking an apple pie for dessert."

Michael took hold of her shoulders and leaned down
until his nose was nearly touching hers. "Ya bake an apple
pie, lass, and I'll bring the ice cream. And a good bottle of
wine."

His voice was guttural, almost seductive, and Libby
couldn't decide if his passion was directed at her or at the
meal she was planning.

A giggle sounded beside them, and Libby looked over
to find Irisa, her hand covering her smiling mouth, staring
at them.

Michael straightened, and Libby quickly turned away to
hide her flaming face. She took off the hat and jacket,
handed them to Irisa, gathered up her purse, and dug
inside it for her list of things to buy.

"What time?" Michael asked.

Libby looked up. "What time for what?"

"Supper. What time do you want us to come over? And
thank you for including John."

"Oh, I wouldn't think of not inviting John. I'm anxious
to meet him. What time is good for you?"

"Six."

"Then six it is," Libby agreed, walking to the counter with her list.

Michael followed. "Did ya get the box Robbie sent?" he asked, stopping her before she could reach Harry and Dwayne. "If ya don't wish to do whatever it is he wants, the boy will understand."

Libby smiled ever so sweetly. "The note said you'd compensate me," she whispered, so only he could hear. "And I'm warning you, I don't come cheap."

Michael raised one eyebrow and looked at Libby so intensely it was a wonder she didn't burst into flames. She quickly stepped back, trying to push down the blush climbing her cheeks. What had possessed her to say such a thing?

"Leysa just came in," Dwayne said, walking up to them. "She can show you the storefront now. Mornin', MacBain."

With one last heated look, Michael turned and nodded to Dwayne. "Have those .270 shells come in yet?" he asked. "And I'm ready to order that knife we talked about for Robbie. Are ya sure it will be here in time for Christmas?"

Libby tried to stifle her gasp, she really did. But it came out anyway. Michael looked down at her, pinched the bridge of his nose, and sighed with weary patience.

Libby held up her hand before he could speak. "Don't say anything. I don't want to know why you're buying a child a knife for Christmas."

Taking her at her word, Michael turned and followed Dwayne to the counter, leaving Libby to gape at his back.

Dammit. She did want to know. Why was he buying Robbie such a dangerous weapon? And what kind of Christmas present was a knife, anyway? The boy should be getting toys, a Walkman, a bike, or socks and sweaters— not something he could maim himself with.

Irisa drew Libby's attention and introduced her to Leysa, Dwayne's wife. Leysa was maybe ten years older than Libby, a good foot taller, with lots of long, wavy hair held away from her face by two beautiful wooden barrettes.

She was cradling a young infant in the crook of her arm.

"My sister-law, Leysa," Irisa said. "Her job to care for store. She deal you the rent."

Libby couldn't contain her curiosity any longer. Both women were absolutely beautiful, neat as an operating room, and such unlikely wives for Harry and Dwayne that she simply had to know more about them. "Hello, Leysa. I'm Libby," she said, nodding as she lightly touched the sleeping infant's hand. "Are you and Irisa from Russia?"

Leysa smiled warmly and held out her child for Libby to take. Surprised but delighted, Libby carefully cradled the baby in one arm and fingered its wrinkled little chin with the other.

"I am Ukrainian," Leysa told her in heavily accented but perfect English. "And Irisa is from Croatia. We came here four years ago, after meeting Harry and Dwayne at a party in Moscow," she continued at Libby's questioning look. "They were searching for wives, and we . . ." She looked at Irisa and smiled, then back at Libby. "We were searching for husbands."

"We pick good men," Irisa added. "And now live in beautiful place and are happy." She patted her flat belly. "I give Harry a son next spring."

Libby was speechless. They'd met Harry and Dwayne at a party in Moscow? She'd seen a story on television about such parties, where American men would travel to Russia or Asia to find wives.

"Am I holding a boy or a girl?" Libby asked, looking down at the infant in her arms.

"A girl," Leysa said. "She is named Rose, after our husbands' mother."

"She's beautiful," Libby murmured, walking to the counter and stopping beside Michael. "Look at what I've got," she whispered. "Isn't she precious?"

Michael set down the catalogue he was leafing through and turned his attention to Rose. He reached over and picked up the infant, cradling her against his chest, covering her head with one broad hand, and burying his nose in her hair.

Libby went weak in the knees at the sight of Michael handling the child with such confidence and genuine affection. And Leysa, instead of being horrified to see her daughter in the arms of the huge man, was pulling Libby toward the front door of the store.

"Come," she said. "I'll show you the space we have to rent, and you can decide if it will suit you."

"But . . . but what about Rose?"

Leysa kept walking. "She'll scream her head off if I take her away from Michael now," she said, turning to smile at Libby. "I think she is in love with him. He can't come here without picking her up. I only have to watch that he doesn't try to sneak her home." She leaned over and whispered, "I think Michael is in love with her as well."

Not only did Libby's legs feel like noodles, but her heart skipped several beats. She looked over her shoulder as Leysa pulled her along and saw that Michael now had Rose nestled against his shoulder and was rubbing a lazy hand over her back as he studied the catalogue again.

He was a towering mountain of a man who could kill a deer in the morning and cuddle an infant a few hours later. He could walk into a room and take her breath away, say something to send her temper flying, and make love to her as if the world would end tomorrow. He thrilled her, inflamed her, and sent her hormones into overdrive with just a look.

And his warning the night he'd come to her room to scare her away finally hit Libby with the force of a locomotive.

Yes, she would be wise to be very afraid.

Chapter Eleven

Libby just didn't want *to* get out of bed. She snuggled deeper into the warm quilt and covered her cold nose with the blanket. She had stayed up past midnight to paint Robbie's plaque, then fallen into bed like a zombie.

Coffee wouldn't help. Libby doubted even aspirin would do the trick. Two or three fresh scrambled eggs might work, along with a thick slab of toast from the loaf of bread she had bought at the bakery conveniently located right next-door to her new studio.

She'd run into Michael again coming out of the bakery. The man's arms had been loaded down with bread and cakes and a bag that looked to have two dozen cookies in it. He'd been chewing on a doughnut at the time and had only nodded and held the door open for her with his foot.

Libby threw back the covers with a moan and stumbled into the bathroom like an old woman. She had another hundred million things to do today, not the least of which was cooking dinner. Thank heavens she had seen some old cookbooks on the shelf in the kitchen. It had been a few years since she'd baked an apple pie.

Libby turned on the shower and waited until the room warmed up with steam before she stepped under the water, letting the driving spray beat the kinks out and the eucalyptus shampoo wash the fog from her brain. In half an hour, she was dressed in her new blaze orange jacket and hat and was ready to face the girls in the coop—this morning, she was wearing blaze orange gloves to protect her hands from striking beaks.

Libby was surprised to find seven eggs in the nesting boxes. It was like Christmas morning, seeing those seven perfectly formed brown ovals just sitting there, waiting for her to collect them. Ian had warned her not to expect any for maybe a week, until the hens had settled down from their move.

But she had seven eggs. She felt like the richest woman in the world.

With her treasures carefully stowed in her pockets, Libby slowly walked back to the house but stopped in the middle of the driveway to stare at Pine Lake.

And her wealth suddenly increased tenfold.

A sense of rightness, of peace and contentment, settled over Libby like a warm blanket of security. She could feel the strength of TarStone Mountain at her back, as she drank in the beauty of the lake cradled in the valley below.

This was as real as it got.

It was good that she'd come here. From this place of strength, she would be able to deal with her gift. She would learn its parameters and begin to understand it. From here, with the support of these good people, she would accept what she could not change and embrace it for the miracle it was.

For the first time in almost two weeks, Libby felt

balanced. And blessed instead of cursed. Something had driven her search, guiding her computer to find this home in Pine Creek.

Grammy Bea?

Or a young boy with a plan?

"It's a mighty fine view, ain't it?"

Libby whirled, then had to scramble to catch the egg that came flying out of her pocket. She bumped it instead and watched as the tiny missile sailed through the air and landed with a sickening plop against Father Daar's chest.

Both horrified speechless, they stared at each other in shock. Libby felt her cheeks warm and quickly pulled off her gloves and used them to wipe the mess off his jacket.

The old priest took the gloves from her and stepped back, brushing his own chest.

"I'm . . . I'm sorry, Father. You startled me."

"Aye," he agreed, handing back her soiled gloves. "And I'm wearing my penance." He looked at her suspiciously. "Ya got any more eggs ya're wanting to throw? 'Cause I'm thinking they'd be better off in my belly instead of on it."

The man was looking for breakfast. He had a lot of nerve, after being so rude to her the other day.

"I have six more," she told him, tucking her hands in her pockets, letting him worry about what she intended to do with them.

He lifted one bushy eyebrow at her. "Are ya a Christian woman, Libby Hart?"

"Sometimes," she said, pointedly looking at the white collar around his neck. "When people act Christianly toward me."

He ducked his head, and his cheeks reddened above his neatly trimmed beard. "I've come here this morning to apologize for my behavior the other day," he said contritely. He looked at her hair. "I was just startled, is all."

"By this?" Libby asked, touching her white curl. "Father, it's a genetic trait. Lots of people have it."

"Aye," he said, nodding. "I've seen such a thing before. Now, are ya gonna hatch them eggs, girl, or cook them?"

The man was tenacious. Libby sighed, turned, and waved him along. "Come on, then, Father. I'll make you breakfast."

He fell into step beside her, his crooked wooden cane keeping time with his limping steps. Libby looked at him from the corner of her eye. "Did you walk all the way down the mountain?" she asked, wondering how old he was.

"Aye," he said, smiling, apparently quite pleased that he was getting fed. "I like walking. It's good for the soul."

"Why do you live up on the mountain and not in town? Don't you get lonely?"

His smile widened. "Solitude is also good for the soul. Besides, I don't much care for people."

Libby stopped and looked at him curiously. "But you're a priest. You're supposed to like everyone. Isn't it in your vows or something?"

"I spoke my vows so long ago I've forgotten half of them. And I'm old now. I've earned the right to be picky."

Well, she couldn't argue with that. Grammy Bea had been eighty-nine when she died, and the old woman could have given audacious lessons to a peacock.

Libby led her guest into the house and waved him to a chair at the kitchen table. Father Daar sat down with a pained sigh, cupped his hands over the top of his cane, and looked around.

"This place hasn't changed much," he said. "But I feel the old house's joy at being lived in again. Can ya feel its energy, Libby?"

Libby finished pulling the eggs from her pockets and put them in a bowl. She looked at Father Daar and found him studying her with a strange, calculating expression in his surprisingly crystal-clear blue eyes. She decided not to answer his question.

"Have you been to see a doctor about your joint pain?"

His eyes narrowed, and his weathered face wrinkled into a frown. "I don't like doctors. All they do is poke and pinch and give ya a list of things ya can't do and can't eat."

"They would also give you something for the pain."

"Ain't nothing wrong with a little pain," he rebutted. "Lets a man know he's alive."

"So does opening your eyes every morning." Libby set the frying pan on the stove and turned on the burner, then grabbed her loaf of bread. "There are some very good treatments now, Father. You don't have to suffer."

"You a doctor?"

Libby stopped slicing the bread and looked at him. What sort of trouble did a person get into for lying to a priest? "I know something about medicine. Enough to realize that you're riddled with arthritis."

"Is that what they're calling it now?" he asked. "In my day, it was called growing old."

Libby popped the bread into the toaster and broke the six remaining eggs into the frying pan. She found a spatula, stirred the eggs, and shut off the burner, leaving them to cook by themselves. She set the table and poured juice into two glasses, buttered the toast, and served up breakfast like a short-order cook, all the while trying to ignore the penetrating stare of her nosy houseguest.

"Do you stay on the mountain all winter?" she asked as she set their two plates of food on the table and took a seat across from Father Daar. "What would happen if you got hurt or were snowed in?"

Libby folded her hands and waited for the priest to say grace, but he dove into his breakfast without even answering her question. It was several bites later before he looked up and frowned at her.

"Dig in, girl, before it gets cold. I blessed the food while you were cooking it. And if I need help, the MacKeage or MacBain would find a way to get to me."

"But how would they know you needed help? Do you have a radio or something?"

He couldn't answer because he was too busy eating again. Libby gave up and went to work on her own breakfast, but she ate slower, savoring the taste of fresh eggs cooked in home-churned farm butter that she had bought at the bakery.

Her cholesterol level was going to skyrocket, living here. And she would probably gain five pounds this winter.

"Am I smelling coffee?" Father Daar asked, pushing his empty plate away, leaning back, and brushing the toast crumbs off his black wool cassock.

He'd been wearing an orange hat for his walk down the mountain and had hung it and his red plaid jacket by the door when they'd entered the kitchen. He stood up now and walked toward the living room.

"We could drink our coffee on the front porch," he suggested. "It's such a fine morning, and the sun is warm."

Libby set their dishes in the sink and poured two cups of coffee. "How do you take yours?" she asked.

"Black," he answered, walking through the living room and heading out the front door.

Libby imagined he was making himself at home because he'd visited Mary Sutter often and had decided to revive the habit with her. She smiled as she followed him out. It seemed she had inherited a priest with an appetite.

They sat in companionable silence, drinking in the view while they sipped their coffee, and Libby decided she was more amused than annoyed by Father Daar. He said the most outrageous things and showed up out of nowhere when least expected.

She still couldn't decide how old he was. He dressed like a priest from the sixteenth century, was obviously a Scot like half the people she'd met here, and appeared positively ancient.

"Have you lived in Pine Creek long, Father?" she asked.

"A bit over eleven years now," he told her. "I came here with the MacKeages."

"From Scotland?"

"Aye."

Realizing he wasn't going to elaborate, Libby decided to head their conversation in a different direction. After all, she had a man of God at her disposal. Why not pick his brain? She was entitled, considering four of her precious eggs were in his belly, not to mention the one decorating his coat.

"Do you believe in magic, Father?"

The old priest choked on his coffee as he shot her such a confounded look Libby didn't know whether to be embarrassed by her question or alarmed by his response.

"It's an innocent question, Father," she defended. "Considering we're looking at this beautiful landscape."

"Oh," he said, relaxing back into his seat. "Ya mean, do I believe in the magic of nature?"

"Yes. That. But I was also wondering if you believed in a more . . . well, a more mystical kind of magic, too."

"How mystical?" he asked, giving her a crooked look. "Like witches and warlocks and . . . wizards?"

"I wouldn't go that far," Libby said, waving her hand in dismissal. "I was talking about things like reincarnation, intuition, and . . . well, maybe a person being gifted. Have you ever met anyone who claimed they had a special gift?

What with you being a priest and all, you must have had people come to you with such concerns."

She was blathering like an idiot. Her cheeks felt hot, and she was almost sorry she'd brought up the subject.

But only almost. Dammit, she was stumbling onto sacred ground here. But if she was going to fall flat on her face, why not do it in the presence of a priest? Wasn't he bound by those vows he couldn't remember not to tell anyone about their conversation?

"Gifted?" he softly repeated, turning fully in his chair to face her. "Like what? Give me an example of what you think of as gifted."

Libby set her cup of coffee down on the porch rail and rubbed her sweating palms on her thighs. She took a shuddering breath, and, as was becoming her habit, she jumped into the fire with both feet—but only partway.

"I'm talking about a mother coming back as an owl," she said, dancing around her own personal problem, trying to get a feel for Father Daar's thinking. "Have you seen Robbie's pet?"

"Aye," he said, nodding, eying her suspiciously. "He calls her Mary."

"And do you believe she's Mary, Father?" Libby asked. "That the woman's spirit has come back to be with her son?"

"I believe that if Robbie MacBain needs his mama right now and the boy feels that the owl is her, then aye, Mary's here."

"Like an imaginary friend?"

"Nay. The owl is real. And that she's attached herself to Robbie is also real. Everyone experiences things that can't be explained sometime in their lives. Haven't you?"

For a crisp November morning, Libby was feeling quite hot under the priest's probing stare. This had not been a good idea.

"I've experienced things I can't explain," she admitted. "But I don't know if I would go so far as to say I believe in magic."

Libby saw his gaze lift to her white lock of hair, then back to her eyes. His face wrinkled into a smile.

"Aye, Libby, I'm thinking ya do believe," he softly contradicted. "And that it bothers ya when ya can't explain something that's happened. But that's the point of magic, isn't it? Ya needn't understand it, only accept it for the gift it is. Why have ya come to Pine Creek?"

His question was asked so subtly, and because she was still trying to deal with what he was saying, Libby answered without thinking. "Because I got scared."

"Of something that happened to you in California? Something ya can't explain?"

She was in for a penny, so she might as well spend the whole dime. "Yes. Something happened that I can't explain."

Father Daar rose from his chair and stood in front of her, leaning against the rail, his clear blue eyes looking directly at her. "Something big enough to turn your entire life upside down," he speculated. "And ya think that by coming here, ya can hide from it?" He shook his head. "Libby, the questions ya're asking me and the evasive answers ya're giving make me believe that ya have been given a gift ya don't want. Am I right?"

Libby stared down at her folded hands in her lap. "I don't think I have a choice," she whispered. She looked up at him. "And that's what scares me. I don't know if I can control this gift or if it will end up controlling me."

"Have ya tried?"

"Once," she told him. "After I discovered it."

"And?"

"And it worked. But then it started to . . . I became

scared," she told him honestly. "I felt myself spinning out of control, like I was being consumed by this . . . this thing. Voices were calling me, tugging at me, and I ran."

"And ya haven't tried since."

"No."

"Ignoring it won't make it go away, Libby."

"I know that."

"This gift, do ya consider it to be good or bad?"

"Good," she said, squinting up at him. Libby stood up and paced down the porch, turning back to face him. "But it's not that simple, Father. If I can't control it or don't have the wisdom to apply it properly, then it could turn out to be a bad thing. I could end up hurting people instead of helping them."

"Ah," he breathed, nodding in understanding. "So it's not the gift ya fear but yourself. Ya do not want the responsibility that comes with it."

"I didn't ask for this," Libby whispered, hugging herself. "I was perfectly happy with my life."

He cocked his head at her. "Were ya? Truly? Then why do ya suppose your gift chose now to show itself?"

"I don't know why."

Father Daar straightened and walked into the house, forcing Libby to follow in order to hear what he was saying.

"Since ya're obviously not willing to tell me what happened in California," he said as he slowly made his way through the living room, "then I can't advise you. I can only say that ya gotta experiment with the thing." He stopped at the coatrack in the kitchen and took down his jacket and hat, then turned to face her. "Practice, Libby. Play with it. Learn what it's wanting to teach ya."

"And if I blow up TarStone Mountain?" she asked, smiling lamely.

He studied her for several seconds, trying to decide if she was kidding or not. His eyes suddenly lit with amusement, and he chuckled out loud. "These mountains have exploded once or twice already," he told her. "They can handle whatever energy ya're playing with."

He patted himself as if looking for something and frowned, gazing around the kitchen. "Oh, I've forgotten my cane. Could ya get it for me? I think I left it on the front porch."

Libby walked back through the living room, thinking about what he had said. Play with it? The damned thing wasn't a toy, it was scary. Learn from it? Learn what?

And experiment? Well, darn it, why the hell not? And she just might start with Father Daar and see what he thought about that.

Libby found his cane leaning against the chair he'd used. She picked it up and started back into the house. But she stopped suddenly when her hands began to warm, and the cane started to hum like a tuning fork. Her whole body tingled, and the sunlight brightened to a sharp, colorful glow all around her.

"Don't be afraid of it, Libby," came Father Daar's voice through the fog. "Just feel the energy, and tell me what ya see."

She couldn't see anything but colored light. But she could certainly feel. Emotions engulfed her. Contentment, fear, longing, and passion; all were present, wrapping around her, tugging at her, pulling her in different directions.

"Focus, Libby," Father Daar's voice said again, sounding far away. "Pick one color, and concentrate on it."

His voice was soothing, ageless, and distant. Libby did as she was told and focused on the brightest color and most persistent emotion.

Tendrils of fear rose in her mind, trying to pull her deeper into the maelstrom. Libby fought against the chaos, crying out as she felt herself sinking into its frightening depths.

"Look around you, girl. Find something to hold on to. Anchor yourself, and you can go there without being consumed."

Libby searched for an anchor but saw only pewter-gray eyes staring at her, burning bright with passion. Arms of forged steel wrapped around her. She hesitantly leaned into the security they offered and found herself turning back to face her fear with a new sense of strength.

The energy became voices, coming at her from a hundred different directions, begging, pleading, reaching for help. The arms holding her tightened, and Libby took a shuddering breath and reached into the middle of the maelstrom.

She wasn't consumed. Instead, she found herself able to touch the swirling mass of pulsing colors. And one by one, the voices quieted, the snapping colors faded, and the storm eased.

Libby turned and buried her face against her anchor, and the sound of gentle laughter brought her back to reality. She looked up and blinked and found Father Daar, his eyes shining with amusement, standing a good five paces away. He held out his hand.

"Can I have my staff back?" he asked. "Before ya use up all its power?"

"Staff?" Libby repeated softly, looking down at the gently humming cane in her hand. She looked up at the priest and took a step back. "What . . . who are you?"

The old man puffed up his chest and smoothed down the front of his cassock. "I'm a wizard, girl. Or haven't ya guessed?"

Libby took another step back. "Wizard?" she repeated. "But that's impossible."

"Then explain what just happened."

"No, you explain it," she demanded, stepping toward him. She held up the still warm, still vibrating cane between them. "What just happened?"

"Ya just got a glimpse of your true gift," he told her, grabbing the cane and clutching it to his chest protectively. "And ya discovered that you can control it—as long as ya keep yourself firmly anchored."

She eyed him suspiciously. "And so now you know what my gift is."

"Nay," he said, shaking his head. "I only know that it's a powerful force and that ya have a job ahead of ya to learn to use it wisely. And I also know that ya're smart to be cautious, that it can be just as destructive as it can be good."

"And you say you're a wizard?" Libby repeated, wondering if his age was affecting his thinking. But it shouldn't be affecting hers, and she certainly couldn't explain what had just happened.

"Ya didn't come here by chance, Libby Hart," Father Daar said. "Ya was lured to this magical land on purpose. The secret to controlling your gift is here." He chuckled again. "And I'm thinking ya've already found your anchor." He shook his head. "MacBain won't like it none, though, when he finds out."

Libby stepped up to Father Daar and took hold of the open edges of his red plaid jacket. "Don't you dare say anything to Michael," she whispered, somewhat demanding, somewhat desperately. "He won't understand."

The priest who called himself a wizard tucked his cane under his arm and covered her hands against his chest. Humor still lit his face, and he laughed out loud again.

"Ah, Libby. Of all the anchors you could have found,

MacBain will understand better than anyone." He canted his head, looking off toward Pine Lake. "And I'm beginning to think that the mishap twelve years ago wasn't a mistake at all." He looked back at her. "MacBain was also destined to be here. For several reasons, apparently."

"What mishap? What reasons? What are you talking about?"

"You, girl. He's here for you. And Robbie. The boy needed to be born, and MacBain had to travel here for that to happen."

Becoming more confused with every word he spoke, Libby tried to turn away, but Father Daar still held her hands and wouldn't let go. And he was still grinning like a demented old fool.

"I didn't make a mistake twelve years ago, girl. And neither did you when ya decided to move here."

Instead of disagreeing, Libby turned her hands in his and gripped his age-bent fingers. She smiled back at Father Daar and willed her power to race through his body, seeking out every one of his arthritic joints.

She was able to rebuild cartilage and smooth bone as she swept through his skeleton with the precision of a laser beam. And again, as it had in California, her body warmed, her heartbeat slowed, and she was able to see his pain and make it disperse into the light.

Father Daar gasped in surprise and stumbled back, his complexion as pale as new-fallen snow. "What have ya done?" he shouted hoarsely, taking several steps back. He pointed a finger at her. "Ya stay away from me!"

Libby rubbed her tingling hands on her thighs and shot him a smug grin. "I was just doing what you told me to."

"Doing what?"

She shrugged. "Practicing. Exploring my gift."

"I didn't mean for ya to practice on me!"

"Did I hurt you?"

He had to think about that. He actually patted himself down and bent over to give himself a visual inspection as well, as if he expected she'd turned him into a frog or something. He danced from foot to foot, waved his arms like a bird, and even turned in a full circle, trying to see over his shoulder to his backside.

He suddenly straightened and lifted wide, crystal-clear blue eyes to her in surprise. "God's teeth, woman. Ya're a healer," he whispered. "Ya healed my aches."

Libby sobered and hugged herself. Hearing those words, spoken with such quiet authority, sent shivers down her spine.

Father Daar walked to one of the chairs on the porch and sat down. He braced his elbows on his knees and rubbed his hands over his face several times before finally looking up at her.

"And this is what made you run here?" he asked. "This ability to heal people?"

Unable to move from her spot, Libby merely nodded.

"No wonder ya're shaken. It's a god-awful responsibility, healing people. Ya can't just go around willy-nilly, curing everyone. Some aren't meant to be cured."

Libby wanted to hug him. Finally, someone who understood her dilemma. "And that's why I ran away," she explained. "I was a surgeon, working in a hospital full of people wanting to be healed. Where would it end? When it completely consumed me?"

He leaned back in his chair and stared at her. "Aye," he said, nodding. "I imagine the energy was overwhelming."

"I had this picture of people lined up all the way out onto the street," Libby confessed, still unable to move from her spot, still hugging herself. "Waiting for me to heal them. But what right do I have to play God with their lives? And what right do I have not to?"

"Ya have no right, Libby, to make those kinds of decisions."

"Then why has this happened to me, Father?"

He scratched his beard with the butt of his cane and thought about her question in silence. He suddenly waved at Pine Lake.

"It's all connected—the land, the people and plants and animals, and the energy that makes our very existence possible. Maybe," he said, looking at her, "ya were given this gift for a particular reason. To heal one specific person, whose life force is linked to the continuum."

Libby walked over and rested against the rail in front of him. "What person?" she asked, leaning forward. "Who?"

"I cannot tell ya that, girl. I'm not a predictor, only a conductor of energy."

Libby straightened and crossed her arms under her breasts. "Then how will I know this person?" she asked. "And in the meantime, do I use my gift?"

Daar shook his head. "I cannot tell ya that, either. But ya already seem to have some control over it. Ya found an anchor in your vision, and that quieted the storm around ya."

"And you're saying that my anchor is Michael? But that he isn't going to like it?"

"Aye," he agreed. "The man's powerfully determined not to let his heart get involved with another woman."

"I don't want his heart."

"But that's what you'll need for this to work, Libby. Ya can't hold on for just a little while and then walk away. You'll be destroyed."

"Then I'll walk away now. I won't use Michael, Father."

He shook his head. "It's too late, I'm afraid. You've already caught MacBain's eye. I'm not sure he will let you walk away."

Well, dammit. Had she lost control of everything?

Father Daar stood up, stretched his newly healed joints like a young man of twenty, and smiled at her. "I'm going to enjoy my journey home," he said, walking to the end of the porch.

Libby followed but stopped when he turned back to her. "I have the good manners to thank ya, Libby Hart. For the breakfast and for making my aches go away."

"Father, if you're a wizard as you claim, and that cane of yours," she said, looking down at it, then back up at him, "has the . . . that energy I felt, why didn't you use it on yourself?"

He smiled disparagingly. "To tell ya the truth, lass, I was afraid I might turn myself into a dung beetle or some other lowly creature." He lifted his cane between them, glaring at it. "It's not my original staff, and this one's so new that I don't trust it."

"How old you are, Father?"

He puffed up his chest and straightened his shoulders. "Fourteen hundred and ninety-five last March," he told her.

"Years?" Libby squeaked.

"Of course, years, girl," he growled. He turned and walked off the porch but stopped in the middle of the driveway and looked back at her, pointing his cane. "Ya'll stop thinking like a surgeon, Libby Hart, and stop trying to put people and things into neat little compartments. Life doesn't work that way, and yar brain's likely to explode from frustration."

He turned slightly and pointed his cane at a frost-killed bed of flowers as he mumbled words under his breath. An arc of lightning shot from the end of the cane, striking the withered flowers with enough force to send a cloud of smoke-laced dirt into the air.

Libby took a step back.

And when the dust cleared, she saw that the flowers were in full bloom, with bright green foliage and colorful blossoms. The entire garden looked as if it were spring.

"And take notice that the passage of time is one of those compartments," Father Daar said. "It exists only for clock-makers. Try to remember that as ya deal with MacBain."

And with that cryptic remark lingering in the air long after he'd left, Libby found herself unable to look away from the fully bloomed flowers.

Wizard?

Hell, maybe her brain had already exploded.

Chapter Twelve

By five o'clock that evening, Libby had done exactly what Father Daar had told her not to—she'd put the unexplainable events of that morning into a neat little compartment that she'd labeled "to think about later."

She was feeling quite pleased with herself right now and somewhat surprised to find that she liked being domestic. She had an apple pie cooling on the counter and potatoes boiling on the stove, and the entire house smelled of roasting chicken. The table was set with an eclectic assortment of dishes that obviously had served many meals in the Sutter home, and the porch light was on to welcome her guests.

Another guest arrived first, uninvited and completely unexpected but just as welcome. Libby was washing her baking dishes in the sink when she heard a noise outside and looked through the window. Robbie's pet snowy owl was sitting on the porch rail, looking back at Libby, a large stick clasped in one of her sharp talons.

Drying her hands on her apron, Libby stepped out the

door and onto the porch. "Hello there," she said as she approached the owl. "What's that you've got?"

Mary spread her wings for balance and opened her talons, dropping the stick onto the porch floor. Libby reached down, picked it up, and examined it under the porch light.

It was a fairly stout stick, about two feet long, and appeared to be hardwood, although she didn't know what kind. It was covered with beautiful, gnarly burls and had been weathered to a smooth, glossy gray. It was heavy. And warm to her touch.

Libby looked at the owl. "I'm guessing you want me to have this," she said, trying not to notice she was talking to a bird. "I don't know why, but thank you for the lovely gift."

She turned to go back into the house but stopped when she realized she was being followed. She looked down and found Mary hopping along the porch floor behind her.

Libby hesitated, then, with a resigned sigh, she opened the kitchen door and stood out of the way. Mary walked into the house as if she owned it. Libby followed but left the door open enough for the eerily silent bird to leave if she changed her mind about being inside.

Oh, if only her colleagues back in California could see her now. Even Grammy Bea would have a hard time believing that her stuffy granddaughter was keeping company with an owl, much less talking to it.

"Make yourself at home," Libby drawled, watching the snowy fly onto the back of the rocking chair at the end of the kitchen.

Mary turned to face her, settled her wings back into place, and gave Libby a lazy blink. Libby wondered if she should offer her guest something to eat. But what? She was fresh out of rodents.

Libby leaned the stick against the wall under the clothes pegs and ran to save her potatoes from boiling over. She checked and found that they were done and looked at the clock on the wall. Twenty minutes before her human guests would arrive.

Libby pulled the chicken out of the oven and inspected it. It looked done. It certainly smelled delicious. She stole a bit of stuffing, popped it into her mouth, closed her eyes, and let out a moan. Damn, she was a good cook.

She grabbed the potatoes and carried them to the sink to drain but nearly dropped the pot when Mary suddenly let out a high-pitched whistle. A truck door slammed, and footsteps sounded on the porch. Libby looked over to see the kitchen door swing open and Robbie MacBain come running through it, holding a dripping brown paper bag away from his body as if it were a bomb.

"I gotta get this ice cream in the freezer," he said, running to the fridge. "I set it on the dash of the truck, and the heater melted it."

He put the ice cream in the freezer and then grabbed a towel from the rack above the furnace. "It made a god-awful mess of Papa's truck, and if I don't clean it up, I gotta walk home," the young boy explained, running back outside.

An elderly gentleman walked in next, wearing blaze orange just as Robbie had been. He hung his jacket and hat on the pegs, took a deep breath, and smiled.

"Now, that's what chicken is supposed to smell like," he said, coming over and stopping in front of Libby. "Hi. I'm John, and it's my pleasure to finally meet you, Miss Hart. This is for you," he added, handing her a tiny potted plant. "For saving my taste buds from self-destructing. It's a cutting from one of Ellen's African violets."

"Oh, thank you, John. It's beautiful." Libby placed the

budding plant on the sink windowsill. "And please, call me Libby."

Robbie came storming back in, tossed the messy dish-cloth onto the floor, and took off his jacket and hat, hanging them on the lower pegs. Holding his sticky fingers out in front of him, he went to the sink and ran them under the faucet.

Michael finally made his appearance. He set a small cardboard box on the floor by the kitchen door and nudged his son out of the way to wash his own sticky hands.

Libby felt as if she were being invaded. Her quiet kitchen was suddenly full.

"Mary!" Robbie exclaimed, seeing his pet perched on the rocking chair at the end of the kitchen.

Michael was just pulling a bottle of wine from his pocket but nearly dropped it when he spun around at his son's shout that Mary was there. He scrambled to catch the bottle and just barely managed to save them all from another sticky mess.

All four of them stared at the snowy owl, which blinked back at them, not the least bit ruffled by the commotion.

"Son," Michael said, "ya don't holler like that." Quickly regaining his composure, he looked at Libby and lifted a brow. "If I had known there would be five of us, I'd have brought more wine."

All Libby could do was shrug. She sure as heck couldn't explain what a wild bird was doing in her kitchen. Only Robbie seemed to think it was natural. Poor John was actually backed up against the wall, looking as if he were expecting the owl to go for his throat. Libby guessed this was his first time meeting Mary.

"It's okay, Grampy," Robbie assured him. "Mary's my pet. And Libby's, too," he said, turning to beam her a smile.

"She's just come for a visit, 'cause I told her we were having supper here tonight."

Libby remembered the stick and walked over to get it. "And look what she brought me," she said, holding it up for all of them to see.

Robbie came over and was just reaching for the stick when Michael took it away from her. "Where did you get this?" he whispered, holding it in his fist at arm's length, looking from it to her.

Libby wondered why he'd turned so pale. "Mary brought it to me," she told him. "Why? Is it a rare wood? From a protected tree or something?"

"Nay," Michael said softly, rolling the stick in his hand and hefting its weight. He looked at the snowy owl, his face drawn taut and his eyes narrowed in suspicion. "Ya say Mary brought it to ya?" he asked, looking back at Libby.

She nodded.

"It appears to be cherrywood," John interjected, coming up and taking the stick from Michael. He also turned it in his hand, holding it toward Libby. "It's full of burls." He traced his fingers over the knots. "See. If you were to cut these off and polish them, you would find a swirling grain that would darken to a deep cherry red."

Michael carefully took the stick away from John, then looked around as if trying to decide what to do with it. He kept his attention divided between the stick in his hand and the owl silently staring at them. Finally, and with what sounded to Libby like a whispered curse, he walked into the living room and headed toward the hearth.

But he stopped when he reached the brightly burning fire and stared into the flames.

"Please don't burn it," Libby softly entreated from the living-room door. "I don't know why it bothers you, but I would hate to see that beautiful wood destroyed."

"Don't burn it, Papa," Robbie added from beside her. "It's Mary's gift to Libby."

Michael continued to stare at the fire, the stick clutched in his white-knuckled fist like a club, and Libby found herself holding her breath. Why was he so bothered by Mary's gift?

Why wouldn't he say something?

Libby began breathing again when Michael set the stick on the mantel and turned to her. "Supper smells good," he said through a tight smile, making no apology and giving no explanation for his actions. He slowly rubbed his hands together as if he were anticipating dinner, but Libby sensed he was trying to rub away the feel of the stick.

"And I'm starved," Robbie said, turning and running to the table. He sat down next to John and immediately reached for a slice of bread.

John took it away from him and put it back. "You have to wait until everyone's seated and grace is said," he instructed in a whisper. "Or you won't get any apple pie."

Libby finished mashing the potatoes and put them in a large bowl while Michael took the chicken out of the roaster and set it on a platter. They carried the food to the patiently waiting guests. There was an awkward moment when they both started to sit in the chair at the head of the table.

Each immediately conceded to the other, but only when Libby sat down facing John and Robbie did Michael finally sit at the head of the table. He busied himself carving the chicken. Libby looked over and saw that John was smiling and Robbie was all but drooling onto his empty plate.

"I can say grace while Papa is carving," the young boy suggested, folding his hands in front of him and bowing his head.

Libby and John did the same, but Michael didn't stop carving, apparently just as anxious to eat as his son.

"Thank you, God, for the food," Robbie began. "And for helping Libby cook it perfect. Amen," the boy said, grabbing back his slice of bread and slathering it with butter.

Dinner went by almost as quickly as Robbie's prayer. Michael, John, and Robbie ate as if there were no tomorrow. There wasn't much conversation, and by the end, there wasn't much food left. The chicken was reduced to a carcass, the stuffing disappeared, and Libby thought Robbie was going to lick the bowl of potatoes clean.

She was just snatching up the last slice of bread when she heard a squeak. Libby looked over at Mary, who was still sitting on the back of the rocking chair, but the bird wasn't making a sound. She was, however, looking toward the wall of clothes by the door with interest.

The squeak grew louder, and Libby heard scratching as well. She decided the noise was coming from the box Michael had carried in earlier.

"What's in the box?" she asked, slowly getting out of her chair and walking around the table until it was between her and the scratching noise.

"I forgot the kittens!" Robbie said, sliding back his chair and running toward the box.

Michael caught him on the way past. "Nay, son," he said, pulling him onto his lap. "Ya can't take them out with your pet here," he told him.

Wide-eyed, Robbie looked at Mary. "Oh," he said. "I hadn't thought about that. She might consider them supper." He suddenly frowned. "But ya told me Mama likes cats."

"She does. I mean, she did. But your pet might be looking at them a little differently." Michael set Robbie off his lap and turned him toward Mary. "Why don't ya see if she's ready to go outside?"

"Do you think that's wise, Michael, for the boy to be handling that owl?" John asked, his worried frown divided between Michael and Robbie. Robbie held out his arm, and the owl hopped onto it.

"She'll not harm him," Michael assured John. "They've been friends for months now."

Libby walked over and opened the door for Robbie. "Good-bye, Mary," she said, reaching out and lightly running her finger over the owl's folded wing. "Thank you for the gift," she added softly enough that Michael couldn't hear. "And come back and visit me again."

Robbie, pleased that Libby was talking to his pet, walked off the porch and into the night with Mary, all the time keeping up a whispered conversation of his own with the bird.

Libby turned to find Michael hunched down in front of the now very noisy box. Robbie must have brought her a pair of kittens. She pushed Michael out of the way, knelt down, and lifted open the flaps.

Three sets of eyes blinked up at her.

Libby caught one of the kittens when it made a leap for her. She picked it up and held it in front of her face. "Well, hello there," she said, smiling at the huge green eyes staring back at her.

The kitten let out an impatient mew and wiggled to be set down. Libby set it on the floor and pulled out the other two kittens, holding them up to get a good look at them. They were such small, squirming things that she laughed out loud and put them down beside the other one.

The first kitten immediately began exploring its new home, another one sat down by the box and watched, and the last little ball of fluff hid under the flap and trembled.

Michael swept the frightened kitten up and cradled it against his chest.

Libby smileed at him. "What am I going to do with three kittens?" she asked.

"That's the entire litter," he told her, caressing his noisily purring bundle. "Robbie didn't have the heart to separate them. Any way he figured it, one would be left alone. So you're stuck with all three."

"He knows which one is the female," John said, coming over and picking up the quiet, watching kitten. "And he's got a list of names a mile long but said you should choose, since they're yours now."

Libby plucked up the brave one trying to climb Robbie's jacket and cuddled it against her chest. Three. She was the proud parent of three gorgeous kittens.

Robbie burst through the door, rubbing his hands together against the chill of the night. "What do ya think, Libby?" he asked, smiling like a proud father. "Ya gotta take all of them, 'cause ya shouldn't separate a family."

"I'll take all three," she assured him, rubbing her chin against the kitten's soft fur. "Which one's the girl?"

"That one," he said, pointing at Michael. "Uncle Ian says she's the runt of the litter and needs special attention 'cause she's scared of everything."

"Why don't ya get the supplies from the back of the truck," Michael suggested to Robbie, "and set them up in the downstairs bathroom for Libby?"

"What supplies?" Libby asked. "I'm not going to feed them in the bathroom."

"The litter box," Michael explained, handing her the female kitten and going to the counter. He picked up the apple pie and carried it to the table.

The man was still hungry after the supper he'd just eaten? John handed her his kitten and joined Michael. Libby turned the box on end and pushed all three kittens inside. The brave one immediately shot back out, but the female and the other one started licking each other.

Careful not to step on the exploring kitten, Libby cleared the table of empty plates and reset it with clean ones. She took the ice cream out of the freezer and brought it to the sink before she opened the sticky bag. The ice cream was a bit soft but still edible. She slid it into a bowl and brought it to the table, along with clean forks and spoons.

Robbie came in carrying two bags and a large bin. He disappeared into the bathroom, and Libby sat down at the table.

John rubbed his hands together. "Oh, boy. You topped it with brown sugar crumble and cheddar cheese," he said, eyeing the pie. "And you didn't skimp on the apples."

More interested in eating it than in admiring it, Michael cut the pie into four pieces and started dishing it out. Libby's eyes nearly crossed when he set one of the plates in front of her. He expected her to eat a quarter of a pie? She watched as nearly a pint of ice cream landed on top of her piece. She wasn't going to gain five pounds this winter, she was going to grow wider than she was tall.

The brave kitten started climbing up her pants leg, and Libby reached down, dug his claws out of her knee, and held him on her lap. Robbie came to the table, wiping his newly washed hands on his shirt, and sat down and grinned at the kitten peering over the top of the table.

"What are ya going to name them?" he asked.

"This one will be Trouble," she told him.

"Nay. He won't be any trouble," he said worriedly. "Ya just have to keep an eye on him, is all."

"I don't mean I don't want him," Libby quickly assured him. "I'm naming him Trouble. And I'm calling the female Timid."

Robbie was surprisingly quick to catch onto her theme and smiled with relief. "Then I think ya should call the other one Guardian, 'cause he's always looking after his brother and sister. And he's really the smartest of the three. Trouble doesn't always pay attention to what's happening around him. Uncle Ian and I had to move a whole row of hay just to get him unstuck, after Guardian alerted us to the problem. And he always stays close to his sister, no matter how much he wants to explore."

Libby noticed that Michael had stopped, his fork halfway to his mouth, to listen to Robbie's story. His features had tightened, and he had gone deathly still.

"Guardian, huh?" she said to Robbie, keeping her attention on Michael. "Then that's what I'll name him," she agreed, setting Trouble down on the floor and pushing him toward his siblings. "How's the pie, Michael?" she asked. "Too tart?"

"What? Oh, no. It's perfect," he said, finally lifting his fork to his mouth.

Libby looked down at her own plate. She couldn't possibly eat another bite. She pushed the dish away and stood up to clear the table of everything but the men's dessert. Michael snatched her own plate closer so she wouldn't take it away.

"If you're not going to eat it," he said, "then I can't see letting it go to waste. Robbie, where did ya come up with the name *Guardian?*" he asked, turning his attention to his son. "Why not *Angel* or *Warrior* or something like that?"

"Ya can't call a boy cat Angel, Papa," Robbie said, rolling his eyes. "And *Guardian* and *Warrior* are different. A warrior has a duty to protect, but a guardian has a higher calling. And the kitten knows this, and so that makes him a guardian."

Libby stared in fascination. The boy sounded more like a philosopher than his daddy did.

She kept an eye on Michael as she walked to the fridge with the butter. His eyes were gleaming, but his fist was clenched tightly, his complexion was pale, and he was eerily still again.

"What higher calling?" he softly asked.

Libby saw Robbie shrug as he ate a mouthful of pie. He swallowed and said, "I don't know, Papa. It's just something I understand but can't explain." The boy shot his father a worried look. "But being a warrior is good, too. And very noble."

"Aye," Michael agreed. "Very noble," he softly repeated.

"How about we call him Noble?" Libby suggested. "That's a nice name."

"Nay," Michael whispered, turning his attention from Robbie to her. "Call him what he is. Guardian."

Libby had never witnessed such an odd conversation. It was as if Robbie and Michael were the only ones who knew what they were talking about. John, apparently having witnessed many discussions like this over the years, was happily eating his pie and ice cream.

Libby turned from Michael's intense stare and started running hot water into the sink of dirty dishes. She added soap, listened to the silence broken only by the clink of forks touching plates, and contemplated the imagination of an eight-year-old boy. She thought about Michael's reaction, both to the stick Mary had brought her and to Robbie's choice of a name for a tiny kitten.

Libby decided that she may have come to a good place when she'd moved to Pine Creek, but it was also a weird place. A little off kilter. Maybe otherworldly.

It was as if she were standing in the middle of the Twilight Zone. She'd actually befriended a snowy owl that shouldn't even be living this far south, she'd met an old priest who thought he was a wizard and claimed to be almost fifteen hundred years old, she'd seen dead flowers brought back to life, and she was trying very hard not to get emotionally involved with a philosophical and very sexy man whose actions and beliefs made her think he was centuries old himself.

And then there was her own gift.

Yes, she fit in perfectly.

Chapter Thirteen

Michael stared down at his two empty dessert plates and considered how long it had been since he'd had such a tasty meal.

Too bad it had settled like lead in his gut.

He glanced toward the living room, toward where the *drùidh's* stick sat on the mantel. He knew it was the other half of Daar's missing staff; the old man had been hunting for it for five years, since it had shot free of the waterfall when Morgan MacKeage had blown up half of Fraser Mountain.

Where had Mary found it? And why in hell had she brought it to Libby, of all people?

"Why don't I take Robbie home?" John suggested, standing up and rubbing his own full belly as he headed for the door. He put on his hat and jacket and went over to Libby and kissed her on the cheek. "That was a wonderful supper," he said, smiling contentedly. "But Robbie and I can't stay to help with the dishes. We both need our beauty sleep. You'll stay and help, won't you, Michael?" he asked, turning to the table. "You don't mind the walk home if Robbie and I take the truck?"

Michael nodded to John. "Robbie, why don't ya collect the kittens?" Michael instructed. "Make a bed out of their box, and lock them in the bathroom for tonight. Then ya can go home with John and tuck each other into bed."

"You want to lock them in the bathroom?" Libby asked from the sink, turning to look at Michael, sending soap suds flying in front of her. "But why?"

"Ya haven't owned kittens before, have ya?" Michael asked, standing up and carrying his two empty plates to the sink. "These are barn cats, mostly nocturnal. They'll keep ya awake all night, get into God knows what trouble, and leave little presents all over the place until they learn where their litter box is."

"Oh," Libby said, looking at Robbie and nodding. "That sounds like a plan. Here," she added, taking two bowls out of the cupboard and handing them to him. "Use these for their food and water."

John started collecting the scattered kittens while Robbie went into the bathroom and made up their new home. Michael helped John search, but it took him a good five minutes to find Trouble. He was in the living room, climbing up the back of the couch.

"Come on, Trouble," he said with a chuckle, plucking the young daredevil off the couch. He turned the scrawny kitten until they were looking eye to eye. "You've been properly named, I'm afraid," he said, carrying Trouble into the bathroom.

"Ya don't have to worry about tucking me in, Papa," Robbie said after John had deposited his kitten and left to warm up the truck. "Mary said she'd follow me home and stay until morning."

Michael looked up from setting Trouble in front of the

food dish and stared into his son's eyes. "Mary told you I would be staying here all night?" he choked out.

Robbie nodded. "Aye. She really likes Libby, Papa, and thinks ya should fall in love with her."

Michael gently took hold of the boy's shoulders. "We've had this talk before, son. I don't want ya getting your hopes up. I cannot love another woman, and I know you understand why."

Robbie patted his cheek. "Ya can if your heart gets healed," the boy contradicted. "And Mary said Libby can do that. She's special, Papa."

"Mary?"

"Nay, Libby." The boy frowned at the wall, obviously thinking. "What did she call it? Oh, yeah," he said, looking back at Michael and smiling. "Providence. She said providence brought Libby to us."

Michael sat down on the floor, leaned against the wall, and scrubbed his face with his hands. He just might return Daar's staff and have the *drùidh* cast a spell that would send that owl back where she came from in a storm of flying white feathers. Dammit, he would not risk his heart again.

Robbie patted his shoulder. "It's okay, Papa. I know it's scary, but you're the bravest person that ever lived. You're a warrior, remember? And warriors fear nothing."

Michael looked up to find the boy grinning at him.

"So ya can't be afraid of one tiny woman," his wisdom-speaking son explained. "And Mary said Libby needs us. Both of us. That we can't spit on providence when it comes calling."

"Mary said *spit?*" Michael asked, eyeing Robbie suspiciously.

The boy shook his head. "Nay, I said *spit*. I think she said *re-rebuke* or something like that."

Michael didn't know whether to hug Robbie or put the

boy over his knee. "Son," he said with a growl, "ya're interfering in matters beyond the both of us."

Robbie nodded agreement. "Aye. That's what I've been trying to explain, Papa. That you're wasting your time being afraid of Libby. Didn't ya tell me, when we buried Gram Ellen, that life happens whether we like it or not?"

The boy was eight, and already he was haunting Michael with his own words. He scrubbed his face again, stood up, and turned Robbie to face the kitchen. But before the boy could open the bathroom door, Michael leaned down and whispered to him. "The next time ya have occasion to talk with Mary, ya tell her for me to mind her own business. Because it's my higher calling to raise you, and I'll do it without interference from her, your aunt Grace, or anyone else who tries to have a say in the matter. Understand, young man?"

Robbie twisted around and threw himself against Michael. Michael lifted him up and hugged him tightly.

"I love ya, Papa," the boy whispered shakily. "And it's my duty to see ya smile again."

Michael took a shuddering breath and buried his face in Robbie's shoulder. "I'm smiling like the village idiot every time I look at ya. And I love ya more than life itself, son."

"Is everyone settled in here?" Libby asked, cracking open the door.

Michael turned, shielding Robbie's tears from her. "Everyone's settled," he said to Libby's startled, blushing face. "We're just saying good night."

"Oh. Yes. Of course," she stammered, backing out and closing the door.

Robbie sat up in his arms, swiped away his tears, and grinned. "How can ya not love her, Papa? She's so . . . so . . ."

"Small?" Michael finished for him.

The boy clasped Michael's face in his hands and tried—but failed—to give him a serious look. "I think her hair has grown a wee bit, Papa. And she looks to be gaining weight. She'll probably have curves by spring."

They were back to their discussion of two nights ago. "And the spring after that, she'll probably be so fat we can roll her down TarStone like a snowball," Michael added, deciding that if he couldn't discourage the boy, he might as well join him.

Robbie shook his head. "Nay, Papa. She won't."

"Son," Michael said with a chuckle, giving him a squeeze. "It's not only beauty a man wants from a woman. It's who she is that's important."

"Mama was beautiful."

"Aye, she was. But that's not why I fell in love with her."

"It's not?"

"Nay. I fell in love with Mary's sass," Michael told him through a smile. "And her compassion and strength of heart." He nodded. "But mostly her sass, which I'm frightened to say you've inherited," he finished, putting Robbie down and turning him to face the door again. He gently swatted his backside. "John is growing old waiting for ya. Go home, brush your teeth, and go to bed. I'll have breakfast cooking when ya get up."

Robbie visibly shuddered. "Cereal," he said, opening the door and finally walking out to the kitchen. "And toast," he added as he sassily swaggered to his coat. "You've gotten pretty good at toasting bread."

Michael followed his son and helped him button his coat. "Tell John to bank the fire in the woodstove," he instructed, setting Robbie's hat on his head. "Don't let him add more wood. I'll do that when I get there."

"Aye," Robbie promised, walking over to Libby. "Thank ya for the delicious supper," he told her. "You're a good cook."

"You're welcome," she said, hugging him good-bye. "Oh, and I finished the little job you gave me," she added, going over to the sideboard and picking up the box, handing it to Robbie. She straightened the collar on his jacket and smiled crookedly. "I hope it's exactly what you wanted."

Robbie looked at Michael. "You'll compensate her, Papa?"

Michael nodded and pushed his son toward the door. "I will. Now, good night."

Robbie finally stepped onto the porch but stopped again to look at Libby. "I'm making ya a surprise for Christmas," he told her. "And even Papa doesn't know what it is. So don't bother trying to get him to tell."

Robbie turned without waiting for a response, carrying his secret box to the waiting truck. Michael watched until their taillights disappeared down the driveway and then softly closed the door and turned to Libby.

She was rubbing her hands on her thighs and looked as if she were carrying the weight of the world on her shoulders.

"You've had a couple of busy days," he said as he approached her. "Ya look tired, lass."

She started backing away. "I like being busy. And . . . and I'm not tired."

Michael followed her retreat. "Then what seems to be bothering ya?"

"You," she said, finally stopping against the wall, her large brown eyes rounded with the caution of a deer. "You're the one who was bothered tonight. By Mary's gift and by Robbie's talk of guardians."

Michael pinned her in place with only his stare, not touching her, not moving any closer. "They're not bothering me now. But you are." He ran his knuckles over her cheek, then leaned forward and lifted her chin to meet his lips. But he didn't kiss her. He whispered mere inches from her mouth, "Ya bother me very much, lass."

She ducked under his arm and scurried away and didn't stop until she had put the table between them. "We have to talk," she said, gripping the back of one of the chairs. "About us."

Michael leaned against the wall and crossed his arms over his chest. He studied her pale complexion in silence.

"I had a visitor this morning," she began. "Father Daar showed up here looking for breakfast."

Michael was careful to keep his expression neutral. "I'm not surprised," he told her. "The old man makes a habit of inviting himself to meals all over Pine Creek. He probably had supper at Gu Bràth tonight."

Libby let go of the chair and nervously rubbed her arms. "We had a very interesting talk."

"Did ya? About what?" he asked conversationally, already knowing he wasn't going to like her answer.

Libby wiped at a crumb on the table. "About . . . about magic," she whispered, looking up at him, her eyes searching his, trying to gauge his response.

Again, Michael refused to betray his alarm. "I hope ya didn't take what he had to say to heart. Daar's quite old and prone to fanciful notions."

"Have you ever touched his cane?" she asked, his negligent pose seeming to calm her enough that she lessened her grip on the chair.

"Aye. Many times," he told her. He shrugged. "It's so delicate it's a wonder it doesn't snap in half."

"Have you ever seen him . . . do anything with his cane?"

Michael straightened away from the wall and walked to the table, keeping it between them. "What are ya getting at, Libby? What happened this morning?"

"Do you believe that Robbie's pet is really his mother?"

Michael closed his eyes and pinched the bridge of his nose. "No," he said softly, deciding this conversation was over. He walked around the table, swept Libby into his arms before she knew his intention, and carried her into the living room. He sat down on the couch and held her tightly on his lap.

She started toying with one of the buttons on his shirt, her troubled eyes reflecting the light from the fire in the hearth. Michael stilled her hand with his and waited until she looked up at him.

"Ya're a doctor, Libby. A woman of science who needs for things to make sense," he gently told her. "And Robbie's pet doesn't fit your concept of reality. But do ya need to question everything around ya? Can ya not simply take some things on faith?"

"That's what Father Daar said," she admitted, frowning. "And I'm still trying to decide if I can or not. But that's not what's bothering me tonight."

"It's not?" Michael asked, surprised. "Then what is?"

"Us. I don't think it's a good idea for us to . . . to, well, to be together."

Michael forced his hands not to tighten around her. "And why is that?"

She started toying with his button again, intensely studying it as she spoke. "I don't want to get emotionally involved with you, Michael," she whispered so softly he could barely hear her. She finally looked up at him. "We . . . we can't be together. I don't know if I can need you for only a little."

"Aye. Need can become a habit."

"And I won't do that to you, Michael. Or to myself. I don't want to cling or for you to feel . . . clung to. And so I've decided we shouldn't be together," she finished, looking at his chest again.

What had happened this morning between Libby and Daar, Michael wondered?

And what in hell had happened to their affair?

Michael lifted her chin and smiled. He tightened his grip on her thigh. "I've never much cared to have someone else make my decisions for me," he told her. He lifted his finger from her chin to her lips to stop her from speaking. "No matter how noble that person is trying to be, lass. Ya leave making up my mind to me."

Michael decided this conversation was over as well. He turned Libby on his lap so that she straddled him, pulled her against his chest, and kissed her.

He was not letting the woman change her mind. He wanted her and knew damned well she wanted him. And a visit from a crazy old priest would not keep them apart.

Libby made a mewling sound not unlike that of her timid kitten, and Michael's heart slammed against his chest. She was such a delicate thing. So tiny and precious and real.

Her hands pushed at his shoulders, desperately refusing his kiss. He felt her thighs squeeze his hips as he pulled her more intimately against him, welcomed her breasts pushing at his own pounding heart, tasted the sweetness of her passion quietly simmering just below the surface. Michael wanted to rip off all their clothes and make love right there on the couch.

He broke their kiss and started unbuttoning her shirt.

"N-no," she shakily whispered, stopping him. "We can't, Michael."

He hesitated, suddenly uncertain about his own intentions.

Was it lust driving him now or something more?

She was just as inflamed as he was. Her breathing was ragged, her cheeks were flushed with color, and her hands on his shoulders trembled with her own barely controlled passion.

"It's going to happen, Libby," he told her, keeping the urgency out of his voice. "If not tonight, then tomorrow or the next day. Our paths have crossed, and what's happening between us can't be ignored. It won't go away, lass. It will only get more powerful."

She cupped his face with her small, delicate hands, her eyes searching his, her whole body tense. And then she smiled and leaned forward and kissed him—so very sweetly.

He stopped breathing and again raised his hands to the buttons on her blouse.

And again, she stopped him.

"Not here," she whispered.

He started breathing again. Not no—just not here. Okay, he decided, standing up before she could change her mind, holding her in his arms. The woman wanted a bed—he'd damned well find her one.

He carried her through the kitchen, his urgency compounded by her hands clinging to his shoulders and her mouth exploring his jaw. Michael captured her lips and kissed her again, keeping one eye on their path so he didn't run them both into the table. He entered the bedroom and all but ran to the bed, set her down and stretched out half on top of her, and started unbuttoning her shirt again.

And again, she stopped him.

"Dammit," he growled. "Now what's the matter?"

"Not here," she whispered. "N-not in Mary's bed."

He reared up in disbelief. "Dammit, woman. This is Mary's house."

"N-not here, Michael," she repeated, pushing against him, her huge brown eyes swimming with emotion. "Please," she entreated. "Find us someplace else."

Michael blew out a frustrated sigh, looked up, and glared at the headboard. Goddammit. There was no place else. It was below freezing outside, his own house was occupied, and he couldn't make love to her in the barn. He rolled to the side and threw an arm over his face, blowing out another sigh, this one resigned. The mattress dipped, and he lifted his arm enough to see Libby standing beside the bed, hugging herself.

He rolled off the bed, gathered up the blanket and two pillows, took hold of Libby's hand, and strode out of the bedroom. She followed in silence as he led her into the garage, pulled her to the back of her truck, and handed her the quilt and pillows. He opened the back door, pulled out the third seat and set it on the floor, walked around to the side of the truck, and folded down the backseats.

He returned to Libby, stopping only long enough to kiss her gaping mouth, and tossed the pillows into the back of the truck. He shook the blanket out to make them a bed, turned, picked Libby up, and tossed her in after it.

And then he climbed in himself, shut the doors behind them, and reached for the buttons on her blouse.

Chapter Fourteen

*L*ibby *blinked to adjust her eyes* to the darkness of the garage. The truck? They were going to make love in the back of her truck?

Well, she had gotten what she asked for; Mary certainly wasn't in here. Libby laughed and threw herself at Michael, reaching for the buttons on his shirt. In more of a frenzy than a coming together, they undressed each other, and as each new body part emerged and each interesting patch of skin was exposed, Libby's urgency grew.

Michael was right—she had no business making up his mind for him. She had warned him, and they would both simply have to live with the consequences. She would not cling to Michael when this affair came to an end—which it eventually must. And if she were destroyed, as the old priest had suggested, she would have no one to blame but herself.

It was liberating, finally giving in to abandon. Libby ran her hands over Michael's body, reveling in the texture and warmth of his skin, not needing any light for her fingers to form a picture in her mind of his sculpted beauty.

Her pants got stuck at her ankles, and Michael worked to take off her shoes. He heated the air with colorful curses. Libby felt the truck move when he banged his knee on the fender well, and she laughed out loud when he twisted and bumped his head on the roof.

"Dammit, woman," he hissed, trying to take off his own boots. "If ya don't quit laughing, I'll see that you're sorry."

Libby snapped her mouth shut—not because of his threat but because her eyes had adjusted to the darkness, and Michael took her breath away.

She'd seen many naked bodies in her career, some of them beautiful, athletic, and fine testaments to the human species. But Michael was . . . he was magnificent—beautifully sculptured bone and muscle perfectly proportioned for maximum strength and mobility. She could see now why Father Daar had called him a warrior.

He dwarfed the back of her cavernous truck, and when he turned to take her into his arms again, Libby's mouth went dry. He was radiating enough heat to steam up the windows. He was so full of vitality, so larger than life, she felt overwhelmed.

But that lasted only until his mouth started doing wondrous things to her collar bone, and his hands introduced themselves to the more sensitive parts of her body. And Libby decided it was time she did the same. She ran her fingers down his solid, rippling torso and then lightly trailed over his hips, slowly inching her way toward his . . . his . . .

Michael reared up, a growl erupting from his throat the moment Libby touched him. He captured her hands just as they wrapped around his erection. There was a short, bittersweet tug of war before he was able to pin her down and glare into her smiling eyes.

"When ya finally make up your mind, ya certainly do so

with zeal," he whispered, lowering his lips over hers. "Slow down, lass. We have all night."

"You can't do all the touching," she complained.

"Ya'll get your chance," Michael promised, sliding down her body and dipping his tongue into her navel.

Squirming, Libby sat up, grabbed fistfuls of his hair, and guided his mouth on its journey over her stomach. Michael couldn't decide whether to groan or burst into laughter. She was so honest about what she liked and so eager to direct him to each sensitive spot.

As he kissed a tiny spot just above her hipbone, her little moan of pleasure told him he was driving her wild. He lifted his gaze and saw Libby's head thrown back against the pillow, her eyes shut tight, her body flushed with passion.

"Oh, my God. Don't stop," she cried hoarsely, trying to push his head back down.

He was not about to stop, but he did change his focus, nuzzling back up her stomach until he came to her firm, delicate breasts.

Her grip on his hair tightened. Her body tensed in anticipation, and Michael began a slow and tender assault on her breasts, moving his tongue in sensual circles around each responsive nipple. She groaned and arched her back. She wrapped her legs around his thighs and lifted her hips until she was centered directly under his shaft.

Michael rolled onto his back, taking her with him. "Not yet," he hissed, guiding her mouth down to his. "All night, remember?" he whispered, stilling her hips before she impaled herself on his erection.

She sat up, blinking, lost in a fog of passion.

"Now it's your turn to touch," he told her, wondering if he hadn't lost his own mind. "Hands and lips only," he clarified. He had to capture Libby's eager hands when she started before he was done giving his instructions. "We're not protected, Libby."

She abruptly pulled back in alarm. "You were supposed to take care of that."

"I did. It's in my pocket," he assured her, folding his arms behind his head, gritting his teeth, praying for some patience of his own and a healthy dose of control.

Libby wasn't sure what to think of his dictate, but she sure as heck knew what to do. She started at his navel and ran her hands up the length of him, sliding her fingers through the silky hair covering his chest. She became fascinated by how his muscles shuddered beneath her touch, how his nipples hardened when she lightly raked her fingers across them, how beads of sweat broke out on his shoulders and neck, how he tensed and growled as if he were in pain.

She knew she wasn't hurting him. In fact, she knew she was driving him wild. And that thrilled her, how just her touch could make a quivering mess of such a strong mountain of man.

She was empowered. Remembering he'd said lips as well as hands, Libby replaced her fingers with her mouth. And mimicking his earlier action on her, she ran her tongue over his nipples. Satisfied to hear his groan, she went in search of other interesting anatomy.

"Have a care, lest ya end this now," he warned, his voice guttural and strained.

She smiled, flexed her fingers on his hips, ignored his suggestion, and gave him a shockingly intimate kiss.

Michael sat up with a shout and took hold of Libby's shoulders, lifting her away before he disgraced himself. This had not been one of his brighter ideas, giving this woman such free rein with his body.

"Find my pants," he ground out. "Now."

Michael couldn't help but smile as Libbly scrambled to pick up his pants. His grin broadened when he heard her mutter an impatient curse as she rifled through his pockets. She held up a small foil packet, stared at it, and then turned and stared at him—or, more specifically, at what she'd just kissed.

She hesitated, looking a bit worried all of a sudden. He took the packet from her, tore it open with his teeth, and set it on the floor, then gathered her back in his arms and ravaged her mouth with a kiss. She melted against him, hugged him fiercely, and kissed him back, opening her sweet-tasting lips to let him inside.

He made love to her senses. His hands roamed over her body and toyed with the curls at the juncture of her thighs. He caressed her intimately, whispered words of anticipation into her cute little ear, and slowly rolled her onto her back, gently placing her beneath him. He slid on the protection while he continued to kiss her and lowered himself until he rested between her thighs.

"Libby," he thickly entreated. "Open yar eyes and look at me, lass, so I can see that ya understand what is happening between us."

She looked at him, and Michael saw the fire of passion burning brightly in her beautiful brown eyes.

"Say it, Libby. Tell me ya want me."

Her hands tightened on his arms as she moved against him, searching for his intimate touch.

"Say it, lass," he ground out, holding on to his control by the barest of threads. "Tell me."

"Yes," she moaned, lifting her hips and straining against him. "Yes, Michael. I want you."

Satisfied, Michael slowly eased into her, mindful of how delicate she was, studying her face for signs of discomfort.

Her eyes widened. Her fingernails dug into his arms.

And he wasn't sure, but she looked as if she was holding her breath. So he reached down between them and gently stroked her passion back into flames.

She relaxed and opened, and he finally slid fully inside her. And Michael felt as if he'd just entered Heaven, he was so warmed and welcomed and deeply embedded. It was all he could do not to move.

Thank God she moved first, wrapping her legs tightly around his waist and lifting her hips. That was all the encouragement he needed. He cupped her face, kissed her lips, and slowly set a gentle rhythm that made her moan into his mouth.

Michael wanted this to last forever. He wanted Libby to feel the strength of their passion as keenly as he did. He wanted her hot and bothered and as wild as he was.

She was definitely bothered. Libby was so focused on feeling him buried so deep inside her, it was all she could do to remember to breathe. Making love to Michael was an unbelievably erotic experience.

But she wasn't quite satisfied. He was moving too slowly, being too careful. She wasn't a china doll—she wanted him to let go of his confounded control.

She raked her fingernails over his shoulders, dug her heels into his back, buried her face in his chest, and licked his nipple. He gave a hoarse shout, bucked against her, and sent skyrockets shooting through her body.

"Yes," she breathed in a shout of her own, urging him on. She arched her back, causing him to withdraw slightly, and then lifted her hips.

He was a quick learner. He moved deeply inside her, then withdrew, then moved deeply again in a tempo that sent her hormones into a riot. Intense pleasure awakened every one of her senses at the feel of his breath against her ear, his body moving against hers, his taste lingering on her lips, and his hands—his large, strong, calloused hands—guiding their bodies together.

She could feel the truck rocking with the force of his thrusts. And for some strange reason, that realization sent Libby over the edge of control. She clung to Michael, cried out, and climaxed so violently she thought she might burst into flames. And just when she thought it was over, he reared up, growled deep from his throat, and stilled. He pulsed inside her, the strength of his own climax a magical thing to witness. She pressed her palms to his chest, felt his heart slamming against his ribs, and her own heart lurched with the realization that more than a simple affair had been started tonight.

So very much more.

Michael was shaken to the very soles of his bare feet. He slowly lowered himself to his elbows, staying inside her, reluctant to let the moment end. He brushed back her damp hair and kissed her forehead, then finally rolled to his side and settled her comfortably against him.

Damn, but it was true—wonderful things did come in small packages sometimes.

Michael lifted his head and found Libby had her eyes closed, her head nestled against his chest, and one hand possessively clutching his neck.

Michael settled against the pillows and pulled the blanket over Libby's back, tucking her firmly against him. He thought about the three other foil packets in his pants pocket, and his smile returned. He wondered if Libby had noticed them when she'd found the first one and if she might be thinking she'd better get some rest now, while she could.

Come to think of it, he was feeling a bit exhausted himself. He stared at the roof, and his smile disappeared. Her damned truck. He couldn't believe he'd brought Libby into the garage, into this damned truck, to make love to her. He was about as romantic as a bull moose willing to rut in a beaver bog.

No wonder she had nothing to say.

Michael was gone. Libby knew this because she was cold. Her nose was running, her feet felt like blocks of ice, and she was wrapped up so tightly in the quilt trying to keep warm that her body ached.

He'd left. The unromantic, insensitive jerk had snuck off in the small hours of the night without even saying good-bye.

He hadn't said thank you, either.

How could a man know so much about a woman's body that he could take her on a fantastical journey to Heaven and back and not know that he was supposed to stick around long enough to tell her he'd enjoyed the trip as much as she had?

Weren't affairs supposed to be flaming things because of the romance? Wasn't that why women usually agreed to have them?

Libby pulled the quilt up over her face to cover her freezing nose and groaned when she discovered aches in places she'd forgotten existed.

Dammit. What had she expected from a self-acclaimed throwback? Flowers? Music and candlelight? A note left on her pillow? Libby pushed the quilt down and looked to her right, half hoping to see a note on the pillow beside her.

Nothing. Only the cold imprint of where his head had been.

She sat up and looked around the shadowed interior of her truck. As love nests went, it could have been worse, considering the options available. She could have been waking up in the barn, she thought with a sigh of self-pity.

Libby loosened the cocoon of her quilt and crawled to the door of the truck. She opened it and backed out, wincing when her bare feet hit the concrete floor of the garage. She pulled the quilt along with her, and something fell on her feet. She looked down, picked up the packet, and stared in disbelief. She looked at the carpeted floor of her truck, saw two more packets, and her disbelief turned to horror.

Four? Michael had brought four condoms with him last night?

Every inch of Libby's body—even her toes—instantly heated with outrage. The man had sat at her dinner table with four condoms tucked in his pocket, fortifying himself for a night of marathon sex.

Well, no wonder he'd left. She'd flopped against him like a drunkard after they'd made love and had fallen asleep before she had even finished yawning. Truth told, it had never occurred to her that he might want to do it again. In her experience with men, they'd have sex, cuddle a few minutes, and then get up and go home—but not while she'd been unconscious and only after a sweet kiss good-bye and a thank-you.

Libby turned on her heel and marched into the house. She stomped to the trash can, lifted the lid, and dropped the three packets inside.

"There. Take that, Mr. Macho Michael MacBain," she muttered as she headed to the bathroom. He'd have to crawl on his knees if he wanted to see her again. And he damned well better have flowers in one hand and chocolates in the other.

Libby opened the bathroom door but stepped back with a yelp of surprise to avoid stepping on Trouble.

She'd forgotten about the kittens.

All three of them went scurrying past her and out the

door, and Libby blew out a resigned sigh as she watched them run into the kitchen. She'd have to make sure they knew where their litter box was.

She walked to the shower, turned it on, and dropped the quilt at her feet. She stepped under the warm spray and let it cascade over her body, determined to wash away all thoughts of Michael.

But as she lathered herself up and heat slowly seeped back into her bones, Libby remembered Michael's strong, sensual hands touching her. She remembered waking once or twice last night to find herself pulled up against Michael's warm body, trapped in his possessive embrace. And she remembered feeling safe and secure and anchored to something more solid than TarStone Mountain.

By the time she dried off, Libby's anger had subsided. With only a towel wrapped around her, she walked back into the kitchen and opened the trash bin. She took out the condoms, carried them into the bedroom, and put them in the nightstand beside the bed.

Dammit. She'd give him one more chance to make this affair work. And if he didn't start living up to her expectations, she just might visit Father Daar and ask the crazy old man to turn Michael into a frog.

Chapter Fifteen

By nine-thirty that morning, Libby had unpacked most of the boxes she'd mailed to herself, and her jewelry studio was beginning to get organized. She was sitting with her feet propped up on the desk that already occupied the store and was contemplating how she wanted to display her product.

She was also halfway through her second warm, gooey, absolutely decadent glazed doughnut, which she'd bought at the bakery next-door. If she wasn't careful, the doughnuts and hot cocoa could become a very bad habit.

She needed displays, she decided, licking her sticky fingers and picking up her cocoa. Maybe some glass-fronted cases she could hang on the wall and a glass and oak counter like the one the Dolans had in their store next-door. But instead of knives and bullets and rifle scopes, hers would be filled with glass birds, acorns, woodland mammals, and colorful beads.

And loons. She should work on designing a nice loon pendant to sell, since the aquatic birds seemed so popular in the Northeast. She'd seen them decorating shirts, hats, and paintings in the Dolans' store yesterday. There had been almost as many carvings of loons for sale as there had been moose.

She should probably design a moose, too. But not as a pendant, maybe a small figurine that could decorate a wooden box or something.

Was there a woodworker in Pine Creek she could team up with? Maybe there were other craftsmen—and women— who could use an outlet for their work. She could form a co-op of some sort, and that way the studio could be open more hours, everyone taking turns manning the counter.

Libby dropped her feet to the floor, picked up her pen, and began making a list of the possibilities. Her spirits soared. She hadn't been this excited since she'd taken a scalpel in her hand for the very first time.

But even that hadn't been this exciting. The scalpel had been just the next step in a long line of steps to become a surgeon. Building a crafts studio was completely different. Grammy Bea had been right. Embarking on a new and creative career was what her soul had been yearning for. There were no rules, no strict procedures she'd have to adhere to, and certainly no one looking over her shoulder and telling her what she could and couldn't do.

It was a very liberating epiphany.

She was thirty-one years old, intelligent, but it amazed her that it had taken so long to realize that she hadn't been happy. She'd been fulfilled as a surgeon—giving traumatized people their lives back was very rewarding—but she'd caught herself more than once over the years yearning for more, secretly searching for something that was missing in her life.

Libby's laugh echoed off the empty studio walls. For all her surgeon's illusion of control, she'd never really had it.

The medical establishment had been dictating her every move—medicine and the people who were supposed to love her, who were supposed to want what was best for her.

Well, now *she* was doing what was best for her.

And she was damned proud of herself.

There was a knock on the door, and Libby looked up to see Grace MacKeage peering between cupped hands through the window, a young child doing the same by her knee. Libby waved them both in, a smile of welcome on her face as she stood to greet her first guests.

"Welcome to NorthWoods Glass Studio," Libby said, stopping in front of them. "And who have we here?" she asked, leaning down to the adorable, shy girl clinging to her mother's leg.

"This is Elizabeth," Grace said, pulling the young child's thumb out of her mouth. "Elizabeth, this is Libby. You both have the same name, but she prefers to be called Libby. Say hello."

Instead of speaking, Elizabeth popped her thumb back between her teeth and hid her face in Grace's plump belly.

Grace sighed when she straightened and smiled at Libby. "We're still working on meeting new people. So that's the name, NorthWoods Glass Studio?"

Libby shrugged. "I'm just trying it out. What do you think?"

"It has a nice ring," Grace agreed, looking around at the bare walls. Her eyes widened when they came to rest on Libby's torch on the workbench. "You've set your equipment up right here in front?" she asked, walking to the workspace, young Elizabeth shuffling along with her. "I expected you'd work out back and fill the front with displays."

"I thought people would like to see how it's done," Libby explained, following Grace. "That way, if they order something special, they can watch me make it."

Grace turned interested blue eyes on her. "You'll take commissions?"

"Sure. Or I'll try," Libby clarified. "Working with glass is not always an exact art, and sometimes I end up with some rather funky-looking pieces."

"Jewelry only?" Grace asked, nodding at the glass blue jay Libby wore.

Libby lifted the bird from around her neck, leaned down, and placed it over Elizabeth's head, deftly shortening the cord and settling it against the child's jacket.

"I can make small figurines that can be displayed," Libby explained. "Just not too big. I have to build up the glass in layers, and there's a limit before it starts to get unwieldy or cools unevenly. Then it just shatters."

Grace looked down at her daughter, who was busy admiring her new necklace, then back at Libby. "Could you make a sword, do you think? Not too big," she said, holding her index fingers about ten inches apart. "With a tartan wrapped around it? Does the glass come in many colors?"

Libby frowned, trying to picture what Grace had in mind. "It only comes in certain colors, but I can usually melt them together, creating a wide spectrum."

"If I draw you a picture of what I'd like, would you be willing to try?"

"Yeah. I'll give it a go."

"Ah—before Christmas?" Grace asked.

"Oh, sure. If you give me something to go by, I can have it done by Thanksgiving."

"Great," Grace said. "Then consider me your first official customer. Do you have any jewelry ready to display?" she asked, peering into one of the open boxes. "Something from nature?" She shot Libby a lopsided grin. "I have a sister-in-law who practically lives outdoors."

Libby started pulling out some of the glass pendants, earrings, and bracelets she'd made over the years, and Grace and Elizabeth immediately started oohing and aahing as they sorted through them. Then Grace stopped and held up a necklace, turning it toward the sunlight streaming through the front windows.

"This is beautiful," she whispered. "The colors are almost alive. It feels heavy to be so delicate, and the raspberries look good enough to eat."

The necklace was made of bright red, bulbous berries interspersed with green raspberry leaves. The glass she'd used was transparent, not opaque, and the sunlight glittering through it cast a colorful prism on Grace's hands.

"It's more rugged than it looks," she told Grace as she dug through the box, looking for the matching bracelet. "I even make key chains out of some of the beads." She gave Grace a crooked smile. "Although the thin leaves might chip if it's dropped."

Grace was only absently paying attention. She was busy clasping the necklace around her neck and looking for something to see herself in. "Oh, I love this," she said, taking the mirror Libby handed her, fingering the raspberries as she admired the necklace in the mirror. "Every August, we spend a whole day picking wild raspberries. They grow wild and abundant around here. What do you think, Elizabeth?" she asked, holding her very pregnant belly while she leaned over for her daughter to see. "Does this look good on Mommy?"

Elizabeth nodded, more interested in her own necklace. "I like my bird," she said, holding it up.

"Then it's yours," Libby told her. She looked at Grace. "If that's okay? I forgot about your other daughters. And it might be small enough for Elizabeth to choke on," she added, looking at the young girl.

"Thank you," Grace said, nodding. "And don't worry. It won't be left around like a toy." She turned Elizabeth to face her and lifted her daughter's chin. "You'll keep it in my jewelry box and only wear it when you're dressing up to go out, right?"

Elizabeth quickly nodded agreement.

"Then say thank you to Libby."

"Thank you, Libby," Elizabeth dutifully repeated, all signs of her previous shyness gone. "I can wear it to my birthday party. And you can come if you want. It's . . . it's . . ." She looked at her mother. "What day, Mama?"

"December twenty-first this year, sweetie," Grace confirmed for Libby. "And since I expect to be quite busy that day," she said with a laugh, patting her belly, "I think we'll have the party a few days early. And you are certainly invited."

Libby was about to thank her and accept when a shadow darkened the interior of the store. All three of them turned just as a large man walked in with two cute, wide-eyed toddlers in his arms.

"Oh, my God," Grace said, rushing up to him. "Don't you dare set them down. They'll be worse than two bulls in a china shop."

"Bird," one of the toddlers said, pointing at her sister.

"Down," the other toddler demanded, wiggling to get free.

"You stay right where you are, Chelsea," Grace said, adjusting the child's blaze orange wool hat. She turned to Libby with a proud smile. "Let me introduce you to some more of my family. This is Chelsea, who's almost four, and her twin sister, Megan. And if you haven't guessed by now, this is my husband, Greylen. Grey, this is Libby Hart."

"Miss Hart," he said with a nod, his smile no less imposing than his size. "It's nice to finally meet you." He took a quick look around her shop, settled his gaze on his wife's neck, and let out a totally male resigned sigh. "You haven't even finished unpacking, and already you have a customer. Two," he clarified with a chuckle, looking at the blue jay Elizabeth was wearing.

Libby was speechless. Was there something in the water around here that made all the men so big? She'd met Michael, Ian, Callum, and now Grey. They were all giants . . . all Scots . . . all overwhelming.

This one, though, had his hands full. Six girls and one more on the way. The man would have seven daughters to deal with by Christmas. Libby realized they were all staring at her while she stood there like an idiot, gawking.

"Er, it's nice to meet you, too," she finally managed to say. She even managed to smile. "And you can't expect a woman—no matter her age—to walk into a jewelry shop and not try something on."

A gleam came into his clear green eyes. "I'm quickly learning the minds of females." He affectionately squeezed his two daughters in his arms, looking from one to the other and then at his wife. "Have you told her your news yet, or have you been too busy shopping?"

"Oh, Lord, I did forget," Grace said, turning apologetic blue eyes on Libby. "Katherine Hart and James Kessler checked into our hotel late last night. And they asked the desk clerk if he knew you, and where you might be staying."

Libby felt a crushing weight land on her shoulders. Her feet were bolted to the floor, her head felt twice its size, and her heart started pounding against her ribs so violently she couldn't breathe.

James was in Pine Creek?

"Wh-what did the clerk tell them?" she whispered, grabbing hold of the desk for support.

Grace stepped closer, her eyes filled with concern. "It's a

small town, Libby. He told them he thought the name was familiar, but he didn't know where you lived."

"Where are they now?"

Grace shot a worried look at her husband, then looked back at Libby and shrugged. "I don't know. I assume they're in town somewhere, looking for you. They'll probably check with the post office, don't you think? Have you signed up for mail delivery yet?"

Grace must have thought Libby was either going to fall over or throw up, because she guided her to the chair behind the desk and made her sit down. She took hold of Libby's shoulder for support.

Dammit. All she had wanted was a little time to get settled before she had to face the scene that would inevitably take place. She wasn't surprised her mother had come, since Katherine had sounded more curious than worried the last time they'd talked on the phone. But honest to God, she had never expected James to track her down and actually come here. And how had he found her, anyway? Libby knew for certain her mom hadn't told him.

But they were both here. Now. In Pine Creek.

"You don't have to see them, Libby," Grace said softly, squeezing her shoulder. "If you're not ready, you can come to Gu Bràth and stay with us until they give up and go back to California. No one has to know where you are."

Libby looked up into Grace's concerned eyes and patted Grace's hand on her shoulder. "Thank you," she told her hoarsely. She shook her head. "You're a good friend, and I thank you for that. I knew my mom would probably come looking for me, but I thought I'd have more time."

"But not this James person?" Grace asked, lifting one curious brow.

"No, not James," Libby confirmed. "I didn't think he would bother."

"Do you fear him?" Grey asked, stepping closer, his eyes narrowed with a different sort of concern.

Libby shook her head again. "I'm not afraid of James, just surprised that he's here."

"Then come to Gu Bràth," Grace repeated.

Again, Libby shook her head. "No. That won't solve anything." She straightened, took a deep breath, and stood, smiling warmly. "I'll have to deal with him sooner or later, and it might as well be now."

Grace took off the necklace she was wearing and carefully set it on the desk. She rounded up Elizabeth, scooted the girl toward Grey, and motioned that it was time they left. Libby watched them walk out onto the sidewalk and toward their truck parked in front of the Dolans' store. Libby could see three other heads sitting in the backseat of the truck.

Grace turned to Libby. "I'm calling Michael," she stated bluntly. "He should know."

"Know what?" Libby asked in surprise. "That my mother's in town? She's just worried about me. And do you blame her? What if one of your daughters just up and moved clear across the country? Wouldn't you be hot on her trail? I'm betting your husband would."

"Not if she's a grown woman, more than capable of making her own decisions."

"But wouldn't you want to understand those decisions?"

Grace conceded with a tender smile. "Yes. I would be on the next plane out," she admitted. "But Michael should know this James guy is in town."

"Why?"

"Why?" Grace echoed in disbelief. "Because he has a stake in this now. He's not going to like the fact that a man has come here looking for you."

"What stake?" Libby asked, honestly confused. "He's my landlord, not my baby-sitter."

"Since when do landlords spend the night?"

"What?" Libby cried. "How could you possibly know that?"

"Grey left to go hunting before daybreak this morning," Grace said. "And he told me he ran into Michael walking back to his house at four-thirty this morning."

Libby returned to her chair and rubbed her suddenly aching forehead. So much for discretion.

Grace patted her shoulder. "There's something you need to understand about these Scots, Libby. They're more old-fashioned than they are reasonable most of the time. They can be so damned possessive when it comes to their women that if it weren't so frustrating, it would be comical. I'll bet you a penny that Grey's on his cell phone right now, calling Michael."

"But why?"

"Because of your reaction," Grace explained. "Grey saw how shaken you were. And to his way of thinking, that means Michael needs to become involved. It's a guy thing," Grace added with a chuckle. "An unwritten code they all live by, to watch out for each other's back. Or their women, in this case."

"That's archaic. We can take care of ourselves. I don't need Michael beating his chest to run James off. I can do that all by myself." Libby stood up, suddenly fortified with anger. "And I'll tell Michael that if he tries to interfere. It's an affair, for crying out loud. A simple, stupid affair that probably won't even happen again."

"Uh-oh. He's already messed things up?"

"I woke up in the back of my freezing truck this morning, all alone, after Michael snuck out. He didn't even say good-bye or thank-you."

"The back of your truck?" Grace repeated, her eyes rounding in disbelief. "But what were . . . why the truck?" she asked, trying hard not to laugh.

"Because it's the only place that Mary hasn't been part of. Good God, Grace. I'm living in Mary's house, sleeping in Mary's bed, trying to have an affair with her former lover."

Grace opened her mouth, but nothing came out.

"I'm sorry. She was your sister," Libby continued more softly, instantly contrite. "But can you understand how weird it is for me?"

"I-I hadn't thought about it from that perspective," Grace said gently, leaning past her cumbersome belly to give Libby a hug. "I suppose it's only natural for you to feel . . . weird." She pulled back and smiled crookedly. "But the truck?" she whispered, covering her smile with her hand.

Libby shrugged. "It seemed logical at the time."

"And he didn't say good-bye. Or . . . or thank you?"

Libby found her sense of humor and smiled sheepishly. "It does sound rather petty, doesn't it?"

Grace picked up her purse and headed for the door but stopped and looked back. "I warned you, didn't I, that he would drive you crazy. So prepare yourself, my good friend. I give Michael ten minutes before he's darkening your doorstep. Welcome to the Highlands of Maine," Grace trailed off with a laugh, walking out to join her family.

Libby stared after her and watched as Grey quickly came around the truck, opened the door, and lifted his pregnant wife into the front seat. Six wool-capped heads were lined up in the two rows of seats in the back, all occupied with Elizabeth's new blue jay necklace.

So, Libby thought with a sigh, walking back to her desk and flopping in the chair. That's what love looked like.

Would she ever have that? A handsome, strong, protective husband and a whole passel of adorable children?

Lord, she hoped so.

Well, maybe not *seven*.

Chapter Sixteen

Considering her options, Libby decided the reasonable thing to do was run. She locked her store, climbed into her truck, and headed out of town before her mom and James found her and Michael could play the knight in shining armor and come to her rescue.

She didn't need rescuing—by anyone. Her mother was there because she was worried about her only child.

James was there on his own agenda.

Libby drove until she saw a sign that had a picture of a picnic table on it. She turned down the dirt road and quickly came to a deserted picnic area on the shore of Pine Lake. She looked around and then eased her truck deep into a young stand of fir trees. Sure it couldn't be seen from the main road, she got out of the truck, sat on top of one of the many picnic tables, and stared at the cold water lapping against the icy shoreline.

She snuggled into her blaze orange jacket, pulled up the hood, and tucked her hands in her pockets. And she sighed, thought about her new life, and compared it with her old life in California.

No matter how she looked at it, she'd made the right decision. Even without this . . . this gift she'd been given, it had been time for a change. Practicing medicine, no matter how honorable and fulfilling, just wasn't enough anymore.

But was making jewelry really what she was looking for?

Seeing Grace MacKeage with her family that morning had stirred something deep inside Libby. Maybe it wasn't medicine she was trying to escape but a new life she was seeking. One that included a husband who loved her, children, and a different sort of fulfillment.

Why couldn't she have it all?

She could practice medicine anywhere. Wherever there were people, there was a need for doctors. California or Maine, it didn't matter; it only mattered that she find more of a balance in her life.

And for that, Maine came out the winner, hands down. There was something about this place—the mountains, the people, the sense of timelessness that seemed to permeate the air. It didn't get any more real than shooting a deer for the dinner table or riding through the woods on a horse or an ATV. Even the weather could not be ignored but counted on to affect daily lives. And neighborliness—that was the most remarkable thing here. Grace had offered her sanctuary that morning, and Libby had been humbled by the offer. That had made her realize she was closer to these people than she had ever been to anyone back in California—except Grammy Bea.

Yes, she had some serious thinking to do about her future.

"Ya're developing a bad habit of running away," Michael said from right behind her.

Libby yelped, jumped up, and would have fallen off the

picnic table if Michael's strong hands hadn't caught her and pulled her up against his broad, solid chest. His warm, demanding lips covered her mouth, swallowing her curse of outrage before she could scold him for scaring her.

This was *so* not right. Michael wasn't on his knees—she was. He was standing, and she was kneeling on the picnic table, and still he towered over her. And since his hands were busy holding her tightly against him, Libby knew he hadn't brought flowers or chocolates.

She didn't want to kiss him back, just on principle. He'd left without saying good-bye that morning, and now he hadn't even said hello before kissing her. He had some nerve, accusing her of running away.

But he tasted so nice. And he felt so warm and solid. Libby sighed into his mouth. She was such a hussy whenever he touched her, so easy and wanton and instantly turned on. So she gave up, opened her mouth to his, and melted.

He was so damned sexy, only a dead woman would be unaffected. Libby wrapped her arms around his waist, inside his unbuttoned jacket, and snuggled against him. She tilted her head back, pushed her tongue into his mouth, and tasted pleasure.

Visions of last night rose in her mind—their naked bodies rubbing together, the feel of him entering her, the explosion of sensations that had followed. Why hadn't she thought to put one of his condoms in her purse this morning? She wanted to feel him inside her again. Right now. Right here.

Libby broke the kiss and buried her face against his chest.

"Good morning," he said with a chuckle, his chin resting on her head, his chest rumbling against her still tingling lips.

"You left without saying good-bye," she muttered.

His arms tightened around her. "I'm sorry ya had to wake up alone, lass, but I wanted to get home before Robbie got up." He leaned back and smiled down at her. "Ya looked so peaceful, sleeping like a babe, I didn't have the heart to disturb ya."

"I was a block of ice when I woke up," she complained, not willing to let him off the hook.

He kissed her nose and pulled his jacket more firmly around her, snuggling her against him as if he could make up for the chill she'd experienced.

And the sad thing was, it was working.

"I'm sorry. I should have carried ya inside."

As apologies went, Libby decided this was a fair one. He was a guy, after all. And what did guys know about romance?

"I'm buying a new bed," she told him. "The truck just isn't going to work."

"Aye," he said with another chuckle, setting her away. He zipped her jacket up to her chin and tucked the hood more warmly around her ears, holding the edges so she had to look at him. "I can see where ya feel awkward about Mary. And if a new bed will help, I'll move her old one to the attic."

"How did you find me?" she asked, pulling away and climbing off the table. She looked up and frowned at him. "I thought you were starting to cut Christmas trees today."

"I left a crew of four men," he said, sitting down on the picnic table, facing her. "John's supervising them. And how I found ya is unimportant. Have ya seen your mother yet?"

"No," Libby said, blushing at the admission that she had run from her as well. "I was just about to head home, figuring she and James have found the house by now."

His expression hardened. "Ya told me ya weren't running from a man," he said with quiet menace. "Am I going to have to drive him off?"

"You are not! I dated James for a while, but that was a

hundred years ago. You leave him alone. His being here is not any of your business."

He stood up, took hold of her hood again, and leaned down as he lifted her face to his. He said, very softly, "You are my business now, Elizabeth Hart. Last night made it a fact. And," he continued even more softly when she tried to pull away, "you will accept the claim I made last night."

"Wh-what claim?"

"That you belong to me now."

"Are you getting philosophical again or just being contrary? We're having an affair, Michael. And women stopped *belonging* to anyone when they got the right to vote."

"Ya can't change the laws of nature, lass," he said, suddenly smiling. "Nor can ya deny your own nature. Ya can try, Libby, to pretend it's nothing more than a simple affair between us, but you're only fooling yourself. I was there, remember? Ya gave yourself freely and completely, and I accepted."

"Well, of all the . . . Michael, you can't just decide I belong to—"

He stopped her protest with another searing kiss that Libby felt all the way down to her toes. The confounding man tasted better than a dozen gooey glazed doughnuts, and Libby was torn between wanting to punch him and wanting to devour him.

Devouring won, probably because one of Michael's hands had found its way under her jacket and was caressing her breast. He ran his thumb lightly over her nipple, and Libby sucked in her breath.

"Stop doing that," she muttered when she finally got her mouth back. "You can't just kiss me whenever you don't like what I'm saying."

He tapped the end of her nose. "I can," he told her. "It's

one of the privileges of belonging. You can do the same, lass, when ya don't care for what I'm saying."

"Even married people don't belong to each other," she instructed, only to realize she was talking to his back. Michael had turned and was walking to her truck. Libby ran to catch up. "And having an affair doesn't even come close," she continued. "So stop acting like a caveman. What are you doing?"

He was holding her truck door open for her. And before she could protest, he picked her up and plopped her down in the front seat behind the steering wheel.

It was quicker than using the apple crate.

"I'll follow ya home, and you can introduce me to your mother," he said, handing her the seat belt. "And James," he tacked on with a glare. "And then the four of us will discuss tonight's sleeping arrangements."

"What do you mean, arrangements?"

"I mean, if James stays, so do I."

"Excuse me?"

He took hold of her chin and made her look directly into his steel-gray eyes. "He stays at the hotel, Libby. Or I'll be in your bed tonight, making sure he isn't."

"Of all the absur—"

He kissed her again.

"Cut that out," she sputtered the minute he pulled back.

"Drive careful," he told her, completely ignoring her glare. "They're hauling logs today," he reminded her, closing the door and walking up the dirt track that led to the main road.

Libby stared out the windshield at Pine Lake, cursing under her breath and licking the taste of Michael off her lips. Dammit. How was she going to explain to her mother that she hadn't been here a week and had already gotten herself *belonging to* an immovable mountain of man? All she needed now was for Father Daar to show up for dinner.

Maybe she could ask the priest to turn them all into frogs.

Suddenly, Michael's statement about making sure James wasn't in her bed dawned on Libby. She opened the door of her truck, jumped out, and started running after him.

"Hey! Wait!" she hollered, trying to get his attention.

When he didn't stop, Libby picked up a palm-sized piece of snow and threw it at him.

It hit him smack in the center of his back. By the time he'd turned to face her with a look of disbelief, she'd thrown another snowball at him, this one hitting him in the chest.

"Are ya toying with my temper so I'll kiss you again?" he asked, his expression fierce, his stance threatening. "Or do ya have a death wish?"

They were standing about thirty paces apart, and he was glaring at the third snowball in her hand. Libby glared back.

"No," she told him. "I'm trying to control my own temper. I do not care for the insult you just gave me."

He broadened his stance and crossed his arms over his chest. "What insult?" he asked, his voice spine-shiveringly low.

"You said you'd be in my bed to make sure James wasn't. You might as well have slapped my face, if that's what you think of me. I do not bed-hop, Michael MacBain. I have too much respect for myself, even if you obviously don't."

He stared at her, his eyes narrowed against the sun. He suddenly uncrossed his arms and opened them wide, holding them out to expose his broad chest as he slowly started walking toward her.

"Throw it," he said, nodding at the snowball in her hand. "Take your best shot, Libby," he softly urged, continuing to walk toward her.

Libby tightened her grip on the snowball and took a step

back. "I-I don't want to throw it. I want you to trust me."

"I do," he said, his pace unhurried, his gaze locked with hers, his arms still spread to provide her with a perfect target. Libby suddenly felt like prey being stalked. She opened her hand, let the snowball fall to the ground, and took another step back.

"I never meant to imply you would sleep with him," he continued. "It's James I don't trust. The man just came clear across the country to find you. He has an agenda."

"But that's just it," she said, somewhat desperately, as she continued to move back. "It doesn't matter if he does or not. I can deal with James."

She looked over her shoulder, trying to judge if she could make it to her truck before Michael could catch her. Lord, what had she been thinking, throwing snowballs at him?

He suddenly stopped. "Ya won't make it," he said softly, reading her intention. "Come here, Libby."

Did he think she was nuts? There was a smudge of slush on his jacket where her snowball had hit him. And he was telling her to walk into his trap?

But he just stood there, his arms held out from his sides.

Libby rubbed her damp palms on her jeans. He was driving her crazy. If he wasn't kissing her senseless, he was insulting her, inflaming her, or confounding her so much that she wanted to scream. In an almost perfect repeat of the afternoon he'd asked her to go riding, he was telling her to come to him, not moving, not saying anything, just waiting for her to concede.

She was damned if she did and stupid if she didn't. This man had somehow engaged her heart while she'd been busy guarding it from him. But if he thought she belonged to him, then he damned well belonged to her, too.

Libby ran and threw herself against his chest. He

wrapped his strong arms around her and buried his face in her hair.

"I did not mean to insult ya, Libby," he whispered into her ear, squeezing her so tightly she squeaked.

"I'm sorry I threw snow at you," she apologized between kisses to his face. "Did I hurt you?"

His laugh shook her. "Nay. But ya did give me a very nice compliment."

Libby leaned back and blinked at him. "How?"

"By showing me you trust me, lass. Ya feel safe enough to let loose your temper, knowing I would never hurt ya."

She blinked again. He was right. She smiled, kissed his chin, and laughed out loud. Yeah. She hadn't given it a thought that he might retaliate.

"I'm not a violent person," she replied. "I don't usually throw things at people."

"Ya have a good arm. And aim," he said, kissing her on the nose. He let her slide down the length of his body, and Libby gasped the moment her belly rubbed over the bulge in his pants.

"You're surprised?" he drawled, setting her away. "I cannot hide how ya affect me, Libby."

She immediately began studying one large button on his wool jacket. "Did you leave so early this morning because you had brought four condoms and only got to use one?" she asked in a whisper, keeping her head down so he wouldn't notice how red her face had become.

He lifted her chin with his finger, and Libby looked into his tender, warm pewter eyes. "I wasn't counting, lass. Nor was I expecting to use even that one. I left because I didn't want Robbie waking up before I got home. I don't want the boy building fairy tales in his head about us."

Too late! Libby wanted to shout. She was already building fairy tales of her own.

"Now, how about I follow ya home, and you can introduce me to your mother?" he suggested.

"You can meet her tomorrow. After the explosion."

"Oh, but I'd rather meet James today," he said, leading her to her truck again. "I can give him a ride back to the hotel."

"He's an old family friend, Michael. How am I going to explain that he can't stay at my house when there are four empty bedrooms upstairs?"

He picked her up, set her back in her truck, and turned her chin to face him. "You'll think of something," he said in deadly seriousness. "Or I will."

"You're being unreasonable."

He arrogantly nodded agreement. "Aye. But not as unreasonable as I will be if he stays." And, without further discussion, he softly closed the truck door and turned and walked back up the dirt road.

Again, Libby stared out the windshield at Pine Lake. But she found herself smiling this time, as Grace MacKeage's words of warning whispered through her head.

Old-fashioned. Protective. Possessive.

Yeah. That was just what this doctor needed.

He didn't care to be indebted to Greylen MacKeage, but he did appreciate the heads-up Grey had given him that morning about Libby's visitors. Michael reached his truck parked on the main road and got in, fastened his seat belt, and rubbed his hands over his face.

He wasn't surprised Libby's mother had come looking for her, but what in hell was her old boyfriend doing here?

What a mess. He'd told Libby that she belonged to him now, and the woman had not meekly, or graciously, welcomed his claim. Michael knew his authority over her was tenuous at best. They weren't married. He couldn't even say they were dating according to modern ways. Making wild, passionate love in the back of a truck parked in a garage was not a date.

No, the only thing Libby had agreed to was a discreet affair. Michael did believe she considered affairs exclusive things, with both parties committed to each other. But that was where his rights ended. Affairs today meant monogamous sex and nothing more—no interfering in each other's life, no formal contract, no recourse if one behaved in a way the other did not like.

He didn't want a modern affair with Libby. He wanted the right to follow her home, meet her mother, and kick James's ass all the way back to California.

Michael's right palm itched for the feel of his sword, and he held up his empty hand and stared at it in silence. It had been years since he'd wielded his sword with intent, and he was shocked that he wanted to now.

Shocked, maybe, but not surprised. For reasons he couldn't explain, Libby stirred his baser instincts. A need beyond his ability to comprehend made him want to possess her completely.

With a twist of the ignition, Michael started his truck and pulled onto the paved road behind Libby's Suburban as she drove past. He rubbed his still itching right hand over his face to wipe away the beads of sweat gathering on his brow. Michael's heart slammed into his ribs, and his muscles tensed with the instinct to flee.

How could he do it? How could he care for another woman? If he gave his heart to Libby and then lost her, he might not survive this time.

And he had to survive—for Robbie.

Aye. It was a hell of a mess, because it was too late.

Because Libby had managed to capture his heart with a simple, well-aimed snowball.

Chapter Seventeen

There was a rental car parked in her yard, and she could see her mother sitting in the front passenger seat. James was standing on the porch, his hands on his hips, the collar of his dress coat turned up against the cold, and an impatient scowl on his tanned face.

Libby drove straight into the garage and quickly walked back to the rental car. She opened the passenger door, waited until her mother got out, and hugged her warmly.

"I've missed you," she said. "I'm so glad you're here."

Katherine Hart hugged her back and kissed Libby's cheek before pulling away. "It took us a while to find out where 'here' was," Katherine returned loudly enough for James to hear, pulling her own collar up against the chilly breeze.

"Elizabeth," James said, turning Libby into his arms and hugging her. He also kissed her on the cheek, then leaned away, still holding her shoulders, and his scowl returned. "Do you have any idea the trouble you're in?"

"That can wait," Katherine said, glancing at the truck

that had pulled up beside their rental car. "Who would this be?" she asked Libby as she stared at the giant stepping out of the truck.

Libby took one look at Michael and quickly pulled away from James. She took hold of her mother's arm and led her over to the truck. "This is my landlord, Michael MacBain," Libby told her. "Michael, this is my mother, Katherine. And this is James Kessler."

"Missus Hart," Michael said, bowing slightly as he took her hand. "Kessler," he said, nodding curtly, then giving his attention back to her mother. "It's nice to see that you've come to help your daughter settle in."

"I've come to take my daughter home, Mr. MacBain."

"Really?" Michael asked, lifting one brow. "It's my understanding that she is home."

With the grace of a woman who'd found herself in many social situations throughout her husband's illustrious career, Katherine Hart set her features into polite amusement. She looked around at the rugged landscape, at the house Libby was renting, and then lifted her assessing gaze to settle on Michael.

"Home is where her work is. And where her family is, Mr. MacBain. And that is in California."

Libby was getting a crick in her neck trying to watch everyone's expression as Michael and her mother talked about her as if she wasn't even there. Which was, Libby realized, a great performance from Katherine for James's benefit. Her mom was playing the worried parent role almost too well.

But it was James who most alarmed Libby. He was being unusually quiet, his golden eyes intent on Michael as he tried to decide exactly how the giant fit in here.

Michael took hold of Katherine's elbow and started leading her to the house. And Katherine, ever the epitome of grace, let him, craning her own neck to give him her attention.

"We needn't stand in the cold," Libby heard Michael say as she tagged along behind them. "I'll get a fire going in the hearth, and your daughter can make ya some tea."

James pulled Libby to a halt. "Who the hell is this guy?"

"My landlord."

"In residence?"

"No," she shot back, pulling away from him. "Will you calm down. He's just being neighborly."

"He's being damned forward, if you ask me. Get rid of him, Elizabeth. We have to talk. Alone."

"Oh, we'll talk, all right," she said, running to catch up with Michael and her mother.

It was just as she was walking through the kitchen that she heard Michael say from the living room, in utter and complete seriousness, "Libby can't return to California until after Christmas, even if she wants to. She's obligated to work for me, in payment for a mishap that occurred the day she arrived here."

"What sort of mishap?" Katherine asked as she sat on the couch facing the hearth. "And what sort of work?"

Michael hunched down and started building a fire. "Libby ran over several of my prize Christmas trees," he said as he laid sticks of kindling over the paper. "And I've agreed to let her pay for them by working in my Christmas shop this season."

Libby realized she was standing in the living-room door with her mouth hanging open. She snapped it shut, darting a look from Michael's broad back to her suddenly speechless mother. James had taken a seat beside Katherine and was now gaping himself.

Only Michael seemed oblivious to the silence. "So she can't leave until her debt to me is satisfied," he continued, turning to smile at Katherine. "If you're staying for a while, I could use your help as well, for a fair wage, of course. Do ya bake, Missus Hart? Or maybe ya do crafts? We're needing Christmas tree ornaments to sell, and handmade ones do very well."

Libby's mouth fell open again. Had Michael just offered her mother a job? For money? Katherine Hart probably hadn't even seen a real dollar bill in years. And she certainly hadn't worked since high school.

"Elizabeth can pay for the trees," James said. "She's a highly successful surgeon and can't be working in a Christmas shop. She needs to get back and salvage her career. How much does she owe you?" he asked, reaching into the inside pocket of his suit jacket. "I'll write you a check right now."

Michael struck a match and lit the paper beneath the kindling, watching until it caught before he turned to look at James. He shook his head.

"Money won't pay for the trees," he told him. "They were prize Douglas fir, ya see, certain to win first place at the state fair next summer. Put your checkbook away, Kessler. I'm needing help more than I'm needing money." He looked from James to Libby. "Besides, she's already agreed."

James and her mother turned on the couch and also looked at her. Prickles of heat rose in Libby's cheeks. Dammit, Michael was crazy.

He was also a genius.

"That's right," she confirmed. "I promised to work for Michael until Christmas."

"Elizabeth," James said, standing to face her. "You're about to be sued for breach of contract. You left without notice."

Michael also stood up.

"We can discuss this later, James," Katherine said, tugging on James's hand to get him to sit down. "Elizabeth, did you put on some tea?" she asked. "And thank you for the offer for a job, Mr. MacBain. I-I'm flattered and will certainly think about it."

"That's good, then," Michael said, rubbing his hands together as he walked into the kitchen, turning Libby ahead of him, and pushing her toward the stove. "I think I'll just go downstairs and check on the furnace, since I'm here. Ya said it was making a funny noise?"

"Yes," Libby snapped. "It's making a lot of noise and blowing lots of hot air."

A startled scream came from the living room just then, and Libby and Michael both rushed to the door at the same time. They saw Katherine standing on the hearth, holding on to the run in her stocking as she stared at Trouble, who was trying to jump up after her.

James grabbed the kitten by the scruff of the neck, holding it away from himself as if it were trash. Trouble let out an angry mew, and suddenly Guardian was climbing up James's pants leg to rescue his brother.

Libby beat him to it and also rescued Guardian while she was at it. "Aren't they adorable?" she asked her mother, holding the kittens against her chest as she faced Katherine. "Robbie gave them to me. There's another one, too," she said, looking around. "Her name is Timid. And this is Guardian, and this is Trouble," she added, turning each one to face her mother. "Kittens, this is my mother."

Katherine let James help her down from the hearth and leaned over to check the run in her stocking. She brushed her hair back from her suddenly embarrassed face and darted a look at Michael and then back at Libby.

"Who's Robbie?"

"He's really my landlord," Libby explained. "He's Michael's son. This is his mother's house."

"And where is his mother now?"

"She died when Robbie was born," Libby told her.

And again, Katherine darted a look at Michael. "Oh. I'm sorry, Mr. MacBain." She looked around the room and then back at Libby. "Where's the other one?" she whispered. "Timid, you called her?"

"She's probably hiding, hence the name," Libby told her, walking over and handing the two kittens to Michael. "Maybe you should go check on the furnace now, before it starts blowing any more hot air."

James came walking into the kitchen, holding Timid at arm's length. "Here's the other one."

"Oh, you're scaring the poor thing," Katherine said, snatching Timid away from him and cuddling her against her cashmere coat. "She's just a baby."

"I can lock her in the bathroom with the others," Michael offered, holding out his hand.

Her mother turned Timid away from his reach. "No, she's trembling. I think I'll just hold her a bit."

And just like that, Libby knew that Katherine Hart had won Michael's approval.

Michael put Trouble and Guardian into the bathroom and then disappeared into the cellar. Libby put the kettle on to boil. Katherine took a seat at the table, still cuddling Timid, and looked around the kitchen.

"This is a wonderful house," she said. "So old New England. How did you find it?" she asked, giving Libby a pointed look that said she was keeping up the charade.

"On the Internet," Libby told her, going to the fridge, hoping there was something hiding in there to eat. She found half a block of cheddar cheese, two apples, and a cucumber. She carried everything to the counter and started cutting it up, arranging slices on a plate for a snack.

"Why Maine?" James asked, sitting at the table opposite Katherine.

Libby shrugged. "Why not?"

"Do you realize the trouble you're in, Elizabeth? You walked away from your contract. And your responsibilities," he told her, his voice scolding. "As it is, your little trip will probably cost you a fortune in fines. But that's nothing compared with what it's already cost your reputation. You walked out of your operating room, Elizabeth. You left a mess."

Libby stopped slicing the apple and turned to look at him. "I sent Randal Peters a certified letter saying I had to leave for personal reasons."

"I talked to Peters, and he doesn't care what reason you cited. He knows you left because of what happened," James said, standing up and coming over to her, taking her by the shoulders. "There's still time to straighten this out, Elizabeth. If you come back right now and apologize to the board and beg their forgiveness, this can be dealt with quietly."

"What exactly happened," Michael asked as he stepped through the cellar door, "that requires an apology and begging?"

James spun to face him. "This isn't your concern, MacBain. It's Elizabeth's."

"And yours?" Michael asked softly, walking up to stand directly in front of James. "Libby doesn't strike me as a woman willing to beg for anything. So, tell me what she's done that needs an apology."

James returned to the table and stood behind the chair he'd been sitting in. "It was a stupid mistake," he said, waving his hand dismissively. "She nearly cut into a perfectly healthy woman in her operating room. But that's not something you throw your career away for."

Michael turned and looked at her, his pewter-gray eyes gently probing hers. "Is that true, lass? Ya left because of this mistake?"

"It's a serious mistake for a surgeon, Mr. MacBain," Katherine said, drawing his attention. "But it wasn't my daughter's fault. They brought her the wrong patient."

Michael looked back at Libby.

She turned to the counter and began cutting the apple again.

"She must have felt responsible," she heard Michael tell Katherine. "Enough to doubt her ability to perform her job."

"I repeat, this is not your business, MacBain," James said tightly. "We will deal with Elizabeth's problem."

"By advising her to beg?" Michael asked so softly that shivers of alarm raced up Libby's spine.

Robbie's arrival interrupted the tense silence. He ran into the kitchen on a blast of cold air, the door slamming loudly behind him.

"Libby! We had a fire at school," he said excitedly in greeting, rushing to tell her his news. "It was in the boys' bathroom, and the whole school filled up with smoke, and we had to leave without getting our coats and stuff."

Almost without breaking stride, Robbie walked over to Katherine and scratched Timid on the head, giving Libby's mother a huge grin. "She'll purr if ya tickle her right here," he instructed, guiding Katherine's fingers to the back of Timid's ear. "She likes ya," he added with authority, his grin widening. "Are ya Libby's mama? 'Cause if ya are, I'll like ya, too."

"Then I guess I am," her mother replied, her warm brown eyes dancing with amusement. "And you can call me Katherine."

Robbie thought about that, studying her for a good long time. "I think I'll call ya Gram Katie," he finally decided. " 'Cause old people like it when I call them things like that."

He turned to face James, completely oblivious to Katherine's horror. "Who are you?" he asked, lifting his young chin. "You better not have come here to take Libby back to California, 'cause she's not leaving. We're keeping her. She's got kittens and chickens to look after, and she signed a lease with me. It's a contract that's . . ." He looked at Libby, suddenly uncertain. "What is it again?" he whispered.

"Binding," Libby whispered back, barely containing her amusement.

Robbie looked at James again, his young features rather threatening. "Yeah. Her contract is binding, and she can't leave for a year."

"Well, if you had checked her references, young man," James said sharply, "you'd know she makes a habit of breaking her contracts."

"James," Katherine snapped. "That's enough."

"Aye," Michael interjected. "It is. Come on, son. You and I have to go buy Libby a new bed."

"What's wrong with her old bed?" Robbie asked, shooting one final glare at James before giving Libby his attention. "Is it lumpy?" he asked her. "Or does it sag in the middle? 'Cause we can put a board under it if it sags."

"It-it's lumpy," Libby said past her blush, keeping her gaze from coming into contact with Michael's. "But I want a new headboard as well," she added, speaking directly to Robbie and hoping Michael was listening.

Why on earth did he have to bring up the subject of her bed now, in front of her mother and James? And dammit, she wanted to pick out her own bed.

Robbie leaned up to speak to his father as he kept a guarded eye on James. "I don't think we should leave right now, Papa," he whispered. "That guy with Gram Katie might try to steal Libby from us. We gotta stay until he's gone."

Of course, everyone heard Robbie, including the subject of his distrust. James sneered, looking at Libby. "The child has no more manners than your cats."

Libby had had enough as well. She pointed her knife-skewered apple at James and decided it was time to tell him what she thought of his own manners. But Robbie beat her to it. The boy rounded on the condescending man and took a step toward him.

"I don't need manners," he told him, his young fists balled at his sides. " 'Cause I've got right on my side. And might," he added, taking another step closer.

"Might?" James sputtered in disbelief, his face darkening with anger.

Libby moved to step between them, but Michael took hold of her arm and silently shook his head, his eyes filled with delight and no small amount of fatherly pride.

"It's my papa's might," Robbie explained, his tone even, his glare filled with challenge. "He's a warrior, and he steps over bigger men than you just to get to a fight."

As threats went, Libby couldn't have come up with a better one herself. For a worldly, sophisticated doctor who was so much at home in an operating room or a board meeting, it seemed James didn't have a clue how to respond to the boy's challenge. He didn't know how to deal with children, period. Which was why, instead of snapping back, he darted a worried look at Michael, pulled out his chair, and sat down.

Katherine reached over, her smile poorly hidden, and patted his hand. "Why don't you bring in my suitcase from the car?" she softly suggested. "Then head back to the hotel and register yourself back in for the night. Elizabeth and I will cook a nice dinner, and you can return at seven o'clock and eat with us."

She looked at Robbie. "Does that sound acceptable to you, young man? You have my word we won't try to steal Elizabeth away from you tonight."

Robbie shot an uncertain look at his father, frowned at Michael's nod, and looked back at Katherine. "That sounds okay, I guess. And her name is Libby, not Elizabeth," he told her.

"It's Dr. Elizabeth Hart," James interjected, attempting to salvage some of his dignity. "She's a very important surgeon back in California."

Libby winced, darting her own uncertain look at Michael when Robbie gasped and spun around to face her.

"You're not a doctor!" he shouted. "Ya make jewelry."

Libby tossed the apple and the knife onto the counter and took the angry boy by the shoulders. "I do make jewelry," she told him gently. "But I'm also a doctor, Robbie. I operate on people who have been in terrible accidents."

He pulled away from her, stepping back and balling his hands into fists again. "Ya can't be," he whispered desperately. "Ya need a hospital to do operations, and we don't have one. You'll leave!" he shouted, spinning around and running out the door as quickly and as loudly as he'd come through it.

Libby ran after him, but Michael caught her before she could step off the porch.

"I have to go to him," she said, struggling to get free. "I have to explain."

"Nay," Michael said softly, turning her to face him. "He'll not listen to ya right now."

"But I have to make him understand."

"He'll calm down once I tell him you're not leaving."

"And just why are you so sure I'm not?"

He pulled her into his arm, lifting her chin to look at him. He smiled and squeezed her until she squeaked. "Because I've decided not to let you," he said, kissing her on the end on the nose and then setting her away.

He stepped off the porch and swaggered toward his truck and Robbie, without looking back.

"Michael!"

He stopped at his truck door and looked at her.

"I want a nice bed, with a fancy headboard and footboard."

The grin he shot her was filled with pure arrogance. "I can't promise ya fancy," he said, sending shivers up her spine. "But I can promise ya it will be large and solid."

Chapter Eighteen

"*What did Robbie mean,* you make jewelry?" Katherine asked as she ran water in the sink and started peeling the potatoes.

They had just gotten back from town and unloaded the groceries and were busy preparing dinner. Libby looked up from sliding the huge roast into the oven and gave her mother a sheepish smile.

"I work with glass. I make pendants and earrings and bracelets."

Katherine stopped peeling. "Those are your creations? The little birds and plants you wear?"

"You mean the ones all your friends have been trying to buy?" Libby asked, nodding. "Yeah. I made them."

"But how . . . where did you learn that? No, wait. My mother, right?" Katherine said with a sigh, shaking her head and turning back to her chore. "I should have guessed when you refused to give my friends the name of the artist." She looked at Libby with dawning awareness. "The wood thrush you gave me for Christmas two years ago? You made it."

Libby nodded again, went to the fridge, and got out the carrots. "And the ivy leaf tie tack I gave Dad five years ago. I made that, too," she confessed, coming to stand beside her mother at the sink.

"But they're beautiful," Katherine exclaimed. "No, wait. I didn't mean for that to sound like it did. Of course, they're beautiful, if you made them. You've always been good with your hands."

"Thank you."

Katherine stopped peeling again and stared at her. "That's why you're such a good surgeon, Elizabeth. You're so damned good you make it seem like magic. Please don't give up your career. What happened in your operating room was a mistake."

"It wasn't a mistake, Mom." Libby took the potato and the knife away from her mother and led her over to the table, gently pushing her into one of the chairs. She sat opposite her and looked directly into Katherine's concerned brown eyes.

"Grammy Bea wasn't just making it up, Mom, and I think you know it. And you know that Aunt Sylvia could heal people, but all these years you've been denying it because you were afraid."

"Afraid of what?"

"Not afraid *of what* but *for whom,*" Libby told her. "You were afraid for me, weren't you? You didn't want me to have this gift because you knew how deeply it would affect me. I healed Esther Brown, Mom, and it was a miracle."

"You perform miracles every day, Elizabeth."

"Not this kind of miracle," Libby said, reaching out and folding Katherine's hands inside hers. "This is the power to heal people without using my skills as a surgeon."

Katherine tried to pull away.

Libby wouldn't let go of her hands but squeezed them

instead. "I felt her, Mom. I actually became part of Esther Brown. I felt her emotions and her determination to live."

"That's impossible, Elizabeth," Katherine whispered. "That . . . it's just not . . . it just can't happen like that."

"But why is it impossible? How many miracles have been documented throughout history? Why can't Esther Brown's unexplainable recovery be one of them?"

Libby finally let her mother have her hands back, which Katherine immediately folded on her lap while she stared at the tablecloth. She finally looked up, her huge brown eyes swimming with worry.

"I don't want Bea to have been right all these years."

"Do you think I do?" Libby asked.

Katherine reached out across the table to Libby. "But it might not even be you, Elizabeth. If it was a miracle, what makes you think you had anything to do with it?"

"Because I did it again."

"What?"

"I did it again, Mom. I was the attending physician for James's patient that morning. Jamie Garcia is only six years old. He'd been hit by a car and was in a coma. But that afternoon, after what happened with Esther Brown, I went to his room, sat beside him, and prayed for him to wake up. And just like before, I felt his emotions, his fear, and his desperate struggle to get back to his parents. And he opened his eyes and smiled at me."

Katherine stared at her mutely. "So you ran," she finally added softly. "Here. But why here?"

"I don't know why. I think the mountains had something to do with it. The distance. The reputation of stoically grounded New Englanders." Libby suddenly smiled. "But mostly it was Robbie MacBain. There was a picture of him in the ad he'd posted on the Internet." She shrugged. "There was just something about him . . . a wisdom that had nothing to do with his age. As if he holds the key to all the secrets of the universe. And I thought—no, I knew I had to come here."

Katherine smiled. "At least, that's something I can understand after meeting him. He's very self-contained for a twelve-year-old."

"Robbie's eight."

"Eight?" Katherine gasped, leaning back in her chair. "He can't be eight, Elizabeth. He's too big."

"He'll be nine in January."

Her mother fell silent again, standing up and going back to the sink to peel potatoes. Libby started setting the table for five people. She was sure that Michael and Robbie would end up eating with them.

"What is James doing here?" Libby asked into the silence. "And why didn't you call and tell me you were both coming?"

Katherine shot her a frown. "I tried. Twice. But you didn't answer, and you don't have an answering machine hooked up." She stopped peeling and turned to Libby. "I didn't tell him where you were, Elizabeth. And I don't know how he found you. But he came to my house and told me he'd tracked you to Maine and that he was coming after you." Katherine shrugged. "So what else could I do? I threw some clothes into a suitcase and came with him."

She stopped Libby from setting the table and took hold of her shoulders. "I spent the entire flight here trying to convince him that Bea's stories were not true. That there was a mix-up in your operating room and that his patient simply woke up on his own. Elizabeth, he can't actually prove anything. If we just stick to our story, he'll give up and go home. Tell him he can have the grant, and he'll stop this . . . this witch hunt."

"Is that what you think this is?" Libby whispered. "A witch hunt?"

Katherine squeezed her shoulders. "Of course not, dear. But James thinks it is. He grew up hearing Grammy Bea's stories, too."

Libby found another knife and started peeling the carrots and tossed them into the pot with the potatoes. "Dammit," she growled to herself. "I am not a witch."

Katherine quietly picked the carrots out and put them into their own pot before setting the potatoes on the stove to boil. "Tell me about Michael," she said, pouring a glass of wine and sitting down at the table to drink it. "He's very . . . ah . . . big. And rather proprietary toward you. Does he have a reason to be acting so possessive?"

Libby dropped her head to concentrate on the carrots, hoping to hide her blush. "He might," she muttered.

There was a long silence from the table, then her mother asked, "He raised Robbie all by himself?"

"Yes. With the help of Grace MacKeage, Robbie's aunt."

"Elizabeth, look at me."

Slowly, reluctantly, Libby turned to face her, lifting her chin as she fought to keep her blush from spreading.

Katherine gave her a warm, motherly smile. "You can't possibly get involved with him, Elizabeth," she said gently. "Not now."

"I tried not to, but it happened anyway."

"Are you sure you're not just trying to distract yourself?"

Libby sighed. "No. Maybe. Oh, dammit, I don't know. Michael is . . . he's . . ."

"All man?" her mother finished. "With more testosterone than is probably healthy? Elizabeth, do you know what you're getting yourself into? Getting involved with a man like Michael MacBain will be all-consuming. I figured

that out within ten minutes of meeting him. Are you willing to give up your career for him?"

"Why do I have to? I can be a doctor in Maine just as
well as in California."

"You really want to live here? You'll have to if you fall in
love with him. Michael doesn't strike me as someone willing to compromise on certain things."

Libby couldn't contain her grin. "Like tonight's sleeping
arrangements?"

Katherine shook her head. "I swear, if I hadn't suggested
that James check back into the hotel, Michael would have,
and not quite as diplomatically. You don't find him a bit . . .
oh . . . a bit domineering?"

"Domineering?" Libby repeated. "He's old-fashioned,
maybe, but he's not really a chest-beating caveman. He's
actually quite civilized—most of the time."

"He's overwhelming."

"He said he won't ever get married," Libby softly confessed, continuing to disclose the mess she'd gotten herself
into. "Not that I'm even thinking about marriage," she
quickly clarified, probably to reassure herself more than
her mother. "Michael and Robbie can live in their house,
and I will be nothing more than a good neighbor."

Bright lights came through the kitchen window, and the
sound of several vehicles pulling up to the house quickly
followed. Libby walked to the door, and Katherine leaned
over the sink to look outside.

Michael's truck was turning to back up to the porch
stairs, its cargo bay filled with what looked like a very
large—and very solid—bed.

Robbie jumped out, came running up onto the porch,
and threw himself into Libby's arms. The impact nearly
knocked her off her feet as she wrapped her arms around
him and attempted to keep them both upright.

"I'm sorry I yelled and ran out," he said into her shoulder, squeezing her so tightly he finished pushing all the air from her lungs. "Papa promised me ya won't leave. Not ever."

"Oh, he did, did he?" Libby whispered, kissing his head. "Then I guess it's settled."

"Aye," he thickly agreed, looking up. "And he said if we act real civilized, maybe Gram Katie will want to stay, too."

Libby ruffled his hair and moved them both out of the way when Michael stepped onto the porch carrying a huge and heavy-looking headboard. She gasped, not because Michael winked at her as he walked past but because the headboard was taller than she was.

She ran after him into the bedroom and slid to a halt when he leaned it up against one of the walls. And she stared, wide-eyed and opened-mouthed, at her new bed.

It was absolutely stunning.

The end posts looked to be solid oak that nearly reached the ceiling. Oak cross members held the posts a good five feet apart, forming a thick frame that surrounded a well-defined, large bull moose cut out of thick steel. The oak was stained a warm honey brown, and the moose was painted black. It was walking through a forest of fir trees painted a crisp green, also cut from steel, with larger trees behind it and smaller ones near its hooves.

Libby lifted amazed eyes to Michael. "It-it's beautiful," she whispered. She ran one finger over the antlers of the moose, shaking her head in disbelief. "It's absolutely beautiful." She looked back up at Michael. "Where did you get it?"

"That's my secret. Do ya like it, lass? It's not fancy."

"It's beautiful," she repeated, unable to think of a better description. "I love it. Is it really mine?" she asked, running her hand over the smooth oak and tracing several of the trees with her fingers.

"Oh, my," Katherine breathed, coming to stand beside her. "It's a work of art."

"I still say ya gotta get the old bed out before ya bring in the new one," Ian MacKeage grouched as he carried in the footboard. "Where do ya want this accursed thing? God's teeth, it's heavy."

Katherine spun to face the unfamiliar voice and let out a yelp of surprise when she was nearly run over by the wild-haired, bushy-bearded giant. She pushed Libby out of the way and scrambled after her, running them both into Michael's solid body. Libby looked up, and Michael leaned down and kissed her on the end of her nose.

"Ya come by your screaming honestly, I see," he whispered. "Now, strip the bed, and then go make sure ya don't burn our supper. Ian and I will have everything moved by the time it's ready."

Libby pushed Katherine out of the way because her mother seemed glued to the floor. And she was staring at Ian.

Ian was staring back.

"Mother, this is Ian MacKeage," Libby told her. "Ian, this is my mother, Katherine."

"Mr. MacKeage," Katherine whispered. "It-it's nice to meet you."

"Kate," he said, nodding politely. He looked at Michael. "Are ya roosting for the night, or we gonna do this job, MacBain? Supper smells good, and I'm hungry," he finished, turning on his heel and walking back through the kitchen.

Michael silently followed, and Libby's bedroom suddenly felt big again. She looked at her mother, who was staring at the door where Ian had disappeared.

"I think there's something in the water that makes them all grow big," Libby told her. "So I've been drinking a lot of water lately. If you want to strip the bed, I'll set another place at the table for Ian."

Katherine stopped her by grabbing her arm. "He—he called me Kate," she said hoarsely. "And his scowl is . . . is . . ."

Libby patted her hand. "Ian can be a bit rough around the edges, but you don't have to be afraid of him, Mom. I promise, under all that hair, he's a cupcake."

Katherine finally shook herself out of her stupor. "I'm not afraid of him," she said. "He's just so . . . he's . . ."

"All man?" Libby finished for her, repeating her mom's earlier words.

"And then some," Katherine agreed, going to Mary's old bed and pulling off the quilt.

Libby took one final look at her new bed, stopping to examine the footboard Ian had leaned against it. It was just like the headboard, minus the moose and half the height, with perfectly matched fir trees lined up like sentinels from post to post.

"Where do you suppose Michael found it?" Katherine asked as she stared at the bed, her arms full of sheets. "It looks to be handcrafted."

"He must know a furniture maker who lives around here," Libby speculated, unable to keep from running her hand over it again. "I wonder if the guy could make me a matching bureau?"

Katherine shook her head and made a *tsk*ing sound. "Oh, boy. You're settling in here faster than frost on a pumpkin."

Libby lifted a brow at her mother.

"What?" Katherine asked, lifting her chin. "Bea may have been your grammy, but she was my mother. I haven't traveled so far from the farm that I've forgotten my roots."

"I miss her."

"I know, sweetie. I miss her, too."

"I'm glad you're here, Mom."

Katherine shifted her load of sheets and straightened her shoulders on a deep breath. "That's good, because I think I just might stay awhile." She shot Libby a smug grin. "And since I'll be gainfully employed, I'll even kick in for part of the rent."

That said, Katherine headed for the bathroom, the sheets trailing after her like a queen's mantle.

"God's teeth, women!" Ian shout from the kitchen. "The potatoes are boiling over out here!"

Libby ran into the kitchen to find a smoking, stinking mess covering the stove, the potatoes completely boiled dry, and the stainless steel pot so black it looked like cast iron. She waved the dishtowel through the smoke and opened the window over the sink to let in fresh air.

Michael quietly took the dishtowel from her, picked up the ruined pot, and carried it outside.

By the time Libby could see again, four sets of eyes were staring at her, all with varying degrees of accusation. Robbie, his arms full of kittens, looked crestfallen at the loss of half his dinner. Katherine appeared dismayed. Ian looked disgusted. And Michael? Well, his eyes were crinkled, and his shoulders were shaking.

James walked into the house, waving his hand at the smoke while his other hand covered his nose in defense of the smell. "I found this gentleman in the driveway," he said. "He claims he's a priest and that he was invited to dinner."

"I may have changed my mind," Father Daar said as he brushed past James. "What in the name of God have ya done to our supper?" he asked, glaring at Libby as he wrinkled his nose. "How can ya claim to keep track of people's innards when ya can't even manage a pot of potatoes?"

"It's nice to see you, too, Father," Libby drawled, turning

and shutting off the heat beneath the carrots. "Mom, maybe it's time you opened another bottle of wine."

"Why is everyone wearing orange?" Katherine asked, looking around the room full of brightly clothed Scots. "Are you trying to match the fall foliage?"

"Oh, for the love of—" Ian huffed in exasperation, wiping his face with a broad hand. "It's hunting season, woman, and we're not caring to get shot."

"Sh-shot?"

Ian went to the counter, found the opened bottle of wine, filled the empty glass on the counter, and carried it over to Katherine. "Would ya like to go hunting with me tomorrow morning?" he asked through his beard. "I have a nice little youth's rifle ya can borrow."

Instead of answering, Katherine lifted her glass and didn't lower it until all the wine was gone. "Th-thank you," she stammered, handing it back.

"I'll pick ya up at four-thirty, then," Ian said. "Dress warm, Kate."

"But I didn't mean . . . I can't . . ." She took a calming breath, straightened her shoulders, and glared at Ian. "I have a previous obligation tomorrow morning, Mr. MacKeage. But thank you for your kind offer."

"Then how about the next morning? It's supposed to snow, but that will make tracking the sneaky critters that much easier."

Katherine snatched her empty glass from him, went to the fridge, and took out the other bottle of wine. Libby decided it was time to rescue her mom.

"Robbie, why don't you put the kittens in the bathroom and wash your hands? Michael, could you take the roast out for me?" she asked, draining the carrots into the sink. "Sit down, everyone," she urged. Looking up at Michael she said, "Somebody should go get John. We can't let him eat alone."

"He's visiting neighbors tonight," Michael told her.

"Oh, that's good, then."

Michael remained unusually quiet throughout the meal, but then, Libby was quiet herself. She couldn't decide if it was because she was overwhelmed by the chaos or amused. In all the hundreds of dinner parties she'd attended in her lifetime, not one had ever come close to providing the joy she was feeling right now.

Her kitchen was full. The food was good, the company was unique, and the setting couldn't be more charming.

Oh, yeah. She was settling in faster than frost on a pumpkin.

Chapter Nineteen

Seeing the car pull up at the end of the field, Michael shut off his chain saw, set it beside the newly cut stump, and signaled his crew to continue working before heading down the row of felled Christmas trees. He pushed up the visor on his hard hat and pulled off his gloves. James Kessler got out of the car, leaned against the fender, and tucked his hands into his coat pockets.

Michael came to a halt three paces away. "I wondered when you'd show up," he said, stuffing his gloves into his back pocket before crossing his arms over his chest. "You're wasting your time, Kessler. Libby's staying."

Michael expected some sort of reaction for such a bold declaration, but Kessler's indifference surprised him.

"If she stays, she'll be ruined," he simply said, without malice and with only a hint of concern. "She has a contract, and if she breaks it, she'll never work as a surgeon again."

"She'll work if she wants to, if she's as good as ya claim."

"She's not good, MacBain, she's brilliant. Elizabeth is methodical, precise, and unbelievably controlled in the operating room. It's only her personal life she's determined to screw up."

"It's her life."

"She won't stay. She'll eventually get over this temper tantrum and realize what she's given up."

"If ya knew Libby at all, you'd know this isn't a tantrum she's having. Tell me, if she did no harm to the woman she almost operated on, why do ya think she ran?"

Kessler took his time answering, giving Michael a long, calculated look. "I don't know," he finally said. "There were rumors that something was strange about the case right from the start. Elizabeth's team was the first to see the woman, and she needed immediate surgery. But she was perfectly healthy by the time she arrived in the operating room."

"And how was this explained? Libby wasn't the only person to see her."

Kessler straightened away from the car. "It wasn't explained. The surgeon of record couldn't be found because she'd run away."

"And you're here to take her back and have her apologize. Exactly what is Libby sorry for?"

"For leaving."

"Ah. So she did nothing ethically wrong, then."

"It's unethical to walk away from her obligation to the hospital. And she has a responsibility to find out what happened to her patient."

"But she has more of an obligation to herself," Michael softly contradicted. "Tell me why you're really here, Kessler."

"Elizabeth's my friend. We grew up together, and since her father died four years ago, I've been looking out for her."

"She's not capable of looking out for herself?"

"Apparently not."

Michael shook his head. "It's more than your concern for a friend that brought you clear across the country. And more than what happened in her operating room. Why are ya here, Kessler?"

The other man's features darkened. "She did something to one of my patients," he said tightly. "The kid was in a coma when Elizabeth went into his room. But when she walked out, he was sitting up and asking for his parents." Kessler balled his hands into fists at his side, his stance defensive. "I want to know what she did to him."

The fine hairs on the back of Michael's neck stirred, and he uncrossed his arms. "What is it you think she did to him?" he asked softly.

Kessler suddenly blew out a frustrated breath. "You're a farmer, MacBain," he said, waving at the field of Christmas trees. "You know nothing about medicine or the politics that goes with it. Elizabeth treated the boy that morning, but once he became my patient, she shouldn't have gone near him. And the kid sure as hell didn't come out of that coma on his own."

Michael thought about the knife tucked inside his boot and wondered what reaction he would get if he pulled it out and held it against Kessler's throat.

"You came here because you're pissed Libby visited your patient?" Michael asked. He shook his head again and crossed his arms over his chest, deliberately relaxing his stance and ignoring his urge to go for the man's throat. "You're leaving today," he said evenly. "And you're leaving alone."

"Dammit. This isn't even your concern, MacBain. I only came here this morning because you seem to have some sort of . . . influence with Elizabeth. And I need to know what she did to my patient."

Again, the fine hairs on Michael's neck stirred at the realization that this conversation was not about medicine or its politics. The man was hiding something.

Or fishing for something.

And suddenly, Michael knew there was more at stake here than Libby's career. Whatever had happened to the two patients Libby had seen that day had affected her so strongly that she'd turned her entire life upside down.

And she had run here to protect herself. Michael rubbed the spot where Libby's snowball had hit him yesterday. Did he really care what had happened in California?

Nay. All that mattered was that she belonged to him now, and that James Kessler had just become more of a threat than an inconvenience.

Michael smiled and stepped forward. "Aye, Kessler, I'm only a farmer," he said evenly. "But I know more about the human body than ya might think. For instance," he whispered, touching Kessler's chest just below the knot in his tie. "I know that if ya poke a man right here, with just enough pressure, ya can crush his windpipe.

"And," he continued, removing his hand and holding it palm forward, ignoring Kessler's suddenly defensive stance, "if I were to shove on the end of your nose, I could drive the cartilage into your brain before ya even realized my intent."

Kessler took a step back, bumping against the fender of the car. "Are you threatening me?" he asked, his eyes widening and his face flushing with anger.

"Aye, I am," Michael growled, taking hold of his tie and pulling him closer. "So, decide, Kessler. Is interfering in Libby's life worth risking your own?"

Kessler grabbed Michael's hand and tried to tug free. Michael simply twisted his wrist, tightening the knot against his throat. "Go home, Kessler. And don't come back. And if I ever hear of ya contacting Libby again, I'm going to hunt ya down and show ya exactly what I know about human anatomy."

His warning delivered, Michael opened his hand and stepped back. Kessler immediately stuck his finger into the knot of his tie and pulled it loose, gasping for air as he took two steps to the side.

"You're actually threatening me," he said, more in disbelief than in horror. "There are laws against that, MacBain."

Michael crossed his arms over his chest again. "I don't particularly care for those laws," he drawled.

Kessler smoothed down his clothes in an attempt to regain his composure. "Look. We're both civilized men. There's no need to reduce this to a pissing contest. I came to see you this morning to explain my concern for Elizabeth."

"There's only one civilized person here, Kessler, and I'm beginning to think it's me. You're pretending concern for Libby when you're really trying to destroy her career."

"Dammit. Don't you get it? Something strange happened to those two people, and Elizabeth's at the center of it. Aren't you even curious about what she did to them? Or are you too blinded by lust to see that you're panting after a damn freak!"

Michael quickly stepped forward and wrapped one hand around Kessler's throat while using his other hand to lift him up by the belt. He threw him onto the hood of the car, shifted his thumb to the pulse in Kessler's neck, and pressed.

"As I live and breathe, I'm going to regret not beating you to a bloody pulp," Micheal whispered into Kessler's flushed face. "But you're worth more to Libby whole and hearty," Michael explained, pressing his thumb deeper. "Because you're going back to California, and you're going to make all those questions about her go away."

Kessler squirmed, trying to pull his neck from beneath Michael's thumb. Michael repositioned his grip on Kessler's tie again and dragged the man across the hood as he walked around the front of the car. Once on the driver's side, he pulled Kessler back to his feet, opened the car door, and shoved him inside.

"Ya have one hour to get out of town," Michael said, leaning down to look him in the eye. "But you'll stop at Libby's first and assure her that you'll smooth things over for her at the hospital."

"You're insane," Kessler whispered, his eyes bulging and his face flushing red as he stared up at Michael in horror.

"Aye," Michael agreed. "I've been told that before. And I've been known to start wars for lesser reasons, which is why you'd be wise to do as I say." He took hold of Kessler's shoulder and squeezed until he winced. "And the news Libby gets from California had best be flattering, Kessler, or I'm coming after ya and finishing this. Understand?" he asked, squeezing harder.

James Kessler frantically nodded.

Michael decided their conversation was over. He gently closed the car door and walked back through his field of Christmas trees, sweat trickling down his back despite it being almost cold enough to snow. And as he returned to work, he wondered what had happened between Libby and the two critically injured people who were now walking the earth as if they'd never been hurt.

"He seemed in a bit of a hurry," Katherine said as she stood beside Libby, both of them watching James pull out of the driveway. "Where do you suppose he went this morning, before he came here?"

"My guess is he went to see Michael."

"Oh," Katherine said, lifting her hand to her chest. "I would love to have been there."

"Not me," Libby said, rolling her eyes. "Michael probably got all manly and clammed up and wouldn't even talk to him."

"That doesn't explain James's decision to leave so suddenly, after coming all the way here and not really accomplishing anything," Katherine said with a frown. "And he looked a little wild-eyed, don't you think?"

Libby lifted a brow. "Are you implying Michael scared him off?" She laughed. "That's ridiculous. He'd never do something like that." She hooked her arm through her mother's and walked them back into the house. "James probably realized how foolish he was being. Now that he's seen I haven't suddenly grown a set of horns or a tail, he's anxious to get home and claim that grant money before I change my mind and go back."

Katherine stopped them just inside the kitchen door and took Libby by both hands. "Do you really think he'll drop it?" she whispered.

"He has to," Libby assured her, reversing their grip and squeezing Katherine's hands. "Like you said, he can't prove anything. And he's beginning to realize he'd only make a fool of himself if he pursues this."

Katherine smiled with relief. "Of course, you're right."

Libby looked around the kitchen, then back at her mother. "So, what do we do for the rest of the day, now that we got rid of James?"

"You take me to town to buy an orange jacket so I don't get shot. And a hat. I want an Elmer Fudd hat."

"Katherine Hart." Libby gasped, giving her mother a wide-eyed stare. "I'm going to take your picture and send it to your garden club."

"No, we'll make a Christmas card with the two of us dressed in orange and holding rifles, looking as if we're about to shoot something. Do you suppose Ian will lend us a couple of guns?"

"So it's Ian now? What happened to Mr. MacKeage?"

Katherine turned and reached for her coat and purse. "I

woke up this morning deciding you're right. He's all bluster, under all that hair."

Libby grabbed her own purse and headed into the garage. She went to the passenger side of her Suburban, took out the apple crate, and set it on the ground.

"I've really got to see about getting some running boards," she said as she helped her mother climb into the truck. "This is getting annoying."

She picked up the crate and carried it to her door, got in, and struggled to set the crate in the backseat without maiming both of them.

"Whatever possessed you to buy such a big truck?" Katherine asked, fastening her seat belt.

"I don't think they have any small trucks around here. Everything in this place is big—the landscape, the mountains, the men. Especially the logging trucks. And you should see Michael's horse. Life is big here. I'm probably going to have a permanent crick in my neck."

"Are you going to show me your studio?"

"Sure. You can help me fix it up. I have to decide what I need for displays."

"Maybe you can hire whoever made your bed to make your displays. And we could cut some bare branches and hang your pendants off them. For Christmas, we can get some white felt and create a seasonal theme."

Libby pulled onto the paved road and darted an amused look at her mother. "You're really okay with this, aren't you?"

Katherine smiled back. "Actually, I'm more than okay. I'm glad for you, Elizabeth. It's been a long time since I've seen you this happy. You're vibrant. Interested again."

"Interested?"

"In life," Katherine said succinctly, only to sigh and shake her head. "And I want to thank you for that."

"Thank me?"

She turned in her seat to face Libby. "Yes. Thank you for having the courage to change your life, for opening my eyes to the truth, and for giving me the courage to do the same."

Libby darted another look at her mother. "That wasn't courage. That was pure, unadulterated fear. I ran, Mom, because I was scared."

"You could have done any number of things besides run away," Katherine said, waving her hand dismissively. "You're made of stern stuff, Elizabeth. And you've reminded me that I have the power of choice, too."

"But what do . . . Mom, what are you talking about?"

Katherine studied her folded hands on her lap. "It's been a long time since I've been truly happy." She shot a worried look at Libby. "Don't get me wrong, I loved your father. But he was so larger than life that he swallowed me up. I forgot who I was, where I came from, what used to be important to me. I became so busy being Barnaby Hart's wife, I forgot to be Kate."

She straightened her shoulders and looked out the window. "My daddy always called me Kate," she whispered. "I'd forgotten that, too, until last night."

"So, what are you saying?"

Katherine looked over and smiled. "I'm saying thank you for giving me the courage to be happy again. If you don't mind, I'd like to stay here with you. I promise not to interfere in your life. Besides, I'll be too busy getting back my own life. Do you suppose Pine Creek could use a florist shop?"

Libby was speechless. But very pleased. She'd weathered the storm that had blown in from California and found a beautiful rainbow at the end. Her mother wanted to stay.

Robbie would love that Gram Katie was staying.

Ian MacKeage likely would be pleased too.

But Michael would not. She'd just gotten a beautiful new bed—and a roommate who was also her mother.

They were all sitting in her living room, happily full from another high-calorie, high-cholesterol dinner. John had Guardian snuggled on his chest and was reading the paper. Kate was gently stroking Timid on her lap while she leafed through a crafts magazine. Robbie was in the kitchen, sprawled out on the floor, teasing Trouble with a feather tied to a string.

And Father Daar, thank their luck, had chosen to bless the MacKeages with his company tonight.

Michael was leaning back on the couch, his long legs stretched out so that his socked feet rested on the lower mantel of the hearth. His eyes were closed, his hands folded over his full belly, and he looked like a contented man recovering from a hard day's work.

Libby was anything but contented. For one thing, her feet couldn't reach the hearth, so she had to rest them on Michael's legs. That was nice, but it wasn't enough.

She wanted to rest her whole body on Michael.

Preferably her naked body. She wanted to try out her new bed.

It had been more than a week since James had left and her mother had announced she was staying. Nine long, sexually frustrating days.

Libby was afraid her hormones were going to explode.

She and Michael had managed to engage in some fairly heavy petting and had worked themselves into a frenzy once or twice, to the point where Libby had been on the verge of suggesting they take a quick ride to the nearest town that had a motel.

As it was, she had two of the condoms tucked in her purse, just in case John went visiting while Robbie was in school and Michael's crew was busy up in the twelve-acre field.

So far, though, things hadn't fallen into place.

"If ya keep fidgeting, lass, I'm gonna send ya out for more wood," Michael threatened, not bothering to open his eyes.

"Mom, when are you planning to go back to California to close up your house and get things straightened away?" Libby asked.

Kate looked up from her magazine. "I thought I'd wait until after Thanksgiving."

Michael opened his eyes and sat up, dropping Libby's feet to the floor with his. "But that's my busy season," he said. "I was counting on your help in the shop. Ya told me you'd work."

"Oh, I hadn't realized things started that soon for you."

"Thanksgiving's still two weeks away," Libby interjected. "Maybe you should go now. It shouldn't take you more than a week to get things in order. You'll be back in plenty of time."

Michael shot Libby a suspicious look, and she answered him with a sweet, innocent smile. His gaze turned to molten, liquid pewter, and she kicked up her smile another notch.

"I can take ya to the airport tomorrow," he said, slowly turning away from her to give his attention to her mother.

Kate sighed, closed her magazine, and cuddled Timid under her chin. "It's such a long flight, I've been putting it off. Libby, do you think you should go back with me? To put your own things in order?"

Of course, she should. But her problems in California seemed minor right now, compared with the problem of getting Michael alone and naked and hot enough to use the three or four condoms tucked under the pillow of her new bed.

"I'm going to wait," she said, getting up and casually stretching her arms over her head. "I've been communicating with Randal Peters about breaking my contract, and he's talking to the board. They probably won't decide anything until after Christmas, anyway. And I'll have to make an appearance then and try to talk them out of suing me."

"Can they really sue you?" John asked, looking up from his paper.

"I did have a contract, and I did break it."

"What happens if they sue you?" he asked.

"It wipes out my savings. And my reputation is ruined."

"Does that mean you can't doctor again?" John asked, frowning with worry.

Libby smiled. "I'm sure a small hospital can be talked into overlooking my sin. Rural communities are always crying for skilled surgeons."

"There's a small hospital in Greenville," John offered. "And another one in Dover-Foxcroft. You could check with them."

"I might, when I feel ready to 'doctor' again. Right now, I just want to get my studio up and running. Which would go much easier," she said with feeling, darting a pointed look at Michael, then glaring at John, "if someone would tell me who made my bed so I can get him to make my displays."

John quickly raised his newspaper back in front of his face. And Robbie, who had just walked into the living room with Trouble perched on his shoulder, spun around and headed back into the kitchen. That left only Michael for her to glare at.

He smiled, stood up, and tapped her on the end of the

nose before following his son into the kitchen. "Is there any pie left?" he asked as he disappeared.

Kate laughed and also stood, settling Timid comfortably into the crook of her arm. "You might as well give up," she said with a lingering chuckle. "They've formed a conspiracy, and when males decide to bond, dynamite won't budge them."

"But what's the great secret? Whoever made the bed should be proud of his work."

"Maybe he's shy," Kate offered. "You know, the humble craftsman who does it for the love of the art, not the glory."

"I can keep his secret, if that's what he wants. I just need some displays."

"Why don't you tell Michael what you need, and he'll tell whoever made your bed?" Kate suggested, heading upstairs to her own bed.

Oh, yes, Libby thought. She wanted to tell Michael what she needed, all right, and it had nothing to do with displays. She needed him.

Michael seemed quite content with the way things were now—a little foreplay stolen at odd times, dinner together almost every evening, going to their separate work every day and their separate beds every night.

Libby had caught him staring at her on occasion, with a speculative, calculated look in his gray eyes. She couldn't tell what he was thinking; he'd been a closed book ever since James had visited him.

And that worried her. What had they talked about?

James hadn't said. He'd come back, said good-bye to her and Kate, wished them well, and left in a cloud of dusty snow.

So, Libby had asked Michael what had happened between him and James. She had gotten only a smile for an answer and a kiss that had not only shut her up but made her forget her question.

Libby poked at the fire in the hearth, pushing the dying embers to the back, banking them for the night. John rose from his chair, folded his paper, and set it over Guardian like a tent.

"We're calling it a night, I'm guessing," he said, coming over and kissing Libby on the cheek. "I just heard Michael's truck start. Thanks for the delicious supper, Libby. It's been a far sight easier going to work every day knowing I'll be getting a decent meal at night. You're a good cook."

With a wave, he walked to the truck, where Robbie waited inside.

Robbie gave her a huge good-bye wave through the windshield, opened the door for John, and scooted to the middle of the seat. Libby noticed that the driver's seat was empty.

Michael walked out of the kitchen, brushing sawdust off his jacket. "I've refilled the woodbox," he told her, reaching out and pulling her into a warm embrace. "Supper was good tonight, lass. Thank you."

"And now that you've eaten all my food, you're leaving."

"I have two trucks headed to New York tomorrow morning, and they're not loaded yet. The crew's arriving at dawn."

Libby sighed and leaned her head on his chest, wrapping her arms under his jacket and around his waist. He pulled the edges closed over her back and hugged her tightly.

"Ya seemed mighty determined to get rid of your mother tonight, lass. Any reason in particular?"

She pinched his side and smiled into his chest when he flinched. "You know why. You're killing me, Michael. I'm in danger of exploding."

His chest under her ear rumbled with gentle laughter. "Aye. And I'm anxious to see that." His arms tightened around her, all but lifting her off her feet. "Soon, Libby," he whispered into her ear, sending shivers down her back, "we'll get to try out your new bed."

"Why won't you tell me who made it?"

"Because he asked me not to."

She looked up and smiled. "Was it Santa Claus? Are you really one of his elves, sworn to secrecy?"

He kissed her on the nose. "If I say yes, then I've blown my cover, now, haven't I? Just enjoy the bed, lass, instead of turning it into a puzzle ya need to solve."

"I'd enjoy it better if I didn't have to sleep in it all by myself," she whispered, running her socked foot up the back of his leg.

"Be good," he growled. "We have an audience."

"We always have an audi—"

He kissed her soundly on the mouth despite their audience. Libby clung to him, kissed him back, and ran her foot up his leg again. His kiss turned into a growl, and she smiled into his mouth.

He might think he knew how to shut her up, but she knew how to beat him at his own game. By the time he walked to his truck, Libby was sure that steam was coming out of his ears. And his walk was a bit stiff, his fists were clenched, and whatever he'd whispered as he stepped off the porch was most definitely not something Robbie should hear.

Chapter Twenty

*I*t took *another two days* for Kate finally to leave for California. Michael had offered to drive her to the airport in Bangor, but Libby had taken her so she could do some shopping in a town that had more than two stores. She spent the entire day in Bangor after seeing her mother off, and the back of her truck was now filled to the roof with shopping bags.

Libby decided it was time she turned her house into a home. She'd already talked with her young landlord and gotten his permission to move some of the old furnishings up to the attic. Libby respected Mary Sutter, and all the Sutters who had come before her, but it was important that she put her own signature on the house.

And she was starting with the bedroom.

Her beautiful new bed was her inspiration. Moose were such ugly creatures they were actually quite endearing, with their massive antlers and dangling goatees, their long, powerful legs and oversized heads. And the fir trees on the bed, painted such a rich, vibrant green, had made Libby decide on a woodsy, outdoor theme.

Somewhere in the back of her truck was a shopping bag containing flannel sheets that had pine tassels and pinecones printed on them. She'd even found a new quilt made of appliquéd blocks of loons, moose, black bears, and chickadees—which Libby had learned were Maine's state bird. She'd bought a checkered dust ruffle, pillow shams, and several matching towel sets.

She'd also bought two new lamps for the sides of the bed, both made from birch tree with carved chickadees perched on the branches. There was a wool rug someplace back there, a framed print of a moose feeding in a bog in the morning mist, and new curtains that matched the dust ruffle.

But her most exciting purchases, and ironically the least expensive, were the glow-in-the-dark stars she'd found at a neat little shop in downtown Bangor. She couldn't wait to get home, stick them up on the bedroom ceiling, turn out the lights, and fall asleep under the stars.

Libby focused past the wiper blades as they tried to keep up with the driving rain that had been pelting the truck for the last twenty miles. It was starting to sound more like sleet than rain, and she was glad she'd made it through Pine Creek before the roads glazed over to ice. Only three miles to go. The whole ride home, the radio had said that a nor'easter was coming up the coast and that the rain would turn to snow in the mountains first, probably by nightfall. It was night now, and the weatherman was being proved right.

Michael had given her his cell phone before she'd left, and he had called her three times already today. The last time, he had been rather blunt about getting her butt in the truck and getting home before the storm hit.

But she hadn't minded his macho attitude, simply because she couldn't seem to get enough of the guy.

Maybe they could go out on an actual date tomorrow night. She'd spend tomorrow rearranging her room, making it pretty and romantic. She'd take a nice, long bubble bath, paint her toenails, and even dig out some of her makeup.

She was a modern woman; she would ask Michael out. She would pick him up, pay for dinner, and bring him back to her bachelorette pad so he could thank her properly for the nice evening.

She might even buy him a whopping bouquet of flowers.

Libby sighed with relief when she finally pulled into the garage. She jumped out and ran to the open garage door, looking through the wind-driven mix of snow and sleet toward the chicken coop. Damn. There was no help for it, the chickens needed tending. She pulled up the hood on her jacket and sprinted across the yard, slamming through the coop door. She waved away a flurry of feathers from the startled birds.

"Sorry, girls. Well, aren't we all nice and cozy in here? Got any eggs for me tonight?"

They blinked in answer and immediately started pecking her muddy shoes. Libby changed the water in their dish and refilled their food pan. She scooped up six huge eggs, tucked them into her pockets, and ran back out into the storm.

She was almost to the garage when she slipped. She windmilled her arms and shuffled her feet for balance, and still she fell with a bone-jarring thud, flat on her back in the middle of a muddy puddle of slush. She heard something crack, and it took Libby a full minute to realize that the eggs had broken, not her bones.

Her head throbbed. Her shoulders hurt almost as much as her teeth did. Her hands were scraped. And when she tried to wipe the mud out of her eyes, she was nearly blinded by sleet.

"Well, hell. Welcome home, Libby," she muttered, rolling over and slowly inching her way back to her feet.

She squished into the garage, took off her muddy shoes, and squished into the house.

Blessed warmth greeted her. Warmth, candlelight, and the smell of burnt food.

Libby couldn't seem to move—either because she was too busy gawking at Michael or because the room wouldn't stop spinning.

He was sitting at her kitchen table, half hidden behind a vase of roses sitting between two glowing candles burned nearly down to their nubs. An open bottle of wine stood beside his fist, which was curled around a nearly empty crystal flute.

"Ya had five minutes left before I came hunting for ya," he said softly as he slowly stood up. "Ya're damn lucky, Libby, that ya got home when ya did."

Part of her wanted to throw herself into his arms. But instinct made Libby want to run back outside rather than face the storm brewing in here. She stood where she was, dripping all over the floor, and fought back tears.

"I-I fell down," she hoarsely whispered. "And you ruined my surprise. I'm supposed to call you and . . . and ask you out and buy you flowers and take you to dinner," she continued, even as he rushed over and snapped on the kitchen light. "And I was paying for it, and you were supposed to pay me back—here, in my new bed."

He silently started running his hands over every inch of her freezing, muddy body, nodding agreement with every declaration she made.

"I had it all planned," she continued, awkwardly trying to help him strip off her clothes. "I was going to paint my toenails. I've got stars. We were going to sleep under them. In the pinecones. With—with the chickadees."

"Ya've hit your head," he said, running his fingers through her scalp. "Aye. That's a bump. Come on, lass, I've got to get ya cleaned up."

The room started spinning again when he swept her into his arms. "You spoiled my surprise," she said, trying to remember if she'd told him that already.

"Nay, lass," he softly contradicted, setting her on the hamper in the bathroom. "Ya spoiled mine. Hold on here," he said, wrapping her fingers over the sink so she wouldn't fall. He started the shower and turned back to her, getting down on his knees and gently feeling the bump on her head again.

"Now you kneel," she whispered. "You were supposed to do that tomorrow night."

"I will," he promised, brushing his thumbs across her muddy cheeks. "How did ya fall, Libby?"

"I nearly drowned in a puddle. I broke my eggs."

"But not yar beautiful neck. That's all that matters."

"Who made my bed?"

"Santa Claus."

"I'm writing him a letter. I want a bureau for Christmas. You have a beautiful chest."

He'd taken off his shirt while keeping an eye on her, still kneeling in front of her. Libby reached out and touched his chest. Then she sighed and leaned forward, intent to kiss his right nipple.

He gently cupped her head, catching her before her lips could land. "Ya have a concussion," he told her.

"I do not. I'm a doctor. I would know that."

"Well, something's rattled yar brain, lass. Come on, into

the shower ya go," he said, lifting her off the hamper and standing her in the tub.

Libby yelped when the warm water hit her, and she would have fallen if he hadn't been holding her up. But she settled down when the heat slowly started to penetrate her bones, and the fog in her head finally cleared as the heavenly spray washed rivers of mud down the drain.

"I-I'm okay now," she whispered, suddenly embarrassed to find herself being bathed like a child. "I can finish."

He ignored her petition and squirted shampoo into her hair, gently working it into a lather, being careful of the bump on her head.

"I've been calling the cell phone for the last hour," he said as he worked, his voice soft, but Libby could still hear the bite in his words. "Why didn't ya answer?"

"I thought I heard it ringing. It's in the back of the truck, in one of the shopping bags, I think."

His sigh raised goose bumps on her skin. "Libby, ya should have stopped and found it. Ya scared the hell out of me, lass."

Keeping her eyes closed so she wouldn't get soap in them was making her dizzy again. Libby held on to Michael's belt with one hand while she foolishly held her other hand over her breasts.

The water suddenly stopped, and Michael lifted her out of the tub and quickly wrapped her in a towel. He threw another towel over her head as he swept her against his chest and carried her into the bedroom.

Candlelight flickered through the room, and dozens of roses tucked into vases sat on every available surface. Libby's tears finally spilled free at the realization that Michael really could be romantic.

Michael set her on the bed, pulled the towel away, and tenderly kissed her on the cheek. "Don't ya dare cry," he whispered, slowly rubbing her hair dry. "You're not hurt, I no longer want to throttle ya, and Santa Claus won't bring ya a bureau if ya cry all over his bed."

"I ruined your surprise," she croaked, throwing her arms around him and burying her face in his chest. "You bought me flowers. And candles. You do know how to be romantic, and I ruined it."

"Shhh," he crooned, laying them both down on the bed and gently tucking her up against his side. "Only supper is ruined, lass. The rest of the night is ours to enjoy. Do ya still have stars in your head?"

"No. They're in the truck."

He pulled back, his eyes probing and suspicious. "In the truck?" he repeated.

"With the chickadees," she added, snuggling against him and closing her eyes. She yawned and patted his chest, letting her fingers rest in the silky hair around his nipples. "You have a beautiful chest."

He threw one leg over her hip and pulled her against him. "You have a beautiful chest, too," he said with another sigh. "You may sleep, Libby, but I'm going to wake you up every hour."

"The condoms are in the drawer."

"To see if ya have a concussion, lass," he said with yet another sigh, this one exasperated.

"I don't."

"I'm glad. But I'm waking ya up, anyway."

Libby lifted her head. "Are you going to sneak out again before morning?"

He tucked her back against his chest and held her there. "Nay. Robbie is staying at the Dolans' tonight. He's going with Leysa and Rose to Bangor tomorrow to do some shopping."

"I shopped in Bangor. My truck's full."

"Aye. Full of stars, ya said."

"And other stuff," Libby mumbled, stifling another yawn.

Michael rearranged her so that her mouth faced up and her breasts pushed against him instead.

"Are ya warming up?" he asked, pulling the quilt over her back. "And are ya hurt anywhere else, other than your head?"

"No, but I am going to ache in the morning."

"Nay. I'll see what I can do about your aches . . . in the morning, lass. Now, go to sleep."

"Promise you'll be here?"

"Oh, yes."

With his words settling over her like a gentle caress, Libby snuggled against Michael and fell asleep in her new bed, content that she was safe from the storm and people-eating puddles.

Michael stared at the ceiling, listening to the gentle rise and fall of Libby's breathing. Sleet pelted the window as the storm continued to rage with blatant disregard for anyone unlucky enough to be caught outside.

Sweat broke out on his forehead. He had just come to the end of his patience when he'd heard Libby drive into the garage. He'd been through two hours of hell waiting for her to come home, and the five minutes it had taken her to come inside had been filled with fantasies of throttling the woman for scaring him.

How the hell could he have guessed she'd go check on the chickens first? And that she'd throttle herself before he could?

Guilt was a terrible emotion but one he was sadly familiar with. He'd failed two women in his life, and he had to take extra care that he didn't fail Libby.

Michael rubbed his chest where she'd hit him with the

snowball almost two weeks ago. She didn't know it, but she had struck him square in the heart—and left a permanent mark that time would not only deepen but spread, until Libby was so much a part of him that he wouldn't know how to live without her.

He already couldn't live without her.

Stars, he thought with a silent chuckle. What had she been talking about? And a date tomorrow night? She'd planned to ask him out, and then she'd intended to bring him back here and seduce him. In her new bed. Which Santa Claus had made.

Well, Santa Claus was suddenly curious.

Michael slowly inched out of bed, carefully wrapping the quilt around Libby and putting one of the pillows up against her back where he had been. He walked softly into the kitchen, put on his boots, and headed into the garage. He closed the huge garage door to keep out the storm and then opened the back door of her truck.

The interior light came on but was shadowed by shopping bags stacked against it. Michael whistled and shook his head in amazement.

No wonder Libby hadn't been able to stay awake. She didn't have a concussion, she was beat tired from shopping. It was a good thing the lady owned a full-sized truck. She needed one for her obvious buying addiction.

Michael started pulling out shopping bags and carrying them into the house, making four trips before he found the chickadees. They were perched on lamps, life-sized little critters flitting around on a birch trunk almost two feet tall. He carried the two lamps into the living room and set one at either end of the mantel. He plugged them in and turned them on, then stepped back to see how they looked.

They looked damned good to him, their light casting a

soft glow on the smooth river stones. Satisfied that he'd found Libby's chickadees a new home, Michael spun on his heel and went back out to the truck.

He tossed the rolled carpet over his shoulder and grabbed two more shopping bags. A thin, colorful package fell out of one of them. He picked it up off the floor of the truck, turned it over, and smiled.

Stars. A gross of stars, the label said, that glowed in the dark and would stick to most surfaces. Michael slid the package into the bag and went back into the kitchen. He dropped the bags onto the table on the way by and continued into the living room, setting the carpet in front of the hearth and rolling it out.

More chickadees, as well as other woodland birds. Perfect. It matched the lamps and fit nicely between the hearth and the couch.

Libby might have ruined his surprise tonight, but when she woke up in the morning, he'd have another one waiting for her. He went back to the kitchen and started unpacking all the shopping bags, pulling out sheets, curtains, a package that said it was a dust ruffle—whatever the hell that was—and towels.

But the stars kept drawing his attention. What did Libby want with stars? He opened them, pouring them out onto the table. One hundred forty-four, all varying in size. He read the label again and slowly started to laugh. Stick to the ceiling, the instructions said.

Libby wanted to sleep under the stars. Well, dammit, she would. Tonight. Michael kicked off his boots and quietly walked into the bedroom, leaning over Libby to make sure she was sound asleep. He covered her face with the edge of the quilt before turning on the light, then carefully reached up and started sticking the stars on the ceiling.

He made the Big Dipper over the north end of the bed, then moved to the foot and laid out Orion. He clustered several of the stars in a long row to mimic the Milky Way and set out as many constellations as he could make.

He needed more stars. There was still half the ceiling to fill. He stepped off the bed and went back to the kitchen table, dumping out whatever shopping bags were left. He found six more packages of stars.

Six? Hell, had she planned on doing the whole house?

Michael sat down at the table and poured the last of the wine into his glass, took a long drink, and stared at all the stuff Libby had bought.

She was nesting. Sitting in front of him were all the signs of a woman settling in. Libby had adopted Maine as her new home and was surrounding herself with its trappings.

She won't stay, James Kessler had said.

From the looks of the stuff she'd bought, Michael knew that he no longer had to worry about Libby's intentions. She was roosting like an old hen sitting a nest.

He was glad. He'd been walking a fine line for two weeks, between being afraid to push her and wanting to get heavy-handed to make her stay. Michael gulped down the rest of his wine and stood up. If the woman wanted to make herself at home, he'd help her do it.

With Trouble, Guardian, and Timid more interested in playing in the empty shopping bags than helping, it took Michael nearly the entire night to finish the job. He washed and folded Libby's new sheets, set out her towels, put her tablecloth on the kitchen table, tossed her new pillows onto the couch, placed the candles she'd bought in strategic places, and hung the huge print of the moose over the mantel.

And he stuck up every damned one of her glowing stars on every ceiling in the downstairs of the house.

It was just daybreak when he finally crawled into bed, pulling Libby up against his tired body in the hopes of getting a bit of sleep himself.

Aye, he'd done a good job of feathering her nest.

"Are ya going to pretend you're asleep much longer? 'Cause if ya are, I'm writing to Santa and telling him not to bring ya anything for Christmas."

Libby now knew where Robbie had picked up the habit of saying *'cause* all the time. "Shhh," she whispered, snuggling against Michael's warm body. "I'm savoring the fact that you're still here."

"I'm still here," he said thickly. "And damned thankful you are as well. Ya scared me last night, Libby. You were supposed to get here before the storm did."

Libby finally opened her eyes and found Michael leaning on his elbow, staring down at her with an accusing glare. "My brain's still a bit foggy, but didn't we cover this subject last night?"

"In part," he agreed, rolling over and pinning her in place. "But I think it's important we go over it again. Libby, ya have to respect the weather and plan your business around it."

"I thought I had." She reached up and ran a finger down the side of his face. "I'm sorry I worried you, Michael. I won't do it again. And I'll keep the cell phone with me next time."

He seemed surprised by her apology and a bit suspicious. He kissed her hungrily as he slid his hand under the blanket and found one of her naked breasts.

"Ah . . . did we . . . you and I . . . did we make love last night, Michael?"

He reared back, both brows lifting in question. "Ya don't remember?" he asked, running a hand over the bump on her head. "You really did take a terrible fall."

"I remember how you took care of me. But I fell asleep. You . . . you said you'd wake me up every hour. Did you?"

He let out a sigh that moved her hair. "I think I've just been insulted." He shook his head. "Ya don't remember anything? Not even telling me where ya'd put the condoms?"

Libby looked at him in horror. "I . . . we did . . . you used *all* of them? Even the two in my purse?"

She bit her lower lip to keep it from trembling. Dammit, they'd finally christened her new bed, and she didn't remember. "Do—do you have any more?" she whispered.

"I might. Why?"

"I thought we could . . . ah . . . do it again. I'm wide awake, Michael. I'll remember this time, I promise."

"I don't know," he said, lifting his gaze to the headboard as if he were thinking about it. "I'll probably disappoint ya so badly that you'll forget again."

Libby reached up, grabbed his hair, and forced him to look at her. "You're lying," she accused, watching him closely. "You didn't touch me last night."

His expression turned wounded. "I touched every inch of ya last night, lass," he whispered gutturally, sending shivers down her spine. "I distinctly remember kissing that cute little birthmark ya have on your left hip."

Her shivers turned to prickles of heat as erotic visions rose in her mind. Oh, why couldn't she remember?

Maybe she did have a concussion.

"Will you kiss it again?" she asked, running her finger down the side of his face, stopping at his mouth and tracing the curve of his bottom lip. "And this one?" she said, pointing to the little mole on her right shoulder. "I'm sure I would have remembered if you had kissed that one. I'm particularly sensitive there."

His deep pewter eyes lit up, reflecting laughter that finally escaped as he rolled over, taking her with him, until Libby found herself sitting astride his waist.

"Maybe it would work better if you kissed my sensitive places," he said thickly, lifting his hips, causing Libby to gasp when his erection touched her intimately. "That way, ya might remember."

"But we used up all the condoms . . . didn't we?"

He nodded toward the nightstand, and Libby leaned over and opened the drawer. Four rows of packets sprang out.

The man had stuffed a dozen condoms in her nightstand?

She sat up and looked at him, her own eyes narrowed in suspicion. "Are we expecting company?" she asked softly. "Or are you just optimistic?"

"Now, lass," he said, rolling them over until she was pinned beneath his body. Shaking with laughter, he said, "I don't want them at home where Robbie can find them and start asking questions. I swear, that boy has more questions than a whole classroom of kids."

He smiled, kissed her on the nose, and wiggled his eyebrows. "But I must say he is right about one thing. Ya do have perky breasts, Miss Hart."

"What?"

Michael kissed her mortified face, letting his lips linger on her scorching cheeks.

"He . . . Robbie said I have . . . oh, God," she hissed, trying to melt into the bed. She pushed Michael's mouth away and covered her face with the pillow. "I don't even want to know how the topic of my breasts came up," she muttered.

Michael pulled the pillow away and threw it onto the floor. "It seems Frankie Boggs thinks small breasts are okay if they're perky," he informed her between kisses.

"Who is Frankie Boggs?"

"The class authority on women," he returned, just as his hands ran up her ribs and covered her perky breasts. "Being a doctor, maybe you should offer to teach a sex education class at school," he suggested, sliding his thumbs across both of her nipples.

Libby sucked in her breath and tried to keep up with the conversation. "To—to second-graders?" she squeaked, just as he lowered his head and took one of her nipples in his mouth.

"Shut up, Michael," she said with a gasp, wrapping her arms around his neck and holding him against her. "Just shut up and make love to me."

He sighed as he moved from one nipple to the other. "If ya insist, lass," he muttered against her skin. "Just try and pay attention this time."

She'd pay attention, all right. She also intended to participate.

With slow and tender attention to detail, Michael and Libby finally christened her new bed. They messed up the bed until only the bottom sheet remained, and that was starting to pull from the corners.

In full light, unhurried by worldly obligations, they explored every inch of each other's body. Libby found more than one sensitive spot on Michael, while he discovered a few more on her.

The foreplay they'd gotten so good at these past two weeks now seemed to last forever, until Libby finally reached over her head and grabbed the hooves of the moose on her headboard. Michael knelt between her thighs, staring down at her with eyes of liquid, swirling metal, sheathed himself in protection, and then slowly lowered his body onto hers.

"Ah, lass, but ya please me," he whispered, carefully entering her, his mouth covering her moan.

Sensations erupted as Libby felt herself stretching, slowly accepting his gentle invasion. She wrapped her legs around his waist and closed her eyes, holding on to the headboard as he set a gentle rhythm that rocked her with pleasure.

But as nice as it was, it just wasn't enough.

"I guess this bed isn't sturdy after all," she whispered in challenge. "You seem to be worried it will break."

He stopped.

Libby smiled up at him. "I won't break, either, Michael."

He gave a small growl, covered her mouth, and moved again, this time with a bit more enthusiasm. Libby clung to his shoulders and moaned her pleasure out loud.

He stopped again. "Don't do that," he hissed, his brow covered with sweat, his eyes dark with passion, and his arms trembling as he held himself off her.

"Do what?"

"That thing," he whispered desperately. "There, that," he hissed, pulling nearly out of her. "I want this to last."

Libby's muscles involuntarily tightened, and Michael hissed again, pulling completely out and rolling onto his back.

"That's a terrible thing to do to a man who's trying to hold on to his control."

Libby turned on her elbow and patted his chest. "I'm not doing it on purpose. I'm not even sure what 'it' is."

He picked her up as if she were a feather and carefully slid her on top of him. Libby sucked in her breath, dug her nails into his chest, and moaned. She set the pace this time and indulged herself in this newfound freedom to wiggle and move and drive them both mad.

And she was doing a fine job of it, until Michael reached down and caressed her, just as he had that first night in front of the hearth.

Libby's last coherent thought as she climaxed was that the moose on her headboard had a silly smile on its face.

Chapter Twenty-one

"*You have six toes* on each foot," Libby told Michael, staring down at the bottom of the tub since she couldn't look anywhere else without getting a face full of soap.

"Nay!" he shouted in horror. "I do!"

He also looked down, his hip pushing Libby into the shower wall. The spray from the showerhead hit her square in the face. She turned so she wouldn't drown and gave Michael a sharp poke with her elbow to keep him from crushing her.

"This isn't working," she sputtered. "You're hogging all the water, and I'm getting squished."

He tried to pick her up to set her in front of him, but she slipped through his fingers like unset Jell-O. Libby shrieked, scrambled to stay upright, and got another mouthful of water. Michael quickly used one hand to protect her head from slamming into the wall and wrapped his other arm around her waist before she could fall.

"And you worry about us wearing a helmet," he said with a laugh. "You're a bit accident-prone, aren't ya?"

"I am not. This shower wasn't built for two people," she sputtered, finally giving up and stepping out of the tub. She peeked back past the curtain at Michael. "Not when one of those people is a giant."

He quickly rinsed off, having to duck to rinse his hair, and stepped out beside her. "Your turn now," he said, holding the curtain back. "I'll just stand here and watch, to make sure ya don't kill yourself."

A loud knocking suddenly came from the kitchen.

Libby gasped and grabbed a towel to wrap around herself.

Michael just closed his eyes. "I know that sound," he said with a sigh. "That's a cane knocking against your door."

Libby didn't gasp again, she shrieked. "Oh, my God. You have to hide," she said, shoving at Michael. "No. Wait. Get dressed, and crawl out the bedroom window."

He gave her an incredulous look. Then he took his time wrapping his towel around his waist before he sauntered into the kitchen to greet their urgently knocking, uninvited visitor.

Libby ran into her bedroom and disappeared inside her closet, not coming out until she was fully dressed. When she walked past a mirror on her way to the kitchen, she noticed her hair was standing on end and she still had soap in one ear.

Dammit. Why did Father Daar have to come to breakfast this morning? If he really was a wizard, he wasn't a very bright one. He was always popping up at the most embarrassing times.

Libby stared at herself in the mirror, watching her face suddenly fill with horror. Oh, God. He knew. Father Daar knew about her gift—and he was in the kitchen, with Michael, who *didn't* know about it.

And he never could know. Michael would think she was a freak or something—an aberration. And he'd probably never let her anywhere near his son again.

She had to talk to Father Daar before he said something. Michael still had to get dressed, and that was her chance. Libby took a deep breath, rubbed the soap from her ear, and ran her fingers through her hair. Suddenly, having Michael greeting the priest wearing only a towel was the least of her worries. So, as calmly as possible and with a smile plastered on her face, Libby finally walked into the kitchen.

"Good morning, Father," she said, going to the counter and starting the coffee. "Did you weather the storm okay?"

Both men eyed her suspiciously.

"Michael, why don't you get dressed while I make breakfast?" she instructed as she sliced the bread. "And could you go check and see if the girls gave us any more eggs?"

He appeared to be rooted to the floor, water dripping from his hair, his arms crossed over his chest, and his towel barely clinging to his hips by one small tuck of its corner.

"I already checked yar girls," Father Daar said, pulling eggs from his pockets. "And I only found these three," he said, glaring at Michael as if he were the uninvited guest. "I'm hoping ya got more in the fridge, 'cause I'm mighty hungry this morning."

Libby shot her own glare at Michael, nodding her head toward the bedroom, silently telling him to go get dressed. He smiled, tucked his thumbs into the waist of his towel, and slowly strolled into the bedroom.

Libby waited until the door shut, then went up to Father Daar just as he was opening the fridge. She grabbed him by the arms, forcing him to face her. "I don't want you to say anything to Michael about my gift," she whispered. "I don't want him to know."

Daar raised one bushy white eyebrow. "And why would that be?" he asked, not bothering to whisper at all.

"He'll think I'm crazy."

"MacBain?" he asked in surprise. "Nay, girl. He's the last person who would think such a thing."

"I'm not taking that chance. Promise me you won't say anything."

Both of his brows rose. "Do ya truly think ya can keep something like that a secret?" he asked, sounding incredulous. "Libby, hiding yar gift from MacBain will cause ya far more trouble than the gift itself. Do ya have any idea what the man is capable of if his temper gets riled?" He visibly shuddered and stepped back, out of her grip. "I'd rather not be a party to that, if ya don't mind."

"I'm not trying to deceive him. I'm trying to protect him."

"From what?" Daar asked, frowning.

"From me. From whatever this is I've got."

"It's not a disease," he snapped. "It's a gift."

"It might as well be a disease," she snapped back, getting a bit angry herself.

He sighed, scratched his beard, and studied her with sagacious regard. "Libby," he earnestly began. "Trying to hide it from MacBain will only compound your troubles. It takes a powerful lot of energy to keep a secret. Energy that could be better spent understanding your gift instead of trying to ignore it."

"What are ya trying to ignore?" Michael asked, tucking his shirt into his belt as he walked out of the bedroom and over to the counter. He poured himself a cup of coffee. "What should Libby ignore?" he repeated when neither of them answered. He turned and looked at Libby, lifting one brow in question.

"Ah—the mystery of who made my bed," she quickly prevaricated, shooting a glare at Daar when he snorted. "Father Daar said I should just let it go. That it probably really was made by Santa, and if I keep pushing the issue, I'll never get my matching bureau."

She was blathering like an idiot, probably because she knew Michael knew damned well she was lying. He sipped his coffee, eyeing her over the rim of his cup, and then turned back to the counter and popped the bread into the toaster.

"I take my coffee black," Daar said, sitting down at the table. "In case ya forgot how I like it," he added, giving Libby a pointed frown. "Did ya get your mama on the plane yesterday?"

"Yes. She said she'll be back by Thanksgiving."

"Well, that will give ya a few days of privacy," the old priest said with a snicker, looking down at the table. "I like yar tablecloth. Is it new?"

Libby had just started to pour his coffee when he asked his question. She turned toward the table and gasped when she saw the blue checkered tablecloth that was decorated with tiny green Christmas trees and bright red balls perched on their points.

"Wh-what is that doing here?" she asked, looking at Michael. "Where did you find it?"

"In your truck," he told her, buttering the toast. "I unloaded everything for ya last night." He popped two more slices of bread into the toaster and pointed the butter knife at the ceiling. "And I put up all your damned stars," he said, turning fully to face her, setting his hands on his hips, the butter knife in his fist. "Do ya have any idea how many seven gross of stars are?"

Libby looked up, and her mouth fell open. Her kitchen ceiling was covered in stars. They were barely visible in the morning light, but come nightfall, they'd probably blind her. She turned her gaping stare on Michael, who was grinning like a boy waiting to be praised, his arms opened slightly, as if he expected Libby to throw herself at him in gratitude.

"You—ah—you put them all up? All seven packages?" she whispered. "In my kitchen?"

"And the living room and your bedroom. Hell, I even put some in the bathroom."

"B-but why?"

"To help ya nest."

"Nest?"

"Aye, nest," he told her, sounding a bit defensive. "Ya went shopping for women's stuff, so that means ya're nesting."

One or both of them were confused, and Libby was afraid it was her. "Nesting?" she repeated.

"I think he means he's trying to help ya settle in, girl," Father Daar said, standing up and grabbing his forgotten cup of coffee out of her hand.

"Settle in?" she parroted, shaking her head as she continued to gape at Michael. "Wh-what else did you do?" she asked, scanning the kitchen.

"I set up yar lamps over the mantel, and put the rug in front of the couch. And I hung that picture of the moose over the hearth."

Libby walked into the living room, stood behind the couch, and stared. There was the print of the moose, hanging over the fireplace, with her chickadee lamps on either side of it. The bird rug was on the floor, right where Michael said it would be, and the quilt she'd intended for her bed was lying folded across the back of the couch.

She looked up. The ceiling was covered with stars.

Libby didn't know whether to weep or laugh. She'd planned to use two packages of stars in her bedroom, and the rest were Christmas gifts for Robbie and the MacKeage girls. The tablecloth was another Christmas gift, for John Bigelow. And the candles that Michael had thoughtfully placed on the end tables—helping her nest—were for Grace.

"Ya bought some beautiful things, lass," Michael said, moving up behind her, wrapping his arms around her, and pulling her against his chest. "And now you've turned this house into your nest."

"Y-yes, it seems I have. With your help," she quickly tacked on, relaxing into him and covering his arms with her hands. "Thank you."

There was nothing else she could say. He must have worked all night putting up, what? More than a thousand stars. She didn't have the heart to tell him the difference. So she turned in his embrace, wrapped her arms around his neck, and kissed his throat—since that was all she could reach.

"The toast is burning out here," Father Daar hollered. "And the frying pan is smoking."

"Wasn't there something ya wanted to ask me this morning?" Michael said, ignoring Father Daar, not letting her go. "Ya mentioned dinner last night."

"Oh, yeah. I thought we could go to dinner and maybe dancing or a movie or something," she whispered, looking at his third shirt button. "If—if you'd like."

"Are ya asking me out on a date, Miss Hart?" he asked, lifting her chin.

His eyes were a deep, warm pewter, filled with a laughing tenderness that bolstered Libby's courage. Why was it so hard to ask the man out, especially considering how intimate they'd been less than an hour ago? She moved out of his embrace and headed into the kitchen, giving him a sassy smile over her shoulder.

"I'll pick you up at six," she told him. "Dress casual."

Father Daar was standing by the door, putting on his coat and glaring at her. "I'm not hungry anymore," he grumbled. "I hate burnt toast."

"Oh, come sit down," Libby said, moving the smoking frying pan off the burner. "I'll make you some new toast."

"I don't know," he said petulantly, running his hand over the top burl on his cherrywood cane, his old, weathered face set in the pout of a recalcitrant child.

"I'll show you a wonderful surprise if you do," Libby offered next. "Something I think you'll find interesting."

That piqued his curiosity, as she knew it would. He might be old, and he might be a wizard, but he was still human—wasn't he?

"What is it?" he asked, taking off his jacket and hanging it back on the peg. He walked over to the table, got his coffee cup, went to the counter, and refilled it. He suddenly stopped on his way to the table and eyed her suspiciously. "It's not one of them blasphemous books on magic, is it, that ya found in a bookstore?" He shook his head. "There's only one book that's worth anything, and I already got it."

Libby moved out of the way so Michael could wipe out the frying pan and start the eggs. "You have a book?" she asked, intrigued. "Of spells?" She ignored Michael's snort and sat down at the table beside Daar. "Will you show it to me?"

"I might," Daar said, his chin lifted in challenge. "If yar surprise really is interesting."

Libby looked down at the cane he'd hooked over the edge of the table. "Did you make that?" she asked.

He frowned at her, his expression guarded. "Aye. From a sapling that grew on Fraser Mountain. Why?"

"Do you suppose that's where my cherrywood stick came from?" she asked Michael, turning to look at him. "The one Mary brought me?"

She quickly turned back when Daar gasped. "What stick?" he all but shouted, standing up. "Robbie's pet brought ya a cherrywood stick?" he asked, looking around the kitchen. "Where is it? What does it look like?"

Libby was confused by his reaction. "It's on the mantel," she said, heading into the living room. "It's about two feet long, it's thick, and it looks very old."

Daar all but ran over her trying to get to the mantel first.

Libby jumped up onto the bottom hearth to get the stick, but it wasn't there. She looked down at Daar, who was wringing his hands and dancing from foot to foot.

"Well?" he said, excitedly. "Where is it?"

"I—er—it was right here. Michael," she shouted to the kitchen. "Did you move the stick when you decorated last night? Where did you put it?"

Michael stepped back from the stove to look into the living room. "It wasn't on the mantel last night," he said softly.

"Where is it?" Daar repeated, going through the living room and looking in every nook and cranny. He stopped and glared at Libby. "Tell me again exactly what it looked like. Was it this long?" he asked, holding his hands two feet apart. "And thick, ya say? Did it have burls all through it?"

Libby jumped down from the hearth. "Yes. It was riddled with knots. But I don't know where it is, Father. The last time I saw it, it was sitting on the mantel."

"And MacBain knew it was there?" he asked harshly, coming to stand in front of her. "He saw it when Mary brought it to ya?"

"Y-yes. He's the one who put it on the mantel."

Libby followed Daar's gaze as he stared into the kitchen. Michael was stirring the eggs in the frying pan, not paying them the least bit of attention.

"Why are you so frantic about that stick, Father? It's only an old piece of cherrywood."

"It's my staff," he said softly, his eyes misting and his expression pained. "I lost it more than eight years ago and only realized it still existed five years ago. I've been searching for it since then."

"Your staff?" Libby whispered in awe. "Can it do what your cane can? Like when I held it?"

He shook his head. "Nay, it's far more powerful than that," he said in a reverent whisper. "It's more than fifteen hundred years old. And MacBain knows where it is," he said, darting a glare toward Michael, then looking back at her, shaking his head. "He's hidden it from me. He knows the power it holds."

Libby was growing more intrigued by the minute.

And a mite scared.

"Michael knows you're a wizard?"

"Of course he does," Daar said. "Why do ya think he's hidden my staff?"

"Why?"

"Because, like the MacKeage, he doesn't want me to have the power."

"What power?" Libby asked, getting more annoyed and even more confused. "What is he afraid of? And what MacKeage? Do you mean Greylen? What's he got to do with this?"

Daar snapped his mouth shut and stomped into the kitchen. He picked up his thin cherrywood cane and strode over to the coat pegs. He put on his coat, walked to the door, but stopped and pointed his cane at Michael.

"Ya destroy that piece of wood, MacBain, and I won't rest until ya're burning in hell. Robbie won't stay a child forever, and then I'll be free to plague ya."

He turned and pointed at Libby.

Michael silently stepped between them.

But Daar spoke anyway. "Ya talk him into giving me back my staff, girl, or ya just might be joining him."

That said, Daar turned and walked out the door, slamming it shut with enough force to rattle the windows.

Silence settled over the kitchen.

"W-were we just cursed?" Libby whispered, rubbing her arms as she hugged herself against the sudden chill of the room.

Michael turned to her. "Nay. He's a priest. He's unable to condemn anyone. People can only do that to themselves."

"Why won't you give him his staff back?"

"Because it's better for all of us if he doesn't ever get his hands on it. His power is only as good as his staff, and as long as Daar has only that thin cane, we are safe."

"Safe? Michael, what are you talking about? What are you afraid of?"

He said nothing, only stared at her with deep, unreadable gray eyes. Libby hugged herself tighter, suddenly feeling sick to her stomach. Michael stepped forward, and Libby stepped back. But he reached out and pulled her into his arms, held her tightly against him, and rested his chin on her head.

"I'll make a deal with ya, lass. When ya're ready to tell me what happened to that woman and boy back in California, I'll tell ya why Daar must never get back his power."

"That's blackmail," she muttered into his chest.

"Nay," he said with a sigh, nearly crushing her. "That's

just how things are. Secrets have no place between us, Libby. As long as they exist, they have the power to hurt us."

"I can't . . . I have to think about it, Michael."

His arms tightened around her. "Shhh. It's okay, lass. I can be patient." He pulled back and smiled down at her. "But can you?"

"Maybe I won't wait for you to tell me your secrets," she said sassily, trying to lighten the mood. "I intend to find out who made my bed, and then I'm going to find out what you and Greylen MacKeage are hiding. I'm a surgeon, remember? We're very good at putting puzzles together."

"Then make sure ya put one more piece into your puzzle," he told her softly, tapping the end of her nose. "Why would Mary bring the staff to you instead of to me or Greylen?"

And with those cryptic words, Michael kissed her soundly on the mouth, grabbed his jacket off the peg, and headed out the door—closing it softly behind him.

Libby stared at the curtain floating back into place and wondered if their date was still on for tonight. She looked up with a sigh and sighed again when she saw all the stars.

They did go on their date, and over the next two weeks, they spent quite a bit of time together. Libby and Michael and Robbie and John quietly slipped into the comfortable routine of having dinner together every night. Sometimes they ate at Libby's house, and sometimes Libby went to theirs and cooked.

And every night after dinner, Michael would either stay and help her do the dishes and make love to her, or he'd walk her back to her house and make love to her.

Libby had discovered two things about the man; he really was romantic, and he could keep a secret better than the Pentagon.

It was Thanksgiving morning, and she was no closer to finding out who'd made her bed and even more stymied by whatever else it was that Michael was hiding.

And as much as she hated to admit it, Daar was right. Secrets took energy, both to keep and to uncover. Libby had been going nuts for the last two weeks. The only time she hadn't been dwelling on what Michael was keeping from her was when they were both naked, in bed, making love.

But, as nice as that was, it wasn't enough.

And therein lay her dilemma. Michael had the patience of Job. He hadn't asked her again what had happened in California, and it was confounding to Libby how he seemed to be able to set the problem aside and get on with the business of life.

She'd hunted everywhere for that blasted cherrywood staff and worried that Michael might have destroyed it already. She even caught herself walking into the woods and calling Mary's name, crazily thinking she actually could talk to the bird. But Mary was keeping to herself lately; only Robbie mentioned seeing her, and even then only on rare occasions.

When she wasn't trying to uncover Michael's secret, Libby was dwelling on her own. He might know about staffs and wizards and magical powers—which was mind-boggling in itself—but how would he react if he learned that the woman he'd been messing up the sheets with was a freak?

Fear came to mind. Would Michael fear her? He didn't seem to be afraid of Daar. But then, he knew Daar was somewhat powerless at the moment and was making damn sure the old priest stayed that way.

Daar hadn't been back since the morning he'd stormed

out in anger. That was fine with Libby; she was a little mad at him herself.

"I hope these taste better than they look," Kate said, carrying a tray of doughnuts into the Christmas shop. "Their holes closed up, and the glaze soaked right into them."

"I think we were supposed to let them cool before we dipped them," Libby said, taking the tray and setting it on the counter.

Her mom had arrived home yesterday. Ian had driven to Bangor to pick up Kate and had joined them for dinner last night at Libby's. The Scot had "taken a shine" to Kate, according to her mother, who also had admitted to Libby that the feeling was mutual.

Now, there was a match that proved opposites attract.

"Wasn't it nice of Michael to let you sell your jewelry in his shop?" Kate said, fussing with the necklaces on the bare branch Robbie had cut for them. "And after Christmas, we can see about finally getting your studio opened."

Libby snorted. "Michael is getting twenty-percent commission and free counter help at the same time."

"And you're getting your product seen," Kate returned warmly. "People are going to grab these up for Christmas presents." She fingered one of the birds, a bright red cardinal male. "This would be nice with a green velvet blouse. Will you make me one to wear at our Christmas party?"

"We're having a party?"

Kate turned and frowned. "Of course we are. We'll invite all the MacKeages, the Dolans, Michael, Robbie, John, and Father Daar." Excitement lighting her eyes, she walked around the counter, found a pen and paper, and started writing. "Let's plan the menu. It should be simple and tasteful. Do you think we can get lobster this time of year?" she asked, looking up at Libby. "And when should we have it? Christmas Eve or a few days before?"

"Mom, we're going to be too busy to have a party. This is Michael's working season. We're going to be in this shop from daylight until after dark every day, including Christmas Eve."

"Oh, nonsense," Kate said, waving that away. "I can plan a party with my eyes closed. Now, we'll need to find a florist." She stopped suddenly, biting the end of her pencil and thinking. "Would sending invitations in the mail be too uppity? They are our friends. Maybe just asking them would be more personal."

Libby had learned a long time ago that it was much easier just to go along with her mother when Kate got a bee up her skirt about something. And parties, for Kate, were the thing of friendships.

"Asking them in person would probably be better," Libby agreed as she returned to decorating the ten-foot Douglas fir Michael had set up in the center of his shop.

It was absolutely beautiful—one of his prize trees, Libby was guessing. One she'd managed to miss with her car. It hadn't been rigidly trimmed this past summer, and the ends of the branches were soft and curving slightly downward, giving it a natural look.

Libby had never thought much about where Christmas trees came from; she'd just gone to the local sales lot and picked out whichever one caught her fancy. She now knew that it took plenty of work and planning and a good deal of artistry to grow them. And patience—which Michael seemed to have in spades. He'd told her this tree was twelve years old, a long time to wait for a return on an investment. Yes, growing Christmas trees took time, care, worry, and skill, as well as a nurturing instinct.

Michael had plenty of that, too.

God save her, she really was falling in love with him. And just as Grace MacKeage had predicted, he was driving her crazy. But it was such a nice, warm, and fuzzy kind of crazy Libby was all but bursting with joy.

"Oh, here come our first customers," Kate said excitedly, looking out the window at the car driving up.

A man, a woman, and six kids got out. The children, ranging in age from about ten down to two, hit the ground running, headed for the closest field of Christmas trees. The woman captured the toddler, picked her up, and slowly started after the brood. The man, his expression resigned, came into the shop.

Kate smoothed down her hair and perked up, her smile warm and inviting. "Good morning," she said cheerily. "Do you need a saw?"

"I do," he answered, eyeing Kate suspiciously as he pulled his wallet out of his back pocket. "Ah, where's John?"

Kate sobered. "He's spending the day with the Pottses, and having Thanksgiving dinner with them," she told him. "We were all worried today might be hard for him . . . without Ellen."

The man nodded. "That's good, then. Ellen was the foundation of this place." He eyed the doughnuts and frowned, looking back at Kate. "And you would be?" he asked.

"Oh. I'm Kate Hart," she said, and then waved her hand toward Libby. "And this is my daughter, Libby Hart," she added.

The man turned, and Libby smiled in greeting.

"Libby Hart?" he repeated. "You the doctor I heard about, living in Mary Sutter's place?"

Libby wasn't sure how to respond, so she nodded mutely.

"Are you going to hang out a shingle in town?" he asked. "We've been trying to get a doctor here for years now."

"I-I'm a surgeon, Mr. . . . ?"

His face tinged red. "Sorry," he said, nodding to both

Libby and Kate. "Alan Brewer. I own the welding shop in town."

"Mr. Brewer," Libby acknowledged. "I'm not really trained in general medicine. I worked in a trauma center."

"We got trauma cases here," he said, suddenly looking even more interested. "Most work in these parts is dangerous, what with the mills and logging operations, not to mention the rugged terrain. I've seen it happen that a person's had to wait more than an hour to be airlifted all the way to Bangor. A few have even died before help arrived."

Again, Libby didn't know how to respond. But she'd bet a penny the next time an accident happened, she'd be getting a call. Well, that was okay, she supposed. She couldn't in good conscience refuse to help when she might be able to save someone's life.

She probably should think about throwing together a triage kit and carrying it in her truck.

"Here's the saw, Mr. Brewer," Kate said, handing it across the counter, smartly saving Libby from having to respond. "And when you're done, bring your children in for doughnuts. We have hot cocoa and warm cider for them, too, and coffee for you and your wife."

"It'll probably take a while," he said with a pained sigh, handing his money to Kate and taking the saw. "Last year, we were in the field for nearly an hour. I swear, everyone's got an opinion on what a tree should look like. I'll see you a bit later, then. Missus Kate. Doc Libby," he said with a nod to each of them, tucking the saw under his arm and leaving to catch up with his family.

"Well, that was . . ."

"Awkward?" Libby finished for her mom, groaning heavily. "I guess word's out that Pine Creek has a new doctor in residence."

"I'd forgotten what small-town life was like," Kate said. "Libby, you know you're going to get called if there's a bad accident, don't you?"

"Yeah, I can see that. Lord, are people going to be calling me Doc Libby now?"

Well, it seemed that they were and that Kate's reminder of small-town life would be proven true. At least, every other person trooping through the Christmas shop that day—and there must have been fifty—knew a doctor had moved into town. Heck, people from out of town knew and asked questions, their eyes filled with hope and a good deal of relief.

By closing time, both Libby and Kate were beat ragged from smiling and fielding questions, making cocoa and coffee, giving opinions on customers' choices of the perfect tree, and apologizing for the sad condition of their doughnuts. And in between all that, Libby had to keep running into the house and basting the turkey, peeling vegetables, and setting the table for their own Thanksgiving feast.

Michael spent his day loading yet three more tractor-trailers with trees headed out of state, so he wasn't much help to Kate and Libby. Neither was Robbie, who had been given the duty of counting every tree being loaded. And Ian MacKeage, when he wasn't inside eating doughnuts and teasing Kate, was outdoors, binding the fat Christmas trees and helping to load them on top of cars and trucks so they could be lugged home.

At seven o'clock, they were finally sitting at the table, ready to feast on a twenty-pound turkey, everyone dog tired and hungry as a bear.

And that was when the phone rang, and Kate's prediction was made a reality, when Michael walked back to the table and quietly told Libby that both Alan Brewer and his oldest son had just fallen off the roof of their house.

Chapter Twenty-two

Libby sat on the passenger side of Michael's truck, staring sightlessly at the landscape passing by in a blur, thinking how she was used to dealing with victims after the paramedics had already done their jobs. And although she had gone on many ambulance runs during her training, it had been a while since she'd had to do triage at the scene of an accident.

And dammit, she didn't have anything to work with.

"What were they thinking, to let a child up on the roof of a house?" she asked for the fifth time. "And I don't have any equipment. You're sure they called the ambulance?"

Michael reached over and covered her wringing hands. "Your knowledge is what's needed. And the ambulance has been called, but it's forty miles away, coming from the other end of the lake."

"My knowledge means squat without equipment. What were they thinking?" she repeated.

Michael squeezed her hands and then had to downshift and concentrate on taking the corner without killing them both. He was driving fast but not recklessly.

"Kids grow up quick here, lass," he said as he shifted and accelerated the truck out of the curve. "We can't afford to keep them sheltered, or they'll get into even more trouble as teenagers." He looked over and smiled. "It's not wise to wait until a boy's grown to put a chain saw in his hand for the first time. Or set him on a snowmobile or let him shoot a rifle. We begin young, when we have the advantage of supervision."

Libby started wringing her hands again. "Ha—has Robbie used a chain saw?" she whispered, fighting back the picture that rose in her mind. "And shot a rifle?"

"Aye, Libby. Under my supervision."

"But he's not even nine."

"If he's big enough to lift a tool, he needs to know how it works in an emergency."

"A gun's not a tool."

Michael gave her a bit longer, more assessing look, as if he were trying to judge her mood. "But it is a tool, lass," he softly countered. "Which is why I've seen that Robbie knows the business end of a gun. When he was only three, I froze a gallon jug of water and shot it. He was properly horrified when it exploded, to realize what would happen to a person."

Libby was properly horrified now.

"Libby," Michael said with an impatient sigh, "Robbie visits friends now that he's in school. And just about every house in this area has a hunting rifle in it. I need to be sure he understands what could happen if his friend wants to impress him by showing off his daddy's gun."

"He should just run like hell and find an adult."

"He will," Michael assured her. "Believe me, that was my first rule. We're here," he said, pulling into a driveway.

Libby was out of the truck before Michael could shut it off, running to the gathering of people at the side of the house.

Worried, helpless, and relieved stares greeted her, along with Mrs. Brewer, holding her two-year-old daughter, tears running down both of their cheeks.

"Please. Help him," she whispered hoarsely. "Al-Alan's hurt bad. I-I think his back is broken."

Libby immediately put on her reassuring doctor's face and smiled at Mrs. Brewer. "I'll do what I can," she promised, turning away and going over to the small group of people kneeling and standing beside the fallen man.

She quickly scanned the area for a second victim but saw only Alan Brewer. "I was told there were two," she said to the small crowd. "Where's the boy?"

"He's here," somebody offered, moving to reveal the child. He was sitting up, leaning against a woman, holding his arm cradled against his chest, his face smudged with dirt and tears. Other than a possible broken arm, he appeared okay.

Libby knelt beside Alan Brewer, thankful to see he was conscious. "Alan," she said, holding his head still when he tried to look toward her. "Tell me where you hurt."

"His back," an unseen voice said from among the onlookers.

"I want Alan to tell me. Where does it hurt, Alan?"

"My back," he repeated gutturally.

"But where on your back? Up by your shoulders or lower, nearer your waist?"

"Low," he hissed. "And my . . . my left shoulder," he growled, closing his eyes.

Libby could see that his left shoulder was dislocated, but it was his back that worried her the most.

"He tried to catch Darren when he slipped," somebody said, kneeling on the other side of Alan. "But the ladder gave way, and he twisted as they fell in order to protect Darren. His son landed on top of him."

Libby assumed Darren was the boy with the broken arm.

"We haven't moved him," somebody else said. "That's the way he landed."

Libby thanked God for that small miracle, absently nodding. She could see that Alan Brewer was in a lot of pain and starting to show signs of shock. Dammit, where was the ambulance?

Her training was useless without equipment to stabilize him, without IVs, a backboard, and a neck brace. Hell, she didn't even have a stethoscope to listen for internal bleeding.

Libby cupped Alan's face and leaned close enough to whisper in his ear. "Just take slow, easy breaths," she told him softly. "Focus only on me. Listen to what I'm saying."

"Darren," he said with a harsh growl.

"He's fine," Libby told him, still whispering in his ear. "He's sitting up and is fine. Listen to me, Alan. I want you to concentrate on my hands. Can you feel my hands on your face?"

"Y-yes."

"They're going to feel warm. Concentrate on the heat. Let the warmth travel through your body, all the way down your back."

Libby closed her own eyes, focusing all of her energy on Alan Brewer. Color immediately lit her mind's eye, a swirling, turbulent mass of black and red and churning blue. Her heart started to beat with pounding throbs, and Libby realized it was Alan's heartbeat she felt. Pain assaulted her in waves. Tension racked her senses.

"Let me in, Alan," she whispered. "I can help you."

The colors swirled in angry chaos, howling through his body and into hers. Alan's fierce emotions kept lashing out at her, blocking her from reaching his injury. For nearly five minutes, Libby tried to get him to let her in, whispering words of encouragement, entreating him to open his mind. And each time, the colors swirled, and his injury danced just out of her reach.

Strong, warm, powerful, and familiar hands took hold of her trembling shoulders, and Libby renewed her effort. But no matter how hard she tried, she couldn't reach Alan's broken vertebra.

A siren sounded in the distance and slowly drew closer, until it finally came to a sudden halt behind her. Voices penetrated the fog of her mind, and Libby sat back on her knees and let go of Alan's face.

Michael lifted her to her feet, wrapped his arms around her body, and hugged her. "Your equipment's here, lass," he whispered as he tucked her head under his chin and tightened his arms, as if trying to still her trembling body with his own.

The paramedics, loaded down with equipment, rushed in. And for a full two minutes, Libby became an onlooker—until her training overrode her shock. She pulled away from Michael, knelt down beside Alan, and started issuing orders to the paramedics. But she stopped the minute she realized they were staring at her.

"She's a trauma doctor," Michael said with quiet authority, moving to kneel beside her.

And from that moment on, she was, using her years of training to guide the two men and one woman as they all worked as a team to stabilize Alan Brewer. An IV was started; he was carefully placed on a backboard and immobilized, then loaded onto the gurney and placed in the ambulance. Libby spoke on the radio to an attending physician in Bangor and was told a helicopter already had been dispatched.

She gave a few more orders to the paramedics, grabbed one of the medical kits, went over to young Darren Brewer, and knelt in front of him. She smiled and brushed a tear off his dirty cheek. "I'm Doc Libby, Darren. Remember me from the Christmas tree shop this morning?"

He wiped another tear himself and then pointed at his left arm. "I-I fell," he whispered.

"Can I see where you hurt yourself?" she whispered back. "Your hand makes a good splint, but I think I can make you a better one."

With worried, pain-filled, and skeptical young eyes, the boy slowly nodded and let go of his injured arm.

Libby smiled at the woman holding Darren. "Why don't you let Michael take over now?" she suggested. "He'll hold him steady for me."

Looking just as alarmed as Darren by Libby's remark, the woman hesitantly nodded and moved out of the way so Michael could take her place behind the boy.

"What were you doing on the roof?" Libby asked as she used scissors to cut Darren's shirt carefully away from his arm. "No, let me guess," she continued, keeping up a steady stream of distracting chatter. "I see Christmas lights hanging off the eave. You were decorating the house, weren't you?"

He nodded and sucked in his breath the moment she exposed his arm. It was broken between his elbow and his wrist, but the bone hadn't pierced the flesh.

Libby let out a long and appreciative whistle. "That's quite a bruise you've got there," she said in awe, smiling at him. "If it were me, I'd be wailing my head off."

"You're a girl," Darren said.

Libby nodded in agreement. "Yeah, I guess that's why I'd be hollering and you're not."

"Is my daddy going to be okay?" he asked, darting a look at the ambulance.

"He'll be fine, Darren. But he is hurt, so we're going to keep him in the ambulance until the helicopter gets here."

"Am—am I going to ride in the helicopter?" he asked.

Libby cupped his face with her hands and shook her head with a rueful smile. "Sorry, chum. Not this time."

He pulled his gaze away from the ambulance and stared up at her. Libby darted a quick look at Michael and then looked back at the boy.

"Close your eyes, Darren," she whispered. "And think about something nice. Do you have a pet?"

"I got Bingo," he said, tightly closing his eyes.

Libby kept one hand on his chin and placed her other hand over the break in his arm. "And is Bingo a cat?" she asked.

"Naw. He's a dog. Ow," he hissed, flinching.

"Shhh. It's okay, Darren. It's only heat you're feeling, not pain."

"Your hands are really warm," he quietly agreed, looking down at his arm.

Libby lifted his chin so he would look at her. "I'm not positive your arm is broken, Darren. I'm hoping it's just a bad bruise. Now, close your eyes again and think about Bingo. Did you get him as a puppy?"

But Libby didn't hear Darren's answer if he gave one. Already, her mind's eye was traveling through his body. She felt his rapid, anxious breathing and his young heartbeat racing with fear. She found his broken bone, pulsing with color, and began to repair it mentally. The break slowly knitted together, the blood vessels stopped leaking, and the swelling eased ever so slightly.

She was just pulling out of his body when Libby noticed something else—an irregularity in Darren's heartbeat, a backwash from one valve. And so she stopped and concentrated and repaired it while she was there. She opened her eyes, lifted Darren's chin, and smiled at him.

"You're a very lucky boy. It's only a bit bruised," she

said, looking over at Mrs. Brewer, who was now kneeling beside her. "A little Tylenol if he complains," Libby told her. "And he'll be good to go in a day or two."

"It-it's not broken?" the woman asked, softly touching Darren's arm.

"No. The swelling will go down quickly, once we get some ice on it," she said, taking an ice pack out of the kit, breaking the seal to mix the ingredients, and then carefully placing it over Darren's arm. "I think he's more shaken than hurt."

Some of the tension eased from the woman's face. "And Alan?" she asked. "He'll be okay, too?"

Libby nodded. "He will," she assured her, remembering the injury she had been able to see but hadn't been able to get near. "He'll have to go through weeks of rehabilitation, but he'll be fine in no time."

"It's all my fault," the woman cried, burying her face in her hands. "I bought those damned lights and wanted them put on the eaves."

Libby wrapped an arm around her. "It's Karen, isn't it?" she asked, trying to remember that morning's introductions.

"Carrie," the woman corrected, nodding.

"It was no one's fault, Carrie. It was an accident. And your husband and son are going to be okay. You'll have a great Christmas."

The woman took her son in her arms. "Thank Doc Libby, Darren," she instructed.

Darren eyed her suspiciously. "My arm don't hurt no more."

"I'm glad," Libby said, standing up and closing the medical kit. "And I'm prescribing that you stay off roofs, young man, for at least three years."

Michael took the kit from her and carried it back to the ambulance, allowing Libby to run ahead and check on

Alan. Being strapped to a backboard was uncomfortable all by itself, and the strain of his ordeal showed on his face behind the oxygen mask.

It was another fifteen minutes before the sound of beating helicopter blades finally broke over the tops of the trees. There was a large field next to the Brewers' house, and people had parked cars and turned on their headlights to illuminate the area. With its own powerful lights flooding the field, the chopper slowly descended, forcing the onlookers to take shelter. Just as it touched down, attendants emerged and ran toward the ambulance.

With her hand placed reassuringly on his chest, Libby climbed down as Alan was lifted out of the ambulance and became part of the parade of paramedics as she shouted an update of vitals to the new arrivals. Just as soon as Alan was placed in the chopper, Libby closed the door and pounded on the side. She then ducked and ran back to the ambulance to avoid being blown away by the downdraft from the blades.

"Do you have someone to drive you to Bangor?" she asked Carrie Brewer. "And someone to stay with your children?"

Carrie nodded, watching the chopper carry her husband away. Finally, she looked at Libby. "Should Darren come with me?"

"That would be best," Libby told her. "He probably should have a more thorough checkup and maybe some X rays."

Carrie pulled her into a shaky embrace. "Thank you," she whispered. "Thank you for helping us."

"The paramedics did all the work. Now, go to Bangor, and tell whoever drives you not to rush. It will take them a while to evaluate Alan. But they'll talk with you before they do anything. And don't worry," she finished, patting Carrie's shoulder, "he'll be fine."

Libby turned and walked to Michael's truck, opened the passenger door, and stared at the chest-high seat. She was too tired and too numb to climb up into it. Strong hands took hold of her by the waist and lifted her up. Her seat belt was fastened, and the door was softly shut.

Libby closed her eyes and leaned her head back against the headrest. Other than to tell the paramedics that she was a doctor, Michael hadn't said one word the entire evening. And he still had nothing to say as he slid in behind the wheel, started the truck, and drove down the driveway. When they got to the paved road, he turned right, not left, and headed toward her home.

Libby was thankful for his silence. Her head was reeling, her stomach was churning, and she couldn't stop shaking. It wasn't until Michael turned on the heater and a blast of warm air hit her that Libby realized she was chilled to the bone.

She probably should say something.

But what?

She looked to her left and could just make out Michael's profile in the dim light from the dash as he watched the road. He silently lifted his right arm. And just as silently, Libby unfastened her seat belt and scooted over until she was firmly against him, closed her eyes again with a sigh, and snuggled into his fierce embrace.

She had been staring up at the ceiling for the last two hours, until the glowing stars were nothing more than blurry dots of light. Libby looked at her clock by the bed, cursed the fact that it wouldn't be daylight for another three hours, and stared at the stars again.

He knew.

Michael knew her secret. He'd been right there with her last night, anchoring her, while she had tried to heal Alan

Brewer. And he'd been holding Darren when she mended the boy's broken arm. Michael had to have felt the energy coursing through her, seen exactly what she had seen, and realized what was happening.

So now he knew.

And he hadn't said a word. He'd brought her home, tucked her into bed, given her a chaste kiss, and left.

What must he have thought? Was he lying in his own bed right now, looking up at his blank ceiling, wondering what sort of freak she was?

Libby tried to imagine how she'd feel if it were Michael who had this gift. Would she be afraid of him? Could she love an aberration if their roles were reversed?

But he did have a secret, and it wasn't just who had crafted her bed, either. There was something mysterious about Michael that had to do with his past. Something had happened to him twelve years ago that had caused the strong, confident man to retreat to the mountains of Maine.

He told her he had been a warrior. Had he seen or done something so unsettling that it had sent him into hiding?

And what was Daar's connection? Michael seemed to accept the priest's claim that he was a wizard. Heck, he seemed actually to respect the old man.

But he wasn't afraid of Daar. Just cautious. And guarded.

And unwilling to talk about her secret because he didn't want to talk about his own?

Damn, what a mess.

Libby tossed back the covers and stumbled to the bathroom, only to nearly step on Trouble when he came scampering out the moment she opened the door. Guardian was right behind him, and she knew the two boys were headed upstairs to find their sister, who was likely sleeping with Kate.

Libby splashed water on her face, fluffed her hair, and brushed her teeth. She went back to the bedroom, dressed in layers of warm clothes, and headed into the kitchen. She found a paper and pencil and wrote her mother a note, telling Kate not to expect her at the Christmas shop until noon. Libby then put on her boots and jacket and hat and gloves, found her flashlight, and headed out onto the porch.

She just stood there for several minutes, staring up at black and silent TarStone Mountain, which rose like a sleeping giant into the star-studded sky.

It looked damned cold. And formidable.

It also looked like a good place to get lost.

Libby didn't dare calculate her chances of finding Daar's cabin, for fear she might get smart all of a sudden and not go. But she had to talk to the old priest before her mind really did explode. And so she snapped on her flashlight and headed across the yard and into the forest.

She couldn't stop thinking about last night, couldn't get past the fact that she hadn't been able to do anything for Alan Brewer.

Why was that? What good was a gift that only worked some of the time? Why had she been able to heal Darren Brewer but not his father?

She needed to talk to somebody, and there was no one else she could turn to except an old priest who brought flowers back to life. The wizard damned well better have some answers for her, if she was foolish enough to brave the dark and scary forest and risk getting eaten by a bear.

Her determination served her well and carried Libby for the first hour of the climb until she heard something off to her left. A branch snapped, and she spun around and pointed her flashlight in the direction of the noise. But all she saw were leafless trees for as far as the flashlight beam would penetrate.

And then she saw two little pinpricks of light.

The eyes weren't moving but staring at her, unblinking, just a few inches above the ground. Was it a tiny animal, a rabbit or a fox or something? Or was it a bear crouching low, preparing to strike?

Dammit. What was she doing out there in the middle of the woods at four-thirty in the morning, with only a flashlight and an overactive imagination?

A white blur suddenly swooped through the beam of her light, and Libby screamed. She stepped back, tripped on a rock, and fell into a growth of fir trees.

"Dammit, Mary!" she sputtered, slapping a branch out of her face. "You scared the hell out of me."

Her only answer was the echo of her own voice.

Libby slowly got up, brushed herself off, and straightened her cap. Well, she wasn't alone anymore—not that an owl would be much help against a bear. She continued walking in the only direction she knew to go, and that was up. But instead of just shining her flashlight on the ground, she now pointed it into the trees every so often, looking for the owl.

"Mary," she called in a singsong voice, feeling more desperate than foolish. "Where's Father Daar's cottage?"

A sharp, high-pitched whistle came from her right, and Libby turned and started in that direction, her singsong turning to whispered curses as she ducked to avoid low branches and tripped over fallen trees. For nearly an hour, she followed Mary, sometimes with only a whistle to guide her, sometimes catching a glimpse of the owl gliding silently ahead. Finally, scratched, cold, and dog tired, Libby saw a faint light up ahead. She stumbled into the clearing but came to an abrupt stop at the sight of Daar standing on the porch of his cabin, silhouetted by the glow of a kerosene lamp hanging on the wall behind him.

"If ya don't have my staff with ya, girl, ya can just turn around and go back down the mountain," he said, his growling voice carrying through the crisp night air.

"I want a cup of coffee."

"Ya can have one if ya brought my staff."

"Michael has it."

"Then have a mind ya don't get ate by a bear on yar way back," he said, turning and walking into his cabin.

Libby stood rooted to the ground, staring at the closed door of Daar's cabin. She knew he had coffee in there; she could smell it, dammit.

She marched up to the cabin, stomped up the four steps and onto the porch, and used her flashlight to bang on the solid wooden door. "I'm not leaving!" she shouted. "I want a cup of coffee, and I want to talk to you."

"Well, I don't want to talk to ya," came his muted reply.

"It's a law that you have to give shelter to anyone lost in the woods," Libby told him. "Along with food and something warm to drink."

"Ya just made that up. Now go away, before I turn ya into a dung beetle."

Libby banged on the door again with her flashlight. When that got her no response, she leaned her head into the wood and quietly started to sob. "My—my gift is broken," she whispered. "It wouldn't work when I needed it last night."

The door opened, and she fell into the arms of Father Daar.

Libby buried her face in his shoulder and continued her soft tirade. "I couldn't heal Alan Brewer. I fixed Darren's broken arm, but I couldn't do anything for his father. There was so much chaos. The colors kept swirling and wouldn't let me reach his injury."

Apparently not knowing what to do with a woman crying all over him, Daar roughly patted her back with one hand while trying to push her away with the other. Finally, he guided them both over to the table and seated her in one of the chairs. Libby looked down at her clasped hands and continued.

"Nothing I tried would work. I even had Michael there, holding me, but I couldn't get through to Alan." She looked up. "It was as if he was fighting me. Why would he do that? He was in pain. Didn't he want to be healed?"

Daar sat down in a chair next to her, scratching his beard, his eyes narrowed in thought. "Of course, he would want to be healed. Ya say ya tried but couldn't get through? But that ya healed the boy?"

Libby nodded. "Darren had a broken arm, and I was able to go in, see the break, and mend it. And I could see Alan Brewer's injury, but I couldn't reach it. The colors kept driving me away."

Daar fell silent. He stood up, went to the stove, and poured a cup of coffee. He brought it back and set it on the table in front of her. Libby picked it up, blew off the steam, and carefully sipped the black, strong-smelling brew.

"Tell me what happened," Daar said, taking a seat beside her again. "I know the Brewers. Ya say they had some sort of accident?"

"Alan and his son Darren fell off their roof while trying to put up Christmas lights."

"And young Darren broke his arm?"

"And Alan broke his back and dislocated his shoulder," she added. "I didn't have any equipment, and the ambulance was taking a long time. So I tried to use my gift to heal him."

"And ya couldn't," he finished softly, frowning in thought. "What exactly did ya see, Libby? Ya entered his body?"

"Yes. Just like all the other times, I—I was actually able

to move inside him. I heard his heartbeat, each breath he took, felt his pain. And I saw exactly where he was hurt and knew just how to fix it."

"And when ya tried? What happened then?"

"Nothing. I could see the broken vertebra, but I couldn't get near it. The colors kept lashing out at me, driving me back."

"And MacBain was there? And still ya couldn't do anything?"

"M-Michael was holding on to my shoulders."

Daar stood up again and paced to the hearth. He silently poked at the slowly burning fire for a time, then turned back and faced her, his brows drawn into a frown.

"Not everyone is meant to be healed, Libby," he said softly. "Or, if they are, it has to come from themselves, not from an outside source."

"But I could have saved him months of rehabilitation."

"Aye. But he was not open to your gift, lass. I know Alan Brewer as a stoic, private man. He's God-fearing, but that doesn't always translate to believing in miracles."

"So you're saying my gift only works on believers?"

"Something like that," he said, nodding. "It's more likely that Brewer just can't comprehend what's not tangible. If he can't touch it, smell it, or see it, then it probably doesn't exist."

"But I didn't believe, and I have the gift."

"Aye. But you were open to the possibility, lass. Ya perform miracles every day in your work, and ya know—deep down, where it counts—that you are not alone in your surgery."

His smile was warm. "As a doctor, ya work with a knowledge of the human body, but each procedure ya do is an act of faith, is it not? Not only faith in the science, but is there not something else guiding yar hand in surgery?"

"I hadn't thought about it in those terms," Libby admitted, frowning into her cup of coffee. She looked at Daar. "I just did whatever I had to."

"And last night, when yar gift failed, what did you do?"

"I used my training."

"Aye. And will Alan Brewer recover?"

"Yes. His back was broken, but I could see that it wasn't a severe or paralyzing break. But what about Darren? Why was I able to help him?"

"Because he's a child," Daar told her. "He hasn't lived long enough for his mind to be closed."

Libby sipped her coffee and thought about what Daar was saying. It made sense, she guessed, in a weird sort of way.

"So I'm just a conduit or something? You're saying I can't force my gift onto someone?"

Daar came and sat back down beside her, his crystal-blue eyes shining with warmth. "Aye, Libby. And that should ease a lot of yar worries. Ya do not have the power to decide a person's fate. Was that not yar greatest fear?"

He was right, that was her greatest worry. Libby nodded and took another sip of her coffee, thankful that her fingers and toes were finally thawing out. Daar suddenly cocked his head as he stared at her, his eyes narrowing in what Libby now recognized as an outward sign that he was thinking.

"I'm just wondering," he mused. "What would have happened last night if ya would have had my staff with ya?"

Libby shot her gaze to his cane, which was leaning against the hearth. "That staff?" she asked, pointing to it. "Why? Do you think I could have healed Alan Brewer if I'd had it?"

"Aye," he said, slowly nodding, his thoughts turned

inward again. "It might not be powerful enough, though. But my old staff would be," he added gruffly, focusing back on her. "With it, ya could have overridden his resistance, I'm thinking."

"But wouldn't that be unethical? Or immoral or something?" Libby asked, growing alarmed. "I don't want a power that can get past a person's own defenses."

"But it's a good power, lass."

"Good for whom?" Libby shook her head. "I'm beginning to understand why Michael won't give you back your staff. He said you could be dangerous if you got all your powers back, and I'm beginning to believe he might be right."

"Dangerous!" Daar growled, his face darkening. "I'll have ya know I've wielded those powers for more than fourteen centuries, girl, and I never once abused them."

"But you have made mistakes," she countered. "That morning on my porch, you admitted as much."

Daar stood up, walked to the door and opened it, and stood to the side, silently telling her their visit was over. Libby got up, shot one last yearning look at the warm hearth, and walked out onto the porch.

The door slammed shut behind her, the bolt sliding home with a resounding thud. Libby walked off the porch and across the clearing, through the slowly brightening light of the frosty dawn.

It took her twice as long to find her way back home, since it seemed that Mary no longer felt like helping her.

And Libby wondered what kind of trouble she was in for refusing to help a wizard get back his power.

Chapter Twenty-three

*M*ichael *slowly rubbed another layer* of wax onto the surface of the tall oak bureau. He'd had precious little time to work on Libby's Christmas gift since his busy season had started, and it would take a miracle for him to have it done in time.

The moose bed, the bureau, and the two matching night-stands still to be finished had been started well more than a year ago. He'd been making the bedroom set for himself, not because he needed a new bed but because working with wood had been a great source of pleasure for him since childhood. Which is why he had made the maple kitchen table two years ago and presented it to Ellen Bigelow on her eighty-fifth birthday. He'd also built Robbie's bed from birch wood, for when the boy moved out of his crib.

Michael looked around his workshop and marveled at the array of tools he'd amassed in just nine years. As a lad growing up in the Highlands, he and his da had possessed only a handful of tools. It was a wonder to him now, how his mama had loved each and every piece of furniture they'd made her, despite their crude but functional designs.

Michael smiled in memory of one piece in particular, a trunk for Isobel MacBain's precious sewing supplies and materials, which he had labored over for nearly five months under the patient eye of his father. He had carved wildflowers into the top of the trunk, which had looked more like weeds than heather and laurel.

His mama had had the same reaction to his gift as Libby, although the two pieces of furniture were worlds—and centuries—apart in craftsmanship. Both women had run their hands over the polished wood in wonder, as if it were precious gold.

Libby.

For the last three weeks, ever since Alan Brewer's accident, she had been distant and unusually reserved. Hell, the woman had made a point of avoiding him. And when they did talk, they usually discussed such inane things that it would be laughable if it weren't so frustrating.

She was just plain scared. Libby knew that he knew her secret, and she was worried he might reject her for possessing the power to heal.

And so, in defense, she was rejecting him first.

That, too, would be laughable if it weren't so maddening.

Michael had been allowing her silent rebellion only because this was one lesson Libby needed to learn by herself. Trust was a tenuous concept to instill in a person and could be taught only by example.

It was just too bad it was taking Libby so long to decide she could trust him.

He'd give her until Christmas. If she didn't come to him by then and openly discuss what had happened at the Brewers', well, he just might steal the woman out of her precious moose bed and take her into the mountains—and not return until she agreed to marry him.

Michael straightened from rubbing the bottom drawer of the bureau and stepped back to admire his work. The rich, warm grains of the oak shone through the many layers of paste wax. He smiled at the tall bureau. Libby was going to have to stand on her tiptoes to see into the top drawer. Maybe he should make her a step stool from the scraps of wood he had left. Hell, she had to get a running start as it was, just to hop into bed.

Damn, but he missed making love to her.

Aye, he'd give her until Christmas to come to her senses. One more week was about all he'd last, he figured, before he went crazy and jumped her beautiful bones in the wreath-making shed.

Michael tossed his rag onto the workbench, shrugged into his jacket, and stepped out into the frosty night air. The cold snow crunched under his feet as he stopped and stared at the hundreds of Christmas trees standing in perfect rows, broken only where felled comrades had been cut to decorate people's homes.

A full moon reflected off the fresh eight-inch snowfall, illuminating a landscape covered in a pristine mantle of white. TarStone Mountain stood cold and silent in the background, with Fraser Mountain nothing more than a distant shadow to the north.

Michael took a deep breath and sighed in contentment. He was at peace with the world for once, he decided as he rubbed his chest where Libby had hit him with the snowball. Actually, he felt more confident than content, that he would live out his natural life in this time, now that he knew the old *drùidh* would never get back his powerful staff. He hadn't destroyed the cherrywood stick but had hidden it where Daar, and especially that interfering owl, would never find it.

Michael chuckled, tucked his hands into his pockets,

and started walking to the house, watching his breath puff gently into the crisp night air. One week, and they'd be a family, brought together by either providence or chance, ranging in age from nine years old to eight hundred and thirty-six.

But this time, he was waiting until after the wedding to tell his bride about his fantastical journey.

"If I have to listen to one more Christmas carol, I swear I'm going to scream," Libby threatened as she dropped several cinnamon sticks into the heating cider. "Why can't we make a switch that turns them on only when a customer walks through the door?"

Kate straightened from putting a log in the woodstove and dusted off her hands, wincing as a rendition of "Jingle Bells" sung by chipmunks filled the Christmas tree shop. "We could accidentally drop the CD player into the pond," she suggested. "Or maybe I could get Ian just to shoot it."

Libby fixed the problem herself by simply walking around the counter, shutting off the player, and removing the disc. She opened the back door and threw the CD like a Frisbee as far as she could.

She nearly hit Robbie, who stopped so abruptly he slid to a halt as the flat, spinning missile disappeared into the snow beside him. He turned his surprised pewter eyes back on her and smiled and shook his head.

"Gram Ellen always did strange things just before Christmas, too," he said, walking past her into the shop. "Papa said my pay envelope is here. Can I have it? Leysa and Rose will be here soon, and I need my money."

"What for?" Kate asked, opening the cash register and lifting out the brown envelope. She waved it in the air. "Why would a young fellow need money at this time of year?"

"It's Christmas," he said, smiling up at her. "And Leysa's taking me shopping in Bangor with her and Rose."

"Again?" Libby asked, turning Robbie, unbuttoning his coat, and buttoning it back up in sequence. "This is the third time this month."

"I wasn't shopping the other two times. I was babysitting."

"Rose?" Libby asked. "You were watching an infant?"

"Not by myself," he said, rolling his eyes. "Leysa just needs me to keep Rose entertained in the stores. I get to push her stroller, and we play while her mama shops."

"And I bet you're a great help," Kate said, straightening his cap and tucking the envelope into his pocket. "What are you shopping for today?"

Apparently having endured all the female fussing he could, Robbie started inching his way to the door. "It's Christmas," he repeated, lifting his chin. "I can't tell you that."

"Can you tell me when you expect to be home?" Libby asked. "Remember, we're having our party tonight."

"Leysa promised we'd be back in plenty of time. She said she wouldn't miss it for anything." He stepped out into the snow but stopped and looked back, scowling at Libby. "Don't ya peek in my workshop while I'm gone," he warned. "Or Santa won't be generous with ya tomorrow morning."

Libby held up her hand in a scout's salute. "I promise not to peek. Robbie," she said, lowering her voice and stepping out the door with him so Kate wouldn't hear, "will you please tell me what I've been helping you make for Michael? I know it's some sort of display case I've been lining with an old piece of wool plaid, but I don't know what it's going to display. And the plaque I painted is for the case, I'm guessing, but what does *Tàirneanaiche* mean?"

The smile he gave her was filled with secrecy and no small amount of satisfaction. "You'll find out tomorrow morning," he said. He leaned in and whispered, "Isn't Christmas fun? All the secrets and surprises? Everything builds up until ya think you're gonna burst, and then it gets revealed all at once. You're gonna love the surprise Papa's planning for ya, Libby." His smile turned up several notches. "I know I am. Tomorrow morning, I'm going to be the happiest boy in the world. And tomorrow night, you're gonna be the happiest woman, 'cause your dream's gonna come true."

"And what dream would that be?" she asked, raising one brow as she returned his contagious smile. "How do you even know what I dream about?"

"Mary told me," he said succinctly. "She knows all kinds of stuff like that."

"Mary told you what I dream about?" Libby asked in alarm.

Robbie patted her shoulder and rolled his eyes again. "She can't see into your head or nothing," he assured her. "She just knows what's good for people." His smile returned. "And she say's Papa's gift is exactly what both of ya need."

He turned at the sound of a truck pulling into the driveway. "There's Leysa and Rose. I gotta go." He turned back to Libby, threw himself into her arms, and hugged her tightly. "I'll see ya tonight. Make sure there's plenty of cheesecake. I really love cheesecake," he said, squeezing her tightly and then letting go, running to the waiting truck.

Michael emerged from his workshop and caught Robbie just as he was opening the truck door. He handed the boy a folded piece of paper, gave him a hug good-bye, and settled him in the backseat, snapping the seat belt closed. He spoke a few minutes to Leysa, tickled Rose's chin, and then softly shut the door and watched as they drove away.

Libby saw Michael turn and cross his arms over his chest. And he just stood there, contemplating her in silence from across the empty yard.

Libby forced herself not to fidget. Lord, but she missed making love to him. It had been four long weeks, with even longer nights. More than the Christmas carols, his stubborn patience was driving her crazy.

She knew what he was doing. She knew he was waiting for her to come to him and talk about what had happened that night at the Brewers'.

But being near him every day, even without the intimacy, was better than not having him in her life at all. And that's exactly what would happen if he ever learned the full scope of her secret.

"I noticed ya sitting on the snowmobile the other day," he said, still standing across the yard, his eyes focused intently on her. "Would ya like to go for a ride, lass?"

"Right now?" she asked, trying to decide if he was being sincere or merely calculating his chances of getting her alone, far away from any distractions. "But what about the shop?"

"It's Christmas Eve and won't be so busy today. Most people have already put up their trees. Kate and Ian can look after things."

She did want to go for a ride, but she really, really didn't want to be alone with Michael. She'd either attack his beautiful body or break down completely and blurt out all her worries.

"I have to help get ready for tonight's party."

He uncrossed his arms and set his hands on his hips. "We won't be gone long," he said, his coaxing voice sending chills down her spine. "I'll have ya back in two hours."

He turned and headed to the machine shed. "Get your coat and mittens," he instructed over his shoulder, apparently decided they were going. "Ya can wear Robbie's helmet."

Libby stood rooted in indecision, rubbing her hands on her thighs. And then she ran into the shop, told Kate where she was going, promised to be back in time to help out with the party, and stormed out through the front door as she slipped into her jacket.

More than her life, she was putting her heart in Michael's hands, but this was one ride she could no longer avoid. They were settling things between them this morning.

And Libby figured she had a fifty-fifty chance of coming off the mountain with a soul mate or walking back alone with nothing but misery for company.

Michael started the engine of the powerful snowmobile and let it idle to warm up while he picked up Libby's helmet and watched her come running from the shop.

She didn't look like a person thrilled with the prospect of riding a snowmobile for the first time. No, she looked like a woman rushing headlong to a hanging, and Michael knew it was her own neck she was feeling the noose tighten around.

His heart ached for her. And for himself. He, too, felt as if this trip might be the death of him, because if Libby couldn't handle what he was about to tell her, his heart probably would break clean in half this time.

"I'm ready," she said, coming to a halt just outside the machine shed. She took the helmet from him, turning it upside down and ducking her head inside. She straightened and smiled tightly and fastened the strap under her chin. "Can I drive?"

"No," Michael said, turning to hide his smile. She might

be suspicious of his motives, but that didn't seem to dampen her enthusiasm for the ride itself.

He climbed onto the sled and revved the engine, inching it out of the shed. He grabbed his own helmet off the handlebars, put it on, and patted the seat behind him. As soon as she hopped on, he tucked both of her feet securely on the foot rails and guided her hands to the handles by her side.

"Just lean against the backrest, and try to relax," he instructed. "Ya needn't worry about keeping your balance. It rides more like a car than a motorcycle. And I'll take it slow."

"Not too slow," she chided, peering at him through the open face of her helmet.

He flipped down her visor and started up through the rows of Christmas trees in the direction of TarStone Mountain. But he turned at the trail that led to her house and pulled to a halt in her yard a few minutes later.

"Why are we stopping?" she asked, lifting her visor.

"I thought we could pick up some lunch to take with us."

"A picnic? In the middle of the winter?"

Michael shrugged and climbed off the snowmobile. "Why not? We'll find a sunny spot out of the wind."

She was running to the house before he could finish and disappeared through the door. Michael turned and looked toward TarStone, thinking about what he intended to do just as soon as he got Libby far enough away from civilization that she couldn't run screaming for help.

For a woman who'd just given birth to her seventh daughter four days ago, Grace MacKeage had still had enough energy last evening to give him a scathing lecture on a woman's need to know she was about to get married.

Michael had visited Gu Bràth last night, on the excuse

that he and Robbie had wanted to see the newest MacKeage bairn. But the moment Robbie had left the room to go play with Heather and the girls and Greylen had left with his brand-new baby in his arms, Michael had sat down in front of the fire next to Grace and told her of his intention to marry Libby on Christmas Day.

He'd expected Grace's surprise but not her anger. She'd stood up, leaned over him, and poked him quite sharply in the chest. And with that same finger waving in his face, she had proceeded to educate him on the finer points of romance, timing, and modern women's minds.

Which was why he was here now with all of Grace's words rattling around in his head, stealing Libby away so that he could propose properly.

Michael snorted, took off his helmet, and rubbed his neck in an attempt to keep the sweat from trickling down his back. Grace also had made him promise that he wouldn't propose until after he'd explained his journey through time.

Which is why they were going up the mountain. He'd learned his lesson with Mary and was not letting Libby out of his sight until she was calm enough not to run.

He turned at the sound of the storm door slamming shut and saw Libby, her arms hugging an overstuffed pack, running back to the sled. He took the pack and secured it on the backrest, climbed back onto the sled, and waited for her to get settled behind him again.

"Do I have to hold on to the handles?" she asked. "Can't I just hold on to you?"

"Whatever's comfortable, lass," he said, starting the engine. "Ready?" he asked, looking over his shoulder.

He saw her take a deep breath, slap down her visor, and nod. The moment her hands came around his waist, Michael set off up the back trail to West Shoulder Ridge.

They rode in companionable silence for several miles, until Libby tapped him on the shoulder.

"I want to drive," she demanded when he stopped to see what she wanted. "It doesn't seem very difficult."

He stood up so she could scoot forward and climbed on behind her. "This is the throttle," he said, placing her thumb over the lever on the right side of the handlebar. "Push softly, as it's quick to respond. And this is the brake," he added, wrapping her fingers over the lever on the left. "Ya must always keep your feet on the rails, Libby, even if it feels as if we're tipping, or ya might break an ankle. It steers just like a bicycle but without the leaning."

She used her elbows to nudge his arms away and pushed on the throttle. They shot off like a rocket. And then they came to an abrupt halt when she slammed on the brakes. Michael braced his feet to keep from crushing her against the handlebars and closed his eyes and prayed for patience.

"It's touchy," she complained in a shout through her visor, just as she pushed on the throttle again.

She didn't brake this time, and Michael was suddenly glad he'd decided not to give Libby her own sled for this trip. For the next two miles, they flew like a drunken jackrabbit up the mountain as she slowly got a feel for the powerful machine. Michael had to intervene only four times to keep them from bouncing off trees.

He finally reached around her and took over the controls, guiding the sled to a small clearing at the base of a south-facing ledge. He shut off the engine and climbed off, pulled off his helmet, and watched as Libby's head slowly emerged from her own helmet to reveal a beatific smile.

"That was wonderful," she said, her eyes gleaming with delight as she patted the sled affectionately. "I'm buying one of these babies. I saw a map at the Dolans' store that showed how you can travel the entire state on a snowmobile."

Michael took her helmet, tossed it onto the ground, pulled her into his arms, and kissed her beautiful smile.

She tasted sweeter than ever, with just a hint of hot apple cider laced with cinnamon. She felt so precious and tiny, even in her plump down winter jacket, that he couldn't get enough of her. He lifted her off her feet and groaned in satisfaction when she wrapped her legs around his waist and her arms around his neck and moaned into his mouth.

He strode up to the ledge and found a place free of snow and covered with dry, fluffy grass. He set her down and followed her, until she was comfortably beneath him—all without breaking their kiss.

Not that she'd let him. She was gripping his hair, wiggling restlessly against him until he thought he would burst into flames, making sweet little mewling sounds of urgency.

Aye, it had been far too long since they'd made love.

With herculean effort, he stopped, pulled Libby's hands from around his neck, and clasped them between their bodies as he stared into her passion-filled eyes.

"We can't, Libby."

"I put three condoms in the backpack. And a blanket."

Michael shook his head, smiling tightly at her obvious want. "Nay, lass. I brought you up here to talk."

"We will. After. Please, Michael, make love to me."

He shook his head again, kissed the tip of her nose, and rolled over until he was sitting upright beside her. He wrapped his arms around his knees and stared at the distant, frozen waters of Pine Lake tucked in the valley below.

"Have ya not wondered, Libby, why I so easily accept Daar as a wizard?" he asked softly.

She sat up beside him, and Michael could feel her eyes fixed on his face. He did not look at her but continued to stare at Pine Lake.

"I wondered," she admitted. "But there was so much I was trying to deal with that I . . . it didn't seem important." She set one tiny hand on his arm. "Why do you believe in wizards?"

He finally looked over and met her turbulent, worried, and somewhat frightened gaze. "He really is a *drùidh,* lass. I know, because I have personally felt his powers. It was in the year A.D. 1200, and I was engaged in a battle with Greylen MacKeage."

"A battle with Grey? Wh-when?" she whispered.

Michael turned and lifted her onto his lap, wrapping his arms tightly around her, bringing her eyes level with his. "I was born in the year 1171, Libby. I'm more than eight hundred years old."

She tried to pull away, but he wouldn't let her.

He continued his tale. "During this battle, I caught sight of an old man standing on a bluff above us, his arms outstretched and a long staff held high in his hand. A great storm broke over us, darkening the sky to night, filling the air with a powerful wind and sizzling bolts of lightning. And suddenly, I was falling, tumbling through what I can only describe as blinding white energy. I felt as if I did not exist for that brief moment of time, merely consumed."

The woman on his lap had gone deathly still, her eyes wide and her complexion pale. Still Michael continued, determined to make her understand exactly who he was.

"My next conscious thought was that I hadn't died, after all. I was lying in a field of tall grass and could hear the moans of my men, broken only by the screams of our frightened horses." He tightened his hands on her arms, more to keep them from trembling than to hold her. "Greylen MacKeage was lying beside me. Five of my own warriors were there, and Callum and Morgan and Ian

MacKeage. Our horses struggled to their feet and stood quivering, breathing hard and snorting in terror, not knowing which way to run to safety. We knew not what had happened or where the threat lay."

Libby lifted one tiny gloved hand to his face and ran a finger down his taut cheek. "Where were you?" she whispered.

"In modern-day Scotland." He captured her hand and held it against his chest, over his pounding heart. "That was twelve years ago, Libby. The five MacBains who were with me are dead now. Only the MacKeages remain from that day. And Daar. His real name is Pendaär, and he is a *drùidh*."

She opened her mouth to say something, but nothing came out. She simply turned her gaze to her hand held against his chest.

Michael lifted her chin and smiled. "Your secret is not so terrible, lass, when compared with mine. That ya have this gift to heal people is a wondrous thing, Libby. And that I can understand your powers is my gift to you."

She was frowning now, staring at his chest again. "You're saying that you traveled eight hundred years through time? That you were born in medieval Scotland, and a wizard cast a spell and brought you here?" she finished softly, raising turbulent, misting brown eyes back up at him.

"Aye, Libby. That is what happened. As God is my witness, I don't know how or why, just that it is. And for the last twelve years, I have been learning to live with the fact."

She threw herself against him, wrapping her arms around his neck and hugging him fiercely, her lips touching his ear as she whispered, "Oh, Michael, I'm so sorry for what happened to you."

He took hold of her shoulders and held her away, staring into her tear-soaked eyes. "Don't ya dare be sorry," he growled. "I have accepted my fate, and it is you who must do the same now."

She blinked, clearly surprised by his anger. "But—"

"You are born of a time when *drùidhs* and magic and miracles are considered suspect, Libby," he continued with gentle force. "Ya cannot comprehend what ya cannot touch or see. But I am from a time where magic was almost a religion and very much a part of everyday life. It is through me that you can come to accept your abilities and embrace them instead of fearing them. It may very well be the reason I'm here, lass." He suddenly smiled. "And Robbie. He was needing to be born, I think, from a wonderful woman who was very special herself. Robbie's destiny is yet to be revealed, but I do know that it's my destiny to be here with him. And with you.

"Which is also why," he continued before she could respond, keeping the steel in his voice, "we're getting married tomorrow."

"Married! Tomorrow!" she sputtered, her own voice cracking with surprise.

Michael nodded curtly.

"But you don't want to get married!" she hissed, scrambling off his lap. She pointed her finger at him. "I will not live with a man who can't love me."

He leaned back against the ledge, crossing his feet at the ankles and his arms over his chest. "But I do love you," he softly declared.

She suddenly looked as if she might explode. "You do not! You can't. You said you have nothing left to give a woman."

"I was wrong."

"I'm an aberration. A freak of nature."

"Then we will be freaks together." He stood up until he towered over her and smiled. "But we will be married freaks, Libby. You belong to me. And we will spend the rest of our unnatural lives as man and wife, embracing our destinies together."

Michael reached for Libby the moment he realized she was about to crumble in a mess of overwhelmed confusion and quickly sat down again, cradling her against his chest.

"Ah, lass. For as much as you've been needing an anchor, so have I. We can ground each other, Libby. Our combined strengths can keep us sane, and together we can help Robbie grow into a fine man as he sets out to find his own destiny."

He lifted a hand and fingered the white lock of hair on her forehead. "And maybe we can have one or two more bairns. Girls if ya want, with cute little locks of white hair and six toes on each foot."

She slapped her hand over his and gave him a horrified look. "My children will be normal," she sputtered.

He tugged on her white curl. "But what's the fun in that? Anyone can be normal."

She had to think about that, and from the look on her face, it was difficult for her to embrace such a concept. So Michael figured he'd help her along by kissing her cute, pouting lips.

"Marry me, Libby," he whispered into her mouth. "Tomorrow at noon, make me the happiest man in the world."

She pulled back with a gasp. "Robbie knows!" she squeaked. "He said those same words this morning." She poked him in the shoulder. "He knew before I did!"

Michael quickly captured her hands and nodded. "So does Kate. And Grace. And John. We've been planning the ceremony for almost a week."

He'd have gotten poked again if she could have freed her hands. "And just when were you going to tell me?"

"I had originally thought to wait until morning," he admitted, feeling heat creep into his face. This was one time he was certainly glad that Grace had interfered. "I have your ring wrapped in a small box, hidden in our Christmas tree. I—er—I was going to surprise you."

"With a ring," she repeated softly, her eyes searching his. She suddenly sighed, all the fight draining out of her. She shook her head. "Every woman dreams of that kind of surprise." She glared at him. "But she usually has a few months before the ceremony to get used to the idea."

"Why wait?"

"Why not wait?"

Michael cupped her face with his hands and rubbed his thumbs over her cheeks as she looked up at him. "Because I want you in my bed at night, lass. When two people decide to spend the rest of their lives together, a long engagement is wasted."

She went back to thinking, and Michael decided that Libby's thinking too long and too hard might very well be a dangerous thing. So he went back to kissing her.

She was hesitant at first, more distracted than responsive, until he was able to wiggle his hand under her coat and find her firm little breast. He also found that she wasn't wearing a bra.

How nice. And how convenient.

Her skin was toasty warm under several layers of clothes and the down jacket. His much cooler hand sent shivers coursing through her body and beaded her soft, silky nipple into a pebble. He ran his thumb over it, captured her gasp in his mouth, and rolled them both over until he had nestled himself comfortably between her legs.

Finally, Libby joined in the love play and darted her sweet little tongue into his mouth as she arched her breast into his hand.

He thought about the blanket and the condoms in her pack and decided they were no longer needed. They were lying on a soft bed of dried, sun-warmed grass, and it was okay now to start making Robbie a brother or sister.

With tenderness and a newly declared love, they undressed each other in a wonderfully erotic dance that slowly stripped away all the barriers that had stood between them.

Finally, with both hearts fully engaged, Michael slowly entered Libby. Passion flared in her eyes as she lifted her hips to take him deeper, and her smile, which outshone the sun, hit him smack in the center of his heart—in exactly the same spot her well-aimed snowball had hit him just five short weeks ago.

Chapter Twenty-four

Libby sat on the top step of her porch, bundled up to her nose in wool, enjoying the serenity of the night. Huge snowflakes were falling with quiet intensity, steadily building a pristine blanket over the slumbering land. The silence was absolute, broken only by the muted sounds of conversation coming from inside the house.

Kate was in there, sitting in front of a roaring fire, cuddling four-day-old Winter MacKeage. Grace was sitting beside her, sipping tea. Greylen had deposited his wife and new baby about an hour ago but had left to get his six other daughters before Libby could ask him why he hadn't brought them in the first place.

Which was why she was out there now, waiting to see what Greylen had said would be a wonderful surprise.

It seemed all these Scots were big on surprises.

While she waited, embraced by the peace of the night, Libby thought about Michael's secret. And Greylen's. And Ian's and Morgan's and Callum's. They were all men born in another time, Michael had told her. Once enemies, they were now united by their determination to make new lives.

How was it possible they had traveled through time?

What had Daar said that morning when he'd zapped her flowers awake? Time, he had told her, existed only for clockmakers.

And, apparently, it could be manipulated by wizards.

How unsettling. And frightening. Could Daar send Michael back to his natural time?

No, the old man must never get hold of his powerful staff. She was glad Michael had taken it, and she hoped he'd had the presence of mind to destroy it.

With no sound of warning, Mary quietly glided out of the darkness and landed on the porch rail above Libby.

"Well, hello there," Libby said to the owl. "I see you got my invitation to our party."

Mary blinked, then turned her head toward the living-room window.

"Have you seen your newest niece yet?" Libby asked. "She's quite an adorable little bundle of joy."

The silent snowy sidestepped along the porch rail until she was even with the window. She sat in silence and watched her sister and her niece.

Another sound gently echoed through the night, a soft jingling that slowly drew closer, interlaced with faint voices.

Libby stood, suddenly excited beyond words. Those were sleigh bells. And carolers, their song keeping rhythm with the beautiful bells. Heavily plodding hoofbeats added to the chorus, the symphony resounding through the air.

Libby ran down the length of her driveway to the road and watched as the huge sled slowly came into view. Two giant horses were pulling it, their bells jingling loudly and the lights hanging from poles at the corners illuminating more than a dozen people.

Libby continued to run down the road. The sled was full of MacKeages, some singing, some laughing, the children bouncing around like Ping-Pong balls. Ian was driving, the slash of his grin showing through his beard peppered with snowflakes. He pulled the horses to a stop, and Libby took his offered hand and climbed up beside him.

"Oh, my God. This is wonderful," she said, turning to smile at the others. "What a perfect way to go to a party on Christmas Eve. Where's Michael? And Robbie?"

"We thought they were here already," Ian said, slapping the reins to move the horses forward. "No telling what Michael's up to," he said with a snicker, giving Libby a wink. "They'll be along soon, I reckon."

Libby grabbed the side of the seat as the sled jerked forward and couldn't quit grinning as they turned into her driveway, the horses breaking into a trot to power them up the steep incline.

They stopped in front of the porch, and Kate came out, her hands on her cheeks as she stared mutely in awe. The men jumped off first and started handing down children before helping their wives.

Libby refused to budge from her seat. "Go inside, everyone. Ian's going to take me for a short ride," she said, weaving her arm through his, giving him a sweet, pleading look.

"Only if yar mama can come," he said gruffly, crowding against her and patting the seat beside him. "Come on, Kate. Get yar cute little behind up here."

"I need to get my coat."

"Nay. I'll keep ya warm, lass," Ian countered, patting the seat again. "We'll just go for a short jog around the field."

Kate needed no more coaxing. She stepped off the

porch, waving their party guests into the house as she ran past, and raised her arms for Ian to lift her onto the sled.

Libby eyed the reins. "Can I drive?" she asked, again smiling sweetly at Ian. "It doesn't look that difficult."

He scowled at her, holding the reins protectively against his chest. "Nay. They're temperamental beasts and will act up if they realize a woman is handling them."

Libby scooted over, all the way to the edge of the seat. He could have just said no, without the woman comment. She was hiding the apple pie Kate had baked especially for him, and she was putting a good amount of cinnamon in his cider.

The chauvinistic old coot.

They made one full circle around the field before Kate's lips started to turn blue, and Libby and her mom ran into the house and left Ian to deal with his precious horses.

Boisterous chaos greeted them; children were running and crawling after the overwhelmed kittens, the men were standing around the food table filling their mouths more than their plates, and the MacKeage women, holding babies of varying ages, were telling their men to save some food for the guests yet to arrive.

Libby's eyes immediately went to Sadie MacKeage. Her height was like a magnet, and her blond hair shone like a beacon in the crowded room. Libby had met Sadie and Morgan just last week, when they'd come to the shop to buy their Christmas tree. She'd noticed then, when Sadie had taken off her mittens to pay, that the palm of her right hand was covered with burn scars.

The tall, beautiful woman set her daughter on the floor, and the toddler immediately took off in a tear after Trouble. That was when Libby realized her mistake. She never should have tied red ribbons around the kittens' necks. The child—Jennifer, if she remembered correctly—

nearly strangled Trouble. Jennifer's grandmother Charlotte came to the rescue, quickly untying the ribbon and picking up Trouble for Jennifer to pet.

Libby immediately found Guardian and Timid and removed the dangerous decorations.

A glass of wine was handed to her, and Libby looked up to say thank-you but instead found herself smiling into the glaring eyes of Father Daar.

"Don't say a word tonight, girl, about my staff," he whispered through a tight smile of his own. "I don't want Greylen knowing it still exists."

"Oh? Why not?" she guilelessly asked, giving him back an equally quelling grin.

"Ya just never mind," he muttered. "Is the eggnog spiked?"

Libby thought about telling him it wasn't, then quickly thought better of getting a wizard drunk. "There's a whole fifth of rum in it," she told him. "Maybe you should stick to apple cider."

He harrumphed and headed to the table of food.

Libby scanned the room, her gaze landing on Greylen MacKeage, who was wearing a pack that sat on his shoulders and draped over his chest. Grace was tucking Winter into it.

Libby watched as Greylen cuddled the newborn's bottom with one of his large hands and turned and used his free hand to start eating again.

Grace looked at the grandfather clock standing in the corner, then back at Libby. "I would have thought Michael and Robbie and John would be here by now. This party is the only thing Robbie's been able to talk about all week."

"And I wonder what's keeping Dwayne and Harry," Sadie MacKeage said, joining the conversation. "The house looks wonderful, Libby. You have stars on the ceiling in your bathroom," she added, tilting her head in question. "When I went in, the whole ceiling sparkled just before I turned on the light. So I ran back out, got Jennifer, and showed her. You should have seen her face when she noticed. Where can I get some? I'd love to put them on the ceiling over her bed."

"There's a neat little what-not shop in downtown Bangor," Libby told her, waving the two women toward her bedroom. "Come on. You have to see my bedroom ceiling."

The stars were a hit, but not nearly as much as her moose bed. Sadie couldn't stop running her hands over it. But Grace . . . Grace couldn't stop smiling like a woman who knew a secret.

"You know who made this bed, don't you?" Libby said, looking her directly in the eye.

Grace's smile turned impish as she tapped her chin with her finger. "Let me see. I remember seeing it in someone's workshop . . . now, where was that?" She shook her head and shrugged in unremorseful apology. "Nope. I just can't seem to remember whose shop it was."

Libby sighed. She almost didn't care anymore, as long as Santa brought her a matching bureau tomorrow morning. The three of them left to rejoin the party and were just walking into the kitchen when the porch door slammed open and Michael came rushing inside.

His face was drawn taut over protruding cheekbones, his skin paled gray, and his eyes filled with a sharp anguish that bordered on terror.

"I need help," he said with palpable urgency to the crowded room. "There's been an accident two miles east of Pine Creek. Leysa Dolan's truck left the road. She's being taken to Dover-Foxcroft by ambulance."

The collective silence lasted mere seconds before the men in the room moved almost as one. They handed off children to their women and rushed to find their jackets, no questions, no comments, only concern darkening their features.

Libby ran up to Michael. "Robbie?" she asked, grabbing the lapels of his coat. "Is he okay?"

The men stilled. The silence returned.

Michael took hold of her shoulders. "I donna know," he thickly told her. "When Dwayne found the accident, there was no sign of him. Robbie and Rose were not in the truck."

Libby tightened her grip on his jacket as his words started her heart racing. "Then where are they?" she cried. "They were with Leysa."

Michael gently pulled free, turned, and took her coat from the peg. With steady, rock-solid movements, he slipped it on her, wrapped his arm around her shoulders, and pulled her tightly against him as he turned his attention to the men.

"I'm thinking he's on foot, trying to make it home by way of the woods. I was able to find faint tracks leading northwest, but the snowfall quickly covered his footprints."

"Why wouldn't he have stayed on the road?" Libby asked, frantic now. "Why go into the woods?"

"He's not even nine years old," Kate said, coming to stand beside Libby, gripping her arm in support. "He's confused."

"Nay," Michael contradicted. "He's acting on instinct. It was a shortcut Leysa had taken. A back road that's traveled only through the week to haul logs. He knew the quickest way to find help was over the ridge."

"Then how did they find Leysa?" Libby asked, drawing Michael's attention again.

"Dwayne went looking for her when she was late getting

home." He ran his finger over her cheek, brushing away a tear. "Libby, there was blood on the backseat," he said softly. "Either Robbie or Rose is hurt. I'm guessing that when he couldn't wake Leysa, he decided to take Rose and go for help."

He looked at Greylen. "I need you to start from Gu Bràth and head over the ridge to the logging road. If we spread out, we should be able to find him."

Grey nodded. "We'll turn on all the ski-slope lights before we go. There's a chance he'll see them," he finished, heading out onto the porch. He stopped and let Ian and Callum and Morgan move past. He looked back at Daar. "Come on, old man. You will help us."

Daar was already putting his coat on and quickly moved to join the other men. He came to a halt in front of Libby, his crystal-blue eyes deeply piercing hers.

"I'm guessing you'll have yar answer tonight, girl. And I will pray it's the one ya was hoping to get," he said cryptically before turning and walking out to the waiting men.

Michael stopped Libby from following and looked at the women. "John is home, waiting by the phone. One of you should go stay with him. Harry and Irisa are on their way to be with Leysa, and Dwayne is already searching for his daughter with the state police. Make phone calls to those who can help. Have them concentrate on the area between TarStone and Pine Lake."

With those quiet orders given, Michael finally guided Libby outside. He opened the driver's side door of his truck, all but tossed her inside, and climbed in after her.

He didn't immediately start the truck but sat staring out the windshield, his features drawn and his whole body as still as the night. "There was a lot of blood, lass," he said quietly, still looking forward. "And palm prints the size of Robbie's." He finally turned to her. "He wrote something on the window, in blood, that I can't make sense of."

"Wh-what?" she whispered, covering his clenched hand on the steering wheel with a trembling hand of her own.

"Three words, in Gaelic. One was spelled wrong, but I'm thinking he was trying to tell me what to do."

"What were the words?"

"The first one is simple. *Pet.* He was saying his owl could find him."

Libby shot her gaze to the porch rail. "Yes. Mary!" she cried, looking back at Michael. "She was here. Earlier. But she's gone now."

"She might be with Robbie," he speculated, finally starting the truck and backing it up, turning it around, and heading it down the driveway.

"And the other words?" Libby asked. "What did they say?"

Michael watched the road, deep in thought. "*Fear-gleidhidh.* It's Gaelic for 'guardian.' I think he was telling me his duty to Rose. And *fiodh,* which could mean 'a piece of wood.' Or it could mean 'forest,' like the path he intended to take. Hell," he growled in frustration, looking over at her. "It could damned well mean anything, for all I know. It was spelled wrong."

"But why would he write in Gaelic?" she asked, quickly fastening her seat belt as they sped down the snow-covered road, traveling faster than the headlights could shine.

"Robbie might be born of this time," Michael said roughly, downshifting as he turned, skidding onto an unplowed logging road. "But he has the soul of an ancient. He's in crisis, Libby, guided by an instinct as old as his ancestors." He shot her a desperate look and then quickly returned his attention to his driving. "The boy knows Gaelic, but he's not been taught to write it."

He stepped on the accelerator, pushing the truck dangerously fast over the narrow tote road. "Dammit," he growled, slapping the steering wheel. "He's been out there for hours."

"Hours?"

"Aye. When Dwayne found their truck, the engine was cold, and there was nearly four inches of snow covering it. Leysa was hypothermic as well as seriously injured. Which means the accident happened at least three hours ago." He looked at Libby, his eyes dark with anguish. "How long can he survive in these temperatures, if he's losing blood?" he asked thickly.

"It really depends on his injuries," she told him, laying a hand on his arm. "Sometimes very little blood looks like gallons when smeared around the inside of a vehicle. And he's smart enough to try to stop the bleeding. And he's good-sized, Michael. He has enough body mass to hold heat."

Libby squeezed his arm and then fell silent, fighting the fear rising inside her, letting Michael cling to the hope she'd given him.

Wood. A piece of wood. What was Robbie saying?

"Wait!" she suddenly shouted, grabbing his arm again. "Stop the truck!"

He slammed on the brakes, bringing them to a sliding halt, and stared at her.

"The staff. Daar's staff. Did you destroy it?"

"Nay. I tried, but I didn't dare. Why? What has it to do with finding Robbie? Mary will help us."

"A piece of wood, Michael. What if Robbie meant Daar's staff? What if he was asking you to bring it?"

"It probably means something else, Libby. That he's traveling through the woods. Robbie's not even aware of Daar's staff."

"Michael, we have to get it anyway," she said, tugging at him in frustration. "Remember Alan Brewer? I couldn't help him because I was not powerful enough to get past his defenses. But Daar said that with his staff, I might have been able to."

"Robbie will not fight ya, Libby. He trusts ya."

"But what if we're too late?" she whispered, looking down at her folded hands on her lap.

Only the sound of the idling engine and the beat of the wiper blades broke the sudden silence inside the truck. Fat, flickering snowflakes bombarded them with growing intensity, disappearing into raindrops on the heated windshield. The dash lights glowed in ethereal colors that only added credence to her unthinkable words.

With nothing more than a growl for answer, Michael slammed the truck into reverse and turned on the narrow road, spinning all four tires to gain traction, heading them back in the direction they'd come from.

In silence, they sped through the night, and Libby prayed they were doing the right thing. She knew Michael's reluctance to expose the powerful staff, but even if they all got zapped back to medieval Scotland, it wouldn't matter as long as Robbie survived.

She'd go with them, she decided, sliding her hand gently onto Michael's thigh. Anyplace, in any time, being with the two men she loved was better than staying in this time without Robbie.

They sped past her driveway and continued to Michael's home, coming to a sliding stop in front of his workshop. He set the brake with a jerk and was running inside before the truck had stopped rocking.

Libby was one step behind him.

The woodworking shop stood patiently silent in the sudden glare of the overhead lights Michael snapped on.

Without breaking stride, he went to his workbench, reached up, and took down a small chain saw. He gave one violent tug on the starter cord, and the miniature engine screamed to life.

Libby gasped in surprise when she saw him shove at a beautiful oak bureau, sending its polished face crashing onto the floor. He set the roaring blade of the saw against the back panel and cut through the wood. Sawdust and choking engine fumes filled the workshop, the whine of the deafening blade making the destruction horribly easy.

The top half of the bureau separated cleanly, rolling onto its finished top. The air continued to hum with bone-chilling echoes long after the noise ceased abruptly. And Libby could only stand and watch in horror as Michael used his bare hands to rip apart the bottom half of his beautiful creation.

He stood up, the two-foot-long, thick, gnarled piece of cherrywood clenched in his fist. He grabbed Libby's hand and, without giving the destruction a second glance, pulled her back out to the truck. He lifted her in, handed her the staff, and climbed in and had the truck moving before she could fasten her seat belt.

Libby stared at the heavy, warm-feeling wood in her hands.

It still hummed with lingering energy—from the whine of the chain saw? Lord, she hoped so. They could well be playing with fire, trying to use this ancient piece of old magic to save Robbie's life.

Libby carefully set the staff on the seat by the door and put her hand back on Michael's thigh as she watched the blinding snowflakes rush past the hood of the truck, their reflection in the headlights all but shouting urgency.

This was taking too long.

They might be too late.

Michael suddenly slammed on the brakes when a white blur of feathers crossed the beam of the headlights, swooping low and then lifting back into the forest. The truck slid to a stop, and Michael shut off the engine and rolled down his window. Together, they sat in absolute silence and listened.

A sharp, distant, haunting whistle came from the woods.

Michael looked down the road in the direction they'd been traveling, then over at Libby. "We're still three miles from the accident," he told her, looking back at the woods.

"How far could he travel?" Libby asked. "Carrying a baby?"

"He could probably cover one, maybe one and a half miles in an hour," he told her. "Depending on his injuries. He might already be over the ridge by now."

"Is there a road leading up there?"

"Aye. There are all sorts of woodcutting trails. But there's almost two feet of snow from the last storm and this one. The MacKeages have the best chance of finding him in their snowcats."

"But we have Mary," Libby reminded him, touching his arm.

He started the truck, then slowly let it roll forward, keeping watch through his open window. Libby saw the narrow track the same time he did. He put the truck in neutral, shifted the four-wheel drive into low gear, then gunned the engine and sent them careening through the ditch and up onto the trail.

Libby had to brace herself against the violent upheavals of the rough terrain, holding on to the dash and gripping the cherrywood staff between her knees to keep it from bouncing around the interior of the truck.

They dug and spun and slowly made their way through

the deep snow, climbing the ridge one rock and one fallen tree at a time. Finally, they stopped with a jarring thud, as all four tires screamed and chittered for traction.

Michael shut off the engine. "This is it. We walk from here," he said, opening his door, getting out, and reaching back under the seat. He pulled out a flashlight, clicked it on, and shone it through the interior of the truck.

"Give me the staff," he said, helping her down and holding her until she found her footing. "Listen," he whispered, looking toward the tops of the towering trees.

They heard it again, that faint, haunting cry of urgent desperation, far off to their left, high up on the ridge.

Michael lifted the back of his jacket, tucked the heavy staff into his belt, and let his coat fall over it. "This way," he said, taking her hand and leading her deeper into the woods.

Chapter Twenty-five

$\mathscr{L}$*ibby followed in silence,* letting Michael guide her around large boulders and over fallen trees, trying very hard not to slow down the pace he was keeping. She felt as if she were in one of those maddening nightmares, where she was running as fast as she could but not moving.

They traveled for what seemed like forever, until Libby was soaked in sweat and beginning to shiver. Her breathing was labored, and her muscles ached. Only the urgency of Mary's distant cries gave Libby the strength to keep putting one foot in front of the other.

Michael suddenly stopped and pointed toward the top of the ridge. "There. Do ya see that?" he asked in a winded whisper. "That blue glow?"

"Is it the ski-slope lights?" Libby asked, moving to see better.

"Nay," he said, pointing to their left. "TarStone is to the north. You can just make out the reflection of the tower lights on the clouds. This glow is blue," he said, pointing back at the south side of the ridge. "Can ya see it?"

He didn't wait for her answer but started leading her in the direction he'd pointed. "It's Mary," he said as he lifted her over a fallen tree. "It's her light."

Libby's fatigue disappeared. She started running to keep up with Michael as his long legs began covering the ground with amazing speed. The blue glow intensified as they drew nearer, reflecting off the snow in shimmering waves that turned the night into day.

Michael stopped, and Libby stopped beside him. Mary was perched on a small mound of snow. There was a red knit hat poking through it where the owl had scratched.

"Robbie!" Libby cried, hurling herself to her knees and brushing the snow away.

Michael knelt opposite her and carefully turned Robbie over, lifting him onto his lap. Libby tore off her gloves and gently brushed away ice crystals from the unconscious boy's face. Her fingers touched the crusted blood on his right temple near the hairline. She examined the small cut that was no longer bleeding, and quickly decided it was only a minor scrape and not responsible for his condition now. She let her fingers trail down his neck to feel for a pulse.

There was none.

Libby pried open Robbie's arms and unbuttoned his jacket. Rose Dolan fell into her hands. The infant was limp, her tiny features drawn and pale. Libby leaned over and touched her mouth to Rose's cheek and felt just the faintest whisper of breath.

"She's alive," Libby said. "Just barely."

"Robbie," Michael growled as he placed his own mouth over Robbie's. He gently pushed several breaths into his son and then looked at Libby, his eyes desperate. "Do something," he demanded. "Wake him up!"

Libby pulled off her jacket and set it on the ground

beside the silent owl. She set Rose inside the jacket and bundled her up, then reached for Robbie. Michael placed his son in her arms, then moved them both onto his lap until Libby was astride his hips with Robbie pressed between them.

"Use yar magic," Michael entreated. "Save my son, Libby."

She was already trying. But instead of the now familiar colors that should be swirling through Robbie, Libby found only darkness. There was no light, no colors, not one single emotion that she could feel.

"He—he's not here, Michael," she whispered, looking up. "He—he's gone." She choked on a sob, closing her eyes and pressing her mouth to Robbie's hair.

Michael's arms tightened. "He's not dead!" He held Libby's hand to Robbie's face. "Try harder."

Libby resumed her search for Robbie's life force, only to find herself once again confronting darkness. She mentally roamed through Robbie's empty body, seeking out anything that would give her a reason to continue. She ignored the chill of the void, instead concentrating on each individual organ, looking for even the smallest of sparks.

And deep in Robbie's heart, Libby found hope. Michael's arms tightened around her, and Libby knew he was there, beside her, feeling and seeing what she did—the distant echo of a young and determined desperation.

And she realized the pulse was merely a connection to Robbie, a lifeline to use to return. Libby pulled away, opened her eyes, and looked up at Michael.

"Go back!" he demanded, hugging her fiercely. "He's alive."

"He's not there, Michael," she told him. "He's in Rose."

They both looked at the jacket lying on the snow. Mary was using her beak to gently pull back the folds of wool.

"He's protecting her," Libby said, wiggling free of Michael's embrace. "He's using the last of his strength to keep her alive." She picked up the infant and nestled her between herself and Robbie. "If we want to save Robbie, we have to save Rose. He'll not leave her until he's sure she is safe."

Michael reached behind himself and pulled the old priest's staff from his belt. With amazingly steady hands, he gently wedged the thick cherrywood stick between Rose and Robbie, then reached behind Libby's shoulders in a rock-solid embrace that engulfed her and the children. He looked at Libby, took a deep breath, and nodded.

With her own arms wrapped tightly around both young bodies, Libby closed her eyes and again went in search of the colors.

Brilliant white light immediately pulsed through her mind, making Libby cry out in surprise. Michael's arms tightened as he braced them against the assault, and slowly Libby was able to feel two faintly beating hearts.

She reached for the weaker pulse, bending the white light toward Rose, gently coaxing warmth into her tiny body. The infant gasped for breath and let out a cry of outrage, and her tiny heart began racing with the rapid beat of a tiger cub.

Libby cried tears of relief as she touched her lips to Robbie's cheek. "Come back," she whispered. "Rose is safe now, Robbie. She's going to live."

A turbulent rainbow pulsed through the white light, pulling at Libby as it sped past. Myriad colors danced about in frantic circles, playfully tugging her own heartstrings before speeding off toward Michael.

"Come home," Michael thickly demanded. "Now, son."

The colors stopped and hovered and suddenly wrapped everyone up in a fierce embrace of elation.

"God's teeth!" Michael shouted, his words echoing through the brightness. "Come home!"

Libby slowly inched toward Robbie's faintly beating pulse and gently tickled his heart. The organ shuddered, thumped twice, then started to beat with the strength of a lion.

The blinding light softly faded to a gentle blue glow. Libby opened her eyes to see a flurry of white feathers wafting down through the night. She looked at her jacket on the ground, but Mary was gone.

"I'm powerful hungry, Papa."

Libby turned her gaze to Robbie, who was looking at Michael.

"And so is Rose," the boy said. He suddenly grinned at Libby. "It's after midnight," he told her. "Merry Christmas."

"Merry Christmas!" Libby cried, pulling him to her as she sobbed in relief.

Michael wrapped trembling arms around them, whispering his own Christmas blessing. Rose squeaked in protest and wiggled to get free. Libby pulled back, wiped the tears off her face, and stood up with Rose in her arms.

The infant shot her a lopsided smile and then reached out her short little arms toward Robbie. Robbie started to take her, but it seemed that Michael was not done hugging him yet. So the boy turned his attention to his father and hugged him back.

"I knew ya would come for me, Papa," Libby heard Robbie say. "And I held on until ya did."

"Aye," Michael breathed, his eyes closed against his own emotional storm as he held Robbie close. "Ya did good, son.

Libby picked up her jacket and tented it over Rose, who was now sucking her thumb, then turned at the sound of an engine approaching. Headlights appeared over the top of the ridge, and a double-tracked machine wove through the forest and came to a halt beside them.

Doors opened, and Greylen and Ian climbed out. Ian helped Daar down over the wide track and held his arm as they came over to Libby and Michael.

"You found them," Greylen said, walking up to Michael, touching Robbie to see for himself that the boy was okay. He slapped Michael on the back. "He seems to be hale and hearty."

"Aye," Michael said, nodding, still not putting his son down.

"And Rose?" Greylen asked, turning to Libby.

Libby pulled back her coat to reveal the infant. "She's hale and hearty, too," she told Grey. "And hungry."

"Did ya save me some cheesecake?" Robbie asked, trying to see past his father's fierce embrace. "I—I guess we missed the party."

"You didn't," Libby told him. "We postponed it until tomorrow—I mean, today—at noon."

The boy's eyes rounded. "Noon?" he echoed, turning to look at his father. He leaned in and whispered something to Michael, Michael nodded, and Robbie looked back at Libby, his face lit with a smug smile. "I told ya Christmas was full of surprises."

Libby couldn't have responded if she'd wanted to.

"We're gonna miss Santa, people, if we don't start making our way back," Ian interjected, turning up the collar on his coat and shoving his bare hands into his pockets. "And we still gotta find Dwayne and let him know his daughter is okay."

Libby followed Michael when he walked to the snowcat and placed Robbie in the backseat. He took Rose out of her arms and handed the child to his son. But before Michael turned back to Libby, he lingered long enough to run a hand over Robbie's head, cupping his chin and lifting his face to his.

"Ian will drive ya home," he told him. "And Libby will stay with ya until I get there. Give John a big hug when ya see him," he instructed. "He's been worried sick about ya."

Michael leaned in closer, and Libby edged forward to hear what he was saying. "Ya did good, son," he told him roughly, gently running a finger over Rose's plump cheek. "You were Rose's guardian angel tonight."

Robbie blinked up at him. "It was my duty, Papa."

"Aye," Michael agreed, patting Robbie on the shoulder.

Michael turned to Libby, and she threw herself into his arms. "Come back with us," she pleaded, holding him tightly. "I don't want us to be separated right now."

"There's no room, lass," he whispered into her hair. "Ian will take ya home, and Grey and I will get my truck and go find Dwayne. We'll be at the house in no time." He kissed her upturned face and gave her a reassuring smile. "Feed my son and Rose, give them warm baths, and see if ya can't talk Robbie into getting some sleep."

His orders given, he lifted her up and settled her in the backseat beside Robbie. He leaned inside, gave her a quick kiss, and then turned to the men. "Where's Daar?" he asked.

Ian and Greylen looked around in the beam of the headlights, and Libby also craned her neck to find Father Daar.

But he was nowhere to be seen.

Libby gasped and reached out to Michael. "The staff," she hissed softly. "Where is it?"

He whipped his head around and stared at the spot where Robbie and Rose had been. After only a quick look back at her, he walked over and started scuffing the snow-covered ground, looking for the staff.

"Now, where in hell did he go?" Ian muttered as he walked to the other side of the snowcat, looking for Daar.

Libby climbed out and started helping Michael look for the staff. Greylen came over and stared at them quizzically.

"What have you lost?" he asked.

Michael stopped and faced Grey. "Daar's staff."

"His cane?" Greylen lifted one brow.

"Nay. His old staff. The one ya threw in the high mountain pond nine years ago."

Libby took a step back when Greylen's face suddenly changed from inquiry to a look of dangerous anger. The man pulled himself up to his full height and took a step toward Michael.

"Are you saying that *drùidh's* staff still exists?"

"Aye," Michael confirmed. "It seems it shot free of the waterfall just before Morgan blew up Fraser Mountain."

"And how did it end up here?" Greylen asked, waving a hand at the ground where Michael and Libby had been looking.

"Robbie's pet owl brought it to Libby. But I took it and hid it."

"And?" Greylen asked gutturally.

"And we needed it tonight to save my son's life."

Greylen looked from Michael to Libby, then back at Michael. "And now Daar and the staff are missing," he said, not as a question but a statement.

Michael nodded, and both men looked off toward TarStone, in the direction of Daar's cabin, their faces drawn pale and their fists clenched at their sides. Libby also looked, as did Ian, who had come to stand beside her and listen to the conversation.

There was a sudden detonation halfway up the mountain, and the sky over TarStone lit up like the Fourth of July.

Michael reached out and pulled Libby into a protective embrace as they all watched colorful bolts of lightning sizzle over the summit. There was another powerful blast that shook the ground under their feet, trembling the trees with enough force to dislodge the snow from their branches.

Ian started cursing under his breath.

Michael tightened his hold on Libby.

And Greylen MacKeage started laughing.

"There," he said when they all looked at him in surprise. He pointed halfway up the mountain, at the smoke rising into the still crackling sky. "I'm betting it's Daar's cabin that just blew up. The crazy old fool has been so long without the magic, he's blown his cabin to hell."

"And himself, I hope," Ian interjected.

Libby gasped.

Michael tightened his hold on her, cutting off her words of concern before she could voice them. He turned her around and led her back to the snowcat. Robbie was standing on the track, Rose clutched to his chest, gawking at TarStone.

Michael urged him back inside, helped Libby into the passenger seat, and kissed her soundly on the mouth. "I'll see you in a bit," he said, softly closing the door.

Ian silently climbed in, started the engine, turned the snowcat around, and headed them home.

Daar sat on a half-rotted stump, fingering what was left of his old staff, and stared at the burning remains of his cabin. God's teeth, he'd done it this time. He'd destroyed not only his home but his ancient book of spells.

It would take him nearly a century to replace it. He'd have to petition the powers that be, stand before them and explain what had happened, then beg their forgiveness. He'd have to bribe and barter and beg yet again for the other wizards to let him copy from their own books.

He looked down at the now shrunken staff in his hand. It was useless without his book of spells.

Daar lifted his head as a sound came to him, whispering up from the ridge below. He cursed when he realized that it was Greylen MacKeage he could hear, laughing his head off.

Well, dammit. He'd see who got the last laugh—for Daar would make sure that young Winter MacKeage would lead her parents on a merry and maddening chase through her childhood.

Chapter Twenty-six

It was nearly three in the morning before Michael's home finally quieted down. A perfectly healthy and happy Rose was with her daddy, both on their way to Dover-Foxcroft to be with Leysa. Libby had called the hospital for an update and was relieved to learn that Leysa would recover fully and that she'd most likely be back with her family by the New Year.

Kate had stayed at Michael's house waiting with John, and Ian had taken her home in the snowcat. Robbie had gotten his belly filled and had finally fallen asleep about twenty minutes ago.

And now, Libby and Michael were sitting on the floor in the library, in front of a roaring fire. Michael was leaning against his worn leather chair, and Libby was sitting between his thighs, absently staring up at the oak-paneled hearth.

It suddenly dawned on her exactly what she was looking at, and Libby finally knew what she'd been helping Robbie build for his father for Christmas.

"Tàirneanaiche," she whispered, scrambling to her feet and walking to the hearth. She reached up and ran her finger along the blade of one of the three swords hanging over the mantel.

"Have a care, Libby," Michael said. "It's sharp."

She turned to face him. "This is your sword. From . . . from before."

"Aye," he said, rising to his feet and coming to stand beside her. He took down the sword she'd been touching, grasping it in his right hand, the tip pointed toward the ceiling.

Libby knew she was gawking but couldn't help it. She was seeing Michael the warrior from eight hundred years ago, holding his sword as he was now, comfortable and confident and ready to meet any challenge.

And she fell in love all over again.

"You're staring at me as if you're seeing a ghost," Michael said, quickly replacing the sword over the mantel.

"No, I'm seeing the man I'm marrying today." Libby wrapped her arms around his waist and hugged him fiercely. "I love you, Michael MacBain." She looked up and smiled. "So much so that when we were searching for Robbie and had Daar's staff, I decided that if we all got zapped back in time, I'd still be happy, as long as we were all together."

Michael's arms tightened around her, and he leaned down and kissed her smile. "Aye. I had the same thought myself," he whispered. "It was a hard life back then, lass, but it had its good points."

"Do you miss it?"

"Nay," he said, shaking his head. "Not anymore."

He swept her off her feet and carried her back to the chair, placing her on the floor and then settling himself behind her. Libby snuggled into his embrace and stared at the fire again. It seemed there wasn't anything else that needed saying, and she was content simply to sit in silence.

But just as she was about to close her eyes and nod off to sleep, a package suddenly appeared in front of her nose.

It was a small package, brightly wrapped in Christmas paper and tied with an elaborate bow. Libby reached out and took the gift, leaning her head back to stare up at Michael. He was smiling down at her, his eyes lit with anticipation.

"What would this be?" she asked, waving the package.

He kissed her on the nose. "It's not a bureau to match your bed, I'm afraid," he said, one corner of his mouth turning down in a lopsided grin. "I'll make ya a new one, Libby."

Libby's smile disappeared. "You hid Daar's staff in my bureau," she scolded. "That took more nerve than brain."

He was far from contrite. "Really? I thought it was genius myself," he contradicted with a shrug. "I didn't dare destroy it, and what better place to hide it? I knew you'd look after that bureau come hell or high water and that it would eventually be passed down to Robbie. And what better tool could I give him when he meets his destiny?"

"Daar has it now."

"Aye. But Grey's probably right. I don't think we need fear the old *drùidh*. Not for a good while, anyway. And we'll deal with him then, if that time ever comes."

Libby shook her gift. "What's in here?" she asked.

"Why don't ya open it and find out?"

She needed no more urging. Libby carefully pulled off the bow and tore through the wrapping to find a small velvet box. She opened the lid and gasped.

"It's tourmaline," Michael told her. "Mined right here in Maine." He took the ring out of the box, picked up her left hand, and slid the ring onto her finger.

"There," he said thickly. "You're mine."

"I guess I am," she murmured, holding up her hand to admire the large forest-green stone shaped like a teardrop. She looked over her shoulder at Michael. "So I guess you're also mine."

"Aye," he softly agreed, kissing her nose again.

Libby turned until she was on her knees facing him, wrapped her arms around his neck, and stared directly into his eyes. "I love you, Michael," she whispered.

"Aye," he repeated with thick emotion. "I love ya, too, Dr. Elizabeth Hart. Will ya marry me, lass?"

"Yes."

He smoothed a hand over her hair and let his fingers trail down to her cheek. "Then I'm giving ya a nine-hour engagement, so ya might want to make the best of it."

"Time only matters to clockmakers," she whispered, leaning up and halting her mouth just short of his. "And the only time that matters is what's left of the rest of our lives." She gave him an open-mouthed kiss, then pulled back and smiled into his molten gray eyes. "I've always wanted to make love in front of a noisy, messy fire. Is it finally going to happen?"

"Aye," he whispered, turning them both until Libby was stretched out on the rug in front of the hearth with Michael beside her. He brushed the hair back from her face and kissed her cheek just under her ear. "It's going to happen right now, lass."

A shiver ran through Libby, and she rolled against him, throwing one leg over his hips and capturing his mouth in a kiss filled with the promise of passion. And with careful attention to detail, they undressed each other, enjoying each new patch of skin that was revealed and each small measure of pleasure they shared.

It was just as Michael was slowly entering her that Libby

caught sight of the ring on her left hand as she clutched his shoulder. The firelight hit the jewel, and she was sure she saw a Christmas tree winking at her from the center of the stone.

Libby sighed in contentment.

She was in love with an ancient Highland warrior. Life didn't get any more real—or more magical—than that.